W9-AVH-090

MR. ROCHESTER

SARAH SHOEMAKER

GRAND CENTRAL
PUBLISHING

NEW YORK   BOSTON

*For Kent, who has lived graciously these past few years
with my fascination for another man.*

———

Copyright © 2017 by Sarah Shoemaker
Reading Group Guide Copyright © 2017 by Sarah Shoemaker and Hachette Book Group, Inc.

Cover design by Elizabeth Connor; Landscape (oil on panel), English School, (18th century) / Good Hope Great House, Falmouth, Jamaica / Photo: © Lucinda Lambton / Bridgeman Images. Cover copyright © 2017 by Hachette Book Group, Inc.

Grand Central Publishing
Hachette Book Group
1290 Avenue of the Americas, New York, NY 10104
grandcentralpublishing.com
twitter.com/grandcentralpub

First Trade Edition: March 2018

Grand Central Publishing is a division of Hachette Book Group, Inc. The Grand Central Publishing name and logo is a trademark of Hachette Book Group, Inc.

The publisher is not responsible for websites (or their content) that are not owned by the publisher.

The Hachette Speakers Bureau provides a wide range of authors for speaking events. To find out more, go to www.hachettespeakersbureau.com or call (866) 376-6591.

Names: Shoemaker, Sarah, author.
Title: Mr. Rochester / Sarah Shoemaker.
Other titles: Mister Rochester
Description: First edition. | New York : Grand Central Publishing, 2017.
Identifiers: LCCN 2016057326| ISBN 9781455569809 (hardback) | ISBN 9781478916123 (audio download) | ISBN 9781455569823 (ebook)
Subjects: LCSH: Brontë, Charlotte, 1816-1855--Parodies, imitations, etc. | Governesses--Fiction. | Fathers and daughters--Fiction. | Mentally ill women--Fiction. | Charity-schools--Fiction. | Married people--Fiction. | Country homes--Fiction. | Young women--Fiction. | Orphans--Fiction. | England--Fiction. | BISAC: FICTION / Historical. | FICTION / Literary. | FICTION / Romance / Historical. | GSAFD: Bildungsromans. | Love stories.
Classification: LCC PS3619.H643 M77 2017 | DDC 813/.6--dc23
LC record available at https://lccn.loc.gov/2016057326

ISBNs: 978-1-4555-6981-6 (trade pbk.), 978-1-4555-6982-3 (ebook)

Printed in the United States of America

LSC-C

10 9 8 7 6 5 4 3 2 1

...without esteem true love cannot exist.

—Charlotte Brontë
Shirley

BOOK ONE

Chapter 1

I know little of my birth, for my mother died long before she could tell me—before I ever heard her voice or gazed at her face—and my father banished the woman who helped deliver me, blaming her for my mother's death. Of course, my father himself had no interest in telling me the least part of it, even if he did remember, which he almost certainly did not. There was no room for sentiment in my father's existence. Although my mother had proved her worth by providing him with two healthy boys, he would still have considered it a waste to lose a good broodmare.

But with her gone, who was there to oversee the raising of his sons? Not himself, that was certain, as he was away on business most of the time, so he turned to Holdredge, his butler, and to his housekeeper, Mrs. Knox, and a succession of nursemaids and governesses, who were sometimes bad and other times worse. It was years before I could think of a governess as anyone other than a presence that must be borne. But in large part, my brother and I were left to entertain ourselves, and we did so separately. Rowland was eight years older than I, and as one might imagine, eight years between brothers does not make for a great deal of affinity. I do not recall much of what he did with himself in those days, but as for me, whenever I was released from the schoolroom I was content to ramble the gardens and fields and woods of Thornfield-Hall.

Even now, when I think of Thornfield-Hall, I choose to remember what it was then—the playground of my childhood—and not what it was to become: a place of secrets and threats, of angers and fears. If I had been prescient in those days, I might have attempted to destroy it myself.

My mother was never spoken of; I never heard her name pass anyone's lips, and it was years before I even knew what it was. But one of my earliest memories is of the portrait that hung over the mantel of the front drawing room, a cozy place where a fire was always laid, and which my father rarely entered. He spent his time at Thornfield riding around his holdings, seeing to business here and there. Running an estate as large as Thornfield occupied all of a man's time, and my father had a steward to do the daily work of it, but when he was home, he took part in overseeing it all, leaving early and returning late, grumbling the whole time about the price of grain or the lack of dependable labor. As if I had antennae, I knew what he was about; it was in my best interests to do so. How else is a child to survive?

But how I loved the drawing room—its walls of a soft green, almost like moss, echoing in more muted tones the lawns beyond the window casements; its ivory-colored carpet and white ceiling with moldings of grapevines; the velvet-covered chairs whose dark wood glowed from decades of polish; the gleaming silver candlesticks; and, most of all, the portrait above the fireplace. The woman was fair-haired and fair skinned, with eyes the shade of the summer sky, standing slim and proud in a dress whose color seemed but a poor copy of her eyes. She stood on a terrace— which I did not recognize—and in the distance a pair of peacocks paused in mid-strut, as if taken aback by her beauty. Of course, without having to be told, I knew who she was; my brother, Rowland, was her exact image.

It became my habit, first thing in the morning and just before bedtime, to stand before that portrait, as if standing before the reality, as if waiting for her approbation, or, when I had done some little thing of which I might be ashamed, as if sensing her disapproval. My father caught me at it one day when I thought he was gone from the Hall. He must have come back for some forgotten item and passed the half-opened door and seen me there. "Boy!" he said, startling me. "Come away from there! You have no business in there."

I stepped back, and then, fearing his quick hand, darted past him and up the stairs to the nursery, another place he never came. I stayed away from my mother for two whole days, but I kept hearing her calling me, until finally I crept back to the parlor and pushed the door open—and she was gone. In her place was another painting—a hunting scene, with horses and red-coated riders milling around, dogs nearly underfoot, the master of the hunt with horn in hand—the sort of thing that hangs in public houses. There was nothing familiar or reassuring about it, nothing to fill the aching hole that suddenly came to my gut. It was a painting that should have been in the dining room, or my father's library or his bedchamber, not in this room that I loved so dearly.

I had, after that, only the memory of her portrait. From then on, I stayed mostly in the nursery or the schoolroom, when I was not in the kitchen or the stables looking for a kind word or a pat on the head, or outside wandering through the wood or across the moors. I peeked a few times into the parlor, hoping that I had been mistaken about the hunting scene, but after that I rarely entered that room again.

As the years passed, my father left more and more of the estate responsibilities to his steward, while he traveled far distances. He was building up his business interests, and sometimes he took Rowland with him, but never me. This was a vast relief to me, as I had no idea how to speak with him or whether he would think me impossibly stupid if I tried to do so.

It is true that, though I lacked for love, I was never actually mistreated. I was fed and clothed—perhaps not in the fanciest ways, but adequately. I generally ate what the servants ate; in fact, when I was not being fed in the nursery, I usually dined with them in the kitchen. It was plain fare, and to this day, having tried the other, I much prefer Cook's simple dishes. In dress, I could have been mistaken for the stableboy in a clean set of clothes, and that I preferred as well. Breeches and waistcoats are a damned nuisance, if you ask me.

While Thornfield-Hall was never truly warm in the winter months, it was never freezing, either, and the cupboards harbored goose down enough for anyone's tastes—though more than once I heard my father berating the housekeeper, Knox, over the quilts on my bed. "The boy must learn to be a man, standing on his own, putting up with whatever life brings him," he'd say, and she would gather up a goose down and slowly fold it for storage. Soon it would appear again, but not a word of it passed between the two of us, though I would try to flash her a smile when I could. She was a slim, black-clad woman with reddish-brown hair, and usually a frown above her gray eyes. But despite her stern appearance, she almost never had a harsh word for me, and for that I am grateful. We both understood that her job was to please the master, not to cosset his second son.

And no one beat me, though there were times when the touch of a hand would have been welcome, even in anger—a slap to the head or a good shaking of the shoulders.

Except of course for Rowland, who'd give me a swipe whenever I was within arm's reach, and if I particularly annoyed him, he would take up the cane. He was enough older, and I was naïve enough then, to believe that that was the job of an older brother: to keep the younger one in his place. By the time I learned differently, he was gone. I will have to keep this in mind, for I have learned the ways of second sons and it would be a sore useless experience if I cannot set things aright.

In those days, Thornfield-Hall was an impressive building constructed of the gray stone so familiar in the area. Two bays, one on each wing and running the full height of its three stories, served to prevent the building from looking like a simple square box, and battlements of carved stonework on the rooftop further softened the effect. The front door was of half glass, with black oak shutters against nightfall and inclement weather. Just inside was a large entrance hall with tall doors to the downstairs rooms, and between them hung portraits of people I presumed to be my ancestors. A massive bronze lamp hung in the center, and in one corner stood a carved clock, taller than my father. I loved that clock, loved to run my finger along its carvings. A grand staircase of oak with twin newel-posts the size of a grown man led from the entrance hall up to the family's private chambers and, beyond, the guest rooms, and on the very top floor were storage rooms and the servants' quarters. In all, the place had a masculine appearance, with ornate panel boards on the walls, heavy tapestries at the windows, and rich plasterwork on the ceilings.

As an adult, I always felt that the Hall was built for show. It was only in the nursery—and, of course, in the drawing room, until I was banished—that I felt the comfort one ought to feel in one's own home. Perhaps that was another reason why I spent so much of my time in those early years hovering about the kitchen begging for a scrap of sweetened dough, or in the stables asking Jem and Kip if I could help with brushing down the horses or polishing and oiling the tack. "No, Young Master," they would always say, adding, "Go ask Cook for a bunch of carrots for the horses, there's a good boy." Cook would wink as she handed them over, and I would dash back, eager to deliver my offering of friendship to those patient beasts.

In the storage rooms on the third floor (a place forbidden to me, which made it all the more attractive), I found treasures: cast-off fishing tackle and butterfly nets, but I never caught any fish, perhaps because I had no one to teach me. I did catch butterflies, but I could never bear to stick a pin through the tiny quivering bodies, so I set them free. There were all sorts of other treasures to be discovered in those rooms as well: trunks of clothing from another era, toys I had never seen or played with, vases gathering dust, furniture blanketed with canvas coverings, and various other items whose use or purpose was a mystery to me—and since I was not supposed to be there in the first place, I could not ask about them. I scoured those rooms, searching for the long-lost painting of my mother, but I never found it.

On three sides, beyond the house and its gardens, were fields of wheat and barley, and on the fourth side was the hawthorn wood that gave the Hall its name and that fueled the many fireplaces and the kitchen stoves. In the springtime the wood bloomed with a haze of bluebells and the delicate white starbursts of wild garlic; in the summer it provided cool respite; in the autumn I practiced creeping through fallen leaves as silently as a fox; and in the winter bare branches clawed their way toward the sky.

And beyond the wood and the fields, as far as the eye could see, were the moors: tall grasses bending in the wind; heather seeming scrubby and useless in the springtime but blossoming to brilliant pinkish purple in late summer; lowering skies warning of weather on its way; hawks circling high above; rabbits darting between tussocks; and random outcrops of silent stones.

The nannies and governesses never lasted, for various reasons. The place was remote, with little social life, my father being gone so much of the time and seeming to care little for society when he was home. Rowland could be curt and dismissive of those he considered beneath his station, and I suppose I seemed untamed and unmanageable much of the time. All in all, there was little to recommend it to anyone who might be hunting for work, although the household servants were remarkably steady.

We were insular at Thornfield-Hall, and I imagine I thought life would go on like that forever. But on my eighth birthday, everything changed.

We did not generally celebrate birthdays, but Cook always made a special sweet just for me, smiling as she laid it before me. Her smiles were rare, but when they appeared they were a sight to behold: dimples deep enough to lose a farthing in, and not one but two wide gaps between her front teeth, one up and one below. Once I thought I heard someone call her Susan, but for the most part we called her "Cook." She was extraordinary in her skills, making feasts at short notice and with whatever she had in her larder at the moment. My father nearly always ate by himself, and he wanted only plain food to fill his stomach, the quicker the better; but by the time Rowland was twelve, he was demanding the most exotic items he could think of, probably only to see if he could confound Cook and give reason for a scolding. She always nodded at his outlandish requests and smoothed her apron and set to work, and he rarely found excuse to complain.

Which does not mean he never did so.

Rowland, when he was home, ate mostly in the dining room, in full dress with a white neckcloth, sitting alone when Father was not in residence, reading the trade news from London or abroad, or examining his

butterfly collection. I envied that collection—such astonishing beauties—
but I could never understand how anyone could bear to kill those de-
fenseless creatures. As for myself, once I was released from dining in the
nursery, I usually ate in the kitchen, if for no other reason than that there I
was less likely to offend my brother, and therefore less likely to receive a
box on the head or a rap on the knuckles.

Rowland had had a tutor since he was eight or ten, and I looked forward
to the day when I could have a proper scholar to be teaching me as well.
Rowland's tutor was, no doubt, the second or third or fourth son of someone not wealthy enough or too old-fashioned to provide well for all his
offspring, or perhaps he was the son of a penniless vicar. I was naïve at
that age, but I'd overheard enough gossip among the servants to know that
if there was any fortune to be had in a family, it was vastly advantageous
to be the eldest son. I had not yet thought what that might mean for me, as
I was too enthralled with ideas of knights and pirates to be having practical notions about my own future.

I imagine that Mr. Richards, the tutor, was actually a decent teacher,
but Rowland, who was anxious only to get on with life, was at best an
indifferent student. Except in maths. Rowland loved calculations of all
sorts. The income needed per month to reach three thousand pounds in
two years. The odds at a horse race. The likelihood of being able to buy
some tumbledown building in any given town or city and hire laborers to
fix it up—if only to dab on a bit of whitewash to hide the worst of the
damage—and then sell it at enough of a profit to make the whole thing
worth the trouble. Or the market advantage of planting rye instead of oats,
or raising cattle versus sheep. One of the earliest arguments I ever heard
him have with our father must have been when I was about four and Rowland would have been twelve, and Rowland was trying to talk Father into
inclosing more of his land to increase his crop yields, sending the less-
industrious tenant farmers packing and turning over their fields to more
assiduous ones. "You can charge higher rents," I remember him saying,
"and the crop yields will be better. It is not our responsibility to provide a
living to incompetents."

Father just laughed and gave Rowland an affectionate cuff on the shoulder. He never followed through on any of Rowland's ideas, but even I could see his pride that this first son of his showed such interest in economic betterment.

I had always imagined that when I was old enough for the tutor, I would become as wise in the ways of the world as Rowland, and Father would laugh and cuff me on the shoulder too, and we three would dream up more and more inventive ways to make Father's wealth greater and greater.

CHAPTER 2

I rose early on that thirty-first day of March, my eighth birthday. I had gone to bed the night before with the anticipation of great things in the day or days ahead. There were hints of such possibilities—subtle ones, but even so, I, in my mostly careless abandon, had noticed. Several communications had arrived in the preceding weeks, some of which I managed to snatch a quick peek at before they were whisked away, but while I was not privy to their contents I saw that most were from my father, and I imagined that I, too, would soon begin my formal education. As well, there were whispered consultations in the kitchen and the back stairs, which ended the moment I appeared. I would have been dense indeed not to be aware that change was afoot.

Cook laid out two raisin buns for me at breakfast that day with an indulgent smile and offered to cook my eggs in whatever style I chose. I briefly thought over that momentous decision, and then fell back into what she always fixed: two boiled eggs with extra butter. She gave my shoulder a squeeze at that, and turned quickly away. I was buttering the buns when Holdredge stepped into the kitchen. As butler, Holdredge was much too busy and important most days for the likes of me, so it was a surprise when he strode right up to me. Immediately I wondered what I had done wrong, what mischief he had attributed to me. But he said only, "Master Edward, teatime in the dining room today. Promptly." And then he turned on his heel and left.

The formality of it terrified me. He had called me only "boy" before, as did my father, always. But my father was away, so whom was I being summoned to meet? I scraped through my mind, trying to think of what I had done in recent days to earn such a frightening order. It was true that I had forgotten to clean my boots after slogging through the horse yard on the last rainy day. My father and brother, of course, routinely left their messes for others to clean, but I was not—yet—privileged to do so. And I had tied a cowbell around the neck of Father's prize bull to see if its gentle sounds would render him as docile as the cows. That did not work, I discovered, and in fact he was nearly driven mad by the bell's insistent clanking. Removing it fell to one of the farm laborers, who was almost gored in the process. But that was two or three weeks before, and I had drawn only a sharp reprimand from Ames, my father's steward, and an order forbidding me to come within ten yards of any cattle. Yet I could not think of any other sin or transgression worthy enough to have me called "Master Edward" and summoned to the dining room.

The worry of it preyed on me as I ate my breakfast, and as soon as I finished I fled to the nursery, which was where Rowland found me. He was dressed for riding, which he did nearly every morning on his great black stallion, Thunder. "Well, Toad," he said, as if he were imparting news of which I, a mere child, was unaware, "it's your birthday today."

"It is," I responded amiably, suddenly imagining a gift of some sort in the hand he was hiding behind his back.

But he grabbed me by the collar and, throwing me facedown onto my cot, brought his riding crop from behind his back and gave me eight quick whacks. He left the room then without another word.

It is true that in certain households it is customary to give the birthday child spankings equal to his years, and it is also true that I was fully dressed and the crop left no lasting pain. Yet it was so far from the kindness I had allowed myself to hope for that I could do no other than remain, face in the bedclothes, weeping.

At this distance in time I recognize that my self-pity was perhaps overplayed. So many others have lived in far worse conditions that I cannot excuse it, except to say that I was a child and longed for a loving, or at least a friendly, act from time to time.

When I had recovered, I slipped down the back stairs, shoved my feet into my boots at the side-passage door, and stepped out into the courtyard, where I quickly dipped my head into the horse trough to wash away the redness of my eyes. The water, on that last day of March, was cold indeed, and it helped shock away whatever self-pity remained. I wandered across the rime-covered lawn and into the woods, where the undergrowth was wet and the trees stood bare and black against the cloud-driven sky, and I tore a little switch from a low-hanging branch and beat the trees with it as I passed them, one by one. In all honesty, I don't remember that the beating I gave them made me feel any better, but, again, I was eight years old. At some point, it occurred to me that if indeed the governess should be leaving and if, henceforth, I would be sharing the tutor with Rowland, I would be forced into Rowland's presence for hours at a time every day. I could not imagine how I could stand that, and it suddenly also occurred to me that Rowland might be feeling exactly the same way and was already laying out the terms of our accommodation.

———

I was, by a bare two minutes according to the clock in the Great Hall, early for teatime. But Rowland was already seated in his usual place in our father's absence, at the foot of the table. Pausing just briefly to determine my own appropriate place at that vast mahogany board, I knew two things immediately: one, that to sit at the opposite end would be an encroachment I dared not make; and two, to sit at his right hand, usually reserved for the female guest of highest honor, was to imply something I cared not to. So I chose his left hand instead, pulling out the chair and sitting in it as if I had every right in the world to be there. Rowland barely cast a glance at me.

Holdredge appeared exactly on the stroke of the hour, followed by Emily, bearing the tea tray. Holdredge stood behind Rowland and slightly to his left as Emily poured the tea, added the milk and sugar according to our preferences, which she well knew, and then set down a plate of scones and tea cakes and two small butter pats before slipping out of the room.

Holdredge cleared his throat and pulled a letter from the inside pocket of his waistcoat. He cleared his throat again and stared at the paper in his hand and said, "Your father requests that I read this correspondence to the two of you on the occasion of the young Master Edward's birthday." He cleared his throat a third time, and read:

26 March, Liverpool

For the edification of my sons:

Rowland is now sixteen years of age, high time for him to step out into the world. Edward is eight, time to put away childish things.

I have ordered that Richards be sent off; his work as Rowland's tutor is finished. Rowland will join me in Liverpool as expressly as can be arranged. He is to bring only a small valise of personal belongings. I will purchase for him whatever is needed for his new position in life. He will be journeying with me to Jamaica at the earliest next sailing, to serve and help me as I continue my ventures in that part of the world.

Edward is to go into tutelage with Mr. Hiram Lincoln of Black Hill, near Leeford. He is to pack immediately all his clothes and necessities, and Glover will drive him to Millcote, from which he can take the coach. Mr. Lincoln is expecting him on the third day of April. I charge Edward to comport himself in such a way that he will not be an embarrassment to the Rochester name. He will remain in Mr. Lincoln's care exclusively until I make further arrangements.

Until then, I remain,
George Howell Rochester, Esq.

I heard that letter with astonishment. And with a multitude of questions. Jamaica? Where is that? And then: Where is Black Hill? So far away that

I cannot come back for holidays? Even for the summer? Or will I be finished with Mr. Lincoln by summer?

I looked at Rowland, as if he would be able to clarify everything, but Rowland had pushed his chair back from the table and was grinning as broadly as a person possibly could. And no wonder: he was going to Liverpool, and after that to wherever Jamaica might be. He was going to be with Father, helping him with his business; all his financial calculations could be put into practice. In short, he was going to be in heaven. And I; I was going to be in Black Hill, for better or for worse.

I had two days in which to decide what to pack, and that mostly meant two days in which to decide how much of home to take with me. Fortunately, Knox was kind enough to help me with those decisions. She encouraged me to take the oft-mended cloth dog that I had slept with each night since Cook gave it to me the Christmas I was four. I had thought I should put away such a childish thing, but Knox confided, with a knowing nod, that when one is in a strange place, it can be a great comfort to have something familiar close at hand. Something in her voice made me picture her, as a child, in a situation not unlike my own, perhaps sent into service in a strange house with no one to comfort her. Without thinking, I reached my arms around her waist for the hug that I had so often hoped for, and she held me tight, her cheek against my hair for a moment, and it was all I could do to keep from crying as I lost what I had barely known I had.

———

Glover was waiting with the trap in the front courtyard at seven o'clock in the morning. Cook had already given me as hearty a breakfast as I could eat, and had further wrapped three pork pies and a half dozen ginger biscuits into a square of muslin for me to take, "to keep that stomach of yours from rebelling." She held me close to her ample bosom, careless for once of her floury hands, then hurried me along and turned quickly away. Holdredge and Knox waited at the front door to bid me farewell, the kind of display one might expect for my father or even Rowland but that came as a surprise to me. Holdredge shook my hand wordlessly in good-bye, and Knox put her hands on my shoulders and told me that she would expect me to comport myself in a proper manner, but I thought I saw moisture in her eyes. Then it was down the step and across the paving stones, and I climbed onto the trap, where my rope-bound trunk had already been laid, and I was off. I gazed back at Thornfield-Hall as it disappeared from sight, and Knox remained in the doorway for as long as I could see her.

In Millcote, Glover was kind enough to wait with me at the George Inn until the coach came through, whereupon he put my trunk up and made sure I was settled inside. He told the driver where I was bound before he gave a perfunctory wave and walked back to the trap. I had been a careless child, it is clear. In my yearning for the larger shows of love, I had barely noticed such little kindnesses. I forced back the tears and distracted myself by gazing about me, the cloth-wrapped parcel held possessively in my lap. To my left was a portly gentleman in a brown waistcoat and yellow trousers who smelled of snuff and who had an abundance of whiskers covering his jowls. To my right was a lady in a dark gray traveling outfit who spent most of her time holding her skirts close, as if afraid I might infect her. Across from me sat another woman, with a girl younger than I, and beside them a man, large and red-faced, opened his eyes just enough to see me enter and then closed them again and proceeded to snore.

I had never been farther from home than Millcote, and there only three or four times, so I spent most of the journey staring out the coach windows at moors and fields, hills and dales, and occasional villages with muddy sheep grazing in the commons. The woman and the girl left us at Keighley, but two men took their place, wearing heavy blue greatcoats that seemed the worse for wear. Their entrance disturbed the sleeping man in the corner and caused much grumbling and resettling among the three of them. A few times they glanced across at me and the lady beside me, as if wondering whether one of us, who took up so much less space, could be persuaded to change places, but they never asked. I sat back into my seat as comfortably as possible, sleepy after a night of anticipation and fear. The coach stopped a few more times, but no one got off and the new passengers had to climb up top. The day waned, and shadows spread over the fells and dales around us.

The coach let us all off at the Four Bells, where the others would spend the night, and from which I was to be picked up and driven to Black Hill. By that time it was dark, and there seemed to be no one there for me, so I lugged my trunk into the common room and found a place to sit. It was far from the fire, near which all the seats had already been taken, but it was still warmer and somewhat lighter than it was outside. My stomach rumbled, but with everything else taken care of for me, I had been sent off without money, and I had long since eaten the pork pies and biscuits. The lady who had been sitting beside me had disappeared, but the two men in greatcoats were standing near the fire, engaged in banter with the innkeeper. One of them eventually noticed me and strode over. "You're by yourself, boy?" he asked. "Not with the lovely lady?"

"No, sir, I am on my own."

"And not having anything to eat?"

"They are coming for me," I said, not wanting to reveal that I had no money.

"Who is coming?"

I shrugged, because indeed I had no idea who was coming. "From Black Hill," I said.

He turned away then, going back to his companion and the landlord, who said something to the men that made them laugh, but he looked over at me with a new curiosity. Some minutes later a barmaid brought me a plate of cold roast beef and a knob of bread, but I shook my head, telling her I had no money to pay. She smiled, showing blackened teeth. "Never mind," she said, and she shoved the plate into my hands. I fell to it, thinking it the best meal I had had in months.

I must have nodded off, because the next thing I knew someone was shaking me awake. I opened my eyes to see a man, short and broad and nearly square, grasping my shoulders with both hands. "Master Rochester," he said in a gravelly voice, "is this you?"

I nodded wordlessly.

"And it's me to get you," he said. When, still dazed with sleep, I didn't respond, he added, "For Black Hill."

With that I was up like a shot. He shouldered my trunk and led the way to an old cart parked outside, drawn by an even older horse. There was but one seat—for the driver—so I climbed into the cart and sat beside my trunk as we jolted along in the darkness. Not a star was in sight; even the moon had disappeared, and I wondered how the strange man could find the way in such complete darkness, until I realized that he was probably giving the horse its rein and letting it find its own way home.

It must have been about an hour, though it seemed half the night, before the driver turned to me and said, "There it is, just ahead." I could still see nothing—no candle burning in a window, no slant of moonlight against a brass door handle, nothing. Then I began to hear a difference in the hoof-beats, as if the horse were hurrying toward the stable, and the driver said, "Yee," to stop him. In the sudden silence I could hear only the wind in the trees and a distant owl and the snort of the horse.

The driver climbed down and pulled my trunk from the cart, leaving me to get out in darkness as he walked to the door. He did not pull a bell but just walked in, and as soon as the door opened I could see a faint light—enough to follow him by. He preceded me into a room with a fireplace burning low and a lump of something seen dimly in the glow of a single candle.

As we came closer, the lump stirred and I could make out that it must be a man sitting in a chair, and I stopped. The cart driver dropped my trunk unceremoniously and left. "Come closer," said the man in the chair. "Let me see you in the light."

I stepped as close as I dared, shivering from the cold or from anxiety, or both.

"Closer," he said, and I took another step. "Do you know who I am?" he asked.

"Mr. Hiram Lincoln?" I responded.

"You are young Edward Rochester," he said. It was not a question, so I did not reply.

"Are you not?" he demanded.

"Yes, sir, I am," I said.

"You are very late."

"I had to wait for the cart. I did not know how to come otherwise."

"Hmm," he said. I had gotten a better look at him by then—he seemed a huge man, both tall and heavy, and his voice was unusually high. "We go to bed with the sun here at Black Hill," he said.

"Yes, sir. I'm sorry, sir," I said.

"And we rise with the sun."

"Yes, sir."

He gazed at me for a time without saying anything. There was something about him that I sensed, a kind of latent power, and I realized that not only was I powerless—a feeling I was used to anyway—but I had little idea of where I was, or for how long, or what was to become of me afterwards. "There are three of you boys now," he said. "The other two share the big bed. You will sleep on the cot. Did you bring your own bedding?"

"No, sir, I did not know—"

"You should have known. Your people should have told you."

I said nothing, dismay rising in my throat.

He sighed heavily. "It's up the steps," he said. "Just the one room. You will have to sleep in your clothes tonight, then."

Standing, he proved to be the biggest man I had ever seen, even in the semidarkness. "Are you waiting for a candle?" he asked. "You won't need one; the cot is just at the top of the steps, next to the wall on your left." He turned away, taking the one candle with him, and I scurried to the steps before the candle glow fully disappeared, leaving my trunk where the driver had dropped it.

CHAPTER 3

A thumb and forefinger lifted my eyelid. "He's dark," said a voice.

I shook my head away from the fingers, opening my eyes on my own and raising myself on my elbows. There were two boys. One appeared to be three or four years older than I, with flaming ginger hair; the other was small, with a freckled oval face and light brown hair.

"What's your name?" asked the ginger-haired one.

"Edward Fairfax Rochester," I said. "What's yours?"

"Edward Fairfax Rochester? That's far too much of a name for a boy your size."

I blinked at him. I had little experience with boys my age—only Rowland, who was not my age, and the two stableboys, with whom I had sometimes played horseshoes when their duties allowed.

"How old?" he demanded.

"Eight."

"Eight," he repeated, in a tone that implied I had affirmed his suspicions.

"And how—"

But he was interrupted by a woman's voice from below: "Boys!"

The two immediately began throwing on their clothes. I rose from my cot—despite the cold and my fears of this place, I had slept like the dead—and I set myself to straightening my rumpled clothes and running a hand through my hair and putting on my shoes, and I hurried downstairs after the others.

Mr. Lincoln was already seated at the table, drinking the first of, as I was later to learn, many cups of coffee, a huge globe on a stand beside him. He glanced up as we tumbled down the steps. "You have met Rochester, I presume," he said, as if new boys appeared all the time.

"We have," the ginger-haired boy said. The smaller one nodded silently.

"And," Mr. Lincoln continued, "has he met you?"

There was a moment's hesitation, and Mr. Lincoln spoke into it. "I thought not. That one is Thomas Fitzcharles," he said to me, "but for obvious reasons he's called 'Carrot' in this place. And the other one is William Gholson; we call him 'Touch.' As for you"—he leveled his eyes at me— "I shall have to see. In the meantime, sit down, the three of you, and put something in your stomachs."

I held back, unsure, as the other boys took their places, and then I sat in the remaining chair, the one to Mr. Lincoln's left, next to the globe. A woman, who I later learned was called Athena—but who seemed as little like the Greek goddess as I could imagine a woman to be; perhaps Mr. Lincoln had given her a new name too—brought coffee in mugs for the three of us, and a plate of bread, which the other two fell to pulling apart, leaving barely a crust for me. Mr. Lincoln seemed not to notice, and I took my crust and dunked it into my coffee and hoped my stomach would not complain too vociferously.

"Your father is a gentleman," Mr. Lincoln said, looking at me over his spectacles.

The other two stared at me. "I believe so, sir," I said.

"But he is also in trade."

The boy called Touch looked down at his mug, but Carrot continued to watch me, his eyes slightly narrowing at this last.

"I suppose he is," I bumbled on, too inexperienced to understand the disapproval the phrase might carry.

"He has business interests," Mr. Lincoln went on. "In Liverpool, I believe."

I hesitated.

"Not in Liverpool?" he asked, his eyebrows rising.

"I think he has some business in Jamaica as well, sir," I said, unsure what, exactly, was the case. I felt as vulnerable as one of Rowland's mounted butterflies.

"Jamaica," he said, "hmm." Then: "Do you know where that is?"

"No, sir."

"No, sir, what?"

Panic rose, but nothing came out of my mouth.

"One must speak civilly at all times," Mr. Lincoln admonished, ignoring my discomfort. "A gentleman does not give the shortest possible answer to a question if he is able to phrase it in a more comprehensive manner. 'No, sir, I do not know' is an acceptable response to such a question, although it is the least acceptable of all possible ones." He was still staring at me over his spectacles, and I could hear the other two sniggering into their hands.

"No, sir, I do not know where that is," I said.

"And why not?"

"I hadn't a map that showed it, sir." Not that I would have thought to look for it if I'd had one.

"Not even a globe?" he demanded.

"No, sir, not even a globe." At that, I felt a quick nudge of my foot under the table, and I glanced at the two boys, who were both gazing at me, but I did not know whose foot had touched mine, nor what it had meant.

Mr. Lincoln took a swallow of his coffee and rapped the table with his knuckle. The woman came and refilled his mug. "You're a quick learner, I'll say that for you," he said to me. Turning to the others, he asked, "What do we know about Jamaica?"

There was a moment of silence, and then Carrot said, "I don't know anything, sir. Except where it is."

"I don't know anything either, sir," Touch said, the first words from his mouth that I had heard. His voice sounded rusty, as if from lack of use.

Mr. Lincoln turned to the globe and gave it a spin. "Here we are in

England," he said, pointing a broad finger. Then he looked closely at me. "Do you know where London is?"

"Yes, sir, I do." I laid a finger on the globe.

"*No!*" he shouted. "One does not *touch* a globe with what undoubtedly are greasy fingers!" He pulled out a pocket-handkerchief and rubbed my filth from the face of England.

"I'm sorry, sir," I said.

He stared steadily at me, and I wished I could melt into my shoes, and then he said, "How far from London are we on the globe—if you can tell me without touching it?"

I looked at the globe, afraid to bring my finger close to it, and unable to understand what he was asking.

"How far?" he asked again, leaning forward. "A finger's breadth, two fingers?"

It was a large globe, but still, England is a small country. "It's a finger's breadth, I think, sir," I said.

To my great relief, Mr. Lincoln turned to Carrot. "And where is Jamaica? You said you knew that?"

"Yes, sir, I do know." He pulled a handkerchief from his own pocket and, with it covering his hand, as he had evidently been taught to do, he turned the globe, located the place, and pointed, his finger close to but not actually touching the globe's surface. "Here is Jamaica, sir, in the Caribbean Ocean."

"And how far is that from us, would you think?" Mr. Lincoln asked me. "How many handspans?"

I had no idea.

"Well?"

"Would that be my handspans or yours, sir?" I asked, playing for time.

He leaned back in his chair and smiled. "It's goodly far. Not a distance one travels on a whim. You understand that, I suppose. And what do you know of Jamaica, other than that your father has business there?"

"I know nothing of it, sir."

"We shall have to remedy that. You see those bookshelves?" I could not have avoided seeing them; they almost completely covered the walls of the room. "You will find there books on nearly everything you might want to know, as well as many, many things you never thought to wonder. That is the purpose of a good library. You will no doubt find something there about Jamaica, and you shall report on what you have found at tea this evening. In the meantime, these two shall study with me. You are excused."

I rose and turned, overwhelmed by the task before me. The books—shelves upon shelves of them—seemed arranged in no particular order. How would I find Jamaica in this apparent hodgepodge? I glanced back helplessly, but Mr. Lincoln and the two others had already focused their attention on the tabletop, rolling out sheets of paper that I later learned were maps, and placing little square tokens on them. In desperation, I stepped to the nearest wall and began my search. Eventually I discovered that indeed there was an order to the books—a mostly geographical one—and with that, I was able to find some likely-looking volumes and I sat down on the floor and began reading.

I was soon swept up by that far-off island, and nearly half the day passed before I realized that those at the table were not speaking English. Startled, I looked toward them: Mr. Lincoln was still in his chair, but leaning over the table, while Touch and Carrot stood at each side of him. All were gazing at the display before them, but I had no idea what they were talking about or even what language they were speaking. Curiosity got the better of me for a moment, and feeling exiled, I longed to join them, to see what was so intriguing. But I reminded myself that I had been given a different task, and this first day was the time to prove myself, so I turned back to the book in hand and did not notice anything else until Athena brought me a cheese pie and a glass of watered beer.

The fact that my meal had been brought to me made clear that I was expected to stay in place, and so I did, still feeling the exile. No one spoke to me: it was as if I were not even in the room. Remembering Mr. Lincoln's shout not to touch the globe with possibly greasy hands, I ate cautiously, careful not to drop crumbs into my book. The day slid by, neither fast nor slow, but by the time it grew too dim in my corner to read, I had gone through the Jamaica parts of six books. To tell the truth, at that point I knew more about that island country than I did about England.

At the end of the day, Mr. Lincoln said, "Well?" and I knew by his raised voice that he was speaking to me. "What have you to tell us?"

He did not invite me to the table, so I stayed where I was. "Jamaica was discovered on May 5, 1494, by Christopher Columbus—"

"Discovered?" Mr. Lincoln interrupted. "*Discovered?* Had no one else ever been there before? Was it vacant of any population?"

The sudden vehemence of his attack startled me, and for a moment I struggled for a response. "No, sir," I said. "There were native people there and they came out in seventy or more canoes to greet him, all painted and dressed in feathers."

"Ah"—he leaned back in his chair—"there was a battle."

"No, sir, there was not, because Columbus made a big show of friendship, and even later, when he thought it necessary, he brought forth his crossbows and after a few of the natives were wounded, they left off any more shows of defiance. Also, he had a dog."

Mr. Lincoln raised his eyebrows. "He had a dog?"

"A very big one, sir. A frighteningly big one."

"Did the natives have no weapons?"

"Yes, sir, they did have some, but only lances and bows and arrows. No crossbows, which are more powerful and can be used from a greater distance."

"Come join us for tea and tell us the rest," he said, as if I had piqued his interest. "Athena!" he called. "It's past our teatime."

I gathered up my books and brought them to the table in case I needed to make reference. At some point, Athena brought the tea, but I hardly took notice; I was so busy reporting on all that I had learned. It was the first time such a thing had ever happened to me: one adult and two other boys listening raptly to my accounts of the Spanish colonization, the pirates who circled the Caribbean, the battle with the English for the island and their use of buccaneers against both the Spanish and the French, the great sea battles for control of the island, the slaves and the Maroons and the Creoles—both white and black—the cocoa and later the sugar plantations, the earthquakes and the hurricanes, the slave trade; all of it taking place on this exotic, sand-garlanded island. I had, on that day, fallen in love with Jamaica.

It was nearly bedtime by the time I finished. Carrot was staring at me. Touch was drawing figures with his finger on the tabletop. Mr. Lincoln was beaming. "Very good," he said, nodding. Then he leaned forward. "But there is more, you know."

"I don't understand, sir," I said.

He leaned back and smiled. "But you will," he said. "You will." He gazed at each of the other boys in turn, before looking again at me. "You have made a start at least, and that is enough for one day." He rose then and lifted a candlestick as signal that it was time to retire. He started away from the table but suddenly turned back to me. "Jamaica," he said, "is a very interesting place. Very interesting. Jamaica. We shall be calling you that: Jamaica."

"Very good, sir," I said, not knowing at all whether it would be good or not.

CHAPTER 4

I could not get Jamaica out of my head. As I climbed into my cot—barely noticing that Athena had put a quilt on it—I was already recounting more than I had told at teatime, starting with Columbus' huge black dog, larger than any such animal the natives had ever seen, frightening them so terribly that, after their first attempt, they rarely tried to attack again.

"That's no surprise," Carrot said. "He probably ate some of them."

"No, he didn't," I said. "I'm sure. The book never said it, anyway."

"I bet he did, though." In the dark, I could tell he was grinning.

"Tell again about the buccaneers," Touch said.

"No, tell about the earthquake," Carrot said. "But here, come get in bed with us. Tell about the man who was buried alive and then washed out to sea."

So I climbed in between them, as they insisted, pulling my quilt on top of the three of us, and I whispered to them about Lewis Galdy, who was first swallowed up by a massive chasm when the Great Earthquake erupted, and afterwards, in a subsequent shock, was spat out of the ground and cast into the sea, whence he escaped by swimming to a boat.

"Could you do that?" Carrot asked. "Or would you be too afraid?"

I imagined the earth closing around me, imagined the panic.

"You would be afraid, wouldn't you?" he challenged.

"I would be," Touch said.

"I don't know how to swim," I said.

"I don't either," Touch said.

"We'll have to learn," Carrot said.

We all went to sleep that night imagining ourselves sitting down to dinner and hearing the terrible noise when the ground opened with choking fumes of sulfur, everyone thinking hell was coming forth on earth as the streets washed into the harbor and the sea rose in mighty waves, tearing ships from their anchorages and sweeping them inland over the sunken ruins of the town.

After that, we three always slept together, with me in the middle. It was cozy, and we found it easy to imagine ourselves bunked together in a pirate ship, sailing in the West Indies. Some nights I told stories about Captain Morgan, who quit being a buccaneer when he was made lieutenant governor of Jamaica; and Blackbeard and Calico Jack; and the female pirates Anne Bonny and Mary Read, who were not executed with the rest of their gang because they were both with child at the time.

And sometimes Touch would make up stories of his own for us. As quiet and gentle as he was, he had a powerfully inventive imagination. The sea was full of not only pirates in his tales, but sea serpents and mermaids as well, and more than one sailor lost his heart to those golden-haired sirens, or his life to a beast that rose unexpectedly from the depths of the Caribbean. I marveled at the way he could make my mind see just what his mind saw. He was four months younger than I, yet he seemed to have absorbed so much more of the world's magic. I wanted to see things the way he did—to have his imagination and his kindness—and at the same time I wanted to be like Carrot, too, who was so sure of himself, who never doubted that life would always treat him well.

In those first days, around Mr. Lincoln's map-covered table, I discovered the world. He was consumed by maps—in fact, among ourselves we sometimes called him "Maps," because he had so many and seemed to love them above all else. Meticulous, colorful, hand-drawn maps, printed maps, entire books of maps—the whole world laid out like an architect's drawing, as if one could indeed know all the workings of the universe if one could only devour enough maps. Soon enough I came to notice drawings on those maps: a sea serpent peeking over the waves, a compass decorating a corner, even a schooner in full sail.

Carrot nodded toward the schooner. "Touch drew those," he said.

I glanced at Mr. Lincoln for confirmation, and he smiled and nodded. "Our friend here has a rare talent," he said.

I noticed then that Touch's eyes were downcast, but he was grinning.

"You could be a mapmaker!" I said enthusiastically.

"He could, if he wanted," Carrot said.

"Indeed," Mr. Lincoln said. But Touch did not acknowledge their words, nor did he look up at us, and the smile had disappeared from his face. It would be months before I understood why their encouragement pained him so.

Though he never beat us, Mr. Lincoln could be a most difficult man, and he brooked no foolishness. I quickly learned, as the others already had, to see beneath the surface of his questions, understanding that the correct answer was never enough; it was always more important to know *why* it was correct. He believed in saturating us with learning, so that from the moment we came downstairs for breakfast until the light had faded and we trooped up to bed, we were nearly always studying something, talking about something, learning something.

His teaching was all about war: the wars against Napoléon when I arrived, but later, Julius Caesar's campaigns and other wars that suited his purposes from time to time. What boy does not imagine himself a hero? Five and a half days a week, Monday morning to Saturday noon, we leaned over the maps, aligning our tokens in battle order—red for the British troops and blue for the French, and green and brown and black and purple for the other nations—and we fought those battles. Or we calculated the time it would take a thousand troops to pass a specific point, or the trajectory of a cannonball or the operation of a trebuchet, the weight of a barrel of salt pork or a barrel of rum, and the mechanics of lifting such heavy weights aboard a ship.

For the Napoleonic Wars we spoke French—or the rest did, as I struggled to follow along. Unswayed by my ignorance of the language, Mr.

Lincoln spoke to me in French anyway, asking questions I did not understand and waiting impatiently for answers I could not give, until the others finally supplied the answers for me. The fact that I had no French seemed to matter to no one but me; they gave me no quarter, and thus I learned it to keep myself in the game. Though, in fact, it was no game; every discussion was deadly serious.

Touch came from a village twelve miles away, which distance he walked if the weather was fair when he went home after noon on Saturdays, with part of a loaf of bread to eat en route, returning by dark on Sunday evenings. If the weather was inclement, his brother came for him on horseback and they rode double on the return. Touch never said much about his home, but I learned that he was the elder of two boys, and his father was a vicar, and I could imagine that there were high hopes laid on Touch's narrow shoulders. As I watched him leave each Saturday, I often imagined going with him, sitting down at the vicarage table and enjoying a family meal. I actually asked once, after I had been at Mr. Lincoln's for a few weeks, if I might go home with him sometime, but with less than his usual warmth, Touch just said, "You wouldn't like it," and turned away. I never asked again.

I was far from unhappy, though, to be left with Carrot. We spent our half-Saturdays and Sundays exploring on our own, creeping through the Yorkshire wood as Captain Cabot and his men in the wilds of America, or British scouts spying on the French, or even British soldiers as the French tried to invade at Dover or Hastings or Bournemouth. We fashioned sabers from sticks and imagined muskets slung over our shoulders. Mr. Lincoln didn't even own a musket, but he had taught us exactly the procedure for cocking and loading such a gun. We knew why soldiers need to wear bright-colored clothing: when five or ten thousand troops are firing their muskets and the smoke is intolerably thick, it's essential to be able to discern one's own men from the enemy. We took those times seriously, for we thought, in those days, that we knew all we needed to know to make soldiers of ourselves. Carrot, of course, was always in command: he was a natural leader, admired for his easy authority and his wild abandon.

Despite what Mr. Lincoln had said the night I arrived, we spent many evenings after dark with him reading to us by the light of a single candle. It was always the philosophers, and, for Mr. Lincoln, it was like reading from the Bible—unlike with texts we studied during the day, there was to be no discussion, no argument; whatever he read simply *was*. When the candle guttered out he usually went on from memory, reciting from Plato's *Apology* or *The Republic* or the writings of Aristotle. He particularly liked Thucydides on the Peloponnesian Wars, but he didn't seem to care for the Romans, which was odd, since his Latin was much better than his Greek.

At the approach of Easter, Touch went home for a whole week and even Carrot left for a similar time. Though he would not tell me where he was going, I assumed he was spending the days with his mother, to whom he wrote every week. By then I had been at Black Hill three weeks and would have been glad of a trip back to Thornfield to play again in the woods, employing my new warlike skills, and to tell Knox and Cook about my new friends. Indeed, as I watched Carrot and Touch prepare to leave, I asked Mr. Lincoln if I ought not to prepare as well, but he told me that there was no point in it, for with my father and brother gone to Jamaica, the place had no doubt been closed up. *No one there?* I thought. *Surely that cannot be.* I could not imagine the Hall closed and empty, and that first night, alone in the bed, I held my breath and forbade myself any pity.

Mr. Lincoln suspended studies in the absence of the others, and indeed he himself journeyed to Skipton for the holiday, leaving me in the care of Athena. Though I asked to eat in the kitchen with her and North—the man who had fetched me from the Four Bells, and who served as a man-of-all-work around the little house and grounds—she insisted on bringing my meals to the table as always, and I was left to eat alone. I amused myself those days with inspecting the bookshelves, picking out books at random. Or I unrolled maps and made my own war games, playing one side against the other. Often I wandered in the fields and marshes and woodlands beyond the little cottage. I assumed everyone would return by sunset on Easter Sunday evening, but when darkness fell and I was still alone, I clomped up to bed feeling more dejected than I had the first night they were all gone. I told myself that surely on Monday someone would return. There was a time, before Black Hill, when I had preferred being on my own to being shut up in the schoolroom with a governess, but now that I had known friendship, I missed Carrot's bold ventures and Touch's inventive tales.

The next morning from a window I caught sight of Mr. Lincoln, home at last, squeezing his large self out of a hackney coach and standing before the cottage as if he were surveying it for the first time. I felt a surge of resentment. I thought to ignore his arrival, letting him know I did not at all care that I had been left on my own, but my excitement got the better of me and I was unable to resist opening the door and calling a greeting. "Ah, yes," he responded distractedly. "Jamaica. You're here, then," he added, as if he had expected me to be elsewhere.

Touch came back midafternoon, rosy faced from the exertion of his walk. In the pack he carried were cold lamb left over from Easter dinner and a few currant buns, which he kindly shared with me. I could not stop smiling, so happy was I to be back in the warmth of his presence. I asked him about everything he did while he was at home, and he told me in his usual froggy voice that it was nothing different from any of his other weekly visits, just longer.

"Do you play at war with your brother?" I pressed.

"Oh no," he responded, "we would never do that."

"Do you explore in the woods?"

He shrugged. "Sometimes we hunt for ramps."

I studied his mild freckled face in dismay, and I suppose he sensed my disappointment. "It's nothing there, Jam, really. It's much more fun here," he said. But he had no idea how I pined for a real home, with a real family.

Carrot was the last to return, the candle lanterns of his carriage announcing his arrival long before we could hear the thud and scrape of the horses' hooves. He walked in grinning, trailing a footman carrying his trunk. He seemed to have grown a foot taller in the ten days he had been gone. He laughed and joked and carried on until it was time for bed, and even in bed he was restless and could not stop talking. I asked again where he'd been, and he chuckled. "Well, Jam, I've been to York," he said. "Would have gone to London, but my father was in York on some matter or another."

He had never spoken of a father; I had assumed his mother was a widow. "I didn't know you had a father," I said, stupidly.

"Oh yes," he responded, his voice full of mirth. "And he's the Duke of—"

"*Duke?*"

"Well, I was born on the wrong side of the blanket, but there you are. And the thing is"—he laughed a little—"he may put me aside for now in a place like this where no one can see me, but he can hardly deny me. I have his hair, you see."

Carrot was far wiser in the ways of the world than I. I had no idea what he meant, and hard as I might try, I could not imagine what difference the placement of a blanket could make, but it didn't matter. I was just happy to have the two of them, as dear to me as brothers, back where they belonged.

The weather had turned to spring: fields suddenly were greener, buds on the trees ready to burst; newborn lambs frolicked on distant meadows; and we boys, let off from our studies early some days, ran outside and reenacted our battles in the nearby fields. Seeing we could not be kept indoors, Mr. Lincoln got out paper and laid a quill pen on the table. "Build a siege engine," he said. "Design and build one yourselves."

Grinning, Touch reached for the pen, and Carrot and I began discussing how tall it should be, how large a rock it should throw, how we should place the counterweight. We searched Mr. Lincoln's shelves, pulling down book after book, studying illustrations of Roman siege engines and of the attack on Rhodes. Carrot and I talked, argued, tried to convince each other; and then suddenly, without consulting either of us, Touch began drawing. It was magical, watching the design flow from his pen. Soon Carrot and I had stopped arguing and we were building on each other's ideas, and as Touch drew he added his own ideas, more elegant than either

Carrot's or mine, and we laughed and pointed and slapped each other on the back, and though I did not notice Mr. Lincoln or his expression, I have no doubt that he was leaning back in his chair, satisfied.

None of us would have believed we could do it. It took us weeks, from scouring the wood for the right trees, to sawing and edging the wood, and then putting the whole thing together. But by the end of July we had the machine built, and Mr. Lincoln even came outside to witness the first trial. It was, admittedly, a weak attempt, but after that failure we went back to work with renewed energy, rebuilding the machine until we had cured all its defects. Again we brought Mr. Lincoln outside. We mounted a rock the size of a cannonball into the bucket. It took all three of us to pull down the bucket, but when we released it, the rock sailed directly at the target, and even Mr. Lincoln joined in our cheers. We could not have been more excited if we had stormed Oporto ourselves.

That first Christmas, I was again left to my own devices for ten days. *Ten days.* Alone, I wandered the rime-covered fields and moors; I poked a stick to break the ice over a slow-moving stream; I helped North feed and brush the dilapidated horse; I sat on the floor in a patch of sun and leafed through Mr. Lincoln's books. Sometimes I closed my eyes and remembered Christmas at Thornfield-Hall. My father had never made much of the holiday, but he did see to having a tree set up in the Great Hall, and Mrs. Knox oversaw the decorating, and all the cottagers came on Christmas Eve to receive gifts and to pull at their forelocks in acknowledgment. And I would receive a gift or two, and all the household had a grand dinner of ham and plum pudding. I wondered what Christmas would be like for my father and brother in Jamaica; if there would be a palm for a tree and if one could find plums on the island.

Although Athena did not cook ham on Christmas Day, at least she allowed me for once to eat my dinner of pork roast in the kitchen with her and North. Still, I longed for the others to return. Mr. Lincoln again came back first, with a brief New Year's greeting before he disappeared into his room to read whatever letters had come in his absence. I waited by the window for Touch and greeted him with open arms, and almost immediately I talked him into drawing pictures: a wicked pirate with a huge curved sword and hair more straggly than mine, and a grisly sea monster, and when we trooped up to bed, I put my arm across his shoulders and thought that if I had had a younger brother, I would have wanted him to be just like Touch.

But without Carrot, we felt incomplete. When he did come back the next day, he was laughing and joking and going on and on as if he'd had no thought for how lonely I had been without him and Touch. The more he carried on, the angrier I grew at his good humor in light of my abandonment until, without thinking, I punched him in the stomach. Astonished, he stared at me, and not knowing what else to do, I gave him another, harder, blow. He grabbed my arms to stop me, but I could not be stopped, yelling incomprehensible words and crying at the same time, until Mr. Lincoln came out of his room, took one look, and bellowed, "*Stop!*"

That brought me to my senses at last, and I looked up at Carrot and he looked down at me and said, simply, "I missed you, too, Jam."

I put my arms around him in relief, and Carrot pulled Touch over, and we all three stood in the middle of the room, arms around one another. Mr. Lincoln retreated to his own chamber. None of us ever spoke of my outburst, and with grit and determination I handled the subsequent holidays more stoically.

———

In the spring, Mr. Lincoln brought out the maps of Gaul, and we began speaking Latin for the Gallic Wars. "In every battle the eyes are the first to be conquered," Tacitus wrote. The most important virtue in battle is to visually intimidate the enemy. It was a lesson I would not soon forget.

Human nature is motivated by fear, according to Thucydides. In our day we do it with battalions of smartly dressed soldiers, but in more primitive times it was often done with a ferocious appearance. Caesar reported that the early Britons painted themselves dark blue to attain a more intimidating aspect, and so, for us, blue became the color for the British tribes.

Mr. Lincoln showed us drawings of woad and sent us out into the countryside to gather leaves to make blue dye. We had a hellish time finding the right plant, and in fact we returned to the cottage twice with the wrong thing. Late in the day, we found the distinctive yellow flowers and bent to our task as quickly as possible. Running home, my arms full of woad, I stumbled over a tussock and fell, twisting my foot and feeling my ankle give way. Carrot, who was ahead as usual, ran on, but Touch came up behind me, his face a picture of concern.

Kneeling beside me, he asked, "Is it broken?"

"I don't know," I said, "but it hurts."

He touched my ankle gently, and I winced in pain. "Can you walk if I help you?" he asked.

It took a deal of negotiating for the two of us to walk back to the cottage together, still clinging to our precious harvest. I was half again his size and weight, and I could tell he could barely keep upright himself with me leaning so heavily on him, but we managed, and when we returned, Athena fashioned a poultice for my ankle. Carrot and Touch babied me and brought me books, and Touch drew pictures of Balboa sighting the Pacific Ocean for the first time.

That reminded me that we had never learned to swim, and Carrot promised that as soon as my ankle was healed we would go to the little nearby lake and teach each other. Touch grimaced at that, and when Carrot was distracted whispered that I might have to save him, for he was afraid of water. I nodded and told him never to worry; I would take care of him as he had taken care of me. It occurred to me then, in his secret admission, that a kind boy like Touch should not have been learning the arts of war. He should have been poring over the philosophers and reading the sonnets of Shakespeare and drawing whatever he was able to conjure in his mind. And, to my great loss, it turned out that his father, the vicar, thought so too.

The day after the woad-gathering episode, Mr. Lincoln led us through the complicated procedure of making the blue dye, which involved, to our boyish delight, the fermentation of the crushed leaves in human urine.

We managed to make enough pigment to color ourselves, and Carrot and Touch then crept through the high grass behind the cottage, daring Roman legions to attack. It was great fun for them, and even I, sitting on a bench at the doorstep, felt the thrill of adventure, but it all ended unhappily. At home that next Saturday, Touch, unthinking, let slip the adventures of the previous week. Unfortunately, the vicar did not think that wandering the countryside painted in urine, pretending to be heathen Picts, was ideal for his son's education. Touch did not return the next day; instead, a note arrived on Monday stating that William would no longer be studying at Black Hill.

I was stunned. Of the three of us, Carrot was the leader, always. But Touch—Touch had seemed almost a part of me, as if, indeed, he really was my younger brother. I had taken him for granted all those months, as if he would always be there. How often had I watched him go home each Saturday, wishing I could go home with him. Carrot, who noticed my distress, was more philosophical. "You have to be ready for that, Jam. There is no one you cannot lose, no one other than yourself who can make you the man you will become. And"—here he looked me meaningfully in the eye—"there is no one who can hurt you, if you do not allow it."

I gazed at him—more than a head taller than I, his ruddy face and his mouth set in a determined line—and I wished I could be like that, and I decided I would try. But every night, with just Carrot and me, I still missed Touch and his stories tremendously.

Some time later, as the first chills of autumn turned the leaves to yellow, a new boy arrived. He was the same age as Carrot, though he was not nearly as tall, but what he lacked in height he made up for in weight. Mr. Lincoln named him Pies, because he could—and did—eat four or five of Athena's meat pies at one sitting, until Mr. Lincoln put a stop to it. Pies rarely made excursions outside unless Mr. Lincoln forced him to, but some winter days it was so cold that even Carrot and I remained indoors. Pies' talents, if he had any, lay in the province of food, and thenceforth Mr. Lincoln made him the quartermaster, tasking him with calculating the provisions for whatever army or whatever naval vessel we were discussing at the time.

Another boy came that next spring, a thin boy whose face was pockmarked and whose teeth stuck out in what seemed like a random arrangement, so that his lips did not close over them, and who at first hung his head and stared at the floor and did not say anything, no matter what Mr. Lincoln said or did. He climbed into bed with us that first night, Pies having taken over the cot from the start, and he turned his back to us. Almost immediately the mattress began to shake gently with his sobs.

"It does no good to cry," Carrot said.

"Maybe he's lonely," I whispered.

"Everybody gets lonely, Jam," Carrot retorted. Then he repeated himself in a louder voice, "Everybody gets lonely. You have to play the cards you were dealt."

The shaking of the mattress stopped and in the silence I could hear the boy's breathing. "Does he beat us?" he asked softly after a few moments.

"Mr. Lincoln?" I asked, astonished.

"Of course not," Carrot said. "What kind of place do you think this is?"

"The last place vey did. Mr. Bertrand and his wife boaf."

I felt the room pressing in on me.

"For what?" Carrot asked.

"For anyfing. For not having clean cloves, but it's hard to get vem clean in such icy water and wifout soap. For eating more van our share. For asking to go to the privy in the middle of a lesson. For shivering in the cold; for not knowing an answer to a question."

"He doesn't beat us," I assured him. "No matter what, he doesn't."

Carrot laughed. "He sits in his chair from the moment he gets out of bed in the morning until the moment he goes back at night. He hasn't the energy to beat anyone."

"He's not that kind of man," I said.

"Well, ven, what kind is he?" the boy asked.

There was a silence while Carrot and I considered that. "He knows what boys like," Carrot said after a while.

"He knows *most* of what boys like," I amended.

The boy turned over onto his back, and I could imagine him staring at the ceiling.

"You'll be all right," I said.

But he was not. He was the most fearful person I had ever met—or have since. Mr. Lincoln called him "Mouse," and perhaps it was not the kindest name, but it was not the worst he could have chosen. Despite our assurances, Mouse was terrified of doing something wrong, of being punished, of being sent away. But in the end, he went on his own, barely three months after he had come.

———

For a while after Touch left, he wrote us occasional letters, Mr. Lincoln reading them briskly after North had brought the mail. I would have liked to see them for myself, but Mr. Lincoln considered them his own property and kept them in his room. I responded every time nevertheless, asking each time for a return letter to be sent in my own name, but perhaps Touch never really understood how different life at Black Hill was without him. He was busy in his own world of family and his new tutor, who came to the vicarage and taught both boys, and then stayed on later to lecture Touch in Greek. *Greek?* I had asked once, and Mr. Lincoln gave me a scowl and muttered that a vicar needed to know the language so that he could read the Bible as God had written it. But I never knew whether he was angry because he hadn't the skill to teach Greek well enough to suit Touch's father or if it was because he did not think Touch suited to be a vicar.

In the months and years after Touch's departure, boys came and went, usually three or four of us with Mr. Lincoln at any one time, always someone new trying to learn the languages I now spoke nearly fluently, or trying to understand the orders of battle or to compute the range of a cannon, but there was never anyone new with whom I felt as close as I had with Touch. Nor was there anyone who seemed more like an older brother—in all kinds of ways—than Carrot. And there was also never anyone, other than I, who never went home for any holiday.

CHAPTER 5

Carrot left the year I turned twelve. He was fifteen then, and he departed in high glee at the prospect of coming under his father's care at last. I could not imagine how life at Black Hill would be without him. I had never gotten over the loss of Touch, and now, with Carrot gone as well, I felt I was really on my own.

By that time, I had spent a third of my life at Black Hill, and much more time with Mr. Lincoln than I had ever spent with any member of my own family. I was thoroughly used to his ways. He could be stern, but occasionally one could catch a knowing glance or a proud, subtle smile when one had done an especially good job.

Perhaps because I had lost both Touch and Carrot, it was in that year that I became more interested in modern, everyday life, as opposed to historic battles and heroes and explorations. Sometimes I managed to get my hands on a newspaper of Mr. Lincoln's before he removed it to the forbidden territory of his own room. He did not encourage us to read newspapers; it was as if there was no reason for us to study a subject that did not appear in a book. Nevertheless, he answered my questions the few times I put one to him, more generously if he could illustrate his response with a map. Most often, as he had done on my very first day, he would send me to his library to discover the information for myself. But I was intensely curious to know what real life was like for real people in our modern times, for I was beginning to understand that I had never actually experienced such a thing.

With Carrot gone, the fun of replaying battles had dimmed for me—as I suspect it sometimes did even for Mr. Lincoln—so it was not with a great deal of disappointment that I greeted the letter that arrived on my thirteenth birthday. I had almost forgotten the significance of the date, it never having been celebrated in my time at Black Hill. But at tea that evening Mr. Lincoln handed me an envelope. It had been opened already, yet Mr. Lincoln gave me the rare courtesy of letting me read it for myself:

Son:

You are now thirteen years of age—old enough to learn more of the world. Accordingly, on 3 April you shall arrive at the premises of Mr. John Wilson of Maysbeck. He shall take you under his wing and teach you all you need to know about being a man.

I expect that you will give a good account of yourself and will not embarrass me in your situation and your dealings with Mr. Wilson.

I have directed Mr. Lincoln to entrust you with 1 guinea, which should see you to Mr. Wilson's establishment. Return what is left to Mr. Wilson, and give him an accounting of what you have spent.

George Howell Rochester, Esq.

Maysbeck. *Not Thornfield.* I had only a vague idea where Maysbeck was, but at least, by then, I well knew how to find out. Mr. Lincoln's gazetteer showed it to be a town of fair size, but of no particular distinction. Still, it was exciting—exactly what I had hoped for, because I would actually be out in the world. It was as if my father, all those miles away in Jamaica, or wherever he was, had read my mind, and, because of that,

I felt an affinity for him that I had rarely experienced before, and I became certain that the next step would be joining Rowland and my father in Jamaica.

"It will be a new kind of life for you, Jamaica," Mr. Lincoln said. "I trust that you will make the most of it."

"I will try to, sir. My father is counting on it."

"Yes, he is indeed," he said, "and it is best that you keep that in mind."

He turned away and rose from the table with his usual difficulty, to go to his room. It was a departure from his normal evening activity to go to his room so early, and in my childish self-absorption I imagined he was devastated to have me leave. I glanced around the table at the others: Pox, who had come to us a month before, and who had yet to accomplish even the shortest sentence in French; Buck, who was large and clumsy, and whose smile was infectious; Tip, who was small and quick of mind and body. He would be the next leader of the boys when I left. That thought caught me up—it was true: I had, almost without realizing, become the leader after Carrot's departure. But I would be going to a new place now, and I would be the new boy and I would have to learn my way around the others, as well as learning the ways of a new tutor.

The next morning at breakfast, Mr. Lincoln behaved to me as if nothing had changed, as if there had been no letter from my father, no impending departure. He rolled out the map of Russia and placed the tokens for the Battle of Borodino, a battle I had enacted more times than I cared to think about, and it was clear that his thoughts were not of me on that day, but on the boys who would be there after I left.

At tea I broached the subject that had teased me all day. "Sir," I said.

Mr. Lincoln did not look up at me. "Yes," he said.

"Might I have Touch's real name, that I might visit him one day? I know his village; it's Mapleton, is it not?"

This brought Mr. Lincoln's head up and his eyes on me. It seems astoundingly strange now, but in fact we never used our real names at Black Hill. It was further evidence that Black Hill was a place of its own. Yes, we were properly introduced when a new boy came, but only our nicknames were used beyond that, and I had no memory of Touch's second name, though I recalled his Christian name was William.

Mr. Lincoln stared at me for several moments. Then he said, "William Gholson is not to be visited. Not in this realm at least. He went to meet his Maker less than a year after he left here."

I did not think: *No, it can't be.* Nor did I think: *Why didn't you tell us?* I could not think anything.

He watched me struggle for a time before adding, "It was the fever, Jamaica. He was of a delicate constitution, as you know."

But I did not know. I did not know when we ran across the fields, when we snuggled together in bed against the winter's cold, when he did not complain as I leaned on him so heavily after straining my ankle, he who was so much smaller than I. It seemed there was still too much I did not know. "May I be excused, please, sir?" I asked, refusing to acknowledge the tear that was running, unbidden, down my cheek.

"I was going to read Caesar's *Commentaries*," he said.

"Please, sir." I was begging by then, for I could not bear to face any more talk of war.

"Very well. You are excused to go to your room."

I escaped the table and ran up the stairs, Mr. Lincoln's voice following me. "Life is cruel, Jamaica. All one can do is tread on and make the best of it."

Upstairs, the late winter cold wrapped around me unnoticed. Fully dressed, I climbed under the quilt and pressed my eyes closed and, imagining Touch there beside me, began to whisper, once again, the story of how Captain Morgan transformed himself from the most feared buccaneer in the West Indies to the vice-governor of Jamaica. I told him every pirate story I could remember and tried to invent new ones when my memory ran dry. Above all else, Touch had loved pirates. As long as I was speaking, he was alive next to me. I could not bear to think of him under the cold ground.

When the others came up to bed, I feigned sleep, and the next day—my last at Black Hill—I was like a sleepwalker, going through the motions mindlessly. I only wanted to leave. I only wanted to lose the knowledge that I now possessed of poor, dead Touch, whom I would never in this life see again.

———

Early the next morning, North took me in the horse cart to the Four Bells, from where he had brought me to Black Hill five years before. In those years, I had never been to the village of Arnfield, there being nothing in that place that Mr. Lincoln thought worthy of our interest. Athena had packed for me two cheese pies, and I set them inside my cap and my cap on my head in order to keep them warm and my hands free. The same trunk that had come to Black Hill with me was filled with my clothes and what few other belongings I now possessed: a notebook full of jottings, a small Latin dictionary, two quill pens badly trimmed, a penknife, five or six rocks that I had gathered over the years for no reason that I can remember except that boys like to gather rocks. And, of course, the letter from my father. The guinea coin was in my pocket.

I had understood that the coach would come through Arnfield before noon, but far past midday I was still waiting. At the Four Bells I bought a watered beer and ate my cheese pies and would have eaten more, but I did not dare spend another farthing.

It was midafternoon when the coach arrived, but there was no room for me except on top, where I was forced to cling to the rail with one hand and my trunk with the other, trying not to shiver in the wind and the cold. I put my mind on Touch, who was lying in the still-frozen ground, though if there were a heaven, surely he must have been there instead; and on Carrot, who had left and never sent a letter. I had no idea where he might be now, nearly a year later, or if his father had really claimed him, and perhaps he was in London among all the toffs, at some party perhaps, dancing with a pretty girl, or drinking wine and laughing at some festive table. Or if he knew that Touch was dead. I did not remember Carrot's real name: Carrot had been all the name we needed for him, as Jam was all anyone had needed for me. Hard as I tried, up there on the coach top, I could not remember anyone ever having called me Edward. And I thought, too, of Mouse, who was with us for such a short time, and who, despite our assurances to the contrary, had been so afraid of being beaten, and I wondered, as I often did and still do to this day, if things had at last gone right for him. In short, I thought of whatever I could that would take my mind from the cold.

Well after dark the coach pulled into the yard of the Royal Oak Inn in Maysbeck, and it took some effort for me to loosen my hand from the rail, for it had become nearly frozen in place. I was unceremoniously handed down, stiff all over, and my trunk after me, and I forced my legs into movement to get me inside. The crowd around the hearth made it impossible for me to warm myself, but at least I was indoors, away from the wind, and I blew on my hands in hopes of warming them. It was only then that I noticed a boy, younger than I by a few years and half a head shorter, who seemed to have come out to meet the coach and had followed me inside.

"Master Rochester?" he said in a voice that was an octave too low for his size.

"Yes," I responded. "Are you from Mr. Wilson, perhaps?"

"I am. You are to follow me." He reached for my trunk, but I picked it up myself, as I could not imagine his being able to carry it.

The boy led the way back out into the dark and the cold. The wind blew scurries of sleet across the yard, and I bent my head against it. We walked a few hundred yards or so along twisting streets and through alleys before I asked, "Is it much farther to Mr. Wilson's home?" Surely it was not, or they would have sent a hack for me.

"We do not go to 'is 'ouse," was the surprising response. "I am to take you to the mill."

"What mill?"

"Mr. Wilson's mill. The Maysbeck Mill."

Mr. Wilson's establishment is a mill? Surely there must be some mistake, I thought, but I had no chance to ask, because the boy was hurrying so fast ahead of me that it was all I could do to carry my trunk and keep up with him. When we finally arrived, my feet and hands and nose were back to ice again, and I imagine the boy was just as cold, since he wore fewer warm clothes than I. In the darkness the building presented an imposing mass as we approached it. The boy made straightaway to a heavy oak door and pounded on it until it was opened by a rough-looking man of forty years or so. He was carrying a lantern, which he held up to my face to get a good look at me.

"This is 'im?" he said.

The boy said, "Yes."

"Well, come in, then," he said, motioning us forward. "It's bloody cold outside."

Inside, I tried to glance around, but the light of his lantern spread only far enough to show a cavernous place filled with large, complicated machinery. I followed the man, and the boy came along behind, as we walked to a dimly lit room twenty yards or so away. I could tell it was an office of some sort. There was a desk and, additionally, a high table covered with neat piles of papers. In a corner, a coal grate glowed. The man put down the lantern and took a good look at me. "Rochester, they say your name is."

"Yes, sir, it is," I responded. "Edward Rochester. My apologies for the time, sir. The coach was late in coming. I'm sorry if I kept you up." The man had not introduced himself; I could not imagine that he was Mr. John Wilson himself, but I could hardly be sure, as so much strangeness had already occurred.

"There is a cot for you in the corner," he said, waving his hand vaguely toward a darkened part of the room. "You will sleep there tonight. I have no idea what will become of you after that. Mr. Wilson will be deciding that. But be sharp: they come promptly to work. You will need to be up and ready before six o'clock in the morning."

"How will I know the hour?" I asked.

He laughed. "You will know," he said. "And, in case you are a very 'eavy sleeper, the frames start up promptly at six. There is no doubt you will 'ear them."

"The frames?" I asked stupidly.

"Boy, what do you know of this place?" he asked.

"I know nothing," I responded, "except that it's a mill, I think. But what kind of mill? And what are frames?"

"Ah," he said in a more kindly tone, "well, it's a broadcloth mill. The finest woolen goods you can buy. Beyond that, though, you shall be told what you need to know in the morning." With that, he turned away from me, taking the lantern with him as he put his arm across the shoulders of the boy. They walked closer to the coal grate to warm themselves for a few moments, and then they left.

The room was not nearly as cold as it had been outside, and I lifted my trunk once more, carried it over to the cot, and took off my shoes and lay down, digging my hands into my coat pockets and wondering if there had been some kind of mistake. This was not a school. Mr. Wilson seemed not to be a tutor. But it must be the place my father had intended me to go, for they had known my name; they had been expecting my arrival. Still, what was I doing there?

CHAPTER 6

The night watchman had been correct about my knowing when to rise, but I was so tormented about my new situation—so different was it from what I had expected—that I barely slept. Why was I there? Was I to be an apprentice in a woolen mill? Was this to be the end of a proper education for me? Would I never get to Jamaica, after all? And what about Thornfield? Thoughts slid around in my brain and kept me awake, but even if I had slept like the dead, I would have been awakened by the bell tolling above me.

Within minutes after that, I heard the sounds of foot treads in the mill, the murmurs of voices, and then the loud clattering as the machines started up, and I rose from my cot and stepped to the wall of windows looking onto the mill floor. In the dim early-morning light, people of all aspects and ages—including boys and girls younger than I—moved purposefully, setting up their tasks for the day. Their countenances told me that they were involved in difficult, serious, deadening work, and I felt a chill of fear run down my back. Why would my father send me to such a place? Then, still staring, I was struck with a realization. I had thought they were men and women equally, but now I saw that by far the most were women. Women, in the chill atmosphere of the mill in early spring, wrapped as best they could manage in ragged shawls, hair bound in rags or covered in tattered mobcaps. I had never seen such sorry-looking people; even the stableboys at Thornfield had been better dressed than these. The girls' dresses were faded to nearly colorless, as if they had been handed down from sister to sister or cousin to cousin, and it seemed that many of the girls wore more than one layer of dress, as it was the only way to keep warm. The boys—fewer in number than the girls—wore trousers either too long or too short, worn through at the knees, their hair curling over their collars. The few men, as well, wore ragged sweaters under thread-bare woolen jackets. They grunted greetings to one another and nodded to the women and mostly ignored the children, some of whom seemed as young as six or eight years of age and who were already gathering up spindles from wooden boxes in a far corner.

Despite the commotion and the people in the mill, I was still alone in the room in which I had slept. The fire had gone out in the grate and it was cold indeed. There was no sign of the man or the boy from the night before, but I found a bucket of water beside the grate and I splashed my face and wet down my hair to make myself as presentable as possible. There being nothing further to do, I stepped over to the windows again, fascinated and terrified by this image of how my life was to be in the next months or years. The previous night those machines had seemed merely hulks in the dark, but now—under the light of lanterns hanging from the walls—they were clearly the most complicated equipment I could have imagined, dwarfing the busy people on the mill floor. And when the machines started up, the clatter of them, even with the door to the office closed, was nearly deafening.

I had been standing there only a few minutes when the door opened. Mr. Wilson did not bother to introduce himself, nor did he need to. Clearly, he was in charge. "Rochester?" he said to me as he entered. He spoke loudly, as was necessary above the roar and clatter of the machines. Behind him, another man slipped in and made his way directly to a stool at the high table with barely a glance and certainly not a word to me.

"Yes, sir, I am," I responded, apprehension rising in my throat.

"You came all the way from Black Hill; that's a far distance to ride in the cold."

"Yes, it is, sir." I should have felt relief for his apparent concern with my well-being, but I was still terrified of what was in store for me.

He turned and hung his hat on the hatstand near the door by which he had entered, and before he turned back he asked, "Do you know what this place is?"

"Yes, sir, I think I do, sir. It's Maysbeck Mill, a woolen mill for the making of broadcloth, I think, sir."

Mr. Wilson frowned at me. "A *worsted* mill," he corrected, and he walked to his desk. "And this room?"

I gazed about. I didn't know what the room would be called. "It's the office, I think, sir."

"The countinghouse."

"Oh yes. The countinghouse." I knew the term from the nursery rhyme but had always imagined the king sitting on his throne in a vast and opulent room, counting his stacks of golden guineas, not in a small, spare, noisy adjunct to a mill.

He stared at me over the rims of his eyeglasses.

"Where the accounts are done," I added, extemporizing, "where the payments are received and the bills are paid and the records are made."

He leaned back in his chair. "Very good. And this gentleman working so busily already is Mr. Wrisley. Bob Wrisley to me, but Mr. Wrisley to you."

I nodded at the man on the stool, who seemed younger now than I had thought. I stepped over to Mr. Wrisley and shook his hand. "I'm very pleased to meet you, Mr. Wrisley, sir," I said.

"And I, you," he said, with a quick nod.

"And your job here—" Mr. Wilson said, already reaching for a sheaf of papers on his desk.

"Yes, sir?" It was to come now. I thought of the ragged workers on the mill floor below.

"Your job here is to learn all that is done in a countinghouse, from maintenance of supplies to the receipt of payments and bills, the paying of wages and bills, and the records of correspondence sent and received." He paused a moment to scan through the sheet of paper in his hand, then laid it aside and looked again over his eyeglasses at me. "Indeed, you are correct: this is a mill for the making of worsted wool, but the important thing for you is not what kind of mill it is, but that it is a manufacturing business. Your father has contracted with me that you learn how such a business is run."

I felt a sudden easing of my mind, for it seemed I was not expected to learn how to run the machines. I was not to work on the manufactory floor. No doubt my relief was clearly visible on my face.

"You will, of course," Mr. Wilson went on, "begin with the simplest of tasks, which you undoubtedly already know." He picked up a pen. "This, for example, needs sharpening. When you have taken care to sharpen our pens and fired up the grate, Wrisley will show you around the mill. Though your business is in this room, it is to be expected that you have at least a minimum of knowledge of what goes on out there, else there will be too much that will escape your understanding."

I was already reaching for his pen, but he held out his hand to stay my arm. "Did you sleep well?"

Torn between manners and truth, I equivocated. "I was nervous, sir. I didn't know what was to be expected of me."

"You were frightened."

"I was, a little, sir."

He leaned back in his desk chair. "You might one day have good reasons for that," he said, "but not, we should hope, in the immediate future. You have had a good education, Rochester, have you not?"

"I have, sir." I could have added that I was fluent in French and Latin and knew Greek as well and could recite Julius Caesar's speeches by heart, and could play out the Battles of Borodino or Trafalgar or even Thermopylae on his desktop, or calculate the dimensions of a hundred-weight of wool or the weight of fifty bushels of corn. But I did not know how to write a bank draft, or the procedures to cash one, nor did I know how to keep financial records. "Still, sir," I added cautiously, "I think I have a lot to learn."

For the first time, I saw a smile break across his face. "That is the most important piece of information any person in the world needs to know," he said.

"Would you prefer me to do the pens first or the grate?" I asked.

"It's blasted cold in here, don't you think, Bob?" he said.

"I do, sir," Mr. Wrisley said. So I took the last of the coal from the scuttle, poured it into the stove, and, throwing in a twist of paper, managed to coax a faint glow of ash into a fire.

It was after noon before Mr. Wrisley found time to take me on a tour of the three floors of the mill. The first processes were done on the lowest level, below the ground floor, after the wool was received and graded in a separate shed, where it was washed and dyed and combed. It was relatively quiet in the receiving sheds, but when we returned to the mill itself, I had such difficulty hearing Mr. Wrisley's soft voice above the clatter and roar of the machines as he tossed around unfamiliar terms for the processes and the machines—*slivers* and *slubbings* and *shoddy; water frames* and *draw frames* and *shuttles*—that I despaired of ever understanding half of them, and I was terrified that I would be expected to.

Indeed, it took weeks before some of those terms had much meaning for me. But one of the first things I did learn was that Mr. Wilson employed mainly women and children because they were cheaper labor than men and easier to handle—"much less trouble," as Mr. Wrisley confided. Mr. Wrisley clearly thought himself considerably above those workers, which made me wonder where I stood in such a hierarchy. I had never thought about those things at Thornfield, and at Black Hill there was only Mr. Lincoln and Athena and North, and we boys—except for Carrot, perhaps—occupied a place somewhere between them. But at the mill, it was clear that differences existed, though I had little idea how to negotiate them gracefully, or even, sometimes, to whom I should defer and who should defer to me. This was the real world, and I realized I would have to feel my own way. There was much to learn.

For the most part, the women and older girls ran the machines, sometimes having responsibility for as many as four frames, needing to keep an eye on all those bobbins, even climbing up on benches to replace them while the shuttles kept moving back and forth, taking care not to catch clothing or hair in the machinery, for to do so was to court disaster. The men served mostly as overlookers and loom tuners, watching that the women kept up with the work, and repairing frames that jammed. The women were not allowed to leave their machines for even a moment, so it was the task of the children to fetch new bobbins and run the full ones to the looms where they were needed.

Back in the countinghouse, Mr. Wilson set me to making copies of two letters that he had written. Copies of all letters were kept in letter boxes as records of business dealings, and the job of copying became one of my main responsibilities. As I quickly came to understand, that is one of the best ways to learn the operation of any business or manufactory.

The machines ran from six in the morning until six at night or later, and Mr. Wilson stayed nearly as long almost every day. He took me home with him that first evening; Mrs. Wilson had tea ready for us the moment we walked in the door. It appeared I was to stay at their home—for the time being, at least—and that fact was a great relief to me, as I had begun to wonder, as the day progressed, if the cot in the countinghouse was to be my permanent residence. The Wilsons were both close to sixty years of age, I should guess, and Mrs. Wilson was a delicate woman with pale skin, fair hair gone to gray, and a warm smile. They had no children, and it seemed to me that they had not yet worked out how they were going to treat me—was I a guest or a member of the extended family, the son they might have had or just another employee?

Mrs. Wilson spent a great deal of her time doing various kinds of hand-work, and I had not been there a week before she presented me with a scarf she had knitted for me. By then it had turned unusually warm, and I had no real need of such an item, but nevertheless I wore it to the mill each day (and to church on Sundays) for a month, regardless of the weather. She even admonished me, once or twice, that I did not need to wear it when the days were so warm, but I laughed and told her I liked it, which was true. I refrained from adding that no one had ever done such a thing for me before.

They put me in a little room on the top floor, under the eaves of their town house, which was cozy in cold weather but airless in the summer. There was in fact a second bedroom across the hall from theirs on the floor below, but it was almost never used. A room of my own—on a whole floor!—was an incredible luxury after sharing a room and almost always a bed with one or two or even three other boys at Black Hill. Even back at Thornfield-Hall, I'd shared the nursery with whatever governess was in residence.

Mrs. Wilson asked if she might call me "Eddie," and much as I wished to hear someone use my given name, after being called "Young Master" and "Jamaica" and now "Rochester," I could scarcely object when she confided that it had been the name of her beloved brother, who had died "too young" of consumption. Mr. Wilson, of course, never called me anything but my surname. It was pleasant at their home, and quiet after the constant roar and clatter of the machines, and it was there that I became more fully aware of Mr. Wilson's deficit of hearing. I had not noticed it at the mill, as we all spoke rather loudly to be heard over the machines, but in their quiet house, I discovered, one still had to speak up to be heard. It was a common ailment of mill workers—something they called *cloth ear*—but I was still young enough to believe myself impervious to such ailments.

Evenings after tea were spent in the parlor, Mrs. Wilson at her handwork, and Mr. Wilson reading the newspaper. For the first time, I had regular access to newspapers—the *Leeds Intelligencer* every week, but also sometimes the *Mercury* or the *Times* from London—and the fact that I devoured them seemed to please Mr. Wilson, who was wont to bring me into conversation regarding some piece of news in almost every issue. At first I had little idea what he was talking about: The Corn Laws; the Tories (whom he hated) and the Whigs (whom he tolerated); the Luddites, whom he of course despised; and the Jacobites, whom he dismissed entirely. I thought I had received a decent education at Black Hill, but with Mr. Wilson I realized how narrow had been my previous training.

As Mr. Wilson explained, large landholders throughout the country had been consolidating their holdings—just as Rowland had proposed to my father years before—inclosing the common land and throwing out their renters, who were left with no way to make a living. These folk flooded into the towns and cities searching for work, but at the same time, the introduction of machines to replace human hands further reduced the work available. It was an unfortunate but necessary side effect of a business like Mr. Wilson's, for Maysbeck Mill's machines now did the work that skilled spinners, weavers, and fullers had once done. I could not help feeling pity for the desperate countryfolk who overran every town and city, but at the same time, I saw how it frustrated Mr. Wilson: didn't they understand that in the cities there were not nearly enough jobs for them all?

Given the sorry state of things, it was not surprising that manufactories like ours became the targets of hooligans bent on smashing the machines that had replaced working folk. Indeed, Mr. Wilson employed a night watchman to guard his mill: Bert Cornes, whom I had met the night I arrived. He was rough looking and coarse speaking, with a nose permanently misshapen in fights. I surely would not have wanted to be at the receiving end of his cudgel, but the few times I saw him, he was never less than pleasant to me.

As for the routines of the countinghouse, the importance of the records became clearer and clearer. The wagonloads of wool had to be weighed and classed and sorted, and the tally slips taken to the countinghouse, where the receipts were written and the payments made. Additional accounts were kept of the dyes used, the idle time for machinery repair or rethreading, and of course of the workers' attendance—for a worker who was not at her machine by ten minutes after six would not be paid for that half day. And of course, there were bank receipts reflecting deposits that came in from Mr. Wilson's agents in London and Manchester and abroad. In short, the work of the countinghouse, and indeed the entire work of the mill, could be and was measured in terms of costs and receipts.

Early on, I was tasked with running tally slips from the sorting floor to Mr. Wrisley, and I enjoyed going out into the manufactory, watching amazed as the wool sliver was pulled and twisted finer and finer in each

successive frame, while upstairs the looms magically (to my unsophisti-
cated eyes) turned that thread into plain or plaid or striped cloth. In my
initial ignorance, I imagined the workers my age becoming my friends,
teasing and joking and laughing with me at the break for lunch, as I had
played sometimes with the stableboys at Thornfield-Hall. But the mill
boys were leery of me, and the adults gave me a wide berth.

After a time, I was given other jobs as well, even taking over some of
the tally work from Mr. Wrisley. I was no end of proud of myself, and I
kept the tally books as neatly and as perfectly calculated as anyone could
wish. But that kind of work meant less time spent on the floor of the mill,
and I had by then noticed one particular girl. I had not even seen a girl
when I was at Black Hill, and, earlier, as a young boy at Thornfield I
had occasionally played with Gracie, the older sister of one of the stableboys, but this was different. This girl was my own age or thereabouts, with
wheat-colored hair, strands of which sometimes escaped from the mobcap
she always wore, and the lightest blue eyes I had ever seen before or since.
She worked in the sorting crib, her quick hands adept at classing the bales
as they were brought into the mill, and, as well, she combed the raw wool
with heated combs into the sliver with which the spinning process began.
I don't know what attracted me to her, except that she seemed different
from the others. None of the boys would have anything to do with me, Mr.
Wrisley was twenty years older than I, and Mr. and Mrs. Wilson, while
kind, were even older. I yearned for a companion.

Weeks went by as I tried to catch her eye, further weeks while I imagined all sorts of ways in which I might meet up with her "by accident"
away from the mill, and as time passed, I became more and more focused
on her, on the thought of talking with her, on the thought, to tell the truth,
of just *being* with her. And then Mrs. Wilson, unwittingly, showed me the
way. We had eaten raisin tea cakes one evening, and I had had more than
my share. In the morning Mrs. Wilson sidled up to me, put an arm around
my waist, and smiled at me the way she sometimes did, thinking perhaps
of her dead brother, Eddie. She slipped a hand into my jacket pocket. "A
special treat," she whispered.

But when I arrived at the countinghouse and put my hand into my pocket, I found she had secreted not one but two tea cakes there, and immediately I began to imagine how I might present my gift to Alma— for that was the girl's name—and I pictured her soft lips spreading into a smile.

It was afternoon before I could make an excuse to go to the sorting crib, where in my fantasies she always was waiting for me. But when I found her, she had her hands deep into a bale of wool. Two or three wool brokers were standing around aimlessly, waiting for the tally, which they could exchange at the countinghouse for credit.

"Good afternoon, Alma," I said. It was the first time I had spoken directly to her.

She paused and glanced up, confused and seemingly dismayed.

Nevertheless, I grinned, just as I had imagined I would do. "Good afternoon," I said again.

"Good afternoon, sir," she whispered.

"Not 'sir,'" I said. "Edward."

She stared down at her hands, saying nothing more. I was suddenly aware that the men were watching us.

"You could call me Edward," I said softly, hoping they didn't hear.

Still she said nothing, nor did she look up, but she did turn an unnerving shade of red.

"I have something," I murmured, pulling out the cloth-wrapped packet. "Would you like a tea cake?"

"No, sir," she whispered, her face still turned away. "No, thank you."

"I have two. I can't eat them both." I pulled open the packet so that she could see, but she didn't look.

"I will have one and you may take the other." I made a big show of withdrawing one tea cake and taking a bite, but it was all lost on her because she still wasn't watching.

"Well then," I said, uncertain of my next move. My daydreams had not anticipated this lack of response. Or for an audience of men, for that matter, who stared stone-faced at me. In my imagination, Alma would by now have succumbed to my blandishments, but now I hardly knew what to do. "Well then," I said again, "I will just leave it here for when it suits you to eat it." And I beat a retreat, uncertain what else I could have done or said, but quite sure that this time, at least, there was nothing else left for me. When next I came to the sorting crib, the tea cake was gone and the cloth neatly folded where I was sure to see it.

From time to time, I left a few more gifts for her: a raisin bun, a raspberry tart. Always they disappeared, and though I had no way of knowing who was benefiting from my generosity, I convinced myself it was Alma. After a while, I stopped bringing those tokens and indeed stopped going to the sorting crib at all unless it was absolutely necessary—when in fact it almost never had been necessary. If I happened to come into close proximity to her, I would nod and hurry on, as if a response from her was not only not needed, but neither expected nor even desired. In short, in my clumsy way, I tried to let her think that I had lost all interest. But in fact, it was all I could do to keep myself from stopping to say a word, to hear her voice, to gaze into those blue eyes. Her beauty was all I knew of her, but it would not let me go.

It happened that one mild, summer Sunday afternoon, I wandered down toward the bottoms, that section of the town where haphazard houses leaned against one another and ragged children played amid the middens, and I saw Alma making her cautious way between the streams of offal that encumbered the path. I watched for a few moments, assuring myself that she was alone, for I had no desire to approach her again in front of an audience. I watched longer, curious as to where she was going and why. My body stirred at the very sight of her, at her careful step, the ripple of her skirt as she walked, and I followed her.

In a short while she turned off the path, taking a narrower way that led behind the Crown Inn, and beyond, turning northward toward Newnan. We were into the countryside now; the birds chirped in the hedgerows, and in the distance a cow lowed and, curiously, a lamb bleated in response. Suddenly, as if she sensed she was not alone, she turned and started at the sight of me, but she turned back and hurried on her way. But now that I was found out there was no point in silently following her, so I ran a bit to catch up to her. "Good day, Alma," I said.

"Good day, sir," she whispered.

"Not 'sir,'" I said, "Edward." And with my hand I turned her flushed face toward me. "Edward," I prompted again, insistently.

"Edward," she whispered. What I had dreamed of: the sound of my name from her lips, and I could not help but respond. I did not plan it or intentionally do it, but my lips were on hers almost before she had finished my name, my arms around her, pressing her close.

I felt her body stiffen within my arms, and she pulled back away from me, pushing her hands against my chest. "Sir," she said, "please, please, sir."

Sir? I was not *sir*; I was Edward. I thought she had understood that. Confused, I watched as she turned and fled, and I was left staring after her.

That is what happened, for she was a pretty girl and I was a lonely boy with no older brother to give advice—Carrot would have told me, no doubt, but he was gone from my life, and I would not have dared ask Mrs. Wilson how one approaches girls. It is not enough, but this is the only poor excuse I can give; and I suddenly knew that I had been wrong, though it was some time before I understood how wrong, for it is never right for a man to take advantage of a girl whose living depends on him.

And there would be much worse to come.

That was the last time I saw Alma. She never came back to the mill, and though I always looked for her whenever I was on the street, and even walked a few times down toward the meager cottages in the bottoms beyond the river, where I assumed she lived, I did not see her. I would have liked to apologize, even as I did not fully understand for what, but I knew in my bones that I had wronged her and I wished for a chance to somehow make it right. After that, I began to notice that the other young people at the mill turned their backs to me and never spoke in my presence if they could at all avoid it.

CHAPTER 7

The next autumn my brother came. I had gone to the bank as usual for a record of the week's postings, and when I returned there was a young man, a dandy from the look of him, seated beside Mr. Wilson's desk, and they were engaged in what seemed like a confidential conversation. The room we called the countinghouse was quite small, but it had never seemed a problem, for we were all three working to the same ends and quite often it was convenient to have one another close to hand to answer a query or share a piece of information. Even in that limited space, I could not see the young man's face, as his back was to the door, but I could tell that his hair was fair, held back with a slim ribbon. I set the postings on the edge of Mr. Wrisley's desk, not wanting to disturb Mr. Wilson just then. Still, he glanced at me, back at his guest, then at me again, and a kind of wry smile spread over his face. "Rochester, come here a moment," he said.

I did as I was told, but I did not pay attention to the young man until Mr. Wilson said, "I think you know my visitor."

The face seemed like something I had once seen in an almost-forgotten dream. I stared, the features coming together in a way that should have been familiar.

"Well, Toad," the young man said, grinning, "aren't you going to greet me as a brother should?"

I should have known in the first instant: the hair, oiled and curled, and the bold blue eyes, the insolent mouth, but it was as if my mind wanted to deny the reality.

"Rowland," was all I could think to say.

Rowland was still seated—of course he would be. It would have been a gesture of respect for him to have stood at the introduction. He was looking me up and down, and I felt quite out of fashion, with my plain brown coat and trousers, compared to his tight, cream-colored pantaloons and shirt of cream silk with cravat, and his moss-green cropped jacket and darker green waistcoat.

He said nothing, and I felt compelled to say, "I thought you were in Jamaica with Father. When did you return?" The only answer he gave was a slight shrug. It had not yet occurred to me that it was nearly eight years since the two of them had gone to the West Indies, and they both could have been there and back a dozen times since then.

It was Mr. Wilson who rescued me. "Your father sent him," he said. "He wanted a report of your progress, and I was just telling your brother that you are doing fine, that you make a good account of yourself, that except for a still slight timidity, you are growing into a quite competent businessperson."

It was the most complimentary statement I had ever heard from Mr. Wilson in the two and a half years that I had been at Maysbeck Mill. It was true I worked hard, but he mostly just nodded, as if anything I did was only what he had expected of me. I knew I was not the best he could have asked for, but I had already become aware that countinghouse work was not what I wanted. It was too routine—old man's work, I thought—though I had no idea what else I would have preferred.

"Well," Mr. Wilson said, rising. "I should imagine you young fellows have much to talk about, a great deal of catching up with each other's lives. The Crown is just down the road there, and a fine place it is for a roast or a stew. Why don't the two of you spend a bit of time together?" Then he turned to Rowland. "I think we're finished here. I shall write out a report for your father and send it off to your lodgings. The Royal Oak, is it not, in the High Street?"

"Yes, it is," Rowland said. "I shall be looking forward to it." He rose and reached for his hat, but before he placed it on his head he tipped it in the direction of Mr. Wilson, and walked out the door, which I had already opened. I did not take from the rack the cap I usually wore, it seeming suddenly too childish, or, worse, too much like those the workmen in the mill wore. With my bare head and my ordinary clothes, I felt myself to be Rowland's inferior in every possible way.

We had scarcely started down the road when I turned to him. "It is not necessary, you know, for the two of us to dine together. We can certainly go our separate ways." (I was proud to have thought to use the more formal *dine* rather than my more common *eat*, though at the same time I hated that I had done it only to impress him.)

Rowland laughed. "Of course we must! Why not? We shall put it on Wilson's tab—I'm sure he has one. He would be disappointed if we did not do so, I should think."

I shrugged at that. I could not imagine what Rowland and I could talk about for the full course of a meal. It might seem that I, who had fallen in love with Jamaica since that first day at Black Hill, would be overflowing with questions about the island. But I somehow did not want Rowland to suspect my infatuation, for I knew he would have enjoyed nothing more than dispelling my fantasies.

He ordered a roast with all the trimmings, and I would have liked the same, but to show my independence I ordered a venison stew, which turned out to be surprisingly good.

After his initial attack on the roast, Rowland lifted his eyes to mine. There was an expression in them I couldn't read, and I steeled myself for what was to come. But even so, I couldn't have been more surprised. "I believe I have a friend with whom you are acquainted," he said casually.

I was unable to imagine whom I might know that Rowland would as well.

"Thomas Fitzcharles," he said, but I shook my head. The name meant nothing to me. He frowned. "You were not at Mr. Lincoln's establishment? A ginger-headed fellow?" He shoveled another forkful of potatoes and meat and gravy into his mouth.

Carrot? I stared at him, openmouthed.

Rowland laughed. "You do remember. He called you 'Jam,' insisted on it, despite that I told him your proper name. It seems rather a childish name: Jam. It reeks of the nursery. Still"—he gazed directly at me then—"perhaps it's a fitting name for you after all. Jam."

I ignored the taunt for a more important question. "But how do you know him?"

He shrugged. "We met at some hunting party or another. Or perhaps it was a race. Something in the neighborhood, you know."

"What neighborhood?"

"Why, Thornfield, of course."

"You were at Thornfield?"

"Of course I was—I am. Where else would I be?"

"I thought you were in Jamaica."

He laughed. "Oh my lord, you don't think I would want to be in Jamaica any longer than I had to be. The place is a cesspool, people dying around you all the time, the slaves revolting, the Maroons making the interior impossible. One is lucky to get away from there with one's life."

My mouth hung open; I could not think what to say. I suppose it registered somewhere in my mind that Jamaica might not be all I had dreamed it was, but a more vital thought crowded that out: Thornfield had been occupied all this time—or much of it—while I was at Black Hill and at the mill. I would have tried going home for a visit if I had known.

"Did…did he ask about me—Thomas Fitzcharles?" I asked. The name seemed odd on my lips and in my ears. Surely this was not Carrot.

"Oh, once, I think. Where you were, that kind of thing."

"What did you tell him?"

He smirked. "I said I didn't know."

But surely you must have, I thought.

"Oh, come, Jam—yes, indeed, I like it; it suits you, Jam. But come now, you surely do not think that the nephew of the Prince Regent of England is really interested in what became of a clerk in a countinghouse in Maysbeck, do you?"

There was nothing I could say in response. He was talking about a grandson of King George III—even if illegitimate—and I was talking about Carrot, who was more a brother to me than Rowland had ever been. Never in his life would Rowland understand that.

The rest of the meal was drudgery. The venison turned dry in my mouth, the beer stale and overwatered, the raucous sounds around us irritating. I was glad for it to end. We parted in the roadway outside, he going toward the High Street, I heading back to the mill. He did not encourage me to come to Thornfield, nor did I expect him to. We might as well have been strangers.

———

But I couldn't get Thornfield out of my mind. In the first months and years at Black Hill I had missed it terribly, but eventually the pain had healed over, as almost any wound does. But like a scar remains, thoughts and visions of Thornfield would surface in my mind: the magnificent clock, the grand staircase; the aroma of Cook's kitchen, the stable smell of horses and hay and leather; the fields and woods and moors beyond the house. Now all that flooded back upon me and I longed for it as an abandoned child longs for his parent.

And yet, how would I get there? I had only Sundays to myself—to myself, I say, though of course I was expected to spend mornings and evenings of that day with the Wilsons at services. As well, I had no money, save the two pounds Mr. Wilson gave me each month, which was enough to pay for an occasional pint of beer or meat pie, or to have my boots mended or to save toward the purchase of a new pair of trousers, but not enough to include the cost of a coach to Thornfield and back. Until Rowland's visit, it had not occurred to me to ask what kind of arrangement had been made between Mr. Wilson and my father. Now I wondered about it, and attempting to be sly, I tried asking questions, but Mr. Wilson was reticent in his own way, only telling me not to worry, that he had sent a good report to my father, that all would be well, and that he was sure my father had plans for me when I was ready.

My father. Was he back at Thornfield too? Or had he remained in Jamaica—or was he somewhere else entirely? I had no idea, nor did I know what he would say if I somehow managed to get myself to Thornfield. I knew full well what Rowland would say, but I didn't care.

And then, one evening a week or so later, an astonishing thing happened. "Mr. Wilson," Mrs. Wilson said over rum pudding, "I received the strangest letter today; I hardly know what to think of it."

"What manner of letter?" Mr. Wilson asked, not even glancing up from his dish.

"From Ella—"

"Ella, your sister?"

"Well, really not from Ella herself, but from Mrs. Brewer." She caught the frown on her husband's face. "Mrs. Brewer, her companion. And she seems quite concerned about Ella. She says my sister has been more and more confused with ordinary things, and now she seems to be talking about Mother as if Mother were still alive, even talking about taking Mother to London, or to Bath, for the season."

At this, Mr. Wilson looked up. "You must have read the letter wrong. It's Ella who's wanting to go to Bath and she's set Mrs. Brewer to writing to you as if she expects me to pay for it." He started back in on his pudding.

"I did not misread it!" Mrs. Wilson exclaimed with uncharacteristic passion. "Not at all!" And she pulled the folded letter from her pocket and handed it to him.

He read the letter over quickly, and again more slowly. "This is not good," he said. I imagine he had quite forgotten I was there.

"I hardly know how to respond," Mrs. Wilson said.

"Perhaps it would be best not to," he replied.

"I cannot just ignore it. She's my sister! My only living relative!"

"What would you propose?" he asked. "She's in Harrogate. We are here."

"I feel I must at least go and see her," she countered, "see if she is really as Mrs. Brewer reports. And Harrogate is not so *very* far away."

"The better part of a day's travel," he said. "You are too frail as well to make the journey on your own, and I cannot go with you. I have commitments here. Two days away at the very least; no, it would be impossible for me to make such a trip until after the first of the year. And even so—"

"I could go," I offered. "I could accompany Mrs. Wilson."

Mr. Wilson turned to me. "No, that's impossible," he said. "We are not... We could not... No, it's impossible."

"But—my *sister*. I cannot just ignore her," Mrs. Wilson insisted.

"She has Mrs. Brewer," he said. "And she has a housekeeper, has she not? What more does she need?"

"She needs *me*!" Mrs. Wilson responded, seeming to rise in stature even though she remained seated in her chair. "And I need to see—I need at least to *see*—that she is taken care of properly."

Mr. Wilson sat back in his chair, the rum pudding forgotten, his mind working. "Would you be willing to go with her, Rochester?" he asked at last. "Would you make sure Mrs. Wilson arrives and returns safely? Would you ascertain if her sister is taken care of adequately?"

"Yes, sir, I would be glad to do that," I replied, my mind calculating. Harrogate was more than a half day's travel north of Maysbeck and not exactly on the way to Thornfield, which was mostly east, I was thinking, but it could be a start; surely I could work something out. I had a few pounds saved, and hoped they would be enough.

"Well then," Mr. Wilson said, "you may write to Mrs. Brewer and tell her you are coming at the end of the week. But keep in mind, it is already the middle of November. The weather will not hold and I forbid you to get snowed in there in Harrogate. You may not stay longer than two days."

"Yes, of course," she said.

But I thought: *Two days! How can I get from Harrogate to Thornfield and back in two days?*

CHAPTER 8

We left Maysbeck on a bright, sunny morning. It had poured rain all the previous day and night, and now everything seemed washed clean—even, almost, the unpainted cottages and shacks of the bottoms. As the coach rumbled past, I gazed at them, hoping to see Alma once more, but I saw only crooked, narrow alleys, children shivering in filthy rags and adults bundled against the mid-November cold and damp, and lank dogs, snuffling amid the detritus. Soon Maysbeck was behind us and we were in the countryside, heading toward Harrogate, and I was imagining myself at Thornfield again, not just being in the place that I had last seen half a lifetime ago, but seeing as well Cook and Knox and all the rest, if they were still there. From Mr. Wilson's gazetteer, I had surmised that with even the fastest of coaches it would take me a good day just to make the trip back and forth, without any time remaining to spend at Thornfield itself. I could not think of how I could persuade Mrs. Wilson to extend her stay in defiance of Mr. Wilson's explicit order. And what excuse could I give for being gone so long?

Beside me, Mrs. Wilson was wrapped in her warmest cloak, and I had tucked a blanket around her besides. In less than an hour she was snoring lightly, her head fallen against my shoulder. The coach drove through countryside that looked so familiar that I could almost imagine Thornfield-Hall just over the next rise, with its fires lit and the silver and brass polished. Rowland might be there, hosting a party perhaps—indeed perhaps including Carrot—and an ache came into my gut, and a longing for Thornfield and for Carrot, both.

In Harrogate, at the inn where the coach left us, I hired a carriage to carry our luggage and ourselves to Mrs. Wilson's sister's house, which was not so very far away. Her sister's companion, Mrs. Brewer, greeted us at the door in a flurry of excitement and confusion and, I noted, a kind of relief. She directed the porter upstairs with our bags, and she led us into a small but serviceable parlor, where Mrs. Wilson's sister was seated close to the fire. At first she stared at us with a kind of detached curiosity, as if she had no idea who we were or why we had come, but on seeing her, Mrs. Wilson exclaimed, "Ella!" and hurried right over to give her a hug. The whole time she was being embraced, the sister gazed over Mrs. Wilson's shoulder at me, as if she thought she ought to know me. Not knowing what else to do, I smiled at her and nodded, but her face remained blank.

"Who is that man?" the sister asked, and Mrs. Wilson came to her senses and turned to glance at me.

"Why, that's Eddie," she said.

"That's not Eddie," the sister said.

"Of course it is!" Mrs. Wilson said in her cheeriest voice.

"Not *our* Eddie," the sister insisted.

Mrs. Wilson laughed. "No, Ella, not *our* Eddie. But he is still a very nice young man. He brought me here to you." And she attempted the introduction. "Ella, this is Edward Rochester, whom Mr. Wilson has taken under his wing and who lives with us—"

"Who is Mr. Wilson?" the sister asked.

"My husband. John Wilson. You know him." The sister looked blankly at her, but she continued on. "And, Eddie, this is my sister, Miss Little."

"I'm very pleased to meet you, Miss Little," I said, stepping forward, making a bow.

But Miss Little shrank back, as if afraid I would strike her. "This is not Eddie, and I don't want him in my house!"

"No, dear," Mrs. Brewer put in, "it's not your brother, Eddie. But he is a friend of your sister's; surely he can stay."

"No, he *cannot*," Miss Little said, her voice rising. "I do not want him here, Cassie. He is not Eddie and there is no reason to pretend that he is, and I will not have some strange man staying under my roof!"

Mrs. Wilson glanced helplessly at Mrs. Brewer, for neither one knew how to handle the situation. But I did. "That is quite all right, madam," I said. "I can just as easily stay at the inn. It's not far and, anyway, you two sisters probably have a lot to talk about." Though I had no idea how that could be, as Miss Little seemed to live in another world.

"Would you mind terribly?" Mrs. Wilson asked.

"No, of course not."

"You could come back for tea, surely," Mrs. Wilson said, looking at Mrs. Brewer.

"Maybe it would be best if I stay away," I said. "I seem to disturb your sister; the less she sees of me, the better."

"But, Eddie—"

"I shall be perfectly fine," I interrupted. "Mr. Wilson said you could stay for two days. I shall return to fetch you then."

"But what will you do at the inn all that time?" she asked.

"Don't worry about me," I said. "I have a friend not far from here. Would you mind if I visit him in the interim?"

"Of course not," Mrs. Wilson said. "It will ease my mind if I know you are occupied."

Relieved, I turned to Mrs. Brewer. "Please don't bother to see me to the door. I will just run upstairs and find my bag and be off." I did not even care if I seemed to be in a hurry to leave, for, indeed, I was.

Unfortunately, I had to spend the night at the inn, as it was too late to catch a coach to Millcote, but I took one early the next morning, and shortly after noon I was at the George Inn, which I had not seen in the nearly eight years since I had left for Black Hill. I knew I had limited time, so with most of the "emergency money" Mr. Wilson had given me, I hired a trap to take me directly to Thornfield-Hall, which took another good hour. I was anxious all the way, almost ripping the whip from the driver's hand to urge the horse on faster. The George and the countryside around it all seemed so familiar that I could scarcely believe it was not a dream. I gripped the handrail as the trap rolled over the old hills and across the little bridges, and then, suddenly, Thornfield lay before me, settled into its quiet valley, the November mists curling around it.

At the gate, the trap stopped and I descended, paying the driver and asking him to return by ten the next morning, and I picked up my small bag, opened the gate, and walked up the long drive. All the way from Harrogate I had tried to work out what I would say to Rowland when I turned up at his door, but despite that I could not think what to say, I also could not pass up an opportunity to be at Thornfield-Hall again. As for my father, I did have a good excuse to be gone from the mill, though perhaps not a good one to be at Thornfield. Never mind, I told myself; I was not going to allow myself to miss this chance.

The place was quiet as I approached, no evidence at all of activity. It flew into my head that it had all been a lie of Rowland's, that Thornfield-Hall was indeed closed and empty, but then I saw drifts of smoke coming from the chimneys, and with a lighter step I hurried forward.

It was Holdredge who opened the door for me. After nearly eight years he still appeared the same, but he clearly did not recognize me. "It is I," I said at last. "Edward. Edward Rochester."

He took in a sudden breath. "Master Rochester?" he said. Then: "Master Rochester! Come in. We had no idea. I am so sorry."

I stepped into the entrance hall as he retreated to make room for me.

"I am so sorry," he repeated. "Did you walk? We could have sent a carriage for you! We had no idea—"

"Of course," I said. "You had no way of knowing I was coming. I had no idea myself twenty-four hours ago. I took a trap from the George."

"Master Rochester—that is, Master Rowland—is not here," he said, as if in apology. "It is only Mrs. Knox and Cook and a girl and a footman who are here at the moment."

"And my father?" I asked.

"Oh," Holdredge responded, "he is never here; he spends his time at his residences in Liverpool and in London."

"Yes, of course," I said, as if I had known of my father's residences and trying not to show my relief. Just those I wanted to see, and no one I cared not to. "I had no right to assume Rowland would be here. This is an unexpected visit, and a short one."

"Do come in," he said. "Into the drawing room?"

"The kitchen if you don't mind. I would like to see Cook. And Knox."

He did not react to this at all, so good a butler was Holdredge. "Follow me, please," he said, and stepped forward and led the way down to the kitchen, where we found Cook and Mrs. Knox enjoying an afternoon cup of tea. When no family was present in the house, I could imagine, this was the kind of relaxed atmosphere that prevailed.

"We have a visitor," Holdredge announced as we walked into the kitchen.

Automatically, Mrs. Knox rose before she even turned to look. I can see her face still—shock there, and confusion, and then the dawning. "Master Rochester," she said quietly.

"Oh, my heavens!" Cook proclaimed, rising and running around the table as fast as her bulk allowed. "Master Rochester! Young Master Rochester!" Mindless of the flour on her apron, she pulled me to her bosom, her body suddenly wracked with sobs. "I thought I would never see you again! I thought I would die without ever seeing you again!" When she came to herself and realized how unseemly her outburst had been, she stepped back, her arms at her sides but her face still locked on mine. "It is," she added, still marveling, "it truly is."

"Welcome," Mrs. Knox said.

"Thank you," I replied. "I know you have not planned for me. And I can go back to the village if necessary. I only have until tomorrow morning, as it is."

"Of course not," Mrs. Knox said. "You shall stay here; of course you shall."

"It would be my greatest pleasure," I responded.

"Master Rowland is not here," she added.

"So Holdredge told me."

"He has gone down to Bath, with his friends."

With Carrot? I wondered. "No matter," I said. "In fact, I saw him only a short time ago. I have come to see Thornfield. And you all. Not him."

Mrs. Knox did not react at all. "And we are delighted to have you," she said. "Are you sure you can stay only until morning?"

"I'm sorry, but yes. I must be back in Harrogate by this time tomorrow."

"I shall make your favorite tea," Cook said. "Is it still pork and kidney pie?"

"It is indeed." It was then that my eye was caught by a movement in the shadows of a corner. It was a young woman—perhaps a few years older than I, square built, with a kind of wary cast to her eyes. I had seen such looks on some of the children in the mill. "Hello there," I said, to put her at her ease.

Shrinking back, she stared at me.

Mrs. Knox glanced at her and at me and back at her, but it was Cook who spoke up. "It's Gracie, Master Rochester. Jem's sister."

"Of course," I said, though I would never have recognized her. I remembered my occasional playmate Gracie as something of a daredevil, but her spirit seemed to have deserted her. "Is Jem still here?" I asked, out of politeness—to change the subject—and from curiosity about my other old friends.

The young woman looked at Mrs. Knox to respond to my question, and then turned quickly away, as if fearing I would ask another.

"Master Rowland let Jem go," Mrs. Knox said.

"He doesn't keep horses?" I asked. That did not seem like Rowland.

"Oh, he does," she responded. "But Jem got into a bit of trouble and—"

"Trouble?"

Mrs. Knox shook her head, and I understood not to push the subject. But still— "Where is Jem now, then?"

"He's at the Grimsby Retreat. He has the care of the workhorses there. Mr. Holdredge gave him the recommendation."

"The Grimsby Retreat?"

"I suppose you would have been too young to know of it. It's a place started by the Quakers, a kind of madhouse, but…designed, as they say, for 'moral treatment' of the mad, whatever that should mean. There is a farm there, and gardens which are supposed to help heal sick minds, though heaven knows if it works or not."

"And you," I said to Gracie, taking a step closer, still attempting friendliness, "do you work here?"

She stepped back, as if I had raised a hand in threat.

"She has—" Cook began. I caught a quick movement at the corner of my eye, but when I turned, Mrs. Knox stood as still as a stone.

"Perhaps you could find a place for her here," I barged on.

"I think perhaps not," Mrs. Knox said. Though her voice was soft, her words were firm.

I insisted on having tea that evening in the kitchen, as I so often had done as a child. Holdredge joined us, and they asked me of my life and seemed impressed that I was a kind of assistant to the owner of a woolen mill. I am afraid I rather inflated my importance at Maysbeck Mill, but it seemed to please them that I could make such a good account of my life. Nothing further was said among us of Rowland. It was, truly, like being home again.

I did not see Gracie again during my brief stay at Thornfield, and I had little occasion to think of her. We had been playmates as children, but we were no longer children.

Mrs. Wilson and I rode back to Maysbeck in silence. She was clearly distraught about her sister, and I hardly knew what to say. At first I asked if she had had a pleasant time, knowing that it could not have been anyone's idea of pleasant, but that is the sort of thing one asks after a visit and I thought I should do so regardless of the situation. She barely responded, turning her head toward the window and closing her eyes. She didn't say another word.

Once home, she removed her bonnet and trudged up to her room. Mr.

Wilson would soon be back from the mill, so I did not go there. Instead, I went into the parlor and tried to read the newspaper, though my own thoughts ran far from the page. I realized it had not been difficult at all to go to Thornfield, and I was no sooner back than I was thinking of how to go again. But as easy as it had been this time, it seemed still a difficulty beyond comprehension: how would I find the time and how would I find the money?

When Mr. Wilson arrived, he stuck his head into the parlor and saw me and frowned. "You have returned, I see," he said.

"Just, sir," I said. "Mrs. Wilson has gone to her room, I believe. The trip was a difficult one for her." I said no more and he asked nothing, just turned, and with a kind of harrumph he mounted the stairs.

Some time later, I heard the housekeeper climb the stairs to knock and announce tea, but she came down almost immediately and told me in a softer voice than usual that tea was served in the dining room and not to wait for the mister and missus. I did not take the newspaper with me; it is bad manners to read and dine, even if one is alone, and I was barely able to focus my mind anyway.

I did not see Mr. Wilson again that evening, but in the morning, he was, as usual, already at breakfast when I came down. He did not glance up from buttering his toast when I greeted him, but he did ask, "You met Mrs. Wilson's sister, I understand?"

"Miss Little, yes, sir, I did."

He spooned a dab of marmalade on a corner of the toast, then, his eyes on me, he asked, "And how did she seem?"

I paused before responding. "Of course I met her only briefly," I equivocated. And then I added, "Perhaps Mrs. Wilson told you that her sister seemed unable to abide my presence. I did not stay there at her house."

"She told me." His eyes had not left my face, and I knew he expected more of me than I had already given. But dare I say that the woman had not seemed of sound mind? That was not something one would blithely say to the person's relation.

"Perhaps her distress was due to my having the same name as their unfortunate brother," I suggested. "Perhaps the memory was too much—"

"That was all? There was nothing more?"

I wished I knew what else Mrs. Wilson had told him, but the fact that they had talked in private the whole evening was enough for me to know that she must have unburdened herself to him quite completely. "She seemed...quite fragile of mind," I ventured. "She did not at first recognize her sister, and when Mrs. Wilson told her who she was and mentioned your name as well, she seemed not to know who you were—who John Wilson was. I am sorry that I could not have observed her further, but she was adamant that I leave. And when I returned, she was not in sight."

He seemed increasingly frustrated at my responses. "And Mrs. Wilson said nothing about it on the return?"

"She did not, sir, nor did I think it my place to insist. She was quite distraught."

He took a decisive bite of his toast and chewed it slowly.

I looked down at my plate. I was not used to being the bearer of such disheartening news. My egg was growing cold, the fat of the bacon congealing, but I could not think what else to say.

"This changes everything," he said at last. "I shall have to write to your father."

This brought my head up in alarm. Had Mrs. Wilson told him of my leaving Harrogate on my own? *Oh God,* I thought. Mr. Wilson was going to write to my father of my truancy. I could not imagine what would become of me—nearly sixteen years old and not even fit yet for any trade except for the meanest of them.

I didn't know what to say, so I kept my silence and let my breakfast grow fully cold in front of me. Finally, he nodded at my plate and said curtly, "You'd better eat your breakfast, Rochester; there's no telling what you'll be getting henceforth."

"Yes, sir," I said, but I hadn't the heart to eat now. All appetite had left me.

"You will not come to the mill today," he said, as I by then suspected he would. "You must find other lodgings for yourself. I shall inform your father that you can no longer be accommodated here."

"Yes, sir," I said, just as if I understood what he was saying.

"One day will be sufficient, I should think."

"Yes, sir."

"You will be back tomorrow, then, as usual."

"Sir?"

"At the mill. Tomorrow."

"I don't...I thought...I don't quite..."

"Get it out, Rochester. I haven't all day," he snapped.

"It's just that—if you've dismissed me—let me go, then why—"

"For heaven's sakes, Rochester, I haven't dismissed you." His face softened, but only by a degree, as he understood my foolishness.

"But you said—"

"I said you no longer will stay *here*. Mrs. Wilson has told me, and you have confirmed it: her sister must come here and live with us. God knows, it is not what I—well, not what anyone would choose."

My breath caught in my throat. "Yes, sir," I managed to say.

"You shall have to find other accommodations, and I will write to your father that our arrangement is, perforce, changed, and now that you are to be on your own, he and I shall have to work out who is responsible for your living expenses." He gazed down at his plate for a moment. "Until Miss Little and Mrs. Brewer arrive, you may keep your room here. Unless you prefer to move out sooner."

"I shall do the best I can," I said, my head still reeling. For the first time in my life, I was to be on my own.

He rose to leave, but he turned back, his right hand gone to his pocket. "And I suppose it was necessary for you to pay for your lodgings in Harrogate from your own purse."

"Well, sir—" I started, but he interrupted.

"Rochester," he said, "some advice. If someone offers to give you payment, do not argue." And he placed a note on the table.

"Yes, sir, I will remember that," I said.

CHAPTER 9

In addition to the pound to pay for my supposed lodging expenses at Harrogate, Mr. Wilson had given me a note of five pounds with which to secure a room and to pay for whatever else I needed until he and my father could work out a satisfactory arrangement. I found a room on the third floor of a house owned by a middle-aged widow, wide of girth and constant of smile: Mrs. Clem. "I keep a decent place," she assured me. "There's to be no drinking in the room. No guests after eight o'clock in the evening, no loud noises, no swearing, and no women guests ever, regardless of their marital status or relationship with you."

Though the room was sparsely furnished, it was clean and had an iron-framed bed with a sagging mattress, an upholstered chair (which I later discovered to be most uncomfortable), a commode with washbasin and pitcher, and three pegs on the wall on which to hang my clothes. The one window faced onto the street below.

"Have you work here?" she asked after we had come to an agreement on price and other matters.

"I do," I said. "At Maysbeck Mill."

"Ah," she responded, looking me over, gauging my status. "As an overlooker, I wonder?"

I laughed. "Not so important as that, I'm afraid. I help in the counting-house."

Her eyebrows raised, but her smile never diminished. "All in good time, I should imagine. All in good time."

I moved within a week, not a difficult task, as I still had few belongings. Mrs. Wilson wept when I left, as if she were saying good-bye once more to her beloved Eddie, repeating over and over, "It cannot be helped; it just cannot be helped." And, as I bundled my things into a hired trap: "You will come for Christmas dinner, surely. Say you will come."

"Of course I will," I said, though I wondered if Miss Little would see fit to allow me to stay through the meal.

Mrs. Clem, it turned out, had three other lodgers: Miss Lavinia Riley, a tall, serious woman who worked at a milliner's; and two men, Mr. Matthew Hill, who was in his midtwenties and who traveled much of the time, and the other, Mr. Henry MacMichael, near sixty years of age, I should guess, and who seemed to do nothing but grumble.

I arranged for Bert Cornes—the night watchman at the mill, who, as his last task before going home in the morning, knocked his long pole on the windows of the mill workers' homes to wake them—to come past Mrs. Clem's establishment and knock me up as well.

Less than a week after I moved out, Mr. Wilson announced to me that his sister-in-law and Mrs. Brewer had arrived, though he needn't have bothered, for his changed demeanor made that clear almost immediately. He spoke even less than before, and his work habits altered as well. He took to coming in earlier and staying on much later, even after the machines had shut down, as if he craved that peace and respite.

I was indeed invited to the Wilson home for Christmas dinner, and Miss Little did not drive me away from the table, but even so it was not a particularly pleasant occasion. Poor Mrs. Wilson was in a dither the whole time, and in fact I imagined that she was often beside herself since her sister had come: she gave her cook and her housekeeper one order after another—often countermanding a previous one. As for Mr. Wilson, he buried himself behind his newspapers and appeared at table only long enough to not seem completely unsociable. His distraction was such that I wondered how he managed to stay through the pudding, which I thought was delicious, though Mrs. Wilson complained that it was burned and Miss Little wandered off after only a bite or two, Mrs. Brewer scurrying after her. As they disappeared, Mr. Wilson seemed to lighten, and Mrs. Wilson, though still apologizing for everything, appeared more relaxed as well.

"You can see how it is," Mr. Wilson said to me.

"Yes, sir, I do," I said, knowing that Mr. Lincoln might scold me for such an abrupt and inadequate response, but there seemed nothing more to say.

He stared off into space for a time. "It can't be helped," he said. "It's not what anyone would choose, bringing a person losing her mind into one's own home, but it must be done. Even the fiercest of beasts—wolves and bears—take care of their own."

"Yes, sir," I said, for it seemed all there was to say.

And, to my relief, he changed the subject. "How are you getting on, by now?"

"I have no complaints. Mrs. Clem keeps a tidy place."

"I understand she is respectable," he responded. "You have done very well under the circumstances, I should say. And you have taken hold well at the mill."

It was the first direct approval he had given me since his conversation with Rowland. "Thank you, sir."

"Don't thank me; thank the father who taught you that a gentleman can work hard and still be a gentleman. There are too many in this world who think being in trade is shameful."

"Yes, sir," I said, wise enough not to dispute the point.

"Has your father ever told you what he has in mind for you?"

"No, sir, he has not," I said, suddenly sitting straighter.

"Nor do I know, but it's clear he wants you to be able to run a facility—a mill or a manufactory of some sort—on your own." He smoothed the tablecloth beside his place and waved to the maid for another brandy. "You are too young for such responsibility now, but that is what I think he has in mind. Would that suit you, do you think?"

"Yes, sir, it would, sir," I said, my heart suddenly beating so wildly that it was a wonder he didn't hear it. No one had ever asked me if any plans of my father's, whatever they were, suited me. It would not have occurred to me to refuse them, but, in fact, at the time I could not imagine anything that would be finer. I still had a great deal to learn.

———

A few weeks later, a letter came to Mr. Wilson from my father, announcing his impending visit. I was stunned into panic. I had not seen my father since I was seven years old, before I had been sent to Black Hill. I did not know what I would say to him or how he would react to me or what he expected of me or, worst of all, if I would even recognize him.

"Well, now, that's a welcome bit of news," Mr. Wilson said, after reading the letter. "We'll be settling a new arrangement for you, since I cannot house you as I had originally agreed." Then he looked me up and down. "You'd best get yourself a new pair of trousers and a new coat."

"I don't know, sir," I said. "My father does not truck well with dandies." I had no idea why I said that, since I could not remember my father's opinions on almost anything. And surely Rowland did not dress as if he were concerned about such a thing.

"Well, at least," Mr. Wilson amended, his eyes not having left me, and I now understood that he was seeing me as he thought my father would, and, further, that he would be held accountable if my appearance were less than what my father would be expecting. "You must at least get your hair trimmed up nicely."

I did that, and even wandered past a tailor's shop or two, but I could not bring myself to order anything new. Much as I wanted to impress my father, I didn't want him to be aware of it. I was, still, young and foolish.

I shouldn't have been concerned about not being able to recognize him, or him me. The astonishing thing was that I had not fully realized it until I came face-to-face with him, but I was the picture of what he must have been in his youth, and he, in turn, showed me how I would appear in my later years. I was the taller by a couple of inches, but he was the broader, his face more lined, of course, his black hair paling but not yet gray, his posture still erect, his step firm.

He gazed at me, and I at him. I had been right about the new clothes; my father wore a well-used black traveling outfit with black top boots. With his hat removed, his hair proved to be longish, scraping his shoulders, and slightly waved, just as mine was at that length. We had the same black eyes, the same intent expression. His skin was darker than mine, a result, perhaps, of his years in the Jamaican sun. "Edward," he said to me. It was the first time he had ever called me that, to my recollection, and, as it turned out, the last.

"Sir," I responded. Then I added, keeping Mr. Lincoln in mind, "I'm pleased to see you again after all these years."

"Yes," he said, already turning to Mr. Wilson, who was hovering about us. The countinghouse once again seemed overly small.

"May I get you a chair?" Mr. Wrisley asked solicitously.

"I think not," my father said, not even deigning to glance his way. "We shall be off, I think. It's past noon and I am hungry, and I understand, Wilson, that there's an inn not far."

"Of course," Mr. Wilson said. "Young Rochester here—young Edward, I mean—knows the way."

"I was counting on your attendance as well," my father said.

"Of course," Mr. Wilson said, "I would be only too glad to join you. It is just that I thought—"

"Leave the thinking to me, Wilson, if you don't mind," my father said.

At the Crown Inn, the discussion was awkward for me, and doubly so because I felt it awkward for Mr. Wilson. Clearly, my father was used to giving orders and not to taking advice. I sat quietly, sipping my drink, pushing the roast—which usually was quite delicious—around my plate, and listening to my father question Mr. Wilson as to my suitability for business, paying me no more attention than if I had been a leaden salt-cellar left on the table by mistake. Mr. Wilson gave a good account of me, which was kind. I caught him stretching the truth more than once, and it pleased us both that my father seemed satisfied with his report.

Then it came to the change in my living accommodations, and with the first words out of his mouth on the subject, it was clear that my father was used to driving a hard bargain. But Mr. Wilson, in his own quiet way, held his ground, politely mentioning that perhaps Maysbeck was more expensive than Liverpool, given that we were more inland and thus farther from the port of entry of so many goods, and that it surely would be embarrassing for us all if I hadn't enough funds to pay for my daily needs.

At this my father gave me a baleful glance—almost the only time he had looked at me all the while we were there—and when he turned back, he made a compromise. There were a few more details to be settled between them, and just when I thought he had truly forgotten my presence, my father turned to me. "Well, boy, what have you to say for yourself?"

Surprised by the sudden attention, I stared wordlessly at him.

"Do you have any questions?" Mr. Wilson quickly prompted.

"Sir, what...what do you have in mind for me in the end?" I asked.

"In the end?" My father scowled. "In the end, that you can oversee a manufactory on your own, of course."

I took a deep breath and barged ahead. "Where might that be?"

"Surely you must know I have interests in the West Indies—in Jamaica. Surely that has not escaped your attention."

"No, sir, it has not," I said, and I blundered on. "It's just that I know you have interests in other places as well—Liverpool, and London I presume, and of course Thornfield."

"Thornfield is not for you. Thornfield is Rowland's."

His words struck like a blow. Much as I had always fancied myself visiting Jamaica, I still imagined that Thornfield was my home. My mouth was suddenly dry; I could think of nothing more to say. It must have become clear to him that he needed to clarify my situation so that there would be no mistake.

"You are the second son. I will not divide—and therefore diminish—the family holdings to give you a portion: that is all Rowland's.

Furthermore, I disapprove of sending any son of mine toward one of the traditional routes for fellows in your position. I have no interest in seeing you a vicar of some forlorn parish, or an officer in the king's navy with little to show for himself beyond a uniform, and I certainly will not have you ending up a simpering muffin living at the whim of some wealthy widow. No, I will not have the Rochester name besmirched by someone who cannot hold up his head in good company. I have not arranged your education thus far for nothing. You will go to Jamaica when you are ready—that is, when you have had the education appropriate for someone in your position—and you will build yourself there an empire and a reputation worthy of the Rochester name. I will give advice or direction if needed, but you will build it yourself. It will make a man of you, if you are not one already by the time you arrive."

May I not come to Thornfield even for a visit? I thought to ask, but stopped myself. If I asked, and if he said no, the door would have definitely been closed. But since I was not expressly forbidden...

My father left shortly thereafter, having told the innkeeper to send for a hackney carriage. He shook Mr. Wilson's hand, and mine, his grip hard on mine as he did so, and then he turned and mounted the carriage. Without another glance toward us, he urged the driver forward, and, much as I wish I had not, I watched him go until the carriage was out of sight. Mr. Wilson stood silently beside me the whole time, and then he took my arm. "I see we have our work cut out for us, young Rochester," he said.

I did indeed feel young just then, but I forced back any emotion that had welled up in me and made myself a firm resolve. I would put away any childish dreams and expectations. Henceforth, I would do whatever was necessary to become a man my father could be proud of.

CHAPTER 10

Mr. Wilson, God bless him, was as good as his word. Immediately, he gave me more responsibility, and I strode through that vast mill as if I owned it, and, indeed, I sometimes foolishly imagined that I did. My father's words had made me see myself differently from what I had before I met with him. Once, I had felt more kinship with the children who worked in the mill than I did with Mr. Wilson or even Bob Wrisley, but now, suddenly, I saw myself in company with men of substance, like Mr. Wilson. I imagined I might even someday hold my own beside my father.

It did not take much time for me to become accustomed to this new vision of myself, and to quite enjoy it. Mr. Wilson seemed as proud of me as if I were his own son, and he frequently invited me to dine with him at noontime at the Crown, where he usually ate his dinner, now that Miss Little and Mrs. Brewer had come to stay. Sometimes we were joined by Mr. Landes, a neighbor who owned a flour mill, or others of Mr. Wilson's friends, but as for the people who worked in the mill, I had begun to see them more fully as Mr. Wilson and his friends did—as a caste quite lower than ourselves, quite inured to difficult times, and lucky indeed to hold the jobs they had.

The workingmen at the mill paid me as little attention as possible, save for one: Rufus Shap, a lout built like a bull, who carried an angry face and glared at me when he thought I wasn't looking. I dared to ask Mr.

Wilson once if he had noticed that Rufus seemed to bear me ill will, but he only replied, "That is Rufus for you." Even Mr. Wilson sometimes nearly came to words with Rufus, but Rufus always backed off at the last moment. "Despite everything," Mr. Wilson said to me once, "Rufus is a good worker, with a strong back, if a weak enough mind. There are men, Rochester, for whom anger is a way of life. They wake up angry and go to bed angry; they seem to know no other way to accept their position in this world. As long as he controls himself, we can live with the way he looks at us. And I would daresay, if you or I had been born in his shoes, we might see the world the same way."

But I was not in Rufus' place, and I was wary of him, and he sensed it. I could tell it in his smirks that passed as smiles, in the way he sometimes deliberately turned his back to me as I neared him, and in the way he at other times stared at me directly in the eye in a kind of silent challenge. It was as if he wanted me to know that as far as he was concerned, I was still that young boy who had first come to Maysbeck Mill and always would be. I tried to ignore it, as Mr. Wilson had advised, but there remained between Rufus and me an animus that simmered as if waiting for the moment of boil.

My duties at Maysbeck Mill had absorbed nearly the whole of my life, and while I sometimes imagined myself as a full partner with Mr. Wilson, in fact I was only too glad not to have the entire responsibility of the place. That became even more clear to me one night just a few weeks after my father had paid his short visit. It was a cloud-covered night, the moon only a vague presence in the sky, and I had been asleep, it seemed, for only a short time, when a fierce pounding came on the front door of Mrs. Clem's house—even I could hear it on the third floor. At first I thought, *Fire!* and I leaped from my cot, but I could smell nothing. I was about to climb back under the covers when I heard a commotion belowstairs: shouts and replying shouts, and footsteps running up the stairs and my name: "*Rochester! Rochester!*" Doors opened on the floor below, and then the steps pounded quite close and I heard my name again. I pulled open the door, and it was a boy, a young boy I did not recognize, full out of breath from running.

"It's the mill!" he shouted as soon as he caught his breath. "Men!" he shouted at me. "Villains! Attacking the mill!" And suddenly I realized—it should have registered with me before—the mill bell was ringing, clanging wildly in the night: the most ominous sound—an attack on the mill.

Oh God, I thought. *They've come to Maysbeck—Luddites.* The name had been only a distant possibility, men angry at the mechanizations that had taken their jobs. The newspapers had lost interest: there was little mention of them anymore, and anyway, one always assumes such catastrophes happen elsewhere. I threw on my clothes while the boy stood watching, as if to make sure I would really come. And then I followed him, barreling down the narrow stairs and out into the night. We ran the full distance to the mill—a mile or more, only a pale half-moon to light the dark, the sounds growing louder as we approached, shouts and crashes and even gunshots.

There was a crowd, lighted by the torches they carried. Some were attempting to beat down the double oaken doors while others shouted angrily, waving cudgels or anything else they could use as a weapon. I knew I had heard shots, but at first I could see no sign of a gun. Then I saw, in a third-floor window of the mill, Bert Cornes with a musket, which he shot from time to time—more to frighten the mob away than to kill or injure anyone.

Across the way, on the other side of the crowd, I saw Mr. Wilson and Mr. Landes, both also with pistols in their hands, appearing angry and somewhat frightened. My eyes scanned the mob, but I did not recognize any of them—agitators from elsewhere, I guessed. My gaze fell on Rufus Shap, at the far edge of the crowd, only a couple of yards from Mr. Wilson. His stoic face showed nothing, neither anger nor pleasure, and I was stunned by the equanimity of it. Though Maysbeck Mill was his livelihood, it was as if he'd as soon break down the mill as defend it.

Then another shot rang out—from Bert Cornes, in the window—and this time a cry of pain pierced the night. The crowd stilled for an instant, and then it surged forward, as if by signal, as if by the mere force of their combined strength they would push through those solid oak doors.

Another shot was fired, and another. I saw Mr. Wilson's arm raised, and I thought, *My God, there's going to be murder.* Just then someone near Mr. Wilson turned to face him, grabbed him, and held him to keep him from shooting, and I realized it was Rufus who had done it.

Desperately I pushed my way through the crowd—I, not half as strong as Rufus but not thinking, so set was I on preventing harm to Mr. Wilson. It was difficult to get close enough, the milling crowd shoving me one way and another, but when I finally reached for Rufus to pull him away, it was like reaching for a bull. He turned to me, though, his face dark with fury. "Get him out of here," he demanded. "At least you can manage that." Then he shoved Mr. Wilson toward me, and I grabbed him, pulling him through the crowd and away toward his home. He came almost willingly, as if he were relieved to have someone else make that decision for him. Behind us, Mr. Landes followed.

By daylight it was all over. The doors had held; Bert Cornes' well-placed shots had injured a few but mostly frightened the rioters from doing their worst, and in the end they gave up and melted away into the countryside from whence they had come. Mr. Wilson expressed dismay that he had been pulled away from his place at the battle, but I quoted Tacitus at him about living to fight another day, and he was so surprised that I not only knew it but could say it in Latin that he quite forgot to be angry with me.

Indeed, in the days after, he expressed his gratitude to me again and again, but he was also subdued for a time, as was everyone else at the mill, going about their business with quiet and serious faces. It was only Rufus Shap who glared at me, and I remembered his words: *At least you can manage that.* It was clear he despised me. On the other hand, he had saved Mr. Wilson, and I could not deny that.

And then two completely unexpected things happened: I received a letter from Mr. Lincoln, with whom I had held desultory communication since I left Black Hill; and Mr. Wilson fell ill. Mr. Lincoln's letter was the usual accounting of his present boys, their strengths and their foibles (which always led me to wonder what he had written to others about me).

But at the end, a few simple sentences stopped my breath and quickened the beat of my heart:

> *You will remember Carrot, I daresay. He is the Earl of Lan-ham now, as you may know, and he writes asking of you. I had not been in communication with him as I have been with you, so I did not know if you two had maintained a connec-tion after leaving Black Hill. I am inclosing his address, for I am not aware if you are in a position to want him to know where you are and what you have been about. So I leave that to you.*
>
> *I remain,*
> *Mr. Hiram Lincoln*
> *Black Hill*

For some strange reason, my eyes suddenly watered with tears. *Carrot*...Carrot asking about me. I heard again my brother's terse words: *You surely do not think that the nephew of the Prince Regent of England is really interested in what became of a clerk in a count-inghouse in Maysbeck, do you?*

Perhaps not. And yet, he *was* Carrot and we had shared a great deal to-gether, and he *had* asked about me. He himself had said it: *I missed you, too, Jam.*

Besides, I was no longer merely a clerk, for all the difference that might make to the Earl of Lanham. I sat down a dozen times to write to Car-rot, struggling to find words that would reintroduce us, that would convey my hopes of seeing him again without sounding maudlin, but each time I threw away my attempt, and it was nearly a month after I received Mr. Lincoln's correspondence when I got up my courage and wrote something that might have been suitable. I posted it before I lost my nerve.

Four days later Mr. Wilson crashed down onto the mill floor with *apoplexia*. The mill foreman came for me and I sent Wrisley for a carriage, and the three of us managed to get Mr. Wilson outside and installed into it. I accompanied him, still unconscious, to his home.

Mrs. Wilson was all aflutter and Mrs. Brewer hurried Miss Little upstairs when we arrived. The coachman helped me carry Mr. Wilson into the house, and then I ordered him to collect the physician posthaste. After an examination, the physician shook his head and would not forecast the future but only ordered nourishment when he regained consciousness, and complete rest—as if Mr. Wilson could do anything else. Through it all, Mrs. Wilson clung to me, weeping into my chest, and I comforted her as best I could.

She was determined to spend the night in the parlor with her husband, but I convinced her to go upstairs and sleep in her own bed; I would hold vigil with him. He did recover consciousness the next day, but his speech was muddled—it was harder to tell about his mind—he had lost all control of the limbs on his left side, and that side of his face seemed almost to have melted. After breakfast I felt it imperative to return to the mill to ascertain that all was running properly, though Mrs. Wilson begged me to return as soon as possible. Mr. Landes came as soon as he heard and offered whatever help was needed, which was kind, given that he had his own mill to run and his own house and his own wife, who had been poorly for years.

Mr. Wilson owned the mill outright, and that was a good thing in the respect that there was no doubt who should have been in control, if only he were capable. But now there was only I and Bob Wrisley—who, though he had many more years' experience of the mill than I, was still only a countinghouse clerk—and Jeremy Hardback, the overlooker. Jeremy was a good enough man, as Mr. Wilson had often said, but not cut out to be more than he had already risen to. In other words, it was now up to me to run Maysbeck Mill, with Mr. Landes' help and advice.

Those workers who had been at the mill for many years still saw me as the near child I had been when I arrived, and it was difficult for them—especially the men—to countenance the fact that I was now truly acting in Mr. Wilson's stead. Somehow, I needed to establish myself in their eyes, if only by force of will. Mr. Landes laid it out for me in no uncertain terms: "I imagine these folk are decent people, most of them, but they, like servants, must keep to their places, and you must keep to yours. One cannot converse with them on terms of equality; one must keep them always at a distance, or one will lose all authority."

I worked at doing that, and I was aware that some at the mill disliked it, but steady work was scarce enough that no one dared to leave. It was always the men who grumbled behind my back; women, I thought at the time and still think, are more practical than men, perhaps because they are used to being powerless and therefore bear what they must, and often more honorably. Certainly, I was often nervous about my new responsibilities, worried that I would fail and let Mr. Wilson down when he needed me most, but I also learned that even if one is unsure, one can play the role with no one else the wiser.

Mrs. Wilson insisted I come back to stay at the house, and I did so out of pity for her. However, that was not an easy choice, for Miss Little continued to abhor the sight of me, and she screamed whenever I appeared, until Mrs. Wilson, who could neither abandon her sister nor bear life without my presence, came up with a solution. I was to move into the second-floor guest room that Miss Little and Mrs. Brewer had been using, and they in turn would take up residence in the third-floor room, where meals could be brought to Miss Little, and she would never have need to come down, nor ever accidentally meet me on the stairway. With that resolved, quiet and almost peacefulness returned to the house.

It was weeks later that I heard from Carrot. My letter, sent to him at Lanham-Hall, had followed him to Bath and then to Baden-Baden, which was just gaining a reputation for all the pleasures that aimless young men enjoy. His return letter exhibited a gratifying level of enthusiasm at having heard from me, and he invited me to join him at my earliest convenience. I noted with a kind of schadenfreude that Rowland was not mentioned. I responded that I could not leave my present position, as I was direly needed, but that I would be delighted to see him as soon as possible after he returned to England.

His reply was pure Carrot:

> *Surely you have nothing to do there in that godforsaken town that is as important as reestablishing our friendship. Nevertheless, I know that sometimes one must do what one must, and I look forward to seeing you soonest. At the end of May we will be going to Epsom Downs for the Derby. Have you been? You must join us there; it is wonderful fun! My friend Willy's father owns the favorite, Tiresias. We shall be sitting in his box.*

I badly wanted to do as Carrot urged, but I knew I could not; it was just not possible at the time for me to leave Maysbeck for even as much as a day. *There will be other times,* I consoled myself; *I have the rest of my life.* Some days later, sitting in Mr. Wilson's parlor in the evening, reading the newspaper to him, I discovered that Tiresias had indeed won the Derby, and I imagined the thrill it must have been to stand among the party of the winner's owner. I wondered if Rowland had been there, enjoying the gaiety of the event. I gazed at Mr. Wilson, half-asleep in his chair, and I thought of Carrot, from whom I had received two days previous a letter expressing his disgust over my inability to come to Derby Day. I admit I had been torn, but I had known the responsible course, and I had done it, if for no other reason than to prove myself. I wished I were in Carrot's position—or even Rowland's—but I was not: I could not shed my life at a moment's notice. I was a second son and had to earn my own way.

Slowly, slowly, Mr. Wilson started to regain his ability to speak. In the beginning it was almost meaningless garble, but his face would brighten if his answer to a question ought to be *yes*, and a glower appeared in his eyes if it was to be *no*. And we began to understand his attempts at words, almost like learning a different dialect of the same language. I would come into his room each morning before leaving for the mill, for he was invariably awake, and I would tell him what I had in mind for the day, or remind him what new orders we were working on, and he would smile or glower and give me advice as best he could. I came back at noontime usually, as I knew he would be anxious to hear the latest—if a frame had broken down or if the orders were keeping up, if the quality remained high or if there was too much shoddy. And again in the evening I went first to him to let him know that all had been taken care of, that there was naught to worry about. I suspected that he barely believed me most of the time, but it was true that Mr. Landes stopped in to the mill nearly every day to make sure I had everything under control. I was pleased indeed when his visits tapered off to only two or three times a week, which I took to mean that he thought I was capable of handling most things by myself.

One would think that all this new responsibility would have pleased me no end, but in fact, while I enjoyed the satisfaction of seeing my decisions carried out, it only made me more anxious than ever to move on. My father had plans for me, and I was eager to get on with them. Yet no matter what I or my father might have preferred, I could not leave Mr. Wilson, who had been more than a father to me.

CHAPTER 11

Carrot eventually got over his ire at my missing Derby Day, and he continued—even more forcefully—to urge me to visit. I was pleased that he seemed as anxious as I to rekindle our friendship, imagining the enjoyable time we two would have together. But of necessity I put him off as best I could, for I was still determined to prove myself to my father as well as to Mr. Wilson. And then, in midsummer, I received a short letter from my father:

> I have heard word of Mr. Wilson's unfortunate accident of some months ago, and I presume you have taken over more responsibilities in light of the situation. This certainly will be invaluable experience for you—running a manufactory on your own. I could not have hoped for better. I assume Mr. Wilson will have a speedy recovery—perhaps he already has—and you, with your newfound experience and responsibilities, will remain of greater benefit to his mill operation than either he or I imagined of you at this point. Therefore, it seems only logical that our arrangement has further need of revision. I cannot at the present take the time to come there and arrange a new agreement. Please advise Mr. Wilson to write to me what new arrangements he is prepared to make.

I read the missive with astonishment. Mr. Wilson was far from recovered and was not in a position to express what arrangements should be made. I withheld the news of my father's letter until I had a chance to share it with Mr. Landes, but when that gentleman read it, he let out an impatient breath and looked up at me. "Do you know anything of the understanding between your father and Mr. Wilson concerning you?" he asked.

"I do not," I said, "except that I was to be trained in the running of a manufactory, like the mill, and that Mr. Wilson was to give me room and meals and a small sum to cover my incidental expenses. And when perforce I needed to find lodgings of my own, they made another agreement that would cover my further living expenses."

Mr. Landes frowned. "Did you never ask what exactly that agreement stated?"

"I have never been in the habit of questioning my father," I admitted. And then I added, because that excuse seemed rather lame for a young man of my age and current responsibilities, "I thought everything was quite clear between them."

"I wonder if there is something written," he said. "Perhaps there is something in the ledgers—some accounting of money paid."

Since Mr. Wilson's illness I had had full access to the mill accounts. "I never saw anything, nor heard mention of it," I said. "It must have been a personal arrangement between them." And I voiced what he must have been thinking: "We may be at my father's mercy on this."

"Indeed," he responded. We both knew that without Mr. Wilson, my father would have the advantage in any negotiation.

"He may not be an easy man in this," I warned.

"There's a chance there's something in writing somewhere," Mr. Landes said. "We can hope for that."

"If only Mr. Wilson would recover—" I began, but he cut me off.

"Rochester, that is not going to happen."

I knew it was true, but the fact of it had not yet been mentioned between us. "What will we do?" I asked.

Mr. Landes was silent for a time, and then he said, "You will write to your father and tell him that Wilson is not yet fully recovered but will make those decisions at the earliest opportunity, and that in the meantime, if there are any points of clarity that should be included, to please express them. That ought to hold him for a time while we ponder this."

I wrote that letter, and a week or so later a short note came from my father:

> *Thank you for informing me of John Wilson's continuing situation. I do hope that you are taking advantage of your position to display your full capabilities in handling the responsibility which has fallen into your lap, for responsibility is what makes a man a man.*
>
> *I look forward to a response from Wilson, as soon as possible.*

And there was a note for Mr. Wilson as well, which I shared with Mr. Landes when he came by the mill to see how things were going:

> *My dear sir,*
>
> *I understand you are still invalided and require additional time of healing. Please be aware that my son is yours for as long as you need him. I assume that you recognize how much his responsibilities have increased, and I await your word as to what financial rearrangements you have made to address that issue.*

"I'm sorry," I said, after Mr. Landes had read the letter.

He didn't respond directly to that, just saying, "I will speak to Wilson."

When I came home that evening, the housekeeper told me that Mr. Landes had already arrived and was in Mr. Wilson's bedroom. I went into the parlor and sat down, attempting to read the newspaper but too distracted to comprehend the simplest sentence. I could not imagine the attempt at conversation that was going on upstairs.

When I heard Mr. Landes' footsteps on the stairs, I folded the paper and rose to greet him. He entered the room brusquely and made for the hearth, just the sort of place where my father might stand to dress me down.

"Sir," I said.

"Sit down," he said, and I did. He got right to the point. "Your father seems a . . . a determined man."

"Yes, he is, sir."

"Nevertheless, he has a point. In the last few months, you have been as John Wilson would have been, if he had been able—"

"No, sir," I interrupted, "not at all. He would have—"

Mr. Landes shook his head. "Never mind how he would have handled things. You have done your very best, which is all that can be asked of any of us. It was remiss of us—of me; I cannot put it to poor John's fault—not to have realized that you were owed more than you were being paid. Therefore, I will write to your father immediately and tell him what John and I have decided. He will find it suitable, I should imagine." He stared into the fire for a time, and then he added, "We shall have to sell the place, you and I."

"Oh no. Mr. Wilson would not want that. The mill is . . . is—"

"Indeed he does not. But he has no choice."

I looked away from that hard truth.

"He is more aware than you think," Mr. Landes went on. "He doesn't want to sell. He did not even want to hear me speak of it, but he will not improve much more than he already has. He can think; he can talk, in his fashion. He most probably will never again walk. Nor could he hold his own against another Luddite uprising. In life, one cannot depend on what has always been or, even less so, what has never been. You have your whole life in front of you, Rochester. We know that, John and I, and his life may well be drawing down. It would not be right for us—"

"It would not be right for me to leave him un—un—"

"You will not leave him unassisted. Indeed, I hope you will remain until we have sold the mill—I hope that your father will agree to that. In my letter to him, explaining our arrangement, I will tell our plans, and I hope he can allow to let you stay a bit longer. Would you be amenable to that?"

What could I say? I did not even know what my choices might have been, but Mr. Wilson had been a father to me. How could I turn my back on him? "Of course," I said, "I will do whatever I can."

"Fine. Then, it's settled. Do not speak of this with Wilson, unless he broaches the subject first. It is, as you can well imagine, difficult for him to have reached this juncture, but there it is. He can do little else. And neither can either of us." With that he left.

And I carried a lamp upstairs to my room, where I undressed and got into bed and did not sleep.

———

I was up and breakfasted and out of the house before Mr. Wilson awoke the next morning, so I had a slight reprieve from seeing him, now that I knew more than I wished to know. At the mill, I walked through the day in a daze: all seemed new, and yet terribly familiar. I felt a general unease among the workers, which puzzled me. Rufus Shap stared at me through the window glass of the countinghouse—his gaze black and more defiant than ever. Was I only imagining it, now that the mill was likely to be sold, or was there some sort of worker psychical perception that could read the minds of the managers?

At noon I did not go to the Crown or back to the Wilson home, but sent a boy out for a cheese pie, and though the task fell under his general duties, when he returned I gave him a whole shilling for his trouble. Mr. Landes came by late in the afternoon, full of apologies for not having come sooner, but I was so relieved to see him that I nearly hugged him in greeting. "And how was the day?" he asked.

"It was terrible," was the best I could think to say.

He nodded and smiled kindly. "The first day after a big decision is made is usually the worst. One always thinks of what else one could or should have done. Second thoughts are the destroyers of good ideas. We are doing the best we can."

"But how is it," I asked, "that the workers seem to know things without being told?"

He nodded wryly. "You are young; you imagine outcomes that cannot happen. The mill workers know Wilson's situation; they know he has little chance to recover. And, indeed, they do have a second sense. They have to, for there is nothing for them to fall back on if the mill closes. They are not like us—they have no education: most cannot even read. They have no savings, no property, and their friends and relatives are as bad off as they are. There is nothing for them but the poorhouse—or starvation. They live on the edge of hell and they know it. Before they left their country cottages, they at least had the gleanings after a harvest, or the chance of trapping a rabbit or two. Here, in a town or in the city, they have nothing. You can thank God you are not in their shoes."

But I had remained caught on what he had said at the outset. "Might the mill really close?"

"It is one possibility," was all he said. I had foolishly imagined that the mill would be sold as easily as selling a mince pie, but now I saw that that might not be the case. He said no more, and we walked on in silence.

Some days after that, again late in the day, Mr. Landes came to the mill to say he had received a letter from my father, who made some additional requirements in light of my changed situation. My father had also made clear that by next summer at the latest, I must leave Maysbeck, for he had other plans for me.

"Was that all he wrote?" I asked, eager for fuller news.

"Unfortunately, yes," he responded. "Even I know by now how firm and terse your father can be." He paused, then said, "Rochester, I know you are anxious about your future. Suppose you went to Liverpool and visited your father. Suppose, in the companionship of shared pints at an inn, you got him to talking. Perhaps he would tell you more."

"I can't leave the mill," I said, impatient that he would even imagine such a thing.

"You could, for a few days. Jeremy Hardback is a good man, and I could spend part of the day here, as well."

"I couldn't ask that of you."

He leveled his eyes at me. "You have borne a great deal more in the last year than one should have expected of someone your age," he said finally. "I know Wilson thinks highly of you. He would second this, I am sure."

I shook my head. I envisioned the companionless silence my father and I would surely share over those pints, and I knew that I felt closer to Mr. Landes—and especially closer to Mr. Wilson, even in his infirmity—and more able to talk honestly to him, than I could ever hope to feel toward my own father. I was ashamed to admit it, even to myself, but I had no particular interest in spending any more time than necessary with him. "It's kind of you to offer, but I know it would do no good. My father is set in his ways. He tells me nothing, deals with others rather than with me if he has the least opportunity. It would be a waste of time."

A frown creased his forehead. "You truly have no idea what he has in mind for you? And you don't consider it prudent to visit him to ask?"

"It would make no difference. He has never let me know what he has in mind until it is about to come to fruition."

"And you are content with that? Rochester, you have shown great maturity in recent months. Surely you have a right to know what lies ahead for you." He took his hat from the rack and put his hand on the door latch, then turned back to me. "Still, it would be good for you to get away for a time—even a short time—from what are really quite heavy responsibilities for someone of your age. If not to your father in Liverpool, might there be anywhere else you would like to go?"

I paused before responding. Thornfield-Hall came into my mind. But my father's words came as well: *Thornfield is not for you. Thornfield is Rowland's.* I could count neither on Rowland's being absent another time, nor on his welcome if he were home. And yet—yes—the thought stole into my mind: there was another visit I longed to make. I tried my best to hesitate, as if I needed to think, but I was suddenly so excited I could not have fooled him in the least. "Indeed," I said, "there is a place—an old school friend who lives near Napier has been urging me to visit, and it has never seemed a possibility. I could be there and back in two or three days."

"Two or three days? Surely that isn't enough. You would barely get there before you had to turn back."

Of course it wasn't enough, not nearly enough. But it was better than nothing. "I think I can manage it," I said.

"Well, then, arrange it," he said. "But give me warning enough that I can work out a plan to oversee both mills."

I wrote to Carrot that very evening and posted the letter as soon as I could. A few days afterwards, the response came, brief and direct: I was to come at my earliest convenience. If I could manage to get myself to the village of Napier, Carrot would send a conveyance for me.

I would see my oldest friend again, at last—I felt as if I were suddenly living in a dream. Mrs. Wilson seemed full of trepidation over my leaving, but she still encouraged me to go. Mr. Wilson simply nodded slowly and peered up at me as if he half feared that I should never return. Probably too effusively, I made a point of saying that I would be gone only two days or at the most three, and I assured him as well that Mr. Landes would be stopping by the house each day to report on work at the mill.

I managed to talk a tailor into quickly putting together a pair of pantaloons, which he assured me were all the fashion, though they felt quite uncomfortable; but I could not bring myself to order a new waistcoat as well. And there was no time to order a pair of the slim, stylish pumps that the cobbler had in his window. There was no real rush, of course, but once it became possible for me to leave, I could hardly bear to wait. Somehow, the prospect of being with Carrot again almost seemed like going home.

CHAPTER 12

On the stagecoach, I began having second thoughts. It had been years since I had last seen Carrot. We had been boys then, playing at soldiers in the fields and woods around Black Hill; now we were older, he an earl, no less, and I— What was I? To the world, I was the young manager of a successful worsted mill, but most days I felt like a boy still, trying to give the appearance of a man, capable and dependable—and terrified of being found out. I was convinced I was the only young man in all the world who felt like a charlatan.

More than once on that journey I thought of Touch, he with his quiet and warm presence, his prodigious imagination. *Would that the three of us could be once more together*, I thought, and I wondered, suddenly, if Carrot knew yet that he had passed on. I laid my head back and closed my eyes and tried to imagine what Carrot would look like, what he would *be* like. I did not even know what one calls an earl when he is a friend, but I was certain that it would not be "Carrot." Still, anxious as I was, I could barely contain my excitement.

For many years after that trip, travel excited my spirits—bringing me back to that bright, early September day, the sky a cloudless blue, the fields of oats and barley blowing in the wind, the workers bending to their tasks, swinging their scythes; heather still rosy purple on the moors; and the delicious anticipation of seeing Carrot again.

We were in Napier by late afternoon—the trip as easy as it could have been; a good sign, I hoped. And Carrot's man was already waiting for me with what seemed like a brand-new tilbury. He tipped his hat and stowed away my luggage while I climbed aboard.

Lanham-Hall was a large country house, slightly bigger than Thornfield-Hall, and more graceful in appearance. Coming up the drive, I was struck by the great gables at the front of the house, and as we arrived, I noted the delicate stonework of the pediment above the massive oak door. The scene carved there was—I recognized immediately—a stylized version of a drawing from an edition of Herodotus on the Battle of Thermopylae that had been Carrot's favorite at Black Hill. He had always insisted on being Leonidas to my Xerxes. I smiled to myself: Carrot was, apparently, still Carrot.

His butler opened the door. "His lordship is still out riding, sir," he told me. "He asks that you excuse him this indulgence. He will be with you immediately when he returns."

"Of course," I said, a bit put out at that lack of a grand welcome. When I stepped inside, I paused, taking in the blue-gray entrance hall, the gently curving staircase, the rose and white Turkey carpet. It seemed restful and pleasing to the eye, not at all what I would have expected of Carrot.

The butler, who introduced himself as Matthews, offered to show me to my chamber, and he led me up the broad stairs and down a short hallway to a room that overlooked the front of the house. From the windows, I could see the long, curved drive, lime trees arching gracefully over it, and, beyond, the rolling fields of Lanham. It reminded me something of Thornfield, though it is hard to say why. At Lanham there was no tangled wood of hawthorn approaching the house, nor was there any moor in the distance. It was no wonder that the place was decorated in pale colors: this was a thoroughly domesticated countryside.

"Make yourself at home, please, sir," Matthews said, "and when you are ready, the dining room is just at the bottom of the stairs, to the left. I'll have something put out there for you."

I remained there at the window, feeling even more nervous now that the reunion with Carrot was upon me. Then, as much to ease my mind as anything, I poured water from the ewer into the bowl and splashed my face and washed my hands. I thought for a moment of changing into other clothes, but I had brought too little clothing to be changing at the least excuse. When I had delayed as long as I dared, I left my room and walked down the stairs and into the dining room.

To my surprise, it was a small, intimate room lined with windows on one side and bookcases on the other three. Mr. Lincoln would have been proud. I strolled the length of one wall, gazing at the books and at the paintings above them. The cases rose only five feet or so from the floor, and above them were a series of lithographs and paintings: Columbus setting foot on the New World, a wonderfully engaging painting of Alexander at the Battle of the Granicus, and, not surprisingly, Turner's rendition of the Battle of Trafalgar. I had been there only a few moments and was still gazing in astonishment at the books and the art when a maid brought in a plate of pork roast and potatoes and peas, which must have been quickly warmed up from last evening's dinner. I sat down at the table, suddenly realizing how hungry I was.

I was just finishing when I heard a commotion in the reception hall right outside the dining room, and the door was flung open and Carrot appeared—older, of course, the ruddy complexion having faded somewhat, but the hair just as bright ginger as ever. "*Jam!*" he shouted, as if I were a mile away instead of just across the room. "Jam! At last!"

I rose and he strode forward, his arms outstretched to embrace me, and sudden tears came to my eyes as I stepped into his embrace. Then he leaned back, his eyes full upon my face. "My God," he said, "it really is you, after all this time!"

"I'd have known you anywhere," I said, at a loss for words, though indeed I would have known him anywhere and under any circumstances.

"But not I, you," he said. "No, indeed. You were—what? ten? eleven?—when we last saw each other."

"Twelve," I said, a bit disappointed that he did not know my exact age, as I knew his.

"Twelve, yes, and now here we are! You're a man now; no wonder you look so different!" He turned then, suddenly. "You'll never guess who's here."

I turned as well toward the door, fearing who it would be even before I saw him. "Rowland," I said, trying not to register disappointment in my voice.

Rowland nodded wordlessly. He must have known I was to arrive. I wished at the moment that I had been similarly warned.

"And if two brothers were more completely different, I could not imagine it," Carrot said.

There was a long silence, made more uncomfortable by the fact that Carrot still had one arm around my shoulders. Then I said, lamely, "I take after our father; he, our mother."

Carrot's hand slipped away from me as his mind moved on. "And what's become of the women?" he asked Rowland.

"Oh, you know," Rowland said, gesturing vaguely.

There are women guests as well? I wondered. And, suddenly, it occurred to me: *Did Carrot have a wife?* "You have a houseful," I said.

"When has he not?" Rowland said, laughing.

"Not so many, actually," Carrot said, "but it needn't bother the two of us. We have much to talk about, have we not?" His hand was on my arm and he guided me out of the dining room, across the reception hall, and into a drawing room that was quite different from the rest of the house: swathed in deep reds and dark blues—a man's room. He led me to a vast maroon leather chair and saw me settled in and then asked, "What will you have?"

I did not know exactly what I should say, so I said the safest: "Whatever you are having is fine." I watched as he stepped to a side table and decanted an amber liquid into two glasses, and cocked his head at Rowland. At Rowland's slight nod, he poured a third. I gazed at the two of them— good friends, no doubt of it—and a flood of resentment swept over me. I had desperately wanted to find my same old Carrot, my closest friend, but now it seemed Rowland had taken my place.

Carrot brought me a glass and, handing it to me, said, "A toast! To the three of us, united at last. Like brothers should be."

I rose to the toast and lifted my glass to theirs, looking from Carrot to Rowland, and back to Carrot. *Brothers,* I thought.

Then, surprising me, Carrot turned to Rowland. "If you don't mind, I would like a word or two with your brother."

"Of course," Rowland said, not turning red as I would have done if the circumstances had been reversed. He left us promptly, closing the door behind him.

"Jam!" Carrot said, once we were alone, laying his hand on my shoulder and searching my eyes. I smiled at him but felt somewhat at a loss, still. Carrot seemed to understand. "You are wondering what to call me, I imagine," he said.

"Yes, I am," I responded, relieved that he had brought it up, as I had not had the slightest idea of how to approach the subject. He seemed so much exactly the same and at the same time so different that I hardly knew where I was to be in relation to him.

"Most people call me 'my lord.' Others call me 'Lord Fitzcharles.' My dearest friends call me 'Fitzcharles,' or 'Thomas.' I'm sure all of those seem strange to you, but there you are. Choose from them as you like, but, for your sake as well as mine, please do not call me 'Carrot' in company. I left that far behind at Black Hill. But, with the two of us . . . well, that's different."

"Yes," I said, "of course."

He stood staring at me a moment, until I added, "My lord."

"Fitzcharles, perhaps," he prompted with a grin.

"Fitzcharles," I said. "Thank you for clarifying."

"Jam," he said, "I hope you won't mind—or be hopelessly confused— if I still call you that: you have always seemed like the little brother I wished I'd had."

"I'm flattered," I responded, and in a way I was, though I would vastly have preferred to be called "Edward." "Fitzcharles," I added then, not yet used to the name. We left the room together, his hand on my back, and as we walked across the entrance hall I saw from the corner of my eye Rowland standing in the gallery at the top of the stairs, watching.

I cannot remember how I managed to get through that evening, for it was not at all as I had assumed, beginning of course with Rowland, whose appearance there was a sore disappointment to me. As well, I was uncomfortable with Carrot, since the name "Fitzcharles" meant nothing to me, and "Thomas" even less, and I was piqued at finding myself still labeled with the childish "Jam."

When we came down for dinner, I was mortified that the tailor in Maysbeck had gotten it all wrong: the fashion for men that season was not the pantaloons he had urged on me, but knee breeches, which both the tailor and I had thought had gone all out of style, and their shoes were the slim pumps I had seen in the cobbler's window and not the sturdy shoes I wore. I felt entirely the country bumpkin.

But the women! They came down eventually, as the sun was lowering in the west, turning the reds and blues of the room to the shades of jewels. There were two of them, and like jewels themselves, but something light and bright, perhaps diamonds or emeralds. They were Miss Kent and Miss Gilpatrick, and they were cousins. Clothed in shimmering gowns, they floated around the room like captive butterflies, flirting with each of us in turn, laughing, showing their dimples.

Carrot displayed an ease that was fitting, while Rowland stood off, as an observer, and even when the women approached him, he seemed to maintain a distance from them, as if to demonstrate that he could not so easily be brought into the circle of their enchantment. Nevertheless, it was clear he held an attraction for them: fair of hair and complexion, with azure eyes and an aquiline nose, he was tall and slim and lithe; he surely looked the perfect gentleman, the perfect dancing partner. I could imagine that people would want to trust my brother, take him into their confidence, hope to be his favorite. I marveled that this was how he appeared to others, knowing what was in his heart. Still, I was eager to learn from watching him, if I could—for it was clear to me he had experience with women.

To me as well, the young ladies returned again and again, perhaps because it was clear I was delighted with them—as who would not be? They were lovely creatures, with light, pure voices and lively eyes that danced with delight when one said something especially clever. And I was, I admit, dying to appear clever.

Dinner was mostly full of talk of the ride that morning, which allowed me to sit silently and observe, grateful at least that my pantaloons and shoes were now out of view. Carrot, of course, was seated at the bottom of the table and Rowland at the top, with me on Carrot's right and the two women across from me. It should have been an honor to be seated at the host's right, but I could think only of the honor, instead, that was accorded to Rowland that he took the top of the table as a matter of custom. I thought it must mean that he frequently dined with Carrot, and, indeed, he seemed quite at home at Lanham-Hall. I could not help wondering if Carrot was equally at home at Thornfield. I pushed that thought out of my mind and concentrated on my dinner.

Partway through the meal, the subject arose as to what entertainment we should have for the evening. "Music, of course!" Carrot responded. He smiled at both of the ladies. "With such musical skill in our presence, how could we not!"

Miss Kent turned to Rowland. "And you as well, Rowland; shall we hear from you?"

"A duet, perhaps?" he responded.

"And you?" Miss Gilpatrick asked me. "Do you sing?"

I flushed. "Not in public," I said, laughing to cover my embarrassment.

"Everyone sings," Rowland said laconically. "I'm sure you do, as well." I turned to him in surprise. What did he know of me? Why would he say such a thing?

"I've heard him," Carrot put in. "Many a sea mariners' song we've shared, have we not?" And without waiting for a response from me, he went on: "And he reads. We had a brilliant mentor in the art of reading when we were boys, and I daresay—"

"That settles it!" Miss Kent interrupted. "Music and reading! What better way to spend an evening. In fact, Thomas, I was perusing your library, and I saw—"

"Perusing my library!" Carrot laughed. "And what caught your eye? Tacitus on war? Or was it Julius Caesar? The collected dispatches of Wellington, perhaps?"

"Don't act the fool," Miss Kent admonished. "It doesn't become you."

I was surprised both at the tone of her voice and at Carrot's docile reaction to it. He was, after all, the lord of the manor, and what was she? Well, indeed what *was* she? I had no idea. There had been no title to her name, simply Miss Kent. But she did have a quick wit and a quicker tongue. "Yes, I saw those boring things," she went on. "Though God knows who would want to read *them*. And I surely did not see what I might have been looking for. It seems you have no books by Jane Austen in this house, even though everyone knows she was the best writer England has produced since William Shakespeare—"

Rowland laughed outrageously at that. "Since William Shakespeare? Jane Austen? That simpering little thing who wrote only of women seeking husbands? As if we don't have enough of that in our real lives without having to read about it too?"

Miss Kent ignored him completely. "But I did see a book by the author of *Waverley*. Has anyone read that one?"

"I have, in fact," Carrot said. "But *Rob Roy* is better."

"You have that!" Miss Kent said.

"Yes, I do."

"Then it's decided," Miss Gilpatrick said. "Lydia and I and Rowland shall play and do duets, and later Fitzcharles and the young Mr. Rochester will read."

Carrot shot a glance at me and I nodded assent. We had all been forced to read at Mr. Lincoln's and he did not permit anything but the most professional of performances. We were both excellent readers.

And that is how the evening progressed. After our brandy and cigars—and after the women had returned from doing whatever it is they do when men have brandy and cigars—we had music and reading. Rowland was a strong tenor and he sang with each of the women, who also sang solo, and even Carrot sang once or twice with Miss Kent. Twice I was asked to sing, but I steadfastly refused.

When we turned to the reading, I, as guest, was given the honor of starting the book. It could not have been a more affecting beginning:

> *How have I sinned, that this affliction*
> *Should light so heavy on me? I have no more sons,*
> *And this no more mine own.*

I was transfixed from the first words, but, ever conscious of my place, I yielded to Carrot much sooner than I would have wished. We were all so entranced with the reading that by the time we parted for the night, we had read well into the first book of *Rob Roy*, and I had made a mental note to buy my own copy at the first opportunity.

As the evening ended and the gathering broke up, I was pulled aside by Miss Kent. "You have a wonderful voice for reading, full and powerful," she said. "You have it in you to be a singer, if you wish it," she said.

Flattered by both her words and the attention she was paying me, I gushed, "Of course!"

"Tomorrow I could give you some training," she suggested.

I smiled broadly. She was a lovely person, with a piquant face surrounded by curls, and I could hardly believe the attention she was paying me. "I would like that very much," I said.

"Tomorrow morning, then. Just after breakfast. Thomas will be inclosed in his library for a time and your brother will be off riding. The house will be quiet."

"I should be grateful."

"And you shall practice on your own, and when next you come, you will be adept and surprise all of them!" She clapped her hands in delight at the thought.

At that moment, my heart felt light. I did not know when I could come back to Lanham-Hall, but I vowed it would happen.

CHAPTER 13

I have always been an early riser, and the next morning I was up before dawn and dressed quickly. At Thornfield-Hall, I would have wandered to the kitchen to see what was afoot, but I was a stranger at Lanham-Hall, and no doubt not welcome in the nether regions, so I stepped outside into the chill air and made for the stable.

In my childhood days I especially loved the stables: the damp, musky smell of the horses, the sharp, earthy odor of straw and the sweet perfume of hay, the rich scent of oiled leather. And the wood of the stalls, rubbed as smooth and satiny as the flanks of the animals they inclosed; and the warm touch of an animal's withers, the moist velvet of its nose. The one who caught my eye that morning was a large chestnut filly that nuzzled me as I put out my hand, turning away in disappointment when she found no treat. I took her halter, though, and turned her back, and spoke sweet, soft words to her, and she stretched her neck and nibbled at my ear and I could not help laughing from the tickle of it.

"She's a beauty, isn't she?" I started at the sound.

"Knew I would find you here," Rowland went on. "You used to like them. Horses."

"Yes, I did."

"Ride much?"

"Not really. Is she yours?"

"Oh yes." He drew the halter from my hands. "You will be leaving Maysbeck soon?" he asked, without glancing back at me.

"Perhaps not so soon. Mr. Wilson had a stroke, and now I am more or less in charge." It was vanity on my part to say that; he was no doubt in correspondence with our father and would already have known.

His back to me, he shrugged as if it were nothing to him who was in charge of a mill. I watched as he saddled the filly, not even waiting for a groom to do so. "You'll have to get yourself a horse when you are in Jamaica," he said. "One can't live a proper life there without a horse."

"Am I really going to Jamaica?" I asked. Though it had been mentioned to me, the possibility still seemed distant, unimaginable.

"Of course. It's all settled."

All settled? He knew that and I did not? And, further, what exactly was settled? I should have asked him more, but I was wary of showing too much ignorance of my own fate. Instead, I only asked, "When? When will I go?"

He turned to me, an odd smile on his face. "When you are ready."

When you are ready. My father—our father—had said that. There was a plan for me that even Rowland knew. Why did I not? "Did you like Jamaica?" I asked, though I remembered that he had said something in Maysbeck that had led me to think that he hadn't.

"It didn't suit me. The people there are stupid, and they have stupid rules. It will be different for you, though."

"Why different for me?"

"It just will be. It's all set for you."

Without saying more, he led the filly out into the stable yard and she clopped across the cobblestones as if she were as anxious as he was to be off across the fields on such a bright and promising morning. As I watched him ride away, I wondered: did Carrot really like him so very much? *Brothers,* Carrot had said: was there something to Rowland that I did not understand? Or was it simply that he took the effort to court and charm a friend like Carrot who could benefit him, while I, the younger brother, had nothing to offer?

I wandered back to the house and found the dining room still empty of guests, and a young maid just setting out the dishes. I nodded to her and she dipped a little curtsy and went about her business. We had a housekeeper and a cook and a scullery maid at the Wilsons'. And there had been Athena and North at Mr. Lincoln's, and even Mrs. Clem had a housekeeper and someone to help her in the kitchen. But it had only been back all those years ago at Thornfield-Hall that there had been genuine servants around: a butler and a housekeeper and Cook and chambermaids. In those days I was only a child, with not much more status than a servant myself. So it was nearly a new thing to me to have people around to wait on me, to bow and curtsy at my nods, to provision me almost before I knew I needed provisioning. And I must admit that I found it quite comfortable.

I took a plate and filled it with eggs and ham and fried potatoes and bread, and black pudding. It was to me a clear reminder of Thornfield-Hall and the breakfasts that Cook used to make, and I was just settling into it when Carrot entered the room and greeted me. "Up so early, Jam? Matthews tells me you have already been to the stables to see Rowland off."

"Yes, I was there. That's a handsome filly he has."

"Indeed. He won the bid on her. I was after her as well. As was Willy, in fact. You should have been to that one. Jam, I was really sorry you didn't come to the Derby. We could have…we could have had a marvelous time."

"I'm sorry as well," I said. I wanted to say more, but there was no way Carrot could understand the childish jealousy I was feeling toward Rowland.

"And I suppose you've never been to Newmarket, either. Well, we shall fix that. Next time. You must join us, if I have to come to Maysbeck myself and drag you there."

I laughed, the warmth of Carrot's obvious affection spreading through me, Rowland for the moment forgotten.

"So you and the lovely Miss Kent have a date this morning for a music lesson!" he said as he filled his plate.

"We do," I managed to say, despite that I was having second thoughts, fearful still of making a fool of myself in front of Rowland. Nevertheless, I determined I would not be intimidated. "She so kindly offered that it seemed uncouth not to accept," I added.

Carrot laughed again. "Uncouth. God knows, no one should be uncouth!" Then he leaned forward, closer. "Must you really leave tomorrow? You have only just gotten here."

"I warned it could only be a day or so."

"But, Jam, *tomorrow*? Do you know that Rowland is leaving tomorrow as well? Surely you won't leave me on my own with these two girls? Whatever shall I do with them?"

"I'm sorry, but I must go back," I said. "I have responsibilities there."

He nodded, though I imagined he had no idea what a working life was like. "We have a lot behind us, you and I," he said. "A lot of history. But now, tell me: what is your future?"

That stopped me. I longed to be the determiner of my own fate, but, unlike Frank in *Rob Roy*, I hadn't the courage—or the foolhardiness—to turn my back on what was being offered, and to strike out on my own. Carrot, I told myself, had also chosen the way that his father had given him. As had Rowland. But I was the second son and had to take the lesser portion, whatever it turned out to be. I hadn't the vision for myself that Frank had, and now, only partway through the first book, one did not even know how it would turn out for him. "I don't know for sure. It's in Jamaica, I think," I said.

"But—Jamaica!—it's the place you always dreamed of." He beamed at me.

"Yes, it is." *Though not as much as it used to be,* I thought.

"How soon will you go?"

"I don't know. Not soon, I'm sure. Actually, it's in my father's hands."

He put his hand on my arm. "I'm glad if your father has taken an interest in you. I remember—" He didn't finish, but I knew he was thinking of all the years that his own father had not publicly claimed him.

"And *I* remember your saying one must take the hand one is dealt," I said.

"Ah yes. And I have to admit that in the end I was dealt a fine one indeed. As you have been."

I stared at him for a moment. *I?* Dealt a fine hand? What was he thinking?

"Jam," he said, "what could have been better for a boy than the time we had at Black Hill? We were fed, were we not? And most of the time we were warm enough. And the things we did! The siege engine we built, the blue face paint—what did he call that stuff?"

"Woad."

"Yes: woad. And the weapons we fashioned, and reenacting the battles; what fun we had with all that! It was as if everything were a game. I have met many a man who would give his right arm to have had the time we had at Black Hill. There are so many worse places of education."

"I've never thought of it that way," I said.

"My God, Jam. It was heaven. And, now, look at you, the manager of a woolen mill! I could not imagine how to do the things you must do every day. Your father has done you well, hasn't he?"

"I suppose he has." It was all I could think to say. Carrot saw my whole life so differently from how I did.

He touched his finger to the side of his nose. "Trust me, Jam. Things usually turn out much better than one fears. And you will return for a visit. Soon."

Miss Kent came in just then, dressed in white muslin, her curls tied back with a blue ribbon. We both watched her cross to the sideboard and pour herself a cup of tea. "Up so early?" Carrot asked her.

She laughed. "How can one sleep on such a lovely day! I'm hoping for an outing with the pony trap. We could take a picnic lunch." She placed a dainty slice of ham, a single egg, and a piece of dry toast on her plate, and sat opposite me at the table.

"I thought you two were doing music lessons today," Carrot said, saving me the embarrassment of asking.

"Well, yes, of course we are," she said, smiling gaily at me. "But not all morning, I should think?"

"Not at all. I'm not expecting to turn into another Farinelli," I said, pleased with my ability to throw out the name of a famous opera singer.

Miss Kent's hand rose to her mouth and her face turned red, and at the same moment Carrot burst out laughing. "And thank God for that, is all I have to say," he managed to get out between guffaws. Miss Kent grew redder as Carrot laughed, and she suddenly pushed back her chair, rose, and ran from the room.

I had no idea what had caused those reactions or even how to upend them. Clearly, my attempt to impress Miss Kent had gone badly amiss. At last Carrot stopped laughing, and giving me a final, merry look, he said, "*Farinelli!* Well, one would hope not."

"Why?" I asked. "What—"

"Oh, Jam. What do you know of him—besides his name?"

"He's a famous opera singer, is he not?"

"And—?"

"He's Italian?"

"And—?" His face was nearly in mine. "The most famous singer… of…his…type." He leaned back in his chair, grinning at me. "Jam," he said, "he's a castrato."

"No," I said. "Oh God, what…?"

"What do you say to our poor Miss Kent? You simply tell her you made a slip of the tongue, that you meant to say 'Andrea Nozzari' instead. I think she's actually heard him sing. She will be impressed; she might even forget about the Farinelli thing."

"No. Oh God no." How could I face her now? "I should pack up and leave."

He took hold of my arm. "Don't be ridiculous. By this evening, we will all be laughing—she will be, and you too, I imagine. It's not a fatal mistake, you know."

Not fatal, no, of course, but still—in Carrot's own words, I would be the laughingstock of the evening.

"Jam," Carrot went on, his twinkling eyes boring into mine, "I have seen you in many a daring and brave act. This is simply another kind of bravery: hold your head up and admit to error, force a laugh if you must, and move on. Others only get the best of us when they sense a weakness. One can never hurt a man who refuses to be hurt."

"But what can I say to her?" I asked.

"You will find the words," he said, motioning with his hand. "Go; it will only be harder the longer you wait."

I left the room and walked slowly across the hall and into the drawing room, my mind scrabbling for something to say. Miss Kent was seated at the pianoforte, playing a simple tune that seemed familiar. She didn't glance up even when I was nearly beside her. "I made a mistake," I said, all other possible excuses failing me. "I should have said Nozzari."

She nodded solemnly. "I agree, a better choice." She looked at me then, her eyes merry. "A much better choice. Shall we begin?"

She was a delightful teacher, never taking herself, or the music, too seriously. She said I was a natural musician, and I, flattered, standing at the pianoforte, gazing down at her graceful hands, fell a bit in love.

In the meantime, Miss Gilpatrick popped her head in and out of the drawing room as she arranged a picnic luncheon. I drove the pony cart, with the two ladies as passengers, and Carrot and Rowland ahead on horseback, leading the way. It was a lovely day, the sky the deeper blue of early autumn, the leaves of the trees beginning to turn to yellow, the farm laborers in the midst of mowing and reaping. One could well imagine Constable just over the next ridge, or perhaps down in the dale ahead, painting the scene.

We picnicked under an ancient oak, and I flirted a bit with Miss Kent. She smiled, amused, I now imagine, at my clumsy, boyish attempts. We all talked desultorily until one and then another dozed off, even Miss Kent, with Carrot's head on her lap. But I was infatuated with the day and with my presence there, and I could not think of wasting a moment of it in sleep. Instead, I wandered off on my own, following a path that might have been a sheep trail and whose end was a mystery to me, making it all the more intriguing. I found myself eventually at the bottom of a fell, which I climbed in order to take in the view, and was rewarded with a vast expanse of meadows and fields, ending, at the horizon, with a dark escarpment that I took to be the beginning of the moor. Beyond, I knew, would be the North Sea. I had, as yet, never seen the sea, and the knowledge that it was just there, not so very far away, excited me. I realized, looking off at what seemed like the edge of beyond, how desperate I was for a new life, for Jamaica, for the world to open to me.

Turning back, I saw Carrot not far behind, apparently having followed the same path as I. By the time I returned to the foot of the fell, he was nearly upon me. "I wondered where you had gone," he said in greeting.

"You can see the moors from up there!"

"Jam, there are moors all around."

"But not those, not so vast," I responded.

Carrot grinned and hooked his arm in mine as we headed back. "If you stay another day, we could take ourselves over there."

"I can't," I said.

"You can do whatever you choose."

Carrot could. He had independence, a home, good friends. "Someday," I said. "But Mr. Wilson has been like a father to me; I owe him this, to take charge until the mill is sold."

"Surely you will come back for a visit, before you sail for Jamaica," he said.

"I will," was all I could say. I could not be sure how, but I knew I'd give anything to spend more days like this one.

But Carrot was not finished. "Your brother is really a rather decent chap, once you get to know him." Somehow Carrot had always been able to read my mind. He slung his arm across my shoulders. "Do you remember the time you tried to pummel me to death?"

"Oh God," I said.

"It's what brothers do," he said, laughing. "I have plenty of cousins— it's what they do. The older ones make life hard for the younger ones, and the younger ones fight back in the only way they know."

"But you never—"

"I never understood how difficult it must have been for you—all those holidays alone. I should have."

I shook my head, my mind still stuck on the word: *brother*. "It's over," I said. "That was years ago." And then: "Did you know that Touch passed away not so long after he left Black Hill?"

He squeezed my shoulder. "Mr. Lincoln let me know in a letter. I couldn't believe it...little Touch. The three of us—what a combination we made, what fun we had."

"Indeed."

"I could not imagine being at Black Hill without you," he said.

"Nor was it the same after you left," I responded.

We stood together for a time, gazing over the fells to the moors beyond. I did my best to hold back my tears, and after a while we walked back toward the rest, his arm still across my shoulders.

That evening we dallied over dinner, all of us mellow of mood and rosy of face from the day outdoors. And, later, there were a few songs from the others, especially Miss Kent and Rowland, but I could not bring myself to sing for them. "Next time," I said. "When I've had a chance to practice, so as not to make another fool of myself." And despite their urging and teasing, I did not budge, though many times since I have wished I had.

We lingered well into the evening, reading more of *Rob Roy* when it suited us, and on the spur of the moment I pulled a volume of Shakespeare off a shelf and read a sonnet or two. I meant them for Miss Kent, and when I finished I looked directly at her. Her face grew red and she glanced at Carrot, and it was only in seeing that look exchanged that I realized how mistaken I had been. And how kind they both had been to me.

After that final embarrassment, I could think of nothing to do other than to retire to my room and leave as quickly as I could in the morning. I did not even see Carrot again before I left.

CHAPTER 14

$\mathcal{T}$hough I had been gone but a few days, there were surprises waiting for me at Maysbeck. Mr. Wilson had taken a turn for the worse, having experienced another serious episode. Mr. Landes assured me that there had been no need to summon me back, as nothing that I or my presence could have done would have made a difference, but still I could not help thinking that I should have been there.

I could scarcely bear to see him as he had become, bedridden, somnolent, looking gray and wizened beneath the bedcovers. I spoke to him, and I thought his eyelids twitched as if he recognized my voice, but more than likely it was just my imagination, or my wish. Mrs. Wilson was red-eyed from weeping, and she clung to me as if I were her last and best hope. But just as there was nothing I could do for her husband, there was little I could offer her but comfort.

And that was not the only change. The day after I left for my visit to Carrot, a man had appeared at the door of the Wilsons' home, claiming to be a distant cousin of Mr. Wilson. Mrs. Wilson had no recollection of having heard his name, but Mr. Landes had judged him to be a competent and honest fellow and had established him at the Crown with the idea that he could learn the business while I was still at Maysbeck and then continue to run it when I had left. All of this was accomplished without Mr. Wilson's knowledge, for it was no longer possible to have any meaningful communication with him. It was clear to all that there would be no recovery, nor could he even be asked his opinion of this alleged cousin from Northumberland. But it did seem curiously providential that young Mr. David Wilson had arrived, now that I was set to leave.

I met this cousin the day after I returned. His grandfather was the brother of Mr. Wilson's father, he said, and he seemed a decent enough sort. He had been a manager at a mill that had been forced to close after Luddites had broken in and destroyed nearly all the frames, and he had come to Mr. Wilson in hopes of a position at Maysbeck. On hearing that the mill was now for sale, this younger Mr. Wilson opined that he had a small inheritance, and perhaps he could manage to actually buy the place. The sum he had to offer was much less than what Mr. Landes had hoped, but given the difficult times, it seemed—as the proverb goes—that a bird in the hand was worth quite a bit, and he and Mrs. Wilson were taking the offer under consideration.

It was not my place to argue one way or another, but if I had been asked, I would have thought to wait a bit and see if any additional offers came. Still, I could not blame Mr. Landes for wanting to get out from under the burden, and Mrs. Wilson for having no reason to delay and perhaps much desire to get the whole unpleasant business finished, now that her husband would never run his mill again.

I was sorry to see her suffer, with both her loved ones in such disastrous states, and to distract her mind, as well as to further my fledgling musical abilities, I asked her to teach me to play the piano in the evenings, after tea. She did not have Miss Kent's skill, but she was good enough to teach me and seemed to enjoy it. Even Mr. Wilson appeared pacified by the music.

At the mill, I felt myself in a rather awkward situation—David Wilson was clearly set on taking charge, and it was sometimes difficult for me to be gracious about teaching him so that he could take over what had been my responsibilities, for it seemed I had become more used to being in that position than I had realized. One of the first things David Wilson did was send Rufus Shap packing, for the simple reason that he had not liked Rufus' attitude. Indeed, I had not liked his attitude, either, but I had put up with him, as Mr. Wilson had urged. But David Wilson did not see it that way at all, and it might have been that he was right and I had probably been too unsure of myself to do what needed doing. He reminded me a bit of my father in that way. At any rate, Rufus was gone and the weight of his gaze was lifted, and the whole mill seemed chastened as a result.

Indeed, with fewer burdens at the mill and without the responsibility to recount each evening the activities of the day to Mr. Wilson, I had more time than I knew what to do with. The hard fact was that I had no good friends at Maysbeck. I did still go to services with Mrs. Wilson—it was the least I could do for her—and as always, she took pleasure in introducing me to the local families. I began to take greater notice of the young ladies in the congregation, who glanced at me from under their bonnet brims when I passed. Not so many young men were in attendance, for most of my age and class were at college somewhere or off making their fortunes in larger cities.

I had never gone to the holiday balls that were held at the town hall each year: I did not know how to dance, and I was reluctant to make a fool of myself. But that winter Mrs. Wilson suddenly seemed determined that I escort her there. Her sudden passion for the dance bewildered me, since she was certainly not in the market for a husband, but I was loath to disappoint her.

But in fact, I found the evening perfectly enjoyable. The young ladies saw no obstacle at all in the fact that I had never danced before; indeed, they appeared to make a contest of who could teach me the most. Although I was neither tall nor fair, they seemed to enjoy my company. The evening was half over before I realized that this was what Mrs. Wilson had intended all along. She sat there in her corner of widows, mothers, and maiden aunts, smiling smugly and eyeing each female with a seasoned and critical eye, and when the evening was over, on our way home, she bubbled with excitement. Did I not think Miss Howard was the prettiest? Did I suppose Miss Phillips the best dancer? Did I notice that Miss Grath, while shy, had a lovely smile—and such perfect teeth? Carrot would have had no end of fun with that: judging a woman by her teeth, as if she were a horse. Still, my pleasure in the evening made me realize how much I had been missing.

In the aftermath, there was a sudden flood of dainty envelopes arriving at the house, containing sweetly scented invitations to tea, to an evening musicale, to another ball, and I threw myself merrily into the game, finally putting my foolish, boyish attempts at flirtation with Miss Kent behind me. It's true that some of the young ladies I met seemed to giggle to an annoying degree, and others gossiped as if they thought it mattered whether a dress and a hat matched or as if I cared who was flirting with whom. But there were others with whom I particularly enjoyed spending time, who seemed warm and intelligent and even quick-witted.

It was then that I became serious about learning to play the piano, for so often music was the entertainment at a tea or an evening gathering. I had already managed to pass myself off as an acceptable singer, and I wanted to be able to play as well, to hold that key to a woman's interest. Mrs. Wilson taught me as best she could, and it was not too long before I was playing as well as or better than she.

Now, frequently on the street I would see a familiar face that smiled discreetly as we passed, and middle-aged men took a sudden interest in me and in my future, and such was the pleasure of this friendly attention that I chose not to remember that I was leaving in the summer, and that my future was still unknown to me.

———————

That spring a short missive arrived from Carrot. We were not in the habit of corresponding with great regularity, but in the eight months since I had been to Lanham-Hall, he often let me know where he was bound—to the Continent, to Bath or Brighton or London; never, of course, to Maysbeck. David Wilson had taken hold at the mill, and sometimes I felt superfluous. I hardly knew what to make of that: on the one hand I was eager to get on with my life, but at the same time he had taken on a role that I had considered my own. I did not always think he made the right decisions, but I had to hold my tongue, for he had made it clear that it was not my place to question him. I understood that he and Mr. Landes had come to an agreement on the price, and I reminded myself that the issue did not much matter to me, for my future was not to be in Maysbeck.

The purpose of Carrot's letter was to remind me of Derby Day at Epsom—only a week or so hence—and it clearly served as a summons to attend. I smiled at the presumptive wording, so sure was he that I had nothing to do other than what he was proposing. Indeed, I had been hoping to attend that year, now that David Wilson's presence gave me more freedom from day to day. I wrote back that I would be there and looked forward to it with great anticipation.

However, I had not reckoned on Rufus Shap.

One evening I attended a tea given by Miss Alice Phillips. Over the preceding weeks, I had come to appreciate Alice more and more: she had a lovely singing voice and an intelligent mind. It was a pleasant event, six or eight of us gathered in her cozy parlor on a soft May evening. The curls of Alice's red-gold hair framed a sweet and lively face, and as I played the piano and watched her sing, I wondered what she would think of Jamaica, if she had the daring to cross the sea for a new life with me.

I was the last to leave that evening, and Alice placed her hand on my arm as she walked me to the door and bade me farewell, brushing a finger across my shoulder as if to whisk away a piece of lint. I could have kissed her, but instead, I tipped my hat and she smiled broadly at me and waved her hand in the doorway until I was through the gate.

It had been a perfect evening. Imagining Alice Phillips in my arms, the sweet scent of her lavender enveloping me, I walked to the High Street and then along it, passing a raucous inn and the dark and silent establishments of a poulterer and a baker. Suddenly I became aware of a noisy shuffling behind me, as if I were being followed. Yet, it was the High Street: other folks were no doubt on their way home at this time of night, and so I paid it no more attention, until a rough, gravelly voice called out, "Oy! You!"

I did not think he meant me, so I continued on.

"*Oy!*" he called again, louder. "*You! Rochester, you!*"

I turned and saw a large, dark form coming toward me, but the street-lamp was behind him and I could not make out his face. "*You!*" he called again, still advancing.

I thought to turn and run, and should have, but I felt young and strong and nearly invincible, and I held my ground. "Who are you?" I asked.

"You know me! You 'as cost me my job!"

Of course—I recognized his voice. "Rufus Shap," I said as calmly as I dared. "I did not cost you your job. You did it to yourself; it was your own doing."

"It was *you*," he growled, and he was close enough that I could smell the ale on his breath. "Though you weren't man enough to do it yourself, were you? And my cousin, as well," he added. He was in my face then, his powerful hands suddenly grasping my jacket, and there was no chance of escape.

"I don't even know your cousin," I said, trying to back away.

"You know 'er," he said angrily, shaking me with his huge hands. "You *do*."

I still did not take his meaning.

"You are a coward among men." His spittle sprayed over my face. "You don't even remember, do you?" he growled. "She was nothing to you, she was. And you forced yourself on 'er, you did. You, high and mighty, thinks you have a right to do whatever you want with a poor girl who works for you, you do." *Alma.* Before I could react he brought a practiced knee to my groin. The pain seared through me and I remained standing only because his huge hands held me. When his fist hit me hard in the head, he let me fall to the ground. He must have kicked me and stomped on me, but by then I had lost all consciousness.

He left me there until some kind souls came by, and, drunk themselves, poured a jug of something over me to bring me back to awareness. When I was able to tell them where I lived, they were good enough to stagger home with me and pound on the door until Mrs. Wilson's maid came to the door in her night-robe, her mobcap askew, and let me in. I poured whatever coins I had in my pocket into the men's palms and thanked them profusely, as they, at the same time, explained as best they could to the maid, and then they fled, as if fearing they might be held responsible for my condition.

And what a condition it was: filthy clothes soaked in rum, in pain from head to toe, and contusions and bruises all over me. At the commotion, Mrs. Wilson came downstairs, took one look, and helped the maid get me into the parlor before ordering water and offering me Mr. Wilson's brandy, though I already stank to high heaven. She directed the maid to bring a quilt and a pillow so that I could spend the night in the parlor, as it was clear to all of us that I could not negotiate the stairs. But first she ordered me to take off my dirty clothing before I soiled her furnishings.

In the morning, I woke to Mrs. Wilson staring down at me. "Mr. Rochester," she said (I was no longer her Eddie, it seemed), "would you be so kind as to tell me what happened last evening, when *I thought* you to be at tea at the home of Mr. and Mrs. Phillips?"

"I was there—" I attempted to rise, but the pain seared through my chest. "I was there, and I must have left about nine o'clock or after—"

She clucked at the tardiness of it.

"Yes, and I'm sorry about that, but it was such a pleasant evening, and the company was charming. Miss Phillips sang and I accompanied her. I was the last to leave, and to be honest, I was strolling home in a kind of lovesick daze, when I heard steps behind me, and then someone called out to me by name and I turned, and it was..." Suddenly I realized that I needed not to mention Rufus Shap—not so much, I admit, to protect him as to protect myself in case someone should decide to hold him accountable. "I didn't know *who* it was," I went on, "just...some ruffians. I don't know why they picked on me." It is easy to lie to protect oneself, I realized. "Perhaps someone who once worked at the mill—I don't know," I said. "And—and, I don't know what they had against me, or if it was just the drink, but without warning, they attacked me. I lost consciousness until those other men who brought me home came along. And I think they must have had a jug of rum that they poured over me to bring me back, for when I awoke, the smell was terribly strong."

She stared at me, shaking her head. "I don't know what the world is coming to," she said. "People used to know their places. Such a thing never happened to my John."

"I have no doubt of it," I said. "But Mr. Wilson was usually home with you, wasn't he, not out courting pretty young women?"

"Not since I married him, you can be sure of that."

"She is pretty—Miss Phillips—don't you think?"

"And you, going to Jamaica, you suppose. What good can come of it?"

"Do you think she might go with me?"

"Heaven knows. But—"

"But what?"

"I should not have taken you to the balls," she said with a sigh. "I did not think what would come of it; I just wanted to see you happy."

"Don't apologize; I've enjoyed it thoroughly," I responded.

"Are you sure you want to go all that distance away?" she asked suddenly.

"My father has—"

"Your father!" she interrupted, surprising me, for she never interrupted anyone. "Your father! Do you have any idea what he will have you doing there, so far away?"

"No," I admitted, "but I'm sure he has my best interests in mind."

"Humph!" was all she said. And that was, as well, all that was said of the episode, except that the doctor was called, and after some poking and prodding, he affirmed a broken arm and probably broken ribs. He bound up the arm and put plaster on my ribs and told me to stay home for a day or two. We sent the message around to Mr. Landes and he notified David Wilson, and for a day Mrs. Wilson had another invalid in her house.

It was the next day before I remembered that I had planned to go to Epsom for the Derby in two days' time. Much as I wanted to go, I did not relish appearing in Carrot's company and—worse, if it came to that—in Rowland's, looking as if I had been on the losing end of a street brawl. I had a discolored eye, a bandage on my arm, plaster on my ribs, and bruises all over me. With much regret, I sent a short note to Carrot saying that I had been in an accident and was injured and could not manage a coach ride of that distance. I could have kicked myself: *If only I had fought back,* I thought, though I knew I would have been no match for Rufus, who was much larger and stronger and no doubt used to street brawls. The fact of my powerlessness against him disgusted me.

It was only after Derby Day that I received Carrot's response:

Dear Jam,

I was annoyed with you at first; missing Derby Day for a second time seemed unimaginable to me, and for what seemed like a poor excuse. And then I thought: perhaps Jam is much worse than he lets on. I hope that is not the case: not an accident at the mill, I hope. Not a missing limb or some such. Write soon, and let me know the truth of it, for my own peace of mind.

Your brother-in-arms,
Carrot

I held that letter in my hand, Carrot in my mind, torn by contrary feelings: shame at having overplayed my injuries, and relief and gratitude for his concern and affection. We were indeed brothers-in-arms, and brothers in so many other ways. We had grown up together in those four years at Black Hill—we had played at being soldiers and pirates and explorers; we had fought, argued, and shared a bed.

I responded immediately, downplaying my injuries a bit so that he did not think I was too badly hurt, and regretting most vociferously my not being at the Derby. I even added that perhaps a visit to Lanham-Hall could be arranged if it were amenable to him. It was a blatant hint for an invitation that, unfortunately, never came.

What did come, nearly the next day, was a letter from my father, addressed not to me, but to Mr. Landes:

> *My dear Landes—*
>
> *It is high time for my son to be quit of Maysbeck Mill and his responsibilities there. My plans require that he be with me at my residence in Liverpool by the tenth day of June. I understand that a process for the selling of the mill is under way, and therefore I am sure that this will present no great difficulty to all involved.*
>
>   *I recognize that you have acted in the stead of Mr. John Wilson in many ways, and I am sure that it has been of benefit to my son. I hereby acknowledge that you and Mr. Wilson have satisfactorily fulfilled the arrangements that have been made in regard to him.*
>
> *I remain,*
George Howell Rochester, Esq.

Mr. Landes showed me the letter and watched closely as I read it, and I imagine he must have examined the expression on my face. The tenth of June was less than a week away, not nearly enough time for me to do all that flooded into my mind: say my farewells to Miss Phillips and perhaps ask for her hand (for how could I do that at a distance, if I were to be sailing off to Jamaica soon?), and see Carrot once more, to say nothing of sorting through the belongings that I had accumulated in the past five years and deciding what I needed for the next phase of my life. And, of course, I must say my farewells to Mr. and Mrs. Wilson and thank them for all that they had done for me, for they had, in all ways, stood in the stead of parents, and I was ever grateful to them for that. As I was, indeed, to Mr. Landes himself, who had never contracted with my father to oversee my apprenticeship, but who had done so, nevertheless. What could I ever say to thank him? For a moment I stood in silence, which Mr. Landes must have interpreted as reluctance.

"He is your father," he said to me, "but you are capable of finding your own way now."

I nodded, unsure what he was trying to say.

"Your life is yours. While I would never advise a young man to ignore his father, the time does come when a man must make his own decisions. If you do not want to go to Jamaica, you do not have to go."

"I understand, sir," I responded, "but to tell the truth, I have always had a great curiosity to see Jamaica. I think it would not disappoint me in the least if that is my future."

"Well then," he said, "I pray that you will be happy there."

"Thank you, sir," I said, and shook his hand. "I shall not forget all you have done for me." It seems now little enough to have said, and how different my life might have been if our conversation had not ended there. However, that brief exchange did set me to thinking: Jamaica was indeed a very long way from England, and a very different place. I would have to learn, I realized, what my own prospects were before I could approach Miss Phillips with a marriage proposal. Still, I spent as much time with her in the next few days as I could manage, cementing—I hoped—our relationship. I told her that I was to leave Maysbeck, and barely had the words left my lips when she gasped, her hand flying to her mouth.

"But you will be returning?" she asked.

"Not permanently, but I will return to see you, of course. Of course."

"But where are you going? Is it so far away?"

"My father has many business interests. I do not yet know where I will be going, but, but..." I was stammering then, because I did not know how to go on.

"*But...?*" she whispered, anticipation spreading across her face. "*But...?*"

Gazing into her face, it was all I could do to refrain from asking for her hand right there on the spot, but how could I, when my future was so little known to me? Instead, I stumbled around and said something completely meaningless, and she recovered her composure, but I lost mine, and I made my excuses shortly afterwards and left. It was badly done, I knew, and yet I was not willing to ask for her hand when I was in no position to support a wife.

After that, I could not leave Maysbeck soon enough. I did not see Miss Phillips again, but I did have conversations with Mrs. Wilson, who, knowing my inclinations, promised to keep an eye on Miss Phillips for me; I hugged her and we both wept, not knowing when we would see each other again. I sat for hours with Mr. Wilson, who may or may not have known I was there, and on the ninth day of June, my luggage and I were on a stagecoach bound for Liverpool.

CHAPTER 15

I cannot explain the fullness in my chest that I experienced as I made that trip toward Liverpool, other than the fact that I was at last traveling toward my father, at his behest. I had no notion of how he would treat me, but he had directed me to come, and I could only hope for the best. I could not help but think of Frank's gladsome reunion with his father in *Rob Roy*. How childish—how utterly ignorant—can it be to take one's life lessons from a novel! Looking back now, I see how desperate I was to find my place in the world.

My father was not at his residence when I arrived. I banged the knocker several times before an elderly man appeared at the door and stared at me. Nodding as if confirming that I was not an apparition, he let me in, then turned on his heel, and leaving me to find my own way, he closed a rear door firmly behind himself. I stood in the entrance hall for a few moments before exploring the house. It was a fine town house, as might be expected of a prosperous businessman. There was a parlor and a library and a dining room on the main floor, and above were two large bedrooms, each with its own sitting room. What was apparently my father's room faced the street and could be recognized as his bedroom only by the clothing in the cupboard. Nothing else personal was in evidence.

It was just at this point of my investigation that it occurred to me that perhaps the painting of my mother might be somewhere in the house, and

I retraced my steps, searching each room in earnest. I did not go below-stairs, where I surmised the kitchen and storage rooms and any servants' rooms might be, but the painting was nowhere to be found, and perhaps it was foolish of me, after all those years, to think that it would be.

Still, a strong sense of disappointment burdened me: my father had not been there to greet me, when I had dared to imagine a happier homecoming for a son who had followed his dictates so faithfully. Dusk was falling, and I lit a lamp in the parlor and took up a newspaper, but lonely and miserable, I didn't register the words at all. For this emptiness I had left the comfort of the Wilson home?

In an attempt to throw off my self-pity, I wandered into my father's library, took in the law and tariff books on the shelves, flipped cautiously through the papers on his desk, and slid open each unlocked drawer before wandering back into the parlor. The whole house, as far as I could see, was a man's place through and through: no feminine touches, no fresh flowers or music boxes, nor indeed any elegant little tables on which to place them. A utilitarian house, fit for a man who did little other than sleep and eat and attend to his business. That fact told me something about my father that I should have expected, and it calmed me a bit, for it was clear he had no personal life or interests, no use for anything or anyone who did not pertain to his business goals. I picked up the newspaper and began to read it in earnest.

My father arrived shortly before midnight, breezing into the room as if our separation had been hours, not years. "You've arrived, I see," he said.

"I have, sir," I said, standing.

"Well then, it's time to bed, I should say."

"Yes, sir, I think so."

"Yours is up the stairs, at the back of the house. I daresay you have already made your investigations of the place."

"Yes, sir, I have," I said, not knowing if he would consider it amiss that I had.

But he seemed to have not given it a second thought. "Breakfast is at six o'clock." His eyes narrowed at me. "You are used to early hours?"

"I am, sir."

"Well, that's one good thing." With that, he turned and left the parlor.

The next morning I was in the dining room just before six—though I had awakened much earlier—and my father was already there, eating breakfast and reading the *Mercury*. "Good morning, sir," I said to him.

He nodded a response and went on with his reading, pausing only to say, "Breakfast is there on the buffet."

"Thank you, sir, I see it," I said, pleased that he had thought to point it out to me, as I helped myself. A place had been laid for me at the side of the table, so I took it and unfolded my napkin and began to eat, no other words passing between us.

I was halfway through my meal when my father closed his newspaper, shoved his empty plate forward, and spoke. "You are wondering, no doubt, why you are here."

"Yes, I am," I said, though in fact the only question in my mind was whether or not my father was to accompany me on my imminent journey to Jamaica.

"I have many business dealings, as you probably know," he said. "Some operate here in Liverpool; others are in other places."

He paused and so I nodded and said, "Yes, sir."

"Some—most—are designated for your brother."

"Yes, sir, so I underst—"

"But you are not to be left a pauper. The interests I have in Jamaica are yours, if you can manage to keep hold of them." I wondered what he meant by that, but he went on. "You have had experience now in managing a manufactory, but you know nothing of the law nor how finances are best to be managed. So you will spend the next few weeks following me around, seeing how I tend to my affairs, and then you will be off to"—he looked at me firmly—"to Cambridge."

"*Cambridge?* But I thought—"

"Leave the thinking to me, if you will. Few men in Jamaica of your class—of any class—have university degrees. They do not consider it necessary over there. They have family and position in society to hold them

up. You will not have those advantages, but you will have the education."
He leaned forward, toward me. "You will take law studies at Cambridge,
not so much for the content of the law as for the ability to think clearly,
to see beyond the obvious, to make an argument, if necessary. You understand that?"

I nodded. "Yes, sir," I said, hardly knowing whether I understood or
not, but realizing that that was the answer he expected.

"Life in Jamaica is very different from here. Slaves do everything. I
mean *everything*. If you drop your napkin from your lap, if you want a book
from the other side of the room, from the time you dress in the morning
until your bedcovers are turned down for you at night, slaves will follow
along behind to do what you have always done for yourself. It will take
time to acclimatize yourself to all of that, to say nothing of the climate itself. However, there is one thing—*one thing*—you will have that will be to
your advantage, and that will be your university education. For that reason,
if for no other, you will make the most of yourself at Cambridge."

"Yes, sir," I said again, bewildered. University? I had not been at school
since I was thirteen years of age, and even then it was at Black Hill, which
to my mind seemed more play than study.

As if he fully understood my thoughts, my father interrupted my musings. "You are thinking you have never been traditionally schooled, are
you not?"

"I am."

"You would be correct. And there are reasons for that. I might have said
more accurately that in the next weeks you will be with me in the mornings; in the afternoon you will go to Mr. Horace Gayle, who will coax
your brain back into action. You must be ready for Trinity College in the
autumn."

"I understand, sir," I said, suddenly excited at the prospect. College: no
doubt just as Rowland had done. My father really did have my best interests in mind.

"From Mr. Lincoln's reports, your education was acceptable, if not ex-
emplary."

"He is quite a unique teacher."

"Lincoln's boys do particularly fine at university, I have learned. You are no doubt wondering why I also sent you to Mr. Wilson."

"Yes, sir, I have wondered that."

"You needed some experience of life in your background before going up to university. To my way of thinking there are three kinds of young men at university. The first are the eldest sons, who will inherit money and position and will never have to worry about earning a pound and who only need finishing off, and who can, as well, benefit from becoming acquainted with other young men of their same class, and forming lifelong relationships. The second are the second or third or fourth sons, who will not inherit—boys like you—who need the education so that they will not make wastrels of themselves, or, worse, popinjays who live off wealthy widows." He stared at me for a moment to make sure I was understanding him. "The third are smart boys of poor families, in whom some wealthy person has taken an interest, and who come in hopes of bettering their chances in life. In your case, you will not have to entirely make your own fortune; I have paved the way for you."

"Thank you, sir."

"Keep in mind: Jamaica will not be, perhaps, as you expect it."

———————

We started immediately after breakfast, walking down to the docks, inspecting his ships, of which he owned three, and two happened to be in port. Then it was on to an inn where he conferred with a couple of gentlemen, and to an importer's office, and to dinner with another group of men. When it suited him, he introduced me—always as "my son, Edward Fairfax"—and I would nod and tip my hat and they would nod. I listened, though much of the time it seemed a continuation of a discussion that had occurred previously. My father, of course, never explained anything. If I hadn't had five years at Maysbeck Mill behind me, I would have been completely lost; as it was, I was only half in ignorance.

After dinner, my father sent me off to Mr. Gayle, a short, dumpy man who did not rise when his maid brought me into his room and who gazed at me from behind thick eyeglasses before pointing to a chair. Even after I was seated he continued staring for a time until he said, "Mr. Lincoln, was it? Mr. *Hiram Lincoln*?" He spat the name out as if it had come from the back of his gullet.

"Yes, sir," I said. "It was Mr. Hiram Lincoln, of Black Hill. I was with him for five years." At least Mr. Gayle would not condemn Mr. Lincoln for not teaching the proper way to answer a query.

"And now it has been as many years since you left him."

"Yes, sir, it has been."

He thrust a book at me. "Let us see if you remember anything."

The text was Ovid, whom I had never particularly liked. I was rusty with the Latin, but after a few too many stumbles, I righted myself and was able to make a respectable showing. After a time, he shoved another book at me: Herodotus, whom I had always loved, and I slipped seamlessly into the Greek, despite the fact that my Greek was far worse than my Latin. But again I surprised myself—and Mr. Gayle as well—leading me to silently wonder if he knew Mr. Lincoln's proclivities.

Mr. Gayle let me read for quite some time before stopping me and asking if I had my mathematics as well in hand. I said I did but allowed that my natural philosophy was poorer. "Yes, then," he said, leaning back in his chair—or doing the best impression of leaning back that he could manage, given that his spine was evidently permanently bowed. "And geography?" he asked.

"Fairly good."

"Music?"

"I can play the piano tolerably. And I can sing a bit."

He waved his hand, as if the singing were of no consideration. "Shakespeare?" he asked.

I nodded vigorously. "The histories especially I know."

Instead of being pleased, he shook his head. "Lincoln," he said. "Of course the histories. The Bible?"

"Yes, sir, I am quite at home in the Bible."

"Law? Argumentation?"

"About those I know very little."

He sighed. "We have only a short time; we will leave that to the dons at Cambridge. They must have something to do to earn their keep."

And so we began with natural philosophy.

This became the pattern of my days that summer. I did indeed learn more from following my father around than I would ever have believed possible, although I often wondered what he did in the afternoons and evenings to which I was never privy. He kept his own counsel, and even to the end, I was never made a party to half of his machinations.

Mr. Horace Gayle, by contrast, loved to hear himself talk, and his interests and opinions ranged further than I could have imagined. He was as different from my father as he could have been, except for one thing: both men were intensely serious about their business.

There was no playing out of battles on map-covered tables at Mr. Gayle's establishment. Instead, I read Thales, strengthening my Greek in the process, and Galileo and Newton, and I made computations and diagrams and wrote papers on the philosophy of natural events. For the first week, as Mr. Gayle questioned me on the slightest details, I feared that I would not measure up, but I came to realize that I was a better student than I had held myself to be, and I almost enjoyed the pressure of his gaze, the back-and-forth of our arguments, and the serious manner in which he approached all of life, whether it was the newest theories of magnetic force or simply whether or not to finish his tea with a glass of claret.

My experience with Mr. Gayle led me to wonder once again why my father had sent me to Black Hill. Had he expected me to learn the ways of war? He had made clear that he did not want me in the military. But as I witnessed him in deep discussion with a colleague regarding another whom they both despised, I understood: business, for my father, was a kind of battle, a locking of horns, a demonstration of power. It was not the battles themselves he had wanted to expose me to, but the tactics.

Some weeks later I heard from Carrot, who had been off on an expedition to India. His letter had been sent to me at Maysbeck, and forwarded by Mrs. Wilson to me at my father's residence in Liverpool, and it included, in Carrot's singular enthusiastic style, accounts of elephant rides and fantastic temples and the glorious Taj Mahal at sunset. He concluded with an invitation to visit Lanham-Hall at my earliest convenience, though he added that he would shortly be off to Baden-Baden, but if I missed him now he would be back in the autumn and was planning a trip to Newmarket to look for a horse.

That information couldn't have been more fortuitous, as close as Newmarket was to Cambridge. I could easily hire a horse or take a coach, I thought; I could even walk it if need be. I sat down to write an immediate response, asking exactly when he would be there. I would be at Cambridge by the first of October; it would be perfect. I couldn't help grinning—almost laughing out loud, in fact—at my incredible luck. Carrot and I would have the chance to be equals again, if not exactly of class, at least as young men with freedom and some degree of leisure.

Then I opened the other letter, from Mrs. Wilson, that had come for me in the same post.

My dear Eddie—

I have delayed sending you this letter for too long, and the one that I forwarded to you has now forced me to the inevitable. I am greatly sorry to write that Mr. Wilson faded quite rapidly after your departure, and he left this earth two weeks ago tomorrow. He is, I believe, in a better world with all the dear ones who have preceded him. My sister is the same, God bless her, and she does not even seem to notice that Mr. Wilson has left us. Young David Wilson is making many changes at the mill, I have learned, and I suppose they are for the best—I know nothing of business, as you know—but I am glad that John is not here to see them. And he is building himself a grand house. I regret to say this, but he has begun courting Miss Alice Phillips, on whom I once had placed great hopes for you. But one cannot look back in regret but only forward in hope, and I hope that your father is doing well for you and that you are successful in whatever endeavors you set your mind to. If you are in Jamaica, as I know you so strongly wished, I hope that you are finding it amenable to your tastes.

I often think of you fondly and of the many ways you acted as a son to the both of us.

Rebecca Wilson

I wrote to Mrs. Wilson immediately, expressing my deepest condolences, as well as my gratitude for all the two of them had done for me, how much they had seemed like family to me. I could not praise and thank them enough. Still, the news that letter contained was so disorienting that the next day my father scolded me twice at my inattention and Mr. Gayle frowned at me over his eyeglasses and shook his head and turned to another subject. I kept that letter, reading it and rereading it, for it contained so much emotion in every line that for months I could barely unfold it without a catch in my throat or a tear in my eye.

Indeed, I so strongly felt the need to talk about Mr. Wilson and what he had meant in my life that I brought up the subject with my father. "Mr. Wilson, of Maysbeck Mill…," I said. "He died a few weeks ago."

"Oh?" my father said, wondering, I suppose, what that was to him.

"He was always very kind to me. I was sorry to hear of his passing."

"Yes, of course."

I felt I just had to say more, but I was at a loss for what that might be.

"You may know that, by strange coincidence, a young cousin came forward and was able to buy the mill," I told him. "He—"

"Yes, David Wilson," interrupted my father impatiently. "Fine young man."

I blinked and nodded, determined not to reveal my own misgivings about him. "It would have been very difficult for Mrs. Wilson, I think, if it had been someone from outside the family. How fortuitous that he appeared when he did and had the experience and the money and all. I cannot imagine what might have happened otherwise; if circumstances had been different—certainly it would have been difficult for me to leave them, when they had been so kind to me..." I stopped suddenly, feeling once more the rise of emotion in my throat.

But my father was completely unaware of all of that. He barely looked up from his papers. "Son," he said, "in business there is no such thing as coincidence."

CHAPTER 16

I went up to Cambridge that autumn. It pleased me when my father insisted on accompanying me, though he seemed mostly interested in re-visiting his haunts from forty years earlier. He nodded in approval at my ground-floor rooms in the Great Court, just opposite the Master's Lodge, but as soon as he left I felt the same emptiness as I had that first night at Black Hill. Still, I reminded myself how well that had turned out for me in the end.

This turned my thoughts to Carrot, and I wondered if he had yet come to Newmarket. Surely, I thought, I would hear from him soon, and we could meet again on neutral ground, where I would not feel so much as if I didn't belong. I imagined how that would be: taking him to dinner, perhaps, at some fine inn, probably spending too much of the allowance my father was granting me, but able this time to pay my own way, and Carrot's.

Despite all Mr. Gayle's careful attention in the preceding weeks, nothing had really prepared me for Trinity College, Cambridge. I was not used to the formality of the setting, or to my classmates, nearly all of whom had been to schools like Charterhouse or Eton. They were accustomed to being part of a vast pack of students and knew how to navigate a society that was completely foreign to me. I could understand how Carrot, with his dominant personality and his winning ways, could have gone from the intimacy of Black Hill to accommodate himself at Cambridge, but I was sure that Touch would have felt as I did. Though it had been many years since his death, Touch came to my mind often in those first days, and once again I wished for his warm companionship.

Still, I discovered that I could survive by keeping my head down and paying attention. As I slowly gained my bearings in that new environment, I wondered that I had yet not heard from Carrot. At times I fancied that one day he would just appear at his old haunts in Cambridge to surprise me, and I took to looking for him whenever I strolled through the town. I imagined I saw his distinctive mop of hair amid a crowd on the commons, or pictured him lounging in my sitting room when I returned from a session with my tutor. But none of those things happened, and impatient as I was to be once again in his company, I remained childishly defiant and refused to write him another letter.

And then—not even halfway through the term, when some of my fellow students were already counting the days until the Christmas holidays—I happened to see a notice posted in the town: "Tattersalls October Yearling Sales in Newmarket." Carrot had, I thought, mentioned Tattersalls; surely these were the sales he had planned to attend. Confused, angry, deflated, I stared at the words, wondering. Why had he not invited me to meet him? Had he not come to Newmarket after all? And if so, why had he not written to me? Or had Rowland come with him, and perhaps Carrot, knowing the coolness between Rowland and me, had decided not to include me?

Heart heavy, I read the dates again: early and mid- and late October. The sales were nearly finished, except for the last. My spirit lifted at that realization: perhaps Carrot was attending that one. Perhaps he was planning to surprise me—to arrive in Cambridge mounted on his newest purchase. I could just imagine it: a grand appearance for all the world to note. And that thought gave me an idea of my own: I would do him one better; I would go myself to this last sale. I would surprise him—even if Rowland were with him—for I would rather be with Carrot in Rowland's company than not be with Carrot at all. I did have seminars, but they did not matter. All that mattered was to be at the auction to surprise Carrot.

I had never been to Newmarket, and the sales there brought hundreds—thousands even—into the town. As I walked through Tattersalls' gates, my heart was pounding. I could not contain myself, and I scanned the crowds for the telltale shock of ginger hair, grinning at the thought of surprising him.

But how to find him? I stood for a moment, unsure, and then I hailed a handler carrying a bridle and a riding crop. "How does one find a particular person in all this mass of humanity?" I asked him.

"With difficulty," he said, barely pausing to respond.

I followed along with him. "No, but I must find him," I said. "He's a buyer, he's a lord; surely there's a way to find him."

His eyes narrowed. "Why? What do you want from him?" he demanded.

"He's a friend," I said. "He's here to buy a horse."

"Not likely today, not if he intends to race it. Who is he, then?"

Carrot. "The Earl of Lanham. Thomas Fitzcharles, by name."

"If you were such a friend," he said, nearly sneering at me, "you would have known." And he turned away.

I grabbed his arm. "Known what? *Known what?*"

"Your 'friend,' as you call him, was killed here two weeks ago. There was a horse—"

I did not hear the rest. Later I would learn that Carrot had been tearing across the downs on a horse called—of all things—Jamaica Run, and the horse had stumbled badly and Carrot was thrown and his neck broken.

I could hardly breathe; I could not think. I simply stood and watched the man disappear into the crowd. *Carrot*, dead. And at Newmarket, where I could easily have gone if I had not been so stubborn about waiting to be invited. And only shortly after I had first come up to Cambridge—while I was feeling so miffed that he had not responded to my letter.

I walked around in a fog for days afterwards, and then weeks. How could it be? Carrot, who had called me his little brother, could not possibly have left this earth, I thought. Without my seeing him again. Without my ever seeing him again. My two dearest friends from childhood, both gone now, and I left alone without them.

And yet... And yet... I barely could get past the *and yet*. The burial had already taken place. What had passed between Carrot and me in letters—and in my mind—in the previous months seemed an incredible waste. I should have gone anyway to the Derby in the spring, despite my injuries. Why had I so easily assumed there would always be another time, another chance? I should never have waited for an invitation from him, but just gone to Newmarket and surprised him. My mind caught on that: if I had been in Newmarket earlier, with Carrot, all would have been different, would it not? He might not have ridden that horse, at least not at the same time, under the same conditions. He might not have been thrown, would not have died.

I could not get past those thoughts. There was no place now, other than a lonely grave, where I could once again come close to Carrot's laughter, his brotherly arm around my shoulders. I went to a bookseller and bought another copy of *Rob Roy*. I had more than enough to occupy myself in the way of studies, but I still found time to read it, and I kept the book at my bedside as a visible promise to myself that I would not let Carrot's memory fade from my mind. Nor would I let fade the understanding I took from it: that warmth and companionship are more precious than gold, and that the future is as uncertain as the weather, knowable only as far as one can see on each day, and therefore just as unpredictable and, at times, just as unkind.

I thought, a time or two, of Rowland, who must certainly have heard of Carrot's death—could he have been with him, that day in Newmarket?—but I did not reach out to him, nor he to me, each of us perhaps jealous of the other's attachment to Thomas Fitzcharles, Earl of Lanham. *Carrot.*

I spent the rest of the term attending lectures, meeting with my tutor and my coach, spitting out answers when required, all the while wrapped in my own private grief. It neither surprised nor disappointed me that my father sent word late in November that while I could come to his town house in Liverpool for the Christmas holidays, he would be occupied elsewhere. It was almost a relief: in Liverpool, on my own, I could let all pretense fall away.

From then on, my life at Cambridge changed. Studies and lectures for six hours a day seemed beside the point, and I began following my own pursuits: sometimes reading at random, but just as often taking countryside walks. I played truant once with a group excursion to Newmarket to watch the races and to gamble. But Newmarket felt riddled with Carrot—and I could not watch the races or turn a corner in the town without sensing his presence—as the last place on this earth he had been. I felt even more bereft than ever, and I could not wait to leave. I never went again.

I was, in those years, rudderless, with no one to push me in one direction or another. My tutor was a brilliant man but no teacher, and he often left me to my own devices. I became one of those faceless men in a crowd, always willing to go wherever the others dictated, willing to do whatever was at hand. I learned to play a role, to be whatever kind of man was needed at the moment. I don't remember much in particular about my college life, and I imagine that none of my classmates remember anything in particular of me. If a person can be a cipher, rolling along with the crowd, having fun, hoisting a mug, causing neither admiration nor dismay, I was that cipher.

I did manage to join the Cambridge Union Society, and although I was told I had a good voice and a quick wit, I no longer had the patience for the study that was required for a killing argument. And I joined a theatrical group, finding it soothing somehow to dress up as another, to play a role, to forget for a time that I was Edward Rochester, alone in the world. As well, I took up riding, my one pleasure above all else in those years. I loved feeling the power of a horse beneath me, the wind in my hair, the sun on my back, as if I were in another world entirely, as if I were totally free of all care or burden.

After years of drifting, of late parties and groggy mornings; of simple romances with town girls that never led to anything, of mad rides over the downs, and, finally, five days of eight-hour exams, I did manage to pass my tripos—if just barely—and come down from Cambridge with exactly what I had been sent there for. There was much I could have learned that I did not, but I did learn two things: that one can hide oneself behind a mask, and that, more than anything else, I longed for a real home of the sort that I had had for such a short time at Maysbeck, and for companionship that I had not known since Black Hill.

CHAPTER 17

Ⓜy father came for my graduation, and although he frowned at my apparent lack of zeal as a student, he said nothing, which I took to mean either that that meant little to him or that I had not done any worse than Rowland. Over dinner that evening, he informed me that I was ticketed on the *Badger Guinea* in two weeks' time, bound for Jamaica. After all that had passed in the preceding years, the lure of Jamaica had faded for me, but as it became clear that he was not to accompany me, my perspective changed. I would be on my own; I would, for the first time, be free.

Perhaps sensing the direction of my thoughts, he cautioned me: "This is a serious business, and I presume that you are up to it."

"Yes, sir, I am, sir," I said, hoping to hide my excitement.

"You must know what Jamaica is: it's a gold mine, but the gold is white—'white gold,' they call it in fact, whole fields of it, growing higher than a man's head. I have a plantation there—a small one, and without an estate house at the moment, but you will have the opportunity to vastly expand that holding if you are wise enough to do so. And a shipping business in addition, as you already know. For"—he leaned across the table—"the 'gold' must be brought to market, must it not? You will take over these interests; they will become yours. Any profit will be yours, any loss yours as well. It is your future, son, to do with as you choose. As you know, my interests in England are Rowland's, but those in Jamaica are entirely yours. Do you understand?"

"Yes, sir," I responded.

"I am aware that you spent too much of your time at university in pursuits other than studies, but that is past now. Now you are a man who will sink or swim on his own merits. If you end up having to rent yourself out as a book-keeper, or, worse, if you return to England in rags and penniless, that is your own account. Is that clear?"

"Yes, sir, it is."

"Fine," he said, tucking into his roast, "we understand each other. Two weeks from today you depart. Whatever must be done must be completed by then."

"Yes, sir."

He looked up at me suddenly. "You haven't made any promises to any young ladies, I presume."

"No, I have not." Miss Phillips had been married to David Wilson for nearly two years, and I had no idea what had happened to Miss Kent.

"Good," he said, taking another bite. "Because there is a young lady you must meet when you get to Spanish Town. A beautiful and charming person, really, and her father and I have had several business dealings together. He is interested in seeing her married, as his health is not the best, and his wife is...gone. The girl has a brother, but he has not the head for business that you have already shown, and the father—Mr. Jonas Mason by name—is quite interested in you as a possible successor. Mason is thrilled that you have finished with Cambridge and made a good accounting of yourself there. A beautiful wife and an extremely generous arrangement: I cannot recommend this situation highly enough." This last was accompanied by a shake of his fork to emphasize each word. "You will find," he went on, "once you get to Jamaica, that a young man who arrives there with nothing but his good name and a willingness to work will find no position of value open to him. The best he can hope for is to be hired as a book-keeper at a plantation—the basest position for a white man, for he works directly with the slaves. If, on the other hand, he arrives with letters of recommendation to individuals of substance on the island, he will find a welcome. And if, as *you* are positioned to do, he comes with connections and with a plantation and a town house in Spanish Town, and shipping interests already in hand, nothing can stop him from making the very best of himself, unless he does not take advantage of all that is waiting for him." His eyebrows rose at the end of that last phrase, but I had caught his meaning well enough.

I nodded, as it seemed there was not much more to be said on the subject, and he dove again into his plate, while I fiddled with my food, my heart already pounding with enthusiasm and anxiety at the opportunities before me.

My father said nothing else until he had finished eating. As he placed his fork down, he said, "I shall be leaving on the coach for London in the morning. I have business there, but I shall return to Liverpool in less than a week. I trust you will have arrived by then."

"Yes, indeed, I will."

"Fine. You have sufficient funds, I presume."

"I believe so," I said, wondering in fact if I did.

He rose and started away, but turned suddenly back, pulling out his purse as he did so. "Young men never have sufficient funds, I have come to learn," he said. He laid a couple of banknotes on the table for me. "This should take care of whatever debts you may have around town and get you back to Liverpool. You will give me an accounting when you return. Take care you are not delayed." And with that he left.

———

I had not known my father to be a generous man, but he was a businessman and he knew the value of a good name. I did have a few debts, and what he gave me would more than cover them, and I was grateful for that. I had nearly gotten used to my father's abruptness, but I felt sure that underneath his manner, he truly did care about me and my future, or else he would not have taken such pains—and expense—to prepare me for it. I left the inn nearly as soon as he did, but I saw no sign of him, and by the end of the day I had indeed paid off my debts and was packed and ready to leave.

The next morning I rose early to see my father off and to arrange to have my belongings shipped to my father's town house in Liverpool. I kept out only what I needed to carry me through the next few days, and these items I placed in a small knapsack of the sort soldiers use. It was perhaps an inappropriate choice of luggage, but I was determined to travel by horseback and therefore to carry as little as possible. I did not expect to see anyone I knew or needed to impress; I was traveling only to visit old friends who had seen me in much worse states and had loved me anyway.

The weather was fine: a lovely day in mid-June, and as I urged my hired horse a bit faster, the meadow grasses, daisies and cowslips among them, nodded in the breeze. I had come to love riding, and I came to understand how Carrot could have died in such a way, atop a racehorse at full speed, pushing the both of them to the edge of danger. Young men tend to be fools in that respect.

My ride took the better part of a week, and my first stop was Mapleton, where I found the little church where the Reverend Gholson had been the vicar. He had departed years before, and I had no knowledge of his destination, but it was not he I had come to see. I wandered in the grave-yard at the side of the church until I found the grave: *William Andrew Gholson—Beloved son of the Reverend Richard and Ann Gholson—"Into God's hands we commend him"*—and I knelt and placed my hands on it, filling my mind with thoughts of that small, gentle boy beneath the ground. *We three,* I thought, and kneeling there in the grass I wept.

But I had more to do, and I mounted my horse again, riding for two days, reaching the little church at the edge of the park at Lanham-Hall just as the bell was tolling the evensong. I did not have difficulty finding the grave in that small churchyard, and the carving on the stone still seemed fresh: *Thomas George Alfred Fitzcharles.* I wept for him as well, and for the time we had not spent together, the letters he had sent, urging me to come, and how I had put him off, and the times he had told me that I was like a little brother to him and I had not responded that he was a better brother to me than the one I had. I told him that now, too late, standing over his grave.

I gazed down the long drive, bowered by lime trees, toward the Hall itself, wondering who would live in it now. It looked empty, forsaken—perhaps there was no one at all there, which seemed fitting to me. Who, after all, could ever take Carrot's place? I turned away and walked back to the grave once more, caressed the stone, and then returned to my mount and hastened off toward Cambridge to return the horse, and to find a coach toward Liverpool and, ultimately, start my journey to Jamaica.

I might have made a detour to ride past Thornfield-Hall one last time, but I could not bring myself to do so. There was no way in the world that I could have managed to face a final farewell to Thornfield-Hall.

CHAPTER 18

I preceded my father to his town house by only a few hours, but a few hours was enough time for me to settle in and to pace the floor in anticipation. He had said, *Take care you are not delayed*, and I understood that to mean that he had plans for me before my departure, as indeed he did. First thing the next morning he took me to his tailor and ordered a complete outfitting of clothing suitable to the life of a Jamaican planter. I had thought that after Cambridge I was finished with tutorials, but I could not have been more mistaken. Even before the tailor's, over breakfast, he started me on the last set of lectures I would ever receive, and they kept on for much of the next week or so, preparing me for the life I was henceforth to lead.

"You are used to our social order here in England," he said, "the upper classes who wield influence and power—and below them the merchant classes and the other educated people and lastly the working people and the cottage folk, and at the bottom, the poorhouse dwellers. Do you know where you fit in this scheme?"

"Yes, sir, I do," I said.

He chuckled dismissively. "Do you? Do you really?"

"We are of the merchant class, surely."

"Surely. *Surely?* What of Thornfield?"

"But...you are—"

"I am what? And what of Rowland, what is he?"

What of Rowland? "He is... You are..."

"Ah, yes, there it is. Rowland is landed gentry: Thornfield is his. He has no need to work and he chooses not to, which is indeed his choice. For generations the Rochesters have held Thornfield and its lands, but living in a manor house and the life it entails has never suited me. By choice I am also a merchant—*in trade*, as is said; I am not ashamed, and, indeed, I like the challenge of it. It will suit you as well. The day will come when members of the gentry are only too happy to marry their sons and daughters to members of the merchant class. Times change, boy, and men must change with them."

I nodded uncertainly. Was he telling me that I was to wind up more fortunate than Rowland?

"You have no experience with slaves yet, of course."

"No, sir, I haven't," I said.

He looked straight at me, his eyes holding mine. "It is different now from what it was when the slave trade was legal. You were but a child when that was ended—so let me clarify: Parliament made illegal the *importation* of slaves, but the institution of slavery survives, and it is the only way that the economy of the West Indies is able to survive. I suppose you find that difficult to comprehend, but you will see soon enough the truth of what I say."

He went on to describe more fully the slave system, and I listened carefully, for I thought he was trying to smooth my way. But now I know differently; now I realize it was simply his way of ensuring that I would understand the world just as he did.

"At this point," he said in conclusion, "you may assume that your purpose will be to act as a plantation manager or even an overseer, as you are surely equipped to do, but that would be lowering yourself. However, many a landowner discovers that he has entrusted too much power to his manager, and as a result that he has been cheated of his due. With your training and experience, you will prevent such a likelihood happening to you, and your neighbors will learn to take advantage of your expertise, which will be to your own benefit.

"That, son, is what you have been educated for. You will move in the highest of society; you will learn quickly the operation of a plantation and thus become an adviser to many. There will be no dearth of opportunity for you. There will be nothing you cannot accomplish, and with a beautiful and charming wife at your side, you will have a life in the West Indies that you have never imagined possible for yourself."

I hardly knew what to say. He had planned and provided for my entire future, it seemed, and, after wishing my whole life for my father's care and attention, I felt one part of me wanting to rebel and refuse and make my own way. But another, larger part told me I would be a fool to turn my back on all that he offered.

I *was* a fool. That day I smiled at my father and thanked him and promised I would make the most of the opportunity that had been laid out for me. I regret now to say how much I gushed my gratitude and how I praised him for all he had done for me. I would like to think that, knowing what he did, he was embarrassed at my effusiveness. Embarrassed and ashamed.

But most likely not. Most likely he smiled to himself to think how well he had arranged things. But I wonder, even today, *did* he know? Could he have, even in his darkest self, known what might come of it? Or was he simply pleased to have this younger son—the one who looked so much like him—out of the way, taken care of? And the older son delivered to safety.

I still struggle to think of it, and I cannot say that it is possible now to harbor good thoughts of him. But then I remind myself that if I had turned my back on my father's plans, my journey would have been entirely different, and while I might have found a satisfactory sort of life much sooner, I would never have found Jane.

BOOK TWO

CHAPTER I

$\mathcal{T}$he ship—the *Badger Guinea*, a barquentine—sailed more or less on time, rather a rarity as maritime schedules go. With my father, I had gotten used to wandering down to the docks and seeing the ships moored with their myriads of lines fastened to the stone walls of the quay, green with sea growth. The *Badger Guinea*'s masts stretched mightily toward the sky, her sails furled on her yards, her crew either busily loading or else off somewhere getting drunk. My father and I had stepped aboard a few times since it had come into port, and he strode about at will, as was his right as the ship's owner. He called the captain by his last name in private, but within hearing of the crew used "Captain." In return, the captain called him "sir."

The vessel had a large hold for cargo but few cabins, and there were only a dozen or so passengers. Despite my father's ownership, he had not instructed that I be given any special treatment, for which I was grateful; I did not care much to be the center of attention, and I was sure I would be most comfortable as it was. I shared a cabin with two other young men—Daniel Stafford and Geoffrey Osmon—who were both about my age, warm and outgoing fellows, all of us traveling to Jamaica for the first time. I fell in easily with them. Osmon was bearing letters of introduction, which I already knew would be a great advantage to him. Stafford did not have such a benefit, but he was pleasant and intelligent and would be quick to make friends. He talked of becoming a book-keeper on some plantation, which made me wonder if he knew what that entailed. Remembering my father's description of a book-keeper's work, I urged him to think of finding something in the city instead. Because I was fortunate enough to come with connections and my path already set, I naïvely imagined myself by far the luckiest of the three of us, for my father had provided me with my own trading company, with three sailing ships, a sugar plantation, and, as well, the education to make the best of all that. I was determined to take advantage of my opportunities, to show that I was ready to take on whatever came my way. In my musings everything seemed golden. I never once doubted that my father had planned it all with my own best interests in mind.

There was only one other young male passenger, Walter Whitledge, a Creole who made such a point of his recent graduation from Oxford—in an accent that dripped with pretension—that we did our best to avoid him, though on a ship of that size it is well-nigh impossible to evade any particular person. A ship is a world in miniature, sufficient unto itself: if one is to eat, one eats what is provided; if one is to be entertained, one must make one's own diversion; if one is to have society, one is confined to those on board. Indeed, all the passengers developed at least a nodding acquaintance with one another, but Stafford, Osmon, and I noted with childish glee that we were not the only ones on board who studiously ignored Whitledge.

There is not much to say for a sea voyage: the days are quite the same, except for the weather. I was fascinated by the billow and clatter of the sails, by the creaks and groans of the ship as wood slid against wood, expanding and contracting and turning and wrenching, and by the assured manner of the captain and the skill and daring of the crew. From Liverpool we sailed southward along the west coast of France and Portugal and then of Africa, until we picked up the trade winds before turning westward. I reminded myself that this was the same route that Christopher Columbus had taken, and I could not imagine the uncertainty faced by the men in those three small ships; the admiration I felt for their courage was immense. Of course, I had no idea of the very different sort of maelstrom I myself was sailing into.

Two days after we turned westward, we experienced dead calm—no wind at all, the sea as smooth as a fishpond. And then, later, as we approached the western Atlantic we were caught up, as I had feared, in hurricane weather. I had told my bedmates at Black Hill of the devastation that hurricanes can wreak, but it is quite another thing to actually find oneself in the midst of such a storm. For three days winds tossed us about mightily and the sea poured over the rails, but the ship and its crew bent to their task of getting us safely through, and they succeeded admirably. Beyond that, the trip was mostly uneventful, which is just about the best that can be said for a sailing expedition from the North Atlantic to the Caribbean.

Although I enjoyed the company of Stafford and Osmon, I often preferred being on my own. It was a pleasure to spend time alone, with no pressing responsibilities, and at those times I could not help but imagine what lay in store for me in Jamaica. Once more I took up *Rob Roy*, imagining Carrot voicing the words in my ear, reading it this time for Touch, who would have loved it, but who had died before it was even written. I was in the depths of such reading when I heard unusual sounds coming from the deck: a quick pounding of footsteps, rumblings of voices, and loud shouts followed by banging and thudding. Curious, I put my book aside and ventured to the deck, but by the time I arrived, a strained silence prevailed. It felt as if the whole world were holding its breath, as, indeed, the whole world of the *Badger Guinea* was. I moved closer to the crowd that had gathered—mostly sailors, but a few passengers as well, including Osmon—and I could see then Mr. Rowe, the first mate, whip in hand, glowering over one of the sailors. Bent over a stanchion, his back bare, the sailor awaited his punishment, but Mr. Rowe was speaking. I could not hear the words—the rush of the wind blew them away—but as his mouth moved I saw some of the sailors nodding in agreement, while one or two others glared behind Mr. Rowe's back. I could not restrain myself from creeping closer, my eyes wide, my heart thudding, for I knew what I was about to see.

Mr. Rowe raised his arm, and with it the whip—a cat-o'-nine-tails, I realized—and brought it down smartly on the man's back. The man made not a whimper that I could hear, and the cat came down again and again. By the second or third stripe I could see blood, and by then the sailor was making a kind of groaning noise. I clenched my teeth as I watched, sensing that it would be unmanly to turn away. It was the first time I ever saw someone whipping a human being as if he were an animal, but of course it would not be the last.

When it was over, Osmon and I stood together at the starboard rail, staring wordlessly into the ocean depths. "I suppose we shall have to get used to sights like that," he said after a time.

"I can't imagine it," I responded.

"I had expected it with slaves," he mused, "but among whites—"

I thought of Rufus Shap and wondered if a good beating would have made a difference. Mr. Wilson and Mr. Landes had made it clear that the working classes were quite different from us, but I still could not imagine being the one to administer the whip, and I hoped that I would not be called upon to do so.

Later, in our cabin, we three tried to fathom what kind of infraction on board a ship required a whipping. "Theft, I imagine," Stafford said, "or insubordination. I suppose it happens."

"Mutiny," Osmon suggested.

The conversation moved on, but the scene haunted me for some time. I thought of poor Mouse, who was so afraid of being beaten by Mr. Lincoln at Black Hill. He had seemed a pitiful figure to me at the time, but this whipping made me understand that a spirit might be crushed in just such a manner.

But there was a great deal of beauty in the trip as well. On the forty-first morning, the rising sun shed a golden light upon the islands of Montserrat and Nevis, and between them the monstrous rock named Redonda, covered with seabirds. And the flying fish! Whole formations of them, slim and silvery, flinging themselves from the turquoise sea and just as quickly disappearing again under the waves. And dolphins, bounding in and out of the water, followed alongside the ship like a joyful honor guard.

I realized then that I was truly at last in the Caribbean, the place I had so often dreamed of at Black Hill, and I could not wait to see how my life would unfold. In the next few days we encountered other islands, to which we sailed close for safety, in case we should find pirate ships bearing down upon us. At Black Hill, pirates had seemed impossibly exciting, but now I understood what terrors they might hold. That part of the Caribbean was still infested with such ships, often schooners—favored for their speed and maneuverability—armed with a single twenty-four pounder that moved upon a swivel. Under Mr. Lincoln's eye we had once built a wooden model of such a weapon, which is perhaps how I was able to notice that one of our *Badger Guinea*'s guns was itself an imitation. When I questioned the captain, he confessed that the ship had indeed lost one of its guns in a fierce storm on its last sailing, and this replacement was what they called a "Quaker," for, even if ordered into battle, it would not fight.

Finally, more than six weeks after our departure, we sailed into Kingston Harbor. My heartbeat slowed and my eyes watered and I felt my hands gripping the rail as I stared at the pale, colonnaded buildings along the harbor, and saw palm trees up close for the first time. Stafford and Osmon were still below, packing, but I had done that the evening before, as I was determined to be on deck when we sailed into a place about which I had read and dreamed so much.

"Will someone be meeting you?" came a voice from behind.

I turned and saw it was Whitledge. I had had so little conversation with him that I had not even recognized his voice.

"I am not sure," I said, a bit embarrassed to admit that I had no idea.

"Where will you be staying?" he persisted, and it dawned on me that he was actually being kind—was truly interested in me—despite all my rebuffs of him during the voyage.

"There is a house in Spanish Town I have access to," I replied, not quite able to bring myself to say that it was, indeed, my own house now. I had the key to the house in my possession, and the address of it, as well as that of my father's attorney—now mine—on papers in my purse.

"You ride, I assume," he said.

"Of course."

"I go beyond Spanish Town, to Clarendon. We can ride together as far as Spanish Town, if you wish."

Suddenly I was grateful for an opportunity for companionship, and I turned more fully toward him. "I'd like that very much," I said.

"Your friends are not traveling with you beyond Kingston?"

"No, they have other destinations."

He raised his eyebrows at this but said only, "Meet me at Harty's Tavern at noon. You will see it soon enough when you get ashore; it's close to the customhouse. We shall have some dinner and then make our travel arrangements from there."

"Very good," I said with genuine gratitude.

He turned away and I watched him go. He did not seem like such a bad sort after all, and in this unfamiliar place I would need all the companionship and advice I could get. Stafford and Osmon, fine enough friends as they were, were even less able to make their ways in Jamaica than I was. In that respect, Whitledge was a godsend that I should have taken advantage of earlier.

CHAPTER 2

Che first thing one notices when one arrives in the West Indies from England is the light, and what it does to everything one sees. It is as if one has entered into a different world, where a veil has been removed, and the sky is suddenly more intensely blue, the sea the deepest turquoise, the buildings starker white, the flora more vibrantly colored. One is assaulted with so much at once: the dialects of the citizens, the screech of strange and brilliant-hued birds—even in the city—and the vast array of exotic fruits and vegetables laid out for purchase: pomegranates, pineapples, avocados, mangoes, coconuts; the sheer variety of it all bewilders the mind while entrancing the senses. And the smells! They were not the odors of an English summer: roses and strawberries and new-cut hay. Although I could not yet identify the ones that greeted me now, they were richer, more intense— well matched for the kaleidoscope of colors on the island. Only the smell of horse manure in the streets was the same, and even there, with the hotter sun, the odors were stronger and sharper. A passing shower struck— a downpour, really—but nearly as soon as it had started it was over and the sun shone strong and clear again. It was not at all like a gentle summer rain in England, and I could not have been more disoriented.

I had expected to see Africans on the island, of course, but I had not anticipated Chinese and East Indians as well, for there was at that time in the West Indies an unquenchable thirst for workers who could be paid near-slave wages, and shiploads of them had been brought in from East and South Asia.

I said hurried farewells to Stafford and Osmon, with vague promises among us to remain in contact. I gave them the address of my town house, and I watched them leave, making their ways in opposite directions. I did notice that they were nearly the only whites walking down the street, but it was only later that I learned how shameful it is to be a "walking buckra"— a white pedestrian—in Jamaica.

Harty's Tavern was, as Whitledge had said, quite easy to find, but it was not yet noon, so I found myself a bit of shade and spent much of an hour just watching the bustle around me. Despite the August heat and humidity, which I found quite oppressive, negroes were hard at work on the docks nearby. They were as black as night, most of them, bare chested and dressed in only rough-cloth trousers, torn and faded. They wore no shoes, and yet they seemed to walk carelessly about without complaint. There was a gang leader, brown skinned instead of black, and wearing a sleeveless jacket and a hat, but still barefoot, holding a whip in his hand, but he seemed not to use it except to crack it above their heads to keep them moving, as one might do to a cart horse.

Few people were on the street at early midday, and those women who were in sight—nearly all of them negroes—carried parasols against the sun as any English lady would. Carriages that might have been seen in Maysbeck or Liverpool passed, carrying white passengers and driven by black men, and, strangely, there was generally a black man trotting along behind. I felt entirely disconcerted by these familiar trappings of English life exported to a world so different: the intense sun, the heat, the aromas, the constant reminders of slavery; and I wondered if I would ever get used to it all.

Shortly after noon Whitledge appeared with a dray, and he immediately set the driver to loading up my possessions beside Whitledge's own pile of boxes and wooden trunks. He watched the operation for a few minutes, until he seemed satisfied that all was being done properly, and finally the two of us made our way into Harty's. The dray set off toward Spanish Town ahead of us, its negro driver hunched over in his seat.

By way of conversation, I noted cheerfully that that was a good amount of baggage Whitledge had brought.

"Ah yes," he said as we entered the indoor gloom. "My father is a magistrate in May Pen—that's the central town of Clarendon. He requested me to bring a number of official papers and books of record." We found a table in the crowded tavern. "And," he added, "I have two sisters who of course desire the newest fashions from London. It will seem Christmas in August when I arrive home."

"How long have you been gone?"

"Four years."

"You never returned in four years?"

He smiled at that. "You have learned how lengthy a trip it is, I should think, and sometimes it can be quite dangerous. Of course," he added with a sly smile, "there are charms in England that one does not want to miss."

I ignored the implications, for I had more immediate interests. "You were at Oxford, were you not? What will you be doing now that you have returned?"

"I studied law there," he said. "I shall begin as an attorney and see what that brings for me. It is how my father started and it has served him well."

"An attorney who manages plantations for absent landowners?"

"Ah then, you understand," he said with another smile. "There is money to be made in that capacity, as I am sure you know. And you? What are your prospects?"

"My father has a small plantation near Spanish Town, and some other business interests there, and here in Kingston. He owns the *Badger Guinea*, for example," I could not resist adding. I had not revealed that to my other shipmates.

Whitledge's eyebrows rose and another expression came upon his face. "Oh? In the slave trade—before it was outlawed?"

"What makes you say such a thing?" I asked.

"*Badger Guinea*. The name means it was a Guineaman—a slave ship. You did not know that?"

No, of course I did not. "And they could not change the name after the slave trade ceased, because it's bad luck," I mused.

He nodded. "You can count on it. If you had gone belowdecks you might have seen the remains of the fittings that had once held the shackles."

I could not think what to say. My shock must have shown, for Whitledge leaned closer across the table. "We all have things we prefer not to think about, Rochester. Here, slavery is a necessary evil. It was slavery, after all, that built this beautiful island, and that makes life here so very pleasant for us. It no doubt helped pay for your education at Cambridge. It produces the sugar you have been putting into your tea all your life, and the rum that will be a staple of your life from here on. And speaking of rum, it's high time to have a bit, is it not?"

"Indeed," I murmured. I should not have been shocked, but I had not realized the degree to which slavery had infiltrated even my life in England. Sitting there in that busy tavern, I tried to steel myself to the reality that Whitledge took so casually: I could not avoid becoming dependent upon the work of slaves. It was an uncomfortable proposition.

The grog was brought soon enough, but I did not drink it right away. I had never been fond of rum, and that first taste of grog in Jamaica nearly gagged me, but in time I did get used to it. And to the way of life that produces it, I am not proud to say.

After a bounteous meal and more drink than I really wanted, Whitledge and I finally left Kingston on hired horses. It was only a short trip to Spanish Town, even at our slow pace and with occasional pauses as Whitledge pointed out views and characteristics of the island. One of the first things I had learned all those years ago at Black Hill was that escaped slaves, called "Maroons," often fled to the mountainous center, which was a wilderness into which no white man ever ventured. Now, as we rode along, I saw that region for myself—it is background to everything on the island, in more ways than one—and it does indeed look forbidding: mountains thick with trees and vines, a bluish haze lying over them. But the rest of the island, from the foothills to the sea, is almost entirely domesticated into plantations and cattle pens.

At that time of year the cane stalks had grown higher than a man's head, rustling and clattering against one another in the wind, and the air was filled with the sounds of hoes chopping weeds in the cane rows and the occasional work chants of the negroes. The fields needed to be weeded constantly, for the weeds benefit from the same conditions that enable the cane to grow so prodigiously. I paused occasionally to watch the back-breaking work, realizing that I would not last half a day working in such humidity and intense sun.

Whitledge was not well acquainted with any of the owners of the plantations we rode past, but he was able to point out each plantation's great house—which the negroes called the buckra house. There was another new and unsettling experience on that ride: we were rarely out of earshot of the crack of whips. A negro driver strode behind each gang, snapping the whip over their heads every few minutes, and when his whip found a target, there was often a cry of pain, a sound that made my skin flinch in my first few days on the island. I never fully got used to that sound.

By the time Spanish Town came into view, I had become so attached to my friendship with Whitledge that I urged him to stay the night with me and continue on the following morning. But he was adamant, for he was anxious to return to his family and his own home. So we said our good-byes at the edge of Spanish Town, and I watched him go on his way, wondering if in the years ahead I would ever become as attached to Jamaica as he. I had not forgotten my father's enticing description of Mr. Mason's daughter, and I hoped that a happy future with a wife and children would transform this strange and exotic place into a home—despite that the word conjured, still, warm memories of Thornfield and its fields and woods and moors.

CHAPTER 3

Spanish Town is a pleasant enough city, bustling as a capital usually is, but not in the same frenetic way as a port city like Kingston, which itself is a mere shadow of Liverpool or London. Spanish Town's government buildings overlook a wide and placid square, and nearby was my father's small and utilitarian town house. As in Liverpool, he had clearly seen little need in Spanish Town to entertain lavishly. Yet, once I had dropped my portmanteau in the entrance hall and surveyed the place, I was struck by how comfortable it seemed. I felt pleased with what had been provided for me, and I could not wait to go over once again the papers that he had sent with me, for they contained all that my life was to be, and I was in a great hurry to get on with it.

I had barely turned around when a young mulatto woman appeared from belowstairs and introduced herself as Sukey. She had been accustomed to running the household when my father was in residence, she said, and I recalled my father mentioning something of the sort. But it was not until I began quizzing her as to what her duties had been and what she expected in the way of payment that the realization struck me: she was a slave and she was mine.

It is an uncomfortable thing to discover that one owns slaves, but I managed to hide my discomfort and forced myself to see her merely as a servant. Indeed, I realized, in Jamaica, where everything was so unfamiliar, she could serve as a guide in my ignorance. "Tell me, please," I asked her, "what was my father's daily routine when he was here?"

"Your father rose early, because buckras do not like the heat," she said. "And after breakfast he goes to his office—you know where that is?"

"I have not yet been there, but he gave me directions."

"I'll show you the way. Tomorrow?"

"Tomorrow would be good. Thank you."

She lifted my portmanteau to carry it to my room, but I wrested it from her. "I can manage," I said, mounting the stairs.

"I show you around the house?" she said from behind me.

I turned, realizing she was as unsure of her position with me as I was. "That would be kind," I said, though I was perfectly capable of exploring the place myself.

While she was showing me the house, a young man by the name of Alexander appeared and carried the rest of my baggage up to my room, but instead of unpacking immediately, I left the house to explore the city that was to be my new home. The sun was low in the sky, but the air was still quite warm, and I spent the waning hours wandering. All was so different: the way the sunlight pierced a path between the buildings and heated their surfaces so that they radiated its warmth, the way the sky could be cloudless one moment and dropping buckets of rain the next, the calls of the street vendors, the sounds and colors of strange birds. I could not have felt less at home.

When I returned to the town house it was late, and a pitcher of grog had been set out for me, along with the calling card of one Richard Mason, with a handwritten note saying that he would come the next morning to make my acquaintance and to offer whatever help I needed to accustom myself to my new life. I could only assume that my father was behind this kindness, and I went to bed that night overwhelmed by all the strangeness that surrounded me.

Richard Mason taught me one of my first lessons of Jamaica that next morning by arriving almost before I had risen from bed. I was learning that Creoles indeed make the most of early mornings, because the heat and humidity enervate a person within only a few hours after rising. Sukey provided us enough breakfast for an army: potatoes, plantains (to which I had to be introduced), yams, turtle steak (also a new delicacy), pickled salmon, and bread—and coffee, of course—more like an English dinner than a breakfast, but one the English Creoles believe will fortify them against the strain of the heat. It seems that so many Europeans die within their first few years from the inhospitable climate or the various fevers that afflict the place that it is called "the graveyard of Europe." My father had never warned me of that.

However, what I had most to fear was being carried off by mosquitoes. Despite the netting around my bed, the constant whining of those devilish insects had kept me awake nearly the whole night, and in the morning I was covered with bites. Richard took one look at me when he arrived and chuckled knowingly. "They do like fresh English blood," he said. "But don't worry, they'll get off you as soon as you begin to taste like the rest of us, and then they'll be gone searching for fresher meat." He suggested I tell Sukey to burn tobacco or Indian corn in my bedroom to drive out those nasty night flyers.

Richard had a pleasant and easy manner, and I quite liked him straight-away. Though the Mason family estate was some ten miles west of the city, Richard told me that he made his home in Spanish Town, intimating that he hated country life and was bored with plantation operations. His lack of interest struck a note with me: I remembered my father mentioning that his friend Jonas Mason had a son who was not fit for overseeing a plantation. But Richard and I got on quite well, and I found his friendship and knowledge to be invaluable in those first days while I was trying to get my bearings.

As we spoke, our conversation came around to the topic of his sister. Richard enthused that a more beautiful woman could not be imagined—those were his exact words. Older or younger? I asked, in an offhand sort of way. He smiled, and his gaze went off in another direction, as if he were remembering fond childhood scenes. A bit older, he said. Well, I was a bit older than he, I guessed, and that seemed to me a very good sign. "Ah," I said casually, "and is her husband also a planter?"

Richard's smile changed slightly, not so fond anymore. "She is not married," he responded. "Nor promised."

I let it go then, but after he left I played the conversation over and over again in my mind. A more beautiful woman could not be imagined, and neither married nor promised. What young man in my position would not rise to that? And, all the better, she carried already my father's blessing.

I also learned from Richard that the "small" plantation I had come to own was "only" seven hundred acres, what in Yorkshire would have been a good-size farm. Though it lacked a great house, it was adjacent to the Mason plantation, which went by the name of Valley View. Valley View was two thousand acres and stood at the head of a river valley, from which one could see all the way to the sea.

In time, Sukey came to take the dishes away and replace them with a pitcher of grog. I was already beginning to like the stuff, perhaps because in Jamaica one always adds lime and sometimes sugar as well. As she moved around the table, I noticed Richard's eyes following her; she was indeed an attractive woman, her skin smooth and walnut colored, her dark hair pulled back into a bun from which a few tendrils had escaped, her expression both pleasant and modest. I could guess where his imagination had gone—or for all I knew, it was a memory from experience. For my part, I had never cared for dark women; I saw enough darkness every time I caught my reflection in a glass. From the time I had had a crush on little Alma at the mill, I had always preferred light skin and hair.

When Sukey had finished and retreated, Richard leaned close to me and grinned. "She was your father's, you know."

"My father's?" I repeated stupidly.

"She could be yours, if you want her. She has good breeding." He leaned back in his chair, grinning. "A handsome woman, quite pleasant to be with, sweet voice, does not ask for much. And yes," he went on, "I know Sukey well. I grew up with her; she came from our plantation, but the time came when my father found another place for her. Your father took her."

I looked back at the doorway through which Sukey had disappeared.

"Don't tell me you're surprised," Richard went on. "Men do not always get away from the plantations to the city as often as they might wish, if you understand my meaning. And their wives are often spoiled and not so interested in pleasing a husband once he has been caught. Of course," he hastened to add, "my sister is not such a woman, not by any means."

But Richard's sister was not at all what I was thinking of. "Sukey was your father's mistress?" I asked.

He laughed. "No. No, not at all. She is his daughter."

CHAPTER 4

After Richard's revelations, I saw Sukey with new eyes, but lust was no part of it. I had no interest in bedding someone my father had had before me. How cavalierly one can, in ignorance, make assurances to oneself!

Still, it was pleasant to have her around the house and to accompany me around the town that day. She showed me the major sights and buildings, as well as the market, and then she left me at what had been my father's office and was now mine. One whole wall of the office was intimidatingly covered with legal and tax books, and a middle-aged man by the name of Drew worked there, clearly running the place in my father's absence. We introduced ourselves, I already realizing that I would have to become a student again, for my apprenticeship under my father in Liverpool had not been nearly extensive enough. We chatted that first day, though he seemed quite guarded, and I was not sure how he would take to serving someone as young and inexperienced as I. But over time, as I let him school me about the business, we both learned to accept the arrangement my father had made.

It was clear that my father intended for me to build on the business he had founded and to prove myself an insightful and canny businessman. There were three ships in total: The *Badger Guinea*, on which I had arrived; the *Mary Rose Guinea*, apparently another former slave ship; and the *Calypso*. Ofttimes they carried cargo to and from the United States or the Canadas, but mostly it was between Jamaica and England, and while the outbound cargo was invariably rum and sugar, the inbound could be anything from cloth goods to fine china to salt cod. In fact, a bill of lading came to my attention concerning the transport of seven hundred yards of osnaburg to a plantation east of Kingston, and I was reminded of a letter I had copied once for Mr. Wilson at Maysbeck. A plantation attorney somewhere in the West Indies had written complaining of the quality of the fabric that had been sent, that it was too good for the use of negroes and in future more shoddy should go into the manufacture of such materials. It seemed a strange and loathsome request, since the price remained the same, but it was not my place to comment. I copied with diligence Mr. Wilson's reply: a gentle admonition that Maysbeck Mill was not in the habit of using shoddy in the manufacture of worsteds meant to be used for clothing but would, in future, try to keep his preferences in mind. It dawned on me, sitting in my office in Spanish Town, that that must have been how my father had known Mr. Wilson—that Mr. Wilson had used my father's ships to export his worsteds to Jamaica.

As those first days slipped by, Sukey kept herself out of my way for the most part, but I became used to her ability to foresee my needs and even my wishes. It seemed there was always a tray of grog and sugar and limes close to hand. Each morning when she brought in breakfast, I made a point of exchanging pleasantries with her, and she came to understand how much I loved pork pies and seemed able to know my mind enough to produce one or two whenever I had a yearning. We did not converse much, but her quiet presence alleviated some of my loneliness in those early days, when I knew almost no one.

In addition to Sukey, there was the young man—Alexander—who hovered around the house, though at first I could not imagine what his function might be. Surely he was not a butler, or even a footman, but he seemed determined to follow me wherever I went. Richard at last explained that Alexander's responsibility was to be my "walking boy," the person who accompanied me in case I had need of his services, whatever those services might entail. And he did follow behind as I went to my office, or to a tavern when I had lunch, sitting down outside the door, waiting patiently.

Richard stopped by most days, for breakfast sometimes, but more often in the evening, when the sun was going down and the heat started to dissipate, and we would sit on the veranda with our grog on the railing and talk about nothing in particular. Nearly everyone in Jamaica retired by eight o'clock and rose accordingly early in the morning.

From the start, Richard urged me to go with him to see my plantation, which was under the care of his father's overseer, and, of course, to see Valley View as well, which he described as one of the most fertile plantations in Middlesex County. Anxious as I was to see my own property, I was still busy learning my way around importing and exporting routines and regulations and taxes. As well, I was mining Richard for as much as he could tell me about plantation operations, for I was determined that my first meeting with Jonas Mason would not reveal complete ignorance and inexperience.

To that end, I quietly but persistently pushed Richard to speak about plantation life, especially about how the places were run and their annual routines. He might not have been interested in such a life for himself, but he knew more than I, and he enjoyed his position of superior knowledge on the subject. He also made sure I knew that I, like all white men on the island, was expected to join the militia, for the purpose of defense against invasion or insurrection. After those years at Black Hill, the idea of being in a militia was intriguing, but from Richard's description it sounded more like grown men playing at the kind of war games I had grown out of by the time I left Black Hill.

Eventually, Richard won out in his push to get me to Valley View. A ball was to be held at Monteith, a plantation nearby, and the whole neighborhood was invited. The invitation seemed to me an ideal way for me to slip gracefully into the local scene, and Richard assured me that his sister would be in attendance and that she was "dying to meet" me, an assurance that convinced me that it was time to make my appearance. Richard was to leave the next day for Valley View, but I had a few things to attend to, so I planned to go separately and meet him there.

The sky was a clear and crystalline blue that morning when I started out, Alexander trotting behind, and I was looking forward to being in the countryside and viewing for the first time my own cane fields. It was late morning when I approached Valley View, and the moment a little pick-aninny saw me, she darted toward the plantation great house to announce me. And what a house it was! Perched on a hill to catch the breezes coming down from the mountains behind it or the southeasterlies from the sea some ten miles away, it was a large, square white house of two stories, with a tiled roof and galleries on all four sides. Sheep grazed languidly on the lawn in front, and nearer to the road were the buildings of the sugar works. Some distance to the west of the house, far enough away from it that any sounds or odors would be dispersed, were the cane-and-daub huts of the negroes, and beside them the little gardens that they maintained for their own use.

I was still thirty yards from the house when Richard came running down the steps and across the lawn to greet me. At the same time, I thought I caught a movement in a window of the house behind him, and I realized I was no doubt being observed. I dismounted, and Richard greeted me profusely, as if we had not just seen each other two days before. "Rochester!" he exclaimed. "At last!"

"What a charming place you have," I said.

"Charming?" he replied. "Beyond charming, I would say. Turn around, Rochester; look."

He had told me that the view down the river valley was lovely, but I had had no idea how spectacular it was. Over time the river had found a path toward the sea, carving its way as it went through thick stands of ancient trees and tumbling over boulders, its water frothy with the effort. The quicksilver water, the deep green of the woodlands, the brighter green of the pastureland and the cane fields against the blue sky and sea, made a landscape that both rested the eye and enlivened the mind.

"Beautiful," I said. "And where is mine?"

"Over there," he said, pointing to the west. "But come along. You must be starved."

Alexander was already leading my horse toward the stables: beauty, pleasure, a carefree life—these were my first impressions of Valley View, and it turned out that they were truly emblematic of plantation life, at least for the planters. As I mounted the steps to the great house, it crossed my mind that I had been wasting my time in Spanish Town.

While we were seating ourselves into wickerwork chairs on the veranda, a negress was at my side with a tray containing a pitcher of rum and a glass, a bowl of sugar, and another bowl of cut limes. I had already gotten used to this manner of living, to appreciating grog, whenever or however it was served, and the delicacies that had at first been so unfamiliar to me: the turtle steaks and soup, the plantains, the shellfish. Gentlemen in Jamaica spend a great deal of their time visiting one another and talking around plates of food and mugs of drink. A visitor to a plantation may come for a few hours and end up staying three days. The women of the household—the wife and the daughters, if there are any—are more often than not out of sight. But when they appear—at dinner, for example, or at a ball—they are costumed as if for a coronation.

Soon, Richard's father stepped out onto the veranda and joined us, cigar in hand. He was a tall man, brown haired like his son, and with observant brown eyes that seemed to catch every detail. Despite their physical similarities, his entire manner was completely opposite to that of his son, whose indolent posture and attitude conveyed disinterest in almost everything around him.

I rose as he approached. "Edward Fairfax Rochester, Mr. Mason."

"Ah yes," he said. "I have been interested in meeting you, young Rochester. Your father is a fine friend of mine."

"And I in meeting you," I responded. "My father told me a great deal about you and about Jamaica."

"And I suppose Richard has been trying to tell you about Valley View?" he asked. "Though he is hardly a worthy instructor."

I laughed warily. "He knows a great deal more than I," I said.

Jonas Mason's eyebrows rose at that, and he turned and walked to the nearest chair. "I have no doubt that Richard is anxious for the two of you to be on your way. His interests are more in the social life than in anything to do with the plantation. Always have been."

Richard sat silently beside me; I had the idea that he had heard this type of comment before and was pointedly ignoring his father.

"You are finding your accommodations in Spanish Town to your liking?" Mr. Mason went on.

"Indeed. The house could not be more comfortable, nor more conveniently situated."

He nodded approval to my response. "And I understand you have the same housekeeper?" He leaned forward in his chair. "By the name of Sukey, I believe?" He asked the question casually, as if he had no connection to her.

"Yes, sir, and she is a very capable person," I replied. "I feel fortunate to have her. And Alexander as well," I added.

Mr. Mason settled back into his chair and puffed on his cigar. "Fine," he said, the smoke drifting from his mouth as he spoke. "Very good." He may well have wondered about the nature of my relationship with Sukey, but I was not about to embarrass myself by trying a clarification, and I said nothing more.

A few moments later Richard rose. "We must be on our way," he said. "Dinner will be on the table and the musicians warming up by the time we arrive."

"And Richard could not bear to miss out on anything like that," his father added sardonically. "But you would be wise," he said to me, "to wait an hour or so if you don't want to be caught in a downpour."

"Don't tease us, Father," Richard said. "Anyone can see there's not a cloud in the sky."

"And as anyone who has lived here all his life should know, that makes no difference at all," his father responded.

I sensed that I was in the middle of a low-level battle that had been going on for a long time, and I sat back in my chair to await the outcome. But once energized to go, Richard would not back down. "Come on, Rochester," he said. "We have diddled here more than we should have already."

"So?" his father said. "You have diddled all your life."

Ignoring him, Richard was already descending the steps, and I had little choice but to follow. I gave Mr. Mason a departing tip of my hat and asked if he would be following soon. He responded that he would come when it was appropriate, which I did not quite understand, but I left him there and hurried after Richard.

It should have been less than an hour's trot to Monteith, but twenty minutes into our journey the skies opened and we urged our mounts forward until we could find shelter under the fat fronds of a banana plant. "He is always so sure of himself," Richard grumbled. "It makes a person want to defy him just as a matter of principle."

I said nothing, which seemed the soundest policy, until Richard turned on me. "I suppose you think I am a fool."

"What goes on between you and your father is no concern of mine," I said. It was perhaps not the wisest thing to have said, but I had no interest in taking sides between them.

"Fathers!" he said in a dismissive tone. He had lived since birth in close quarters with his father; I, on the other hand, had spent nearly my whole life wishing for a connection with mine. Neither of us could fathom how the other felt.

The rain stopped as quickly as it had come, the sky was blue again, and by the time we arrived at Monteith we were nearly dry. Once inside, I could not help stopping to gaze about. I had not gone indoors at Valley View, so this was my first plantation house.

Most of the big houses in Jamaica seem built with the weather in mind. The breezes flow through the many open windows, and indoors from room to room. Roofs overhang enough to keep the sun from shining directly in and the rain from soaking the veranda furniture, and the floors are bare of carpets. A massive repast was laid out on a large table, and a staff of negro house servants was busy filling and replacing platters and bowls as the guests—who were already quite numerous—nibbled and drank and chatted. I was interested in seeing if I recognized anyone there, for I had harbored hopes of seeing at least one of my fellow passengers from the *Badger*—Whitledge or Osmon or, less likely, Stafford—but none was in evidence.

With his hand on my arm, Richard guided me through the room, stopping now and then to introduce me to clusters of gentlemen. They were mostly planters from nearby, and a few merchants from Spanish Town and one from as far away as Kingston. I discovered I could almost always tell the planters from the merchants, for the planters had the same kind of languidity about them that I had noticed in Richard, while the merchants seemed at the same time intense and easily distracted, as if, like my father and his friends, they were always looking for a way to earn an advantage. It passed through my mind that I was to be a bit of both—planter and merchant—and I wondered how I would appear to others.

As we strolled about the room, a young lady attached herself to Richard's other side and simpered up at him that he had not yet introduced his handsome friend. "Ah yes," he said, turning to me. "This is the recently arrived owner of a small plantation near Valley View, Edward Fairfax Rochester—Miss Mary MacKinnon, whose hospitality we are so much enjoying here at Monteith."

I made a bow. "My pleasure, Miss MacKinnon," I said.

"And mine as well, Mr. Rochester." She had fair skin but a poor complexion, but she did have dimples, which she showed off at every opportunity. "Will you stay for the ball?" she asked.

"Of course," Richard replied before I could respond.

"Lovely," she said, "I will count on it." She was gazing straight at me as she spoke, and I understood her meaning, but I already had Richard's sister on my mind. Had she been the one peering through the window at Valley View?

"Not very attractive," Richard commented rather crudely as she hurried off, no doubt to report to her friends what she had learned of me. "And did you notice? She lisps."

We had been making our way toward another, larger room, and now I could hear the intriguing sounds of unfamiliar instruments. As we entered that next room I saw a half dozen or so negroes clustered in a far corner with two or three drumlike instruments and a fiddle or two and some horns, which they played with nearly professional skill.

In time, the dancing began. Miss MacKinnon claimed me for a reel almost immediately and for several dances thereafter. She was pleasant enough, but not a particularly interesting conversationalist. Her attention was flattering, I suppose, but I didn't want it to appear that I was particularly attached to her. I danced with various other young women as well, though I think it was not that I was so desirable a partner, but simply that their lives were so limited that any stranger was a welcome change. Despite the attention I garnered, I kept my eye on Richard, hoping he would give me some kind of sign when his sister appeared. Yet it was well into the evening before a bustle of activity at the doorway announced the arrival of a cluster of young ladies. Everyone paused to watch them flit into the room like a covey of bright birds. No sooner had I stopped to watch than I felt a hand on my arm. Expecting Richard, I turned—and found myself once more in the company of Miss MacKinnon. "It's your Miss Mason," she whispered.

"*My* Miss Mason?"

"Well, you are staying with them, are you not?"

"In truth, I am not," I said.

"Truly?"

I could not help smiling at her obvious pleasure with that news. "Truly."

But Richard was there at my elbow by then, pulling me away from Miss MacKinnon. "You must meet her; you simply must," he urged.

The circle parted as we approached, almost as if they were expecting us, and I saw in the center of that group the most astonishing-looking woman I have ever seen. She was tall, as tall as I at least, and she had masses of black hair that shone as if it had been oiled and that fell into curls that framed her face and clustered on her shoulders and hung down her back nearly to her waist. She was dark skinned, but not as dark as I, and her eyes were black, with thick black lashes. She wore a dress of brilliant red with some sort of bangles on it, and that dress was cut in such a way as to leave little to the imagination. She stood among her coterie of friends like a queen, proud and elegant and stunning.

"My dear sister," Richard said as we came close, "may I present Mr. Edward Fairfax Rochester. Rochester, my sister, Miss Mason—Miss Bertha Antoinetta Mason."

Bowing over her hand, I said, "I prefer Edward, if you please."

She smiled broadly. "But I *don't* please," she said. "I prefer Fairfax. And you may call me Antoinetta."

It was my turn to smile then. And to be unconventional. "I shall call you Bertha," I said.

Her eyes clouded for a moment, but her smile remained.

CHAPTER 5

We danced a few times that evening, she radiant and glowing, the silk of her dress slipping through my hands as I struggled to hold her in a fashion that would not appear unseemly. I was nervous and found myself nearly stumbling through the sets. She laughed at my missteps, a deep, vibrant laugh, her breath warm against my cheek when the dance brought us close. "You are new to this music?" she asked.

"Yes, I am," I replied. "But I am sure I will learn."

"You will, Fairfax, you will indeed," she said. She smiled at me, her lips parting to reveal perfect teeth, the hint of a tongue flashing between them. I felt as if she owned me already.

I reminded myself as we danced that I had never cared for dark-haired women, but I had never known—never seen—a creature like her. When she stared directly into my eyes, which, unlike so many women, she often did, I felt as if she saw into my soul, saw all that I was, and when she smiled, I felt the kind of approbation I had always hoped for. When she danced with other men, my heart turned in my chest. I knew it was jealousy, and it made no difference at all that I had no claim to be jealous. She was courted at that ball, and at the balls to come, by nearly all the eligible young men in the neighborhood, and some who were neither eligible nor young. I looked for signs that she preferred me, but I never saw any, but neither did I see a sign that she preferred anyone else.

"So!" Richard grinned as we rode back to Valley View the following afternoon, still recovering from the ball, which had lasted through the night. "Is she not the most beautiful woman you have ever seen?"

"Actually," I responded, just to tease him, "I have always preferred fair ladies."

Richard's head turned so quickly toward me that I thought it might fall right off his neck. "Really? *Really?* In preference to my sister?"

I laughed. "She is striking," I admitted. And she was. But I would not allow myself to fall so easily as that. No, it took at least another event or two before I could admit to myself that I must have Miss Bertha Antoinetta Mason as my bride. However, I was sure I wasn't the only young man with such thoughts, for wherever Bertha went, men dropped whatever they were doing and clustered around her as honeybees to clover. But I hoped, given what my father had told me about his friendship and history with Mr. Mason, that my chances might be higher than most. Indeed, it had almost seemed that my father had promised her to me.

It was Bertha's custom to arrive late in order to make the kind of entrance I had seen at Monteith. She would dance for an hour or two and then leave. She did not single me out particularly, but we usually danced together two or three or four times, and she always managed to charm and flatter me to the point where it was all I could do to keep myself from running off with her. But inevitably she would flit away with another man, or with her friends, and be, once again, lost to me.

And then one day I had occasion to arrive at Valley View unexpected and unannounced, for I had developed a business idea that I was eager to discuss with Mr. Mason. Although Jamaica was not on the normal sailing route between England and North America, I had noticed that immigration along that route was increasing mightily. In addition, I knew that abolitionist forces within the English Parliament were growing stronger, and I was sure they would win out sooner or later. Moreover, even the short acquaintance that I had with the sugar plantation system made clear to me that such an economy could not endure once slavery was abolished. *Then what?* I had asked myself: my plantation and the ships that carried its products would be worthless. But, I calculated, the ships could be refitted to carry loads of passengers. I had broached the subject once with Mr. Mason, but he had waved me off, assuring me that while it was true that abolition could end the sugar trade as we knew it, that very fact would prevent Parliament from acting in a way that would endanger such profitable enterprises on both sides of the Atlantic.

At the time I had not been able to convince him otherwise, but I had recently come across a beauty of a ship: a three-masted square-rigged vessel, speedy and reliable for the transatlantic passenger and packet trade. Mr. Mason and I could get our feet into that trade while my current ships were still in sugar. The *Sea Nymph* was at that time lying in Kingston Harbor, available for purchase, but I hadn't the funds on hand for it. Somehow, I needed to convince Mr. Mason to take it on with me.

Since my father had handed over all his interests in Jamaica to me, Mr. Mason and I were partners now, our operations intertwined with each other, and this idea of a passenger venture would only solidify that partnership. In my eagerness to consult with Mr. Mason, I hurried to Valley View without sending advance word to him or to his son; I had visited often enough and discussed business on occasion before leaving for various balls, and I just assumed that Mr. Mason would be there, for he always was; he much preferred it to anyplace else on the island.

But that day, as I climbed up the steps to the veranda, a servant opened the door and welcomed me inside with a wordless smile. The vast reception room was empty but for its furnishings. I turned back toward the servant, but she had disappeared. Muffled voices and even a quick outburst of laughter came from an adjoining room, and, not knowing what else to do, I stepped toward the sound and opened the door. I could not have been more astonished at the sight that greeted me there.

The room's shutters were closed, and in the gloom I could see three or four young women sitting cross-legged on the floor in a far corner, dipping their hands into a bowl of some kind of food and licking their fingers with boisterous appreciation. They were all dressed in the plain and simple shifts that the negro children wore, which all of them—even Bertha—had pulled up above their knees. *Even Bertha.*

She was not facing me, but I recognized her by her hair, pulled together with a string and falling carelessly down her back. She did not see me until the others, caught suddenly in an indiscretion, silenced their laughter, and she turned to look, her fingers still in her mouth. Staring at me, she slowly rose. I saw that she was barefoot, as the others were—the others, all ne- groes, suddenly scattering away out of sight—but she stood her ground. "Fairfax," she said, her low voice caressing my name in a way I had never before heard. "What an unexpected surprise." But there was neither sur- prise nor warmth in her countenance. Instead, she simply watched, her head tipped coyly downward, but her eyes on mine.

I made my bow. "But not an unpleasant one, I hope," I said.

"You have come for my father, I presume," she said.

"Yes, I have, but it's a pleasure for me to have encountered you." That was my manners still speaking, for I hardly knew what to make of the scene I had just witnessed, or of the way she was clothed—barely—or the way she was behaving.

And then she broke into a broad, impish smile, her eyes still holding mine, and she seemed at that moment like nothing more than a child caught with her hand in the biscuit jar. I could not help smiling in return. Then, with another shift equally abrupt, she turned from me and called for the negress who had allowed me into the house. "He has come to see my father, as you should well have known," she snapped as the woman ap- peared. "You will wait for me in the kitchen."

Wordlessly the girl ran out of the room, and without a further glance at me, Bertha left the room as well, her final acknowledgment of me only the words that trailed behind her: "He is not at home. You should have saved yourself the trouble."

I watched her go, stunned at the mystery of her. The outlines of her body were clear through the flimsy muslin of the shift, and at that moment when I should have been shocked, I could not have wanted her more.

Mr. Mason and I were sitting on the veranda, mugs of grog in hand. I had sent him a note the day after my unannounced visit, to ensure his presence when I came this time, and I put my proposition to him immediately on my arrival. I could tell he was not impressed with my notion that abolition would come well within his lifetime, nor was he particularly taken with the idea of partnering with me in the purchase of the *Sea Nymph*. "What do you know about buying boats?" he asked abruptly, and I had to agree that I could only take the word of another shipping agent. He responded to that with a long draw on his cigar. And then he said, "My daughter seems quite taken with you."

"She is indeed beautiful and charming," I responded cautiously.

He turned to face me, and I scrambled for more.

"Any man would be proud to have her on his arm. Any man"— suddenly I threw caution to the wind—"*I* would be proud to have her on my arm. As my wife. If she would have me."

He was still gazing at me. "You come from a good family. I know your father well, and admire him."

"And you know my circumstances," I said. "My plantation is not as big as yours, but, nevertheless . . . And there is the importing and exporting business." I did not repeat a mention of the immigrant trade, though it was heavily on my mind. "I am young and in good health, and, as you have said—"

"You are still stuck on that ship, of course," he interrupted. "You think that this . . . this migration across the Atlantic would be profitable."

"I do."

"But you have never actually started an endeavor on your own, have you. You have no idea of the risks."

"I have not founded anything, it's true, but I have worked closely with men who have. I know the way they think, the way they evaluate opportunities."

"I have two children," Mr. Mason said suddenly. "My wife is gone;

when I die, my son and daughter will inherit all I own, equally." He looked closely at me, to make sure I understood. "And I suppose you would want a dowry as well."

"I . . . I had not thought—"

"I propose thirty thousand pounds," he said.

I was dumbfounded. I did not know what to say.

"Yours. To do with as you choose."

"You are very generous," I said. "But—what of her? Does she want to marry me?"

"Of course she does. I would not have made this offer if I did not already know that. What kind of father do you think I am?"

"I'm sorry, sir, it's just that—"

"I have only one daughter," he said. "I want the best for her. I expect you to treat her in the way she deserves and has become accustomed to."

"Yes, sir, of course," I said.

"We'll drink on it," he said, raising his mug.

We were to be married on the twentieth day of October, and in those intervening weeks I could hardly think of anything other than that beautiful creature, clothed as simply as a negress, barefoot, her glorious hair tied carelessly back from her lovely face. I lost myself in happy reverie, to know that she had wanted me as much as I did her. Though we were now betrothed, I had little more occasion to spend time alone with her than I had had before, but that distance and mystery only increased my desire. I pined for her, imagining her with one of her many suitors, jealous of all the months or years they had been in her presence and I had not, jealous of the times they had danced with her, their arms at her waist, jealous of her touch, her whisper, her disarming smiles. I imagined her soon tied to me forever in marriage, her wild, mercurial spirit so unlike those docile, simpering, boring, *proper* women like Mary MacKinnon. Life with Bertha would always be new, always exciting. I was mad for her; I was wild with longing. I could not wait to have her for my own.

Her father welcomed me into the family with a smile and a cigar and a toast of rum punch. He seemed to have come to accept me fully as a partner, to see that I did have a head for business, that my education had been all he would have hoped for in a partner as well as a son. So often in marriages such as this was to be, the arrangements are quite drawn out, as the families argue and bargain over every little jot and tittle. But in this case, they were so easily made that I could hardly believe it myself.

I had imagined that we would live in Spanish Town after the wedding, but when she was told, Bertha wept at the idea. Valley View had always been her home; she could not imagine living anywhere else. I gave in on that, for the house there was large and it was clear that Jonas wanted us there. He had expressed a desire for me to begin keeping an eye on the management of the sugar operations on both his large estate and my much smaller one, in addition to our joint business ventures in Spanish Town. It was not a great distance to Spanish Town, or even to Kingston. The thirty thousand pounds had made it quite possible for me to buy the *Sea Nymph*, and I already had plans for refurbishing it.

I saw the whole of it as an astonishingly lucky turn of events. I had been in Jamaica for less than three months, and here I was on the verge of marriage to the most beauteous creature I could imagine, and with a golden future ahead of me. It could not have been better if it had all been planned that way.

Which, I eventually came to understand, it had been. All of it. From the time I was put to work at Mr. Wilson's mill to the time I arrived in Jamaica to the time I had first seen Bertha. The only unexpected event was the one chance encounter I had had with her, and at which, if I had been wiser or more experienced or more prescient, I would have known to flee. As it was, I walked right into it, with my eyes open, believing only that I had been granted an incredible future.

CHAPTER 6

Although we were married in the handsome Church of Saint Jago de la Vega in Spanish Town, the wedding was small: I had no relatives in the West Indies, and I did not know how to contact my shipboard friends, Osmon and Stafford. Whitledge had sent a kind note with his apologies. Mr. Arthur Foster, my solicitor—and Mr. Mason's as well—attended with his wife, who appeared distracted. A few of Mr. Mason's friends came with their wives, and left as soon afterwards as they could. Of course, Richard Mason was there to stand with me. And in my heart Carrot and Touch were there as well, to praise my choice of bride and applaud how well I had done for myself.

We took a honeymoon tour of the island, stopping the longest at the lovely Montego Bay. We spent our days there strolling along the shore and gazing out to sea. It is a wondrous sight, that sea—the deepest turquoise far out, then turning lighter and lighter blue, until near to shore all one sees is sand beneath clear water.

The torrid heat had abated by then, as had the hurricane danger, and the palm trees swayed in a gentle sea breeze, the sand like sugar beneath our feet. I had not particularly noticed the night skies before, but now I saw that the stars seemed brighter than I had ever seen. I felt, truly, as if I had entered paradise; I could not have been happier or more sanguine about my future. It's true that Bertha's moods were somewhat hard to predict—at times the water's vista entranced her and she ran barefoot on the sand, screaming her delight like a child, but at other times that same vastness unsettled her, and she cowered beside the sea, clinging to me and weeping. I did not mind: I would rejoice in her happiness or hold her in my arms to calm her, whatever she needed. My heart was full of love.

I found her on the beach one evening after dinner, when I returned from a solitary stroll. She had been with Molly, her body servant, when I left, but when I came upon Bertha later, she was alone, sitting on the sand, a clamshell in her hand, drawing it slowly and forcefully across the inside of her wrist. She was so absorbed that she did not notice my approach. I bent down beside her. "What are you doing?" I asked, for I could not imagine.

She smiled up at me ingenuously. "It feels so good," she said.

"But does it not hurt?" I asked. "Look, you have made scrapes there. Oh, my darling, you're bleeding."

She smiled more broadly. "It feels good," she repeated, licking the blood from her wrist.

I placed my hand over hers. "I will give you a golden bracelet for that wrist."

She leaned against me. "You will give me gold and jewels and babies," she murmured.

"I will give you whatever you want," I said, and I believed it then. "Bertha," I said, pointing, diverting her attention, "see that flight of birds against the sunset."

"They're beautiful," she said.

"*You* are beautiful," I responded. I took her in my arms and she dropped the clamshell; I held her close and we kissed, and then we walked on down the beach.

I came to learn that, unless she was putting herself on display at a ball, she was uncomfortable in unconfined spaces, and that the presence of people she did not know made her restless and, sometimes, angry. At those times, I could not always calm her, and she would retreat into our rooms with Molly, who had been at her side since childhood and who seemed able to calm her when I failed to do so. They would sit in the semidark, with the shutters drawn, and Molly would sing to her in some African language that I of course did not understand, and perhaps Bertha did not, either, but the repetition of the melody soothed her and in time she was able to rejoin me and smile, both of us pretending that such events were normal.

Near the end of our journey, when we reached Kingston, I could tell from her restlessness that something was bothering her.

"Are you anxious to be home?" I asked, thinking she had found the journey more trying than I realized.

"No...yes," she responded.

"Do you want to leave immediately?"

"Why do you question me?" she shouted. "Is it not enough that I hate Kingston?"

"Hate? Whatever for?"

"You are so stupid!" she screamed, bursting into tears.

A man ought to be able to help his wife, to save her from distress—but I could not think what to do. I sat gingerly beside her on the bed and she fell into my arms. "It is the worst place in the whole world!" she said, weeping, her whole body shaking in despair.

"Kingston?" I was bewildered.

"Do you not know? Do you really not know?"

"Bertha, I—"

"My *mother* is here," she snapped.

What can she mean? "I thought your mother was dead."

"She might as well be."

"Bertha...? I don't understand...your mother?"

"Fairfax," she said, her face twisted in anguish. "My mother is mad. Insane. She is shut up in a lunatic asylum. I have not seen her in years, nor Michael, either."

"Michael?" I asked.

"My brother," she whispered, calmer now but still clinging to me. "My brother Michael, poor thing. He is with her there, the two of them: she a madwoman and he an idiot since birth." She looked directly at me then. "Do you wonder why I hate this place, why I do not want to be reminded of her?"

I held her close, and she wept. I had thought her mother dead, but this, was this not worse? "I should not have brought you here. I'm sorry," I said.

She shook her head quickly, as if to rid herself of the memory of her mother. I could not imagine it, and yet—would not the presence of a living mother, even if her mind is gone, be better than no mother at all? I had no idea, but, *If I had a mother alive...*, I thought.

But Bertha's hand was on my private parts, and I had already learned that sometimes the best way to bring my bride out of a sulk was in the act of intercourse, which she entered into with a wild abandon that I took at the time for passion. We spoke no more of her mother.

A modern man is pleased if his wife enjoys the act of love, and in those early days I cherished Bertha with a grateful heart, thanking God that he had given me a wife who was as lusty as she was beautiful. When we had finished, I gazed at her lying beside me on the sheets, and I said, "We will make beautiful children together."

Unaccountably, she began to weep silently, and I could think of nothing to do except to hold her close until she fell into sleep. But later that night, I woke to her weeping again. *She mourns for her mother,* I thought. "It's all right," I whispered. "I am here; I will take care of you."

"The baby," she muttered between sobs. "I cannot find the baby."

"Hush," I whispered. "You've had a bad dream. It will be all right in the morning. Go back to sleep." I thought I felt her body soften, though the weeping went on and on, until, finally, she wore herself into exhaustion.

The next morning I woke first, and I lay beside her in bed, gazing at her—at her face relaxed in sleep: dark eyelashes against satiny skin; full, red lips that almost seemed to move as if she spoke in her dreams; masses of lustrous black hair. *When she does have a child,* I thought, *it will be as beautiful as she.* The thought roused me, and as if she sensed it, she murmured in her sleep and reached for me. I kissed her, and she pulled me into her with a passion. When our ardor had spent itself at last and we rose from the bed, I vowed not to mention the dream she'd had in the night, for there was no reason, I thought, to ruin the last day of our honeymoon.

———

We might have stayed longer in Kingston; I might have taken Bertha down to the docks to see the *Sea Nymph*. She might have been excited to see that sleek ship that was soon to be mine, but I could not insist she stay where she was so ill at ease. In Spanish Town I had legal papers to sign regarding the ship's purchase, so we moved into my town house for a few days. I was surprised that she seemed familiar with the place, but there was no reason she might not have visited before, as a child accompanying her father on business. And of course she knew Sukey, whom she greeted wildly with kisses and embraces and enthusiastic chatter about all we had seen and done—more of what we had done than I considered decent, in fact. But marriage was new to her, I told myself, and I supposed she could not refrain from spilling out whatever came into her mind. And of course I knew enough to understand that, much as we might not prefer it, servants are always privy to whatever happens in a household.

Sukey served us grog in the parlor while Molly and Alexander carried our things upstairs to our bedroom—what had been my father's room, and then mine, and now was ours in this house. When I rose to leave to go to my office, I asked, "Will you be all right here alone?" for I knew she hated being by herself.

She laughed. "Alone? *Alone?* But I am here with my sisters."

Her comment took me aback, but what could I say in response to that? She had, indeed, grown up with Sukey and Molly, and so I left them alone together.

I was gone for perhaps three hours, and when I returned evening was descending. I was eager for a home-cooked meal after all those days of eating in taverns and inns, and I smelled the distinct aroma of Sukey's pepper pot as soon as I opened the door. I heard laughter coming from an upstairs room, so, delighted, I climbed the stairs, imagining myself in five or ten years, hearing children's laughter filling the house as women's laughter filled it now.

I came into the bedroom to see the three of them sitting in a circle on the bed. The curtains were all drawn, but in the gloom I could make out Bertha in her undergarments and the other two in their simple dresses, all three of them barefoot, their heads together, staring at something on the bed. Sukey saw me first and caught her breath. Bertha glanced up. Molly scooped up whatever they had been looking at and kept her eyes focused on the bed.

"My husband has returned!" Bertha exclaimed, stretching her arms out to me. The other two scampered off the bed and out of the room.

I came closer. "What were you doing?" I asked.

She turned around and stared at the bed, as if she had already forgotten. "Oh, just a silly game the Africans play. Come here, my love. Come and kiss me."

She seemed so ephemeral—her mind here and there at random—but I was still so enamored with her, and I assumed she with me, and so hopeful for our future, that I pushed any hesitation out of my mind. Instead, I sat down beside her and she cupped my face in her hands and smiled into it and kissed my mouth. I wrapped my arms around her and she pulled me down onto the bed on top of her, kissing my face and licking my ear. The heat of her rose into me and I was on top of her and she on top of me and if we could have consumed each other we would have.

When we had finished, lying in each other's arms, she sighed, contentedly, I thought. "Fairfax, tell me: whatever happened to the portrait of your mother?"

I was startled into dumbness for a moment. "What portrait?" I managed to ask.

"The one that used to hang here in this house."

"Of my mother?" *My God,* I thought. It could not be. "How do you know it was she?"

She laughed. "You donkey. She looked just like your brother. Like Rowland. You look like your father and he looks like her, with her fair hair and her blue eyes."

"You saw it?"

She laughed into my neck. "She was beautiful, wasn't she?" And then, in her way of flitting from one thing to another, she asked, "When can we return home?"

CHAPTER 7

$\mathcal{T}$he portrait had been here, in Spanish Town, I thought. But it was not there anymore, at least not in the house. Where could it be? In his offices? Had he taken it back to England with him? My mind would not let go of it, and when next I was in Spanish Town I asked Sukey if she knew what had happened to the portrait of my mother that had been in the house. She frowned, shaking her head, appearing genuinely confused. I described it to her, but she still had no recollection of it. Then I asked if she remembered my brother, Rowland.

"He tall?" she asked. "Pretty boy?"

I had to laugh at that. So she did remember him, but not well. She had been only a child herself, she said, living at Valley View.

"How long have you been staying at my father's house?" I asked.

"Eight years, nine." She seemed uncomfortable with my questions, but it was clear she could be of no help in finding the portrait. And, after searching my father's office, I put it out of my mind.

———

We returned to Valley View, and though I still thought both of us would sometimes reside there and sometimes in Spanish Town when I needed to attend to business, it became clear that Bertha had no intention of doing so. Even at Valley View, I began to notice that Bertha's temperament was changing and that she spent much of her time wandering barefoot through the house, as if searching for some lost item, or else closeted with Molly and one or two others, still playing their mysterious games with feathers and knucklebones and straw dolls and other odd items. Her father paid her little attention, preferring my company from the start. I worried some over what Bertha would think of her father's apparent preference for me, but she seemed not to notice it. She rarely ate meals with me and her father, but she did continue to occupy my bed each night and surround me with her caresses, and I was content, enveloped by the scent of her.

Ball invitations for the two of us began to arrive almost immediately on our return. I was thrilled, imagining myself proudly entering a hall, Bertha on my arm, the envious glances of other men, my face wreathed in smiles. I imagined us dancing the night away—reels and contra dances and even waltzes—until we were dizzy with exhaustion.

"When shall we leave?" I asked her the first time. "It will take us most of an hour to get there, I should think."

"*We?*" she replied. "Don't be stupid; wives never go with husbands. The men always come first; surely even you must have noticed that."

"But I thought—"

"Oh, Fairfax, really. It is not done. And *I* would certainly not do it, even if it were. You go, whenever you like, as you have always done. And I will arrive when it suits me."

"But"—I saw the expression on her face but blundered on, nevertheless—"but we will dance together, surely."

She tilted her head downward as she often did, coyly, gazing at me through her eyelashes, a smile spreading slowly across her face. "Of course, my darling. When I have arrived." When she had made her entrance, was what she meant. Marriage had not changed her wish to be seen and admired by all in attendance. Still, I claimed her at the first reel, but after that initial dance, she turned from me and tilted her head at a man I had never seen before. He took her from me, and after that she was with another and then another. I broke in from time to time, but she pouted when I did so, as if I were ruining her evening, and after a time I gave up altogether and stood out on the veranda with a group of planters, smoking cigars and talking about the cockfights.

She did not leave the ball early that evening, as she had done every other time since I had known her. Instead, she stayed to the very end. A few times, she pulled her partner out onto the veranda, leaning close to him and laughing softly. I was tempted to leave, but I stayed on, for I did not want the others to see my jealousy, or how little control I had over my own wife.

She left the ball as dawn was nearly breaking. Kissing her final partner on the cheek, and gathering her wrap against the night air, she mounted her carriage. She did not even seem to notice that my horse followed behind, and that I trudged up the steps to the house in her wake.

Once inside, she turned to me. "I must say, you behaved abominably," she snapped. "I cannot imagine what people thought."

"Abominably? Me?" I countered. "It was you who refused to dance with your own husband."

"Refused? I did not refuse! You were never around. It seemed as if you were never to be found. And leaving me half the night with that horrid Jasper Duncombe while you mooned over that stupid wife of his!"

"*You kissed him!*"

"Kissed him? *I? Kissed him?* That lout! I would rather kiss a tree frog."

I stared at her in astonishment.

She stared back, her eyes locked on mine, her pout slowly breaking into a coy smile, and she stepped closer. "Take me," she whispered.

I could not believe it—my head whirling at the speed with which her emotions changed. Yet, was this not the Bertha I preferred, I asked myself—a loving and lusty wife? She stepped closer and put her arms around my neck, kissing me full on the mouth, and I responded, and together we made our way to our room and fell upon the bed.

When we had finished, spent, I caressed errant locks of hair from her face and kissed her gently until she turned away from me. "You are nothing like your brother," she murmured.

"What?" I asked, suddenly chilled.

"You are nothing like your brother," she repeated slowly.

I moved back from her. I was indeed nothing like my brother, I knew, but I could not think of a response to that.

But she could. "He is tall and slim and fair, and he dances as if he is moving on a cloud, while you—"

"That's enough," I said. I did not need to be told by my own wife how much she might have preferred Rowland. "You were a child when he was here," I said, throwing on my garments. "And you had a child's imagination. But now you are a woman, and you know nothing of Rowland."

"It is *you* who knows nothing!" she screamed. "You stupid… graceless…ugly—" I slammed the door on her words.

———

The next morning, she came to me, contrite, and leaned over the back of my chair as I sat at breakfast, kissing my neck and nuzzling against my ear. "Did we make a baby last night, do you think?" she murmured.

I turned toward her. "Bertha—"

"*Antoinetta!*" she demanded, rising.

I rose as well, pushing back my chair and facing her. "We can only hope God blesses us—"

"*God.*" She spat the word. "God has nothing to do with it." She began weeping, silently. "It's all wrong," she said as she wept. "Everything is all wrong."

I thought I loved her. *I will make it right,* I told myself. But I had no idea.

There were other balls and gatherings after that, but they were all the same. We arrived separately and danced a few times together before she went on to dance with one man and then another, and afterwards we returned, she sullen, or I, or both of us. She spent her days with Molly, playing strange African games. Perhaps they were meant to help her conceive a child, but I ignored them as foolishness. And we came together in acts of passion, if not always love.

Everything to do with my marriage to Bertha had happened so quickly that I had not, fortuitously perhaps, found time to write to my father to tell him the news, that I had indeed married Jonas Mason's daughter. However, by the time I got to the task, I had already begun to wonder what kind of future our marriage held for us—Bertha's mother and brother in an insane asylum, and Bertha herself clearly disturbed—so I wrote to him in simple and civil terms, saying as little as necessary and imploring him not to make my marriage known among his friends and acquaintances.

It was not the marriage I had thought we would have, but it was perhaps no worse than many others. Richard had warned me about Creole marriages, though at the time I paid little attention. One always thinks one is the exception, I suppose.

I saw less of Richard since Valley View became my chief residence, but I did pin him down once on the question of his mother, though he seemed not to understand my concern. "Of course she is mad," he said. "Did you want us to shout it from the treetops?"

"I should have been told," I responded tartly.

"What good would it have done? And anyway," he added as he walked away, "half the women on the island are mad."

But that far from satisfied me, and I confronted Jonas Mason as well. "I ought to have been made aware of Bertha's mother," I blurted out to him one evening as we sat on the veranda. It was not how I should have done it, but perhaps it was as good as I could have managed in my distress.

"You ought," he agreed. "I had imagined...I *thought* you could help her keep from becoming like her mother." He glanced away from me, as if searching for the right words. "I thought new blood...And—"

"She will get worse," I said.

He nodded. "She will."

"And she is afraid of being put where her mother is."

"Please," he said. "We cannot let that happen."

That stopped me for a moment. What could I say? There had been a time when I had thought my presence would always calm her, my words or actions could somehow make her well again, but I no longer thought that, and I could not imagine what my life would become, saddled forever—*forever*—to a woman like Bertha. "I will do my best," I responded, though in truth I did not know how I could manage such a thing for the rest of my life.

But there was one more thing: "Did my father know—did he always know of Bertha's inheritance?"

"He knew of my wife, Rochester," he said gently, "but in those days I hoped neither Bertha nor Richard would follow their mother's course. And I still hold out hope that Bertha...will...not..."

He did not complete his thought, but I knew it was a false hope.

After that, from time to time, I tried writing to my father, demanding to know why he had not warned me about Bertha's inheritance. I wished him to blush with shame at having had any part in sending me to Jonas Mason, for I was certain now that he had known far more than I did from the very beginning, and I could not imagine why he would do such a thing to his own son—bring me up, educate me, for this...this hell. But every time I wrote, I balled up the letter without sending it, for I could never think of how to adequately express my anger and my loss of respect for him. As for Jonas, while of course I wished he had been more honest with me, my sense of betrayal was less acute: I understood his desire to ensure his daughter's care, which was what any father would do. It was my own father who seemed to have sacrificed his son—*me*—for Bertha's sake.

To escape the disappointment of our marriage, I buried myself in my work. True, Bertha was as beautiful as ever, and true, I could not complain of the way she graced my bed. But beyond that, there was nearly nothing. We did not share meals, nor did we speak of everyday things, or our hopes and dreams. She did not care to read or to share her thoughts on any subject, small or large. I did complete the purchase of the *Sea Nymph*, though the ship had become nearly a burden for me, a reminder of the mistake my marriage seemed to have been.

There were other tensions as well in our world, especially between the Creoles and the field slaves in the West Indies. Negroes on the island of Jamaica outnumbered whites by ten or more to one, and there was—

always—the fear of a slave uprising. Such revolts happened on all the sugar islands from time to time—uprisings that saw a great deal of violence and destruction on both sides. At those times slave owners were rarely killed, but often they were shamed by their negroes by being put into the stocks, or shackled—as negroes sometimes were—to iron posts set into the ground, a humiliation beyond bearing. And, of course, the great fear was the burning of the cane fields.

Daniels, the estate manager at Valley View, had informed me early on that it was never allowed for all the whites to be absent from the estate at the same time. He did not say outright that it was to deter insurrection, but I understood. The one weapon the whites had against the negroes was fear. A negro late to the field received ten lashes; a negro who tried to escape was beheaded and his head placed on a pole at the side of the road as a warning.

Does not the effect of unlimited power and the frequent witnessing of such severe punishment tend to harden the heart? Yes, I found, it does, although the whites of the West Indies would have said it is an unfortunate truth that must be accepted, for there is no way to grow and harvest sugar without it. But there is also no doubt that such power destroys the souls of those who wield it every bit as much as it destroys the bodies and spirits of those who suffer under it, and I was no exception, for I too easily slid into acceptance of the way of life of a Jamaican planter.

I followed Daniels around, watching his dealings, learning the routines of a sugar plantation: the planting season, which involves the most difficult work of holing for the new canes; the rainy season, when the canes and the weeds grow most vigorously and the weeds need constant chopping lest they—and the vermin they harbor—get entirely out of control; the autumn and winter months, when the temperature grows cooler and the plantation manager needs to keep an eye on the cane and on the dampness of the soil and when the final repairs to the mill must be completed, so that sometime in the first few months of the year, when the cane is ready to harvest, all is prepared for the long, mad days of harvest and of sugaring.

At that time I was so intent on all that the plantation involved, I often did not see Bertha from dawn until evening, and when we were together there were frequently sharp words between us. "You care nothing for me!" she would scream. "It's only the stupid, idiotic, *bloody* harvest that you care for."

"You know that's not true," I would respond, forcing my voice into calmness. I had gotten used to her foul language and had come to think that if I ignored it she would stop using it, as if she were some kind of child who was only trying to shock.

"You're worthless!" she screamed once. "Ugly! Stupid! You know nothing of women! You can't even fuck right!"

That jolted me into silence, and I stormed out of the room.

———

Crop time was almost a relief. The pressures are heavy on all involved, because sugar is a finicky crop: it must be harvested at just the right stage, for a day or two in one direction or another can ruin the crop and mean the loss of a year's work and thousands of pounds of income—the difference between the life of a prosperous planter like Jonas and that of the poorest landholder in the county.

Although the work of a plantation like Valley View is highly regimented, everyone having his or her own responsibilities, at crop time all work is focused on chopping and transporting the canes to the mill, and on boiling and distilling and curing the sugar that will someday grace the tables of the wealthiest and noblest Europeans, and on the production of the rum that warms many a man the world over.

The harvest lasted about a week, the black smoke rising day and night from the boiling-house chimneys. Book-keepers took twenty-four-hour spells overseeing the work gangs and catching a few moments of sleep wherever and whenever they could. People grew tired and snappish but carried on until the work was finished. I did not see Bertha at all during those crop time days. I was in the fields or the sugar mill or the distillery all day and half the night, and when I did return to the house, I fell into bed, sometimes not even bothering to take off my clothes. Bertha was occasionally absent from the bed, but I assumed she was sitting somewhere in the dark with Molly.

For me, for that brief time, my mind and body were so occupied with all the fury and activity around me that I could not possibly think of anything else. And that was a blessing.

CHAPTER 8

The end of the harvest—"crop-over time"—was always an occasion for great celebration. The negroes received an allowance of sugar and *santa*—a mix of fruit juice, sugar, and rum. First there would be a dinner at the buckra house and a black ball and an overabundance of rum punch. Negro fiddlers would play and drummers drum, and all the negroes came dressed in their finest. They danced with the buckras, and when, sated with rum and dancing, they left to sleep it off, the white neighbors arrived for more food and dancing and rum. Crop over could last for days and days.

I had assumed that Bertha would be in attendance at Valley View's crop-over celebration, for she always attended the neighborhood balls in her usual fashion. But she did not appear at the black ball, nor did she attend the white one that succeeded it. By that time I had not seen her for two weeks and I had become concerned, but I hardly knew where to turn. None of the servants could answer my questions regarding her, and Molly had disappeared as well. I could not bring myself to admit to Jonas that after only a few months of marriage I had lost my wife. After another day, I took myself to Spanish Town to speak with Richard, but he merely shook his head and said, "Bertha is like that. She's probably with one of her Obeah women. She'll be back."

Bertha had become obsessed with Obeah, a kind of religion, or

mysticism, or magic—I hardly know what to call it—that some of the negroes practiced. It involved attempts to control events or to secure good
luck for oneself or bad luck for others, or put curses on others or remove
them from oneself, and included the use of the bones and feathers and
strange concoctions of blood and herbs that I had seen Bertha with on a
few occasions. I did not know how to react to this or what to say, and
whenever I mentioned it she laughed at me as if I were a fool to take any
of it seriously, and yet I saw how much time she spent on it and how far
she would go to meet with an Obeah woman or man. I had asked her father about it once, but he had laughed it off as a childish obsession that
she had not yet outgrown. "Give her a child of her own, and she will forget all that nonsense," he had said, taking another drink of his grog and
looking off over his cane fields.

I stayed over in Spanish Town for a few days, Sukey's calm presence a
comfort, and when I returned I found Bertha in our bedroom, as if she had
been there all along. She was playing, I thought, with a doll. I had not seen
it before, and I assumed it was some precious thing from her childhood,
but on closer examination I saw that it was roughly made from old fabric,
patched in the arms and body, and with hair cut from some animal. Bertha
glanced up at me when I arrived and grinned. "We shall have a baby!" she
announced.

"Really!" I exclaimed, flooded suddenly with conflicting emotions, for
while I was keen to have a family, I worried about Bertha: I was not as
convinced as her father that a baby would bring her back to her former
self.

"You will give me a baby," Bertha said.

"Oh," I said. Not yet, then.

"Now," she said. "It must happen now." She rose and kissed my
mouth, her teeth biting my lips as they often did when she was strongly
aroused.

I meant to step back, for I had great reservations regarding the act of
love with her, for in fact, she was not in her right mind and I had come to
understand that she ought never to become a mother. But before I made a

move, she suddenly began to weep. "What good does it do to have a baby when they just take it away from you?"

I stared at her in confusion. She seemed to be talking gibberish.

Still, I asked, "Who takes babies away?"

"*They* do!"

"Who?"

"*What does it matter who?*"

Her Obeah woman had put hallucinations into her head. *Or perhaps,* I thought, *the worst has happened and she has become her mother.* She reached for me then, her face suddenly softening. "You will give me a baby," she whispered, "and you will not disappear." Her lips were on my surprised mouth, her tongue inside. I felt the heat of her, but I could not rise to her need. When instead I tried to comfort her, her hands pummeled me and she bit me, screaming my worthlessness at me until I turned from her and left.

Later, sleepless, I walked out of the house and into the moonless night, cursing myself, and my father, and all that had brought me to that wretched place.

———

After that night, it seemed that Bertha grew worse by the day. She often had hallucinations—some were garbled and full of fantasy; others were clear. She imagined my brother or my father in the room with her; she imagined a house full of babies; she even imagined she had killed her father and mine. And then she took to cutting herself, and Molly and I had to be ever watchful to keep sharp objects from her reach.

I needed to get away. Far away. I needed new vistas, other persons surrounding me, other thoughts than those crowding my head in the night. I sent a quick message to Whitledge and packed a small valise and made my excuses to Jonas, barely able to look him in the face as I did so, for I had come to wonder if everyone—all of Jamaican society, except me—had known of Bertha's proclivities. I had been an egotistical fool: it was not a contest for Bertha's hand that I had won; it was the contest for her bed, and perhaps I had not won even that.

I rose early, just at dawn, and even though it was chilly and the early-morning air still damp, I was determined to leave at once. The day promised to be fine, the sky that pure Jamaican blue that one almost never sees in England, and the air full of the raucous birdsongs I had become used to. As I started out, I felt a kind of freedom, a release. In the previous few weeks I had felt tied down to Bertha in a way that I had not felt when we first married. I had not before then seen her darker side, did not know the terrors that haunted her. I had once thought that a child of her own might make a difference, but now I knew I could not wish a mother like her on any innocent being. She frightened me, not only because I wondered how life could go on as it had before, but also because I had begun to wonder what demons lay inside *me*—inside anyone—only waiting to be awakened.

I reached Arcadia late in the afternoon. I had expected the great house there to be similar to the one at Valley View, but in fact it was noticeably smaller, set beautifully on a small rise, the road to it lined by a handsome avenue of tamarinds. Whitledge, warned no doubt by some sharp-eyed pickaninny, was on the veranda, waving as I approached.

"Rochester!" he shouted, as if I were some long-lost cousin, rather than a shipboard acquaintance. After our warm greeting, he offered me a tour of the house—an unusual gesture, since most estate owners kept their homes quite private, except for the public rooms where a dinner or a ball might be held. But I accepted gladly.

Arcadia was an architectural gem. Valley View, it was clear, had been built by a man with a practical and mathematical bent, reflected in its stolid, square shape, in the symmetry of its windows, and in its expansive rooms. But in Arcadia alcoves and curves abounded, ceiling heights changed from room to room, doors led into unexpected spaces. Bertha would have loved its surprises and mysteries. Had she seen it in the first days of our marriage, she would have flung her arms around my neck and insisted, "Fairfax, we must build a house just like this! Just exactly like this!" I would have done it for her too, back when I was still under her spell.

Whitledge was rightly proud of it. "My father and I designed it together when I was a child. Its building, I have to say, was a result of a tragedy. There was an uprising of the negroes and the house and most of the fields were burned. None of us was harmed, but my mother never recovered. She refused to set foot in the damaged house, where all her belongings smelled of smoke; she could not bear the memories of those fearful days.

"So we moved in with my grandparents, and my father had the building totally destroyed, the ground leveled off and put into gardens, and he settled on this new location, where he built a house designed for my mother. She never lived in it, though. She died before it was completed." He paused then, and said, "Have I told you I'm to be married soon?"

Of course he had not told me; we had not conversed since we parted in Spanish Town months before. She was a delight, he enthused, a girl he had known from childhood; her parents had been great friends of his own. It had always been assumed that they would marry, and now he and his Elizabeth were to wed in less than a month. He hoped my wife and I would be able to come; he was quite anxious to meet the woman who had captured my heart. I smiled and said it would be a pleasure, while wondering what excuse I could make when the time came, and thanked God that Whitledge had not heard gossip regarding Bertha.

A couple of days later, at a neighborhood ball, I had an opportunity to meet the bride herself. She was not at all what I had expected, I will confess. Whitledge was a handsome young man and I expected Elizabeth to be a beauty—but while she had an attractive figure, her face was quite plain, with a nose too small for her broad forehead. Still, she had a bright smile and was pleasant indeed to talk with. I danced a reel or two with her and found her to be an engaging conversationalist. I could imagine with envy the quiet, contented nights she and Whitledge might spend together.

After four days, I took my leave to return to Valley View. Whitledge was eager for me to visit again as soon as possible, and I wished with all my heart that I could return the invitation, but things were far too uncertain at Valley View. As I began my ride home that afternoon, I reflected that I had not had so many days of pure enjoyment and much-needed relaxation since my visit with Carrot so many years before.

——

After my absence, I had hoped to return to a different Bertha, perhaps even a chastened one. But the moment I put foot to the veranda steps, she ran out of the house, dressed like a harridan, her black curls flying, her mouth spewing the most vile language I had ever heard. She rushed toward me, her face contorted in anger, and when I was within her reach she slapped my face. And then, before I could even react, she accused me, in full earshot of the whole household, of every indecency she could think of: desertion, drunkenness, unfaithfulness, even violence.

Astonished, I tried to place my hands on her shoulders to calm her, but she screamed and backed away as if I had assaulted her. To my relief, Molly materialized at Bertha's side, gently touching her arm and speaking in a language I did not know. Bertha soon turned from me and followed Molly as docilely as a child.

From that day forth I gave up all pretense of a respectful partnership with her. I learned to ignore her demands and her foul words, using only calm language in her presence, and I never had intercourse with her again. She screamed at me and swore and attacked me more than once. But just as she had lost all sense of decency, I had lost all desire for her.

Jonas caught me by the arm one day shortly after that first public outrage and pulled me into his study. "You are not to be blamed for this," he said, and his voice was shaking with emotion.

Still, she was my wife; I had taken her for better or for worse, though none of us imagines beforehand how bad the worse might be. In my despair, I wondered what I might do to free myself of her. But a divorce would have taken an act of Parliament, and how could I drag us both—all of us—through that? No, I could not. When one is young, one imagines all sorts of miracles that might come to pass if one is patient. So I let time pass, still harboring a slim hope that that lovely, vivacious girl I had fallen in love with remained in there, hidden, but alive.

Now, in retrospect, I know that I should have done at once anything necessary to free each of us from our bonds to the other. But at the time, I thought that would have been an unconscionable act of cruelty. I had no idea of what was yet to come.

CHAPTER 9

1 cannot say that my decision was brave or generous or kindhearted, or even humane. It was just that I had nothing behind me in England and nothing ahead of me in Jamaica that I could see except the life I had slipped into in Valley View. I had been linked to Jonas by my father, not only in marriage to his daughter but also in my very way of life: the plantation and the import and export business that we shared. As well, the *Sea Nymph* was doing so well that Jonas and I had together purchased another ship, the *Dragon*, which we had outfitted as another passenger ship in the lucrative immigrant trade from Europe to America.

And, indeed, Jonas had had to deal with a mad wife. I did not ask—nor did I want to know—the circumstances of his marriage, but we shared that situation as well, and, in particular, our concern for Bertha. It might have been easy to blame Jonas for his part in entangling me with Bertha, but his very concern for her taught me that he was simply doing what he thought best for a child he loved. I could not blame him for that. So I simply tried to make the best of my situation.

But my father was a different case. I could not understand how he could have encouraged a relationship between Bertha and me. If anything, it seemed, he should have warned me against it. His actions went against all I understood about a parent's duty to his child. I could not forgive him, and therefore I ceased what little communication had occurred between us.

There would never be anything like a normal marriage between Bertha and me, but, as with many marriages in the world, a person could manage, more or less, with a sham. Sometimes, in Bertha's calmer moments, I tried to make something of what we had left. I would sit down beside her in the evening and try to have a conversation with her, but she knew little of the wider world and cared less. The only things she seemed to care about were the worthless incantations and precepts of her current Obeah man or woman, and the strange games that she played with Molly. Now and then she tried to seduce me, but more often she attacked me. Twice she came at me with the sharp edge of a broken china plate, once managing to draw blood before I was able to wrest the weapon from her.

Sometimes she even turned on her own flesh. Twice she tried stabbing herself with the pin of a brooch I had given her as a wedding gift, and once she shoved a fist through a window in order to cut herself with the glass shards. Molly kept a close watch on her day and night, and for the most part she was successful in keeping Bertha safe.

But one dark night Bertha managed to escape, making her way out of the house with a lighted candle, and before anyone knew it, she had set the nearest cane field ablaze. When the fire was discovered, ten acres were already burning and Bertha was still nearby, her eyes on the flames as if transfixed. It was too late to save that field, and only with the valiant efforts of everyone on hand were we able to save the other nearby fields. By afternoon the next day we claimed victory, though there were still smoldering pockets. As I stood in the midst of the ashes, covered in dirt and soot and smelling like burned sugar, it occurred to me that in nearly all of Jamaica the whites feared an uprising of the negroes that would burn down the fields, but at Valley View it was a white woman who did it and negroes who put the fire out.

The morning after the fire Jonas asked me into his study, closing the door behind me. I sat—uncomfortably, for we had difficult things to discuss—in a chair facing his desk. "My daughter is a danger to herself, to us, and now to the plantation itself," were his first words. "But I refuse to put her into an asylum. It would break her heart. It would kill her."

I felt a sudden surge of rage. "I cannot understand why I was not told!" I charged. "I should have been told! You deliberately—"

"I suppose I did," he interrupted.

"You *suppose*?"

"I hoped...," he said. "I thought marriage would keep her from growing worse. I thought perhaps a baby—"

"*A baby!* She is the last person who should have a baby! Her mother is like this?"

He blanched at my question, but he did respond. "Worse. I imagine"—he sighed—"I fear my daughter will someday fully lose her mind, as her mother did. But if there is any hope for her, it will be in keeping her at home. My wife grew much worse when she was put in care, and, between you and me, Rochester, I've found it difficult to get over that decision; it's irreversible now, but I would give anything to have done it differently, to have kept my wife and son near me, despite it all. We must keep my daughter with us, safely under our eye, here, within the radius of our family. Constrain her within the house if you must, but..." He choked back a word or two, then gathered himself again. "We must treat her with gentleness, Rochester, for she is sick, and we must stop it from getting worse."

Though it seemed impossible to end Bertha's decline, I reluctantly agreed with him, for Jonas' love for his daughter was clear, and I had respect—and envy—for that. But I could not yet completely forgive him for having sacrificed my happiness in his quest to see Bertha cared for—nor, worse, could I understand my own father, who should have warned me of her family history, which he must have known. What reason could have compelled the two of them to use me so?

Devastated, I retreated to Spanish Town as quickly as I could, for the town house there had become almost a sanctuary for me. As always, Sukey almost seemed to foresee my arrival, for there was pepper pot on the stove to welcome me. She was in the parlor, mending a shirt of mine, when I arrived, but she rose immediately when I came into the room. "No, no, sit," I said to her.

As she sat, I said, "It's Bertha," for I needed at that moment to unburden myself, though it is never right to bring servants into one's private life.

She nodded.

"You know her inheritance," I said. "Her mind."

Sukey did not even look at me.

"Why was I not told?" I demanded, as if I expected the poor girl to hold the answers. When she did not speak, I found myself unable to contain my restlessness. "I will be back for dinner."

"Yes, sir," she said, and I left.

I went to my office, where, distracted, I signed the application to the registrar-general for permission to remove the word *Guinea* from the names of the two ships that had carried slaves. I didn't care if it was bad luck or not; I had had enough bad luck in my life anyway. What worse could happen?

The next day I rode to Kingston, though I knew it was a mistake, and asked directions to the asylum—a large, formidable building of gray stone. I paused in front of it for a long time, not sure what I was seeking but knowing I needed to face what lay behind those walls. Finally, I tethered my horse and walked toward the gate, where a squinty-eyed man asked my business. He led me down a dark hallway that smelled of urine and vomit and God knows what else. I could hear, in the distance, shouts and screams and a low, nearly constant moaning. Another man intercepted us and the two had a few words, and then the second man beckoned me forward and I followed him.

"Why do you want to see her?" he asked.

"She is my wife's mother."

He shook his head. "Too late for you, then, surely," he said.

I did not respond.

We passed several cells crowded with women, all of them reminding me of Bertha in one way or another, before we stopped at a cell containing a woman alone, her simple dress askew, her hair matted.

"Here." My guide indicated her with a nod.

I watched her for a time, taking in the three-legged stool on which she sat, the mat on the floor on which she no doubt slept, the bucket for her waste. She was raking her fingers through her hair, as if to groom herself, and she seemed not to notice me. At first I pitied her, sitting there alone. "I have come from Valley View," I said to her. "Your daughter sends her love." My words seemed to make her suddenly aware of the two of us standing outside the bars, and she started to scream, and she rose and lunged toward us with an ear-shattering howl, her face grotesquely contorted, and I inadvertently jumped back.

"This one's right mad," my guide observed.

I stood for a moment, rooted to the spot, horrified. Was this what would become of Bertha? And then I fled.

Bertha there, in that place? It was no wonder her father forbade it and she was terrified of it. I could not blame them. As I rode away, the horror of that place would not leave me, and I, too, became as determined as Jonas to prevent Bertha from ending up there.

I spent three more days in Spanish Town before I could bring myself to return to Valley View.

———

Bertha's rages and her night terrors came and went, and as I grew to understand that they had nothing to do with me, but with her own inner demons, I tried to ignore them. However, her hallucinations grew more frequent and more devastating. She would talk and scream and cry at beings in the room, one moment cowering from them and the next charging around as if to drive them from her. She ate little and bathed less, and sometimes she seemed unsure of who I was.

There were good days—many of them, in truth—and each time I raised a hope of improvement, but her rages came unannounced, and sometimes only Molly's voice could calm her; we were deeply in that girl's debt, all of us. At last, Jonas and I arranged for the plantation carpenter to turn two of the bedrooms into an apartment for Bertha, and that became her private refuge. She rarely left it, and Molly and her daughter waited on her there. Tiso was nearly ten years of age—old enough to be in the fields in the second gang, but Jonas and I agreed her presence in Bertha's apartment was of more importance. She was a sweet girl, and obedient, and was a great help to Molly.

Bertha was immediately calmer, more content, when she could shelter in her rooms, and she didn't seem to mind being away from the rest of the household activity. I visited from time to time, and she would beg me to make her with child, but I was far beyond accommodating her in that respect. Jonas rarely went to see her—he could not bear to, I think. Richard came even less often, and I suspected he and his father had had a falling-out, but neither of them would speak of it.

That was what my life became. I buried myself in the business of the plantation and spent considerable time in Spanish Town and Kingston overseeing my shipping business. Being there was balm for me: the silent house, Sukey fixing my favorite meals without my having to ask for them. As for the *Sea Nymph* and the *Dragon*, they were making regularly scheduled packet and passenger trips, and Jonas and I were pleased with the results of our purchases. Even my father, far away in Liverpool, having heard from Jonas of my venture, wrote that he was glad I was taking advantage of the education he had provided. I read the letter with distaste and threw it into the fire.

Once or twice again I rode out to see Whitledge at Arcadia. I did not attend his wedding, giving some poor excuse at the time, but the fact that he never again asked after Bertha—other than a vague *How is your wife these days?*—led me to assume the gossip had somehow reached him. After a handful of outbursts at balls that shocked half the county and confirmed the suspicions of the other half, no mention of a dinner or a ball was ever made to her again. Even so, she would often dress up in her finest clothes, insisting I dress up as well. She imagined herself going to the governor's ball, but we plied her with sangaree or with something stronger until she became unaware of the passage of time, and when she awoke we told her of the wonderful evening she had had.

Was that cruel? Perhaps it was, but we did not know what else to do. Jonas was with me to the end in this endeavor, but Richard turned against us both, holding me responsible for Bertha's disintegration, even as we did the best we could to prevent it from worsening. Once he even demanded to be allowed to take Bertha under his own care, insisting she would recover and be the woman she had been before I came upon the scene. I might have succumbed to this last resort, but Jonas knew his son better than I, knew he hadn't the will or the stomach to deal with his sister, and forbade it. Indeed, as it was, Richard rarely visited her apartment, always promising to do so the next time.

I spoke to him about it once, saying, as gently as I could, that Bertha might well enjoy an occasional visit from her brother. He, in turn, stared at me in surprise and countered that I was the interloper, coming between his sister and her family. I begged to differ, but he grew quite sullen, complaining that I had taken his sister from him and his father as well. I hardly knew what to say to that, but the coolness between us remained.

In the end, Jonas prevailed upon someone he knew who had migrated from Jamaica to Madeira and asked him to offer Richard some sort of position there. I never knew the whole of it, but I would not be surprised if Jonas had included a monetary offer to entice the move. Jonas was like that. He deeply suffered over the taint that his wife's madness had brought upon his children, and he would have done anything in the world to ease it from their lives. Thank God, I never had to worry over my own children of such a marriage.

Somehow, with Bertha tucked safely away in her apartment and without Richard attacking my motives at every turn, I fell into a more settled, calmer existence. As time passed, I realized how little true satisfaction I received from my business dealings. Yes, the income was rewarding, as were my business decisions in general—I was proud of my investment in the two ships. But I did not enjoy the daily work of it. I could not take satisfaction in besting my competitors as my father did. He reveled in the challenge of the chase, the thrill of the conquest, but I am of a different mind.

One day, in Spanish Town, I turned a corner and ran right into Geoffrey Osmon. We stared at each other, unbelieving, for a moment, and then burst into laughter, our arms around each other. Nothing would do but that we go to a tavern and renew our friendship over drinks. He was in town on business and proudly told me that he had moved up from book-keeper to overseer at an estate, and I was pleased for him. As for me, I revealed as little as possible about my private life, except that I was married but had no children. We spent a pleasant evening together reminiscing, and when we left, we promised to keep in touch, though I doubt that we really intended to.

Also, I joined the militia. One could choose one's regiment, and I wisely chose the mounted, as had Richard before me. Although we practiced regularly on the parade ground under the watchful eye of the governor, looking right smart as we did so, I learned far more strategy around Mr. Lincoln's table than I ever did in the militia. I had thought I might make friends in that group, and they were certainly fine fellows, but their interests did not match mine, except for one who had a particular fondness for horticulture. From him I learned the pleasure of gardening, and the orchard at Valley View soon became my real interest and occupation.

That garden had been planted in Jonas' father's time but had fallen into disrepair over the years. It boasted the usual tropical banana plants with their cascades of fronds; avocados, whose shiny, bright green leaves never failed to lift my spirits; and citrus trees and ornamental palms and tamarinds, frangipani and mangoes; and it was there I became acquainted with the glorious Jamaican rain tree and its brilliant yellow flowers. As well, there was a magnificent cedro, whose aroma far exceeds that of the common cedar, and there was ginger and orchids of all descriptions, some native and others imported from Africa and Asia. I cherished the time I spent there, pulling up weeds, sitting on the little bench I had placed there, and reading. Sometimes I could even imagine myself in the orchard at Thornfield.

That summer Daniels announced he was leaving us. He had accepted an offer to manage a much larger plantation in the north. There was a time when I had pictured Valley View's two thousand acres, plus my seven hundred, as nearly as large as a plantation could be, but by the time Daniels left, I knew of places twice our size. Jonas and I were sorry to see him go, for he had been a fine manager, and I had learned so much from him.

"The full burden will be upon my shoulders," I said to Jonas. "I confess I'm rather looking forward to it."

He turned toward me in surprise. "You do not mean to take Daniels' place, surely?"

"Why not?" I asked.

"It's not done," he responded.

"But I was trained for it, was I not?"

Jonas laughed. "Rochester, your father wanted you to understand how a prosperous operation works, not to run it yourself. The owner never runs it; only the lowliest of plantation owners operate their holdings. No, of course not."

"Then I am nearly useless here," I protested.

"So, you think *I* am useless?"

"No, but—"

"You will take my place one day. Surely you know there must always be a master."

I did not know how to respond to that. Despite that I did not feel myself to be a businessman, I still wanted to be useful.

"Rochester," he said gently, "most men work all their lives for what you have."

What I had. A mad wife who looked and acted like a harridan. No one with whom to sit of an evening and read, or sing or play an instrument. No chance for children, unless I were to take a mistress, as Jonas had done, but I could not imagine bringing children into the world who would be destined only to become servants, like Molly, or like Sukey.

And then I thought to hire Osmon to replace Daniels. It was a risk, because Osmon had only been a book-keeper and later an overseer for a short time, and I did not know how well run the plantation where he had worked had been. Still, I desperately wanted for someone my own age to talk with, and I imagined I could spend at least part of my time in overseeing the plantation under the guise of teaching Osmon. As it turned out, we were a good pair. Despite that he had not been to university, he was well-read and had an abiding curiosity about the world. Many were the evenings that we would sit on the veranda, grog at our elbows, and talk, especially about literature. He had a distinctly different view of *Rob Roy* from mine, and he appreciated Jane Austen more than I ever had, and we spent a good part of a month reading and talking about a book by an American, James Fenimore Cooper.

I was surprised at this interest of his, and how deeply he understood the works, for he had made no mention of it on board the ship. To him, I probably appeared at first as unthinking as Bertha seemed to me, though I strove to make up for it. He told me his father had been a day laborer, too poor to educate him properly, but Osmon had always found pleasure and relief in reading. He had come to Jamaica as the next best thing to college—a place, he had hoped, where he could continue his education on his own. We both laughed at that, although he did insist he had learned as much in the past four years as he would have done at Oxford.

With Osmon at hand, I was able to feel as content as possible in my life at Valley View. Even Jonas seemed more at ease, usually joining Osmon and me in the evenings on the veranda. Though he said little, I know he also felt a kind of peace settling down into Valley View. "I was skeptical about your bringing on this green hand, but he is doing well," he told me after a few weeks. "Things could not be smoother, and of that I am abundantly glad."

CHAPTER 10

Some months after Daniels left and just before harvest, Jonas passed. It was a quiet death: he rose as usual, early in the morning, had some breakfast, but complained nearly right away of indigestion. I suggested he lie down for a while, and as he was making his way back toward his room, his legs suddenly gave way under him and he fell. I rushed to help him up and found his face gray and his body nearly limp, and it was all I could do to prop him up against me on the floor. I called out for help, and his walking boy came in. He took one look and ran back for damp towels with which to swab Jonas' face. He was nearly gone by the time the boy returned to place a cool cloth on his forehead. Jonas' eyes opened and he tried to speak, but he seemed not to have the strength even for a word. "I have sent for the physician," I said, nodding at the boy to go immediately. "Relax, you will be fine," I added. "It's just a little something."

But he and I both knew better. His hand raised slightly and clutched at my shirt, and his mouth moved urgently. I leaned closer to make out his guttural whispering, and at first I could make no sense of it, but then I heard the word, "Promise...promise."

"Yes, yes," I said, imagining his concerns for Valley View in his absence.

"Promise me...," he murmured again.

"Yes," I said soothingly.

He must have known I didn't understand. Summoning the last of his strength, he pulled me closer, and he said, "Promise…you will never… never…abandon my daughter."

These last words were barely more than a sigh, but they ran through me like a jolt. At the same time, I saw the light begin to fade from his eyes. "Yes," I said, "of course."

As if I had given him permission to pass, his hand released my shirt, his head slumped, and he was gone.

I held him in silence, feeling, somehow, as if the floor had given way beneath me. I could not imagine him gone. I stayed with him until the physician arrived, but finally I rose and left the house. There was nowhere to go, but I walked anyway, into a cane field, the stalks rising above my head, leaves brushing against my face, losing myself, losing for a while all sense of time and place.

———

We debated whether Bertha should be told, Osmon and I. Bertha now led a life quite opposite from that of the rest of us, rising at dusk, pacing through her little apartment, sometimes talking or even shouting at imagined beings, and sometimes playing childish games with Molly and Tiso while the rest of the world slept. She still had her fits of anger and attempted destruction, but she had ceased demanding my attention as a price for her imprisonment. Indeed, I didn't believe she saw it as such. When she wasn't at the center of a ballroom, she had always preferred dark, inclosed places, and now she lived a dark, inclosed life, which seemed to comfort her as little else could.

I was wary of disrupting her precious equilibrium with this tragic news, for I had no idea how she would react, nor if she would even be able to comprehend it. But Osmon thought that she should come to the burial as any daughter would. When we retired that night, the issue was still undecided.

In the morning, with great trepidation, I went to Bertha's apartment.

Molly let me in, and I crept into the little bedchamber, where I sat down on the bed beside my sleeping wife. As always, the shutters were closed, yet even in the gloom, relaxed in sleep, she was nearly as beautiful as ever. I did not then fully understand the weight of Jonas' last words, for Bertha was content in her rooms, or as content as she could ever be. Surely, I thought, we could continue our life at Valley View and go on as we had.

I touched her cheek lightly, running my finger along it from her temple to her chin. I felt her stirring, and then Molly was there with a lamp so that Bertha could see me and I her.

"You came," Bertha said, a slight smile on her lips.

"Yes," I responded, not knowing how to tell her.

"Is this a dream?" she asked.

"No, it is not a dream. I must tell you something." I leaned closer, smoothing her hair away from her face. "Your father . . . passed."

She shook her head slowly. "It is a dream," she said.

"No, I am afraid it is not."

"My father?"

"Yes. I'm sorry to have to tell you."

"But he is a young man."

"Not so very young, Bertha."

"Call me Antoinetta."

"Antoinetta."

"Yes," she said, smiling. "That is my true name." Then she smiled even more widely. "And you have come to me for love."

"I think this is not a good time," I said, starting to move away from her. But she pulled me to her.

Molly set the lamp on a table and quietly left the room.

Bertha held me tight. "Say my name again," she said.

"Antoinetta."

And then she wept, loud, excruciating sobs, and I wept with her.

Chapter 11

We buried Jonas Mason on a hill overlooking his beloved Valley View. We had sent a notification to his son, but there was not time in that climate to wait for him to return from Madeira, and Bertha refused to leave the house in the daylight. Daniels returned from his new position in Trelawny, which was kind of him, but despite our earlier rapport, he gazed across the grave opening at me as if I had been to blame, as if in his presence Jonas would never have left this mortal coil. After the burial he shook my hand brusquely, stared at Osmon appraisingly, and left. The neighbors who had come for the service followed me into the house, and we ate and drank the day away, sharing reminiscences of Jonas. Sukey came and stood in the background, and it only served to remind me that there had not been, as far as I ever saw, any relationship between the two. Is that what it becomes? A man fathers a child and has no sense of connection with her—or him—except perhaps to make sure she does not work in the fields? That she is not subject to the blows of the whip? That the child's life is at least not as bad as it might have been?

But no, in Sukey's case, he gave her to his business partner. Or sold her; I did not know which, and did not care to know. But I did wonder about her. She had never spoken of him; I had no idea what she thought of him, or if she thought anything at all. Yet she had come.

When all the guests had left, I walked silently into Jonas' chamber. A few articles were neatly placed on his desk; his riding crop leaned against the wall in a corner, though I could not remember when I had last seen him ride; his boots stood beside the chair.

The next day I sent Alexander for my horse, and I mounted her and rode into town. The house was quiet when I entered, but I could smell pepper pot, and I walked into the kitchen. Sukey was there at the stove. "I don't know what to say," I said, "except that I am sorry."

"Sir," she said softly. "He was a man; that's all."

She said no more, and I could not bring myself to state the obvious, but her words hung in the room between us. Then I said, again, "I'm very sorry."

She gazed at me across the room, and I could not tell what was in her eyes, but I left for my office, where I had papers to sign. And from there, even though it was late, I returned directly to Valley View.

———

Once again it was crop time—Jonas' death could not stop time, or our responsibilities to the land. Work continued around the clock; we slept when and where we could. I kept imagining Jonas' voice in my ear, telling me that it was not my job to oversee the operations, that that was what we had an overseer for, but I wanted more than anything to throw myself into it and to lose sense of all else.

After crop-over time, when things had once again quieted, I realized that I should have informed my father of the passing of his erstwhile partner. Hesitantly, I sat down one evening and wrote to him. It was an uncomfortable letter to write, as I had not forgiven him for the part he had played in encouraging my marriage, for I had become well convinced that he had known of Bertha's inclinations. But I did not mention Bertha. *Let him wonder,* I thought.

———

Richard returned with the spring, ready to be the master of the estate, riding up the valley in grand fashion on an enormous black stallion. It was evening, and I was on the veranda, and I watched him come, at first curious as to who it might be and, when he was close enough to recognize, curious as to what would transpire. In the short time that Richard and I had been friendly before my marriage to Bertha and before he left for Madeira, I had come to understand that his father's blunt assessment of him was, sadly, most likely correct: though there was nothing malicious in him, he was shallow minded, somewhat lazy, and prone to exhibit the trappings of wealth, as if they would convey a kind of distinction. I wondered if Madeira had changed him, but it did not appear so.

I descended the steps to greet him, and he was all smiles as he dismounted. "Everything looks fine," he announced. "Is the crop over?" As if he could see any canes still to be cut.

"It's over," I said. "It was a good crop. Your father would have been pleased."

"Ah then, I am pleased as well."

He gave a flit of his hand, as if his absence at the funeral couldn't have been helped, which it couldn't have been. Had we waited for him for the burial, Jonas' body would have been ripe indeed. "Yes, well," he said, "I am pleased you have kept up your end of the bargain until I could arrive."

"Yes?" I did not know what exactly he meant by that.

"You have already moved into a house on your own property, I presume."

I paused, and he filled the silence: "Oh? You have not yet done so?" A breeze from the east blew just then, ruffling his hair, and I should have taken it for an omen. "It is time, don't you think? You and Bertha cannot always live under the roof of the big house. It is mine now."

"It is not the usual kind of marriage," I said, although, truly, that was not his business.

His eyes hardened. "It is nothing to me what kind of marriage you have, though God knows my sister was a woman whom any man would have been happy to have as his wife. Where you live is not my affair. But this house"—he looked beyond me toward it—"is mine now. And that *is* my affair." He pushed past me and mounted the steps, and I understood then that Richard actually believed that he could so easily replace his father, with whom, during his father's life, he could barely exchange two pleasant words.

I could have let him go. I could have packed a bag and mounted my horse and left him with Bertha and his precious house. If I had known what was to come, I might well have, for in a few years' time slavery would be abolished in Jamaica, and even if Richard had not already run Valley View into the ground, he couldn't have dealt with slavery's end.

But Bertha was still my wife and I had a responsibility to her, no matter what else. And I had a responsibility to Jonas as well, and I knew what his plan had been. "It is not that simple," I called after him.

He had already reached the top of the steps, and he paused, not turning around.

"There is an entailment," I said.

He turned then and gazed at me, his eyes still hard, though I saw a question take root in them.

"You should speak with his solicitor," I added.

"*You* tell me," he said.

"I think you should speak with his solicitor, Mr. Arthur Foster. I'm sure you have met him, and you must have heard from him since your father's passing. You can spend the night here and ride back to see him in Spanish Town in the morning."

"I have no interest in riding to Spanish Town," he countered. "Send for him, if you must." And he walked into the house.

So I sent for Foster to come in the morning, and, having no particular desire to entertain Richard, I retired to my room.

The next morning Richard accosted me at breakfast, blaming me for Bertha's reaction to him and for her so-called miserable living conditions and for her appalling appearance. I listened quietly, for it seemed he had forgotten all about her deterioration before he had left, and he was convinced that her entire situation was due to my neglect. There was no way

I could make him understand what the situation was, or what had gone on before, or even what Jonas had arranged. That latter was not for me to reveal.

At midmorning, Foster arrived, a tall, thin man with a permanent stoop. He carried with him three parcels, bound in black, and I ushered him into the house, where Richard sat at Jonas' desk, trying to pretend he was attending to some sort of business. Foster tipped his hat to Richard, who nodded wordlessly at him, and then Foster said, "My condolences for your father's passing. It must have been a surprise to you. And, as a consequence, we have some matters to discuss."

I could not wait to hear how this would work itself out, but, perhaps mercifully, Richard stared coldly past him at me. "I think it is between you and me, Foster. It is none of Rochester's affair. He is only my sister's husband—if barely that—and not a blood descendant to my father."

Foster tilted his head. "As you wish, Mr. Mason," he said.

So instead I rode to Kingston, where the *Mary Rose* was in port undergoing some minor repairs. I was only too willing to let the solicitor explain everything in terms Richard could understand. I already knew the contents of Jonas' will: he had left the property to Bertha and Richard jointly, with myself acting on Bertha's behalf and in permanent control of operations, and entailed so that it could never be sold or mortgaged. Richard would receive half of all income, but beyond that, he had no material interest in the estate.

I intended to stay away for three days—I had business in Spanish Town as well, regarding the purchase of some additional land in the county—but as it turned out, that was two days more than necessary. Richard appeared at my town house on the second day, pounding on the door before I had even risen from bed. I could hear his voice the moment Sukey opened the door to him, and he did not stop yelling until I descended the stairs.

"You set him against me!" he accused. "You turned everyone against me! You Judas!" His face was red with exertion and I feared for his health.

"Will you have some breakfast with me?" I asked.

He balled his fists and for a moment I thought he was going to strike me. "I would not grace your table for all the tea in China! I will never speak with you again!" he shouted.

"I had nothing to do with it. It was your father's wish." I knew there was no point in saying that; he had already made up his mind. But I felt I needed to say so anyway, in my own defense.

"And you have shut up my sister in a prison!"

It was true; I could not deny it. But she preferred that prison to any alternative, and her own father and I had concluded that it was far better for her there than in the kind of place her mother was kept. And, at any rate, Bertha's mind had become a much worse prison than I could ever have concocted for her. I did not respond.

He ranted longer than I would have thought I could bear, and I listened wordlessly, until his fury abated and he gave me a final black glare and stormed out of the house. Hearing him leave, Sukey came in and refreshed my tea. "Are you all right, sir? Sometimes I think they *all*—"

"It's enough," I said. "We do not need to discuss it."

She nodded.

We never again spoke of that episode. *Sometimes I think they* all *are mad* was what I knew she had started to say. I could not dispute it, but if I had let her finish, I would have had to.

———

I thought I had seen the last of Richard, but I should have known better. That same evening I returned to Valley View and was astonished to find him seated on the veranda, waiting for me, no doubt.

"We are not finished," he said as I mounted the steps. "You have no right to take over *my* inheritance."

"You will receive one-half; the other half is your sister's. I am only the executor."

"It is *I* who should be in charge!" he shouted. He had been drinking, more than he should, I thought.

"It was your father's decision," I said.

"You drove him to it! You turned him against me!"

It seemed nothing I could say would dissuade him, and, unable to unleash his pique anymore on me, he rose abruptly and strode into the house, slamming the door behind him. I remained on the veranda, giving him time to cool down, but within a few minutes he returned, a box under his arm. I could hardly believe what he was proposing. Surely even Richard was not that foolish. Or stupid.

He made a great show of opening the box, displaying inside the two dueling pistols.

"Richard," I said.

"Now," he said. "Now we will settle it."

"Have you ever in your life fought a duel before?" I asked.

"Have you?"

"This is foolish," I said.

"Foolish? *Foolish?* You think I am a fool to demand my own rights?"

"Where did you get those?" I asked.

That stopped him for a moment. He had not expected to be interrogated. "They were my father's," he said in a voice suddenly less agitated.

"Have you ever fought a duel?" I asked again. "Do you know how to load and cock them?" I knew, but only in theory, for Mr. Lincoln had drilled us on all kinds of weapons, but I had never used the knowledge, for in the mounted militia we had only sabers.

He shoved the box toward me. "Take your choice," he said.

"I will not fight a duel with you."

"Coward!"

"Richard. If you should kill me, who will look after your sister? Will you take care of her from now on?"

"She is *your wife*."

"If you kill me," I repeated, "she will be my widow. You will be her only relative. Are you ready for that responsibility?" I remembered that he had tried to claim that custodianship before, but I did not think he would have ever been actually willing to do such a thing.

But, in response, he boasted: "I would take it gladly."

"But don't we need seconds?" I asked. "Don't we need to make arrangements to meet at dawn?" That was what always happened in books.

He stood there in silence until I understood that he was trying to figure out how to get out of such a rash act, and I took a step toward him. "It does neither of us any good to kill the other," I said. "No one gains by that, Bertha least of all. Your father would not have wanted us to end up this way."

"My father," he said, nearly mournfully. "*My father*. He gave me up for you."

"Your father loved you. As he loved Bertha. He wanted only to see the two of you provided for."

He stared at me.

"Is that not right?" I pushed. I could have said more. I could have asked if that was not why Jonas and my father had conspired to bring me to Jamaica, why I was sent at the age of thirteen to apprentice in a manufactory, for even in those days, Jonas had known that his son would never truly want to be a planter, that he would always rather someone else do the work.

"It was...," he started, but then he paused, and I could not tell what was in his eyes. "My father thought I was worthless," he said at last.

"Your father loved you. That is why he tried to make sure you and Bertha would still have Valley View for the rest of your lives."

The opened box was still in his arms. "He came to love you more," he said petulantly.

"He gave me the responsibility; he gave you the living, because you were his son. Without ties, simply because he loved you."

I saw the resignation come into his face then, and I pitied him. And envied him.

Chapter 12

Richard stayed for a few more uncomfortable days before returning to Madeira, and life returned to its usual rhythm at Valley View, with me at the helm. And then, in late July, I received a letter from England. I did not recognize the hand; it was not my father's. I took it from the girl and opened it as I walked toward my desk, but the first line of it startled me into stillness.

> *My dear sir—*
>
> *I am saddened to inform you that your father, Mr. George Howell Rochester, was himself deceased this May last, due to a bout with the fever, his physician tells me.*
>
> *Among his papers, I found your letter, dated 10 February, which he may or may not have answered, as he was, I believe, not yet stricken. Since you are his sole surviving heir, I am awaiting your instructions concerning the Estate that has thus fallen to you.*
>
> *Yours, at your service,*
> *Paul W. Everson, Esq.*

I stood stock-still for some moments, dumbfounded, a sound like the rush of wind in my ears. I cannot even recall the thoughts that ran through my head, and it is difficult now to say what stunned me most: that my father had died or that I was his sole heir. Where was Rowland? If something had happened to him, why had my father not informed me? And, when I got past all that: *my father's estate had fallen to me?* What, exactly, did that mean for me? For my future? My God, for my whole life?

———

Within an hour of reading the letter from Mr. Everson, I found myself riding madly toward Spanish Town, as if to escape from—or catch up with—my own future. I had thought that my future lay forever in Jamaica; now, with this single letter, everything had changed. Over the years, the town house had become a refuge for me, and I had made it my own. There were not just law and tax books, as in my father's day; now there were histories and travel books, novels, and even poetry. There was a globe in the study and maps on the walls. I could not be at Valley View without Bertha remaining at the back of my mind, a burden I was unable to ever fully set down. But in Spanish Town I felt more free. And now; now I needed space to think. *My father dead*: I still could not comprehend it. I wished, not for the first time, that Mr. Wilson were still alive, that I could go to him for advice, for the comfort of his wisdom, he who had been so much more of a father to me than my own had ever been.

At the town house, Sukey had been in her room, I suppose, but she always came at the sound of my hand on the latch, unless she was otherwise fully occupied. This time she stopped and took a step back immediately when she saw me. I must have looked wild with anguish or despair or at least confusion.

"What is it?" she asked. "Has she—"

"My father has died," I blurted, and her face turned suddenly as still as stone. I cursed myself, for in my own shock and confusion I had momentarily forgotten her connection with him. "I am very sorry," I said. "It has been a shock." What else could I say?

She took another step back and put a hand to her cheek, almost as if I had slapped her. "And I am sorry for you," she responded.

I came closer and put my hands on her shoulders, and I felt a shudder run through her, and finally a quieting and a deep breath, and she gazed up at me.

She was only a few years older than I and she had been kind to me since the day I had arrived, and at that moment I felt certain we both needed someone to hold, so I held her. We stood there together in the hall, and it would have been an easy thing to do whatever I chose, and I could have, for she was mine. But I would not. If for no other reason: she had been my father's; I could never.

I remained in Spanish Town for nearly a week, and in that remove I was able to take a close look at my life, at what it had been and what it could become, nearly overwhelmed by what might be opening to me. I wrote to Everson immediately, requesting more information on what had happened to Rowland, and a more thorough accounting of the estate and its buildings—did it contain Thornfield-Hall? It *must*. And what part of it was under management? It was strange to me, to lose my father and brother at the same time, at least in the same letter, and stranger still to think that I might be able to live, again, at Thornfield one day, perhaps even soon.

Thinking back, the choice appears easy, but at the time, it was the furthest thing from obvious. I had a life in Jamaica—if one could call it that—but, yes, it was a life, and in fact a good one in many ways. I had as many responsibilities—and opportunities—on the estate as I chose to pursue, and I had the respect of my neighbors. I had a good friend and overseer in Osmon, despite that many of my equals thought he was beneath me. It was true my wife was no companion and never would be, and I could never bring her into company, but there could be worse burdens for a man to bear.

Still—was Thornfield mine? *Mine?* Were the fields and the woods and the moors that I had once wandered and loved now *mine?*

But I had made a pledge—a promise—to God, and to Jonas, to keep Bertha as my wife, never to abandon her. God knew, she was not my wife in any sense but the legal and the moral, and never would be again, but neither could I abandon her. Given that, what kind life could I have there? What kind of life could I have in either place?

On my return to Valley View, I took a walk in the orchard, the one place on the estate in which I felt true peace. In the evening breeze the avocado leaves brushed against one another in a soothing rhythm and a nearby parrot screeched into the night. The citrus scents of oranges and lemons surrounded me, and I closed my eyes and imagined myself at Thornfield—would that it were so easy to transport oneself from one place to another, with no cares and no responsibilities. After a time, I rose and went to the house and drank a mug of grog and another and another, and I finally managed to find my way to my own bed and fell into a deep sleep.

I dreamed of Bertha, of her setting the cane fields afire, of her attacking me with a machete, of her tormented screams that went on and on, until I woke and realized it truly was her screaming—as she did often enough in the night hours—and I rose, still half-drugged with sleep and overpowered with a sense of hopelessness. I could choose either Valley View or Thornfield; it made no difference: I would always be burdened with a mad wife.

I opened the jalousied window further, expecting a rush of cooler air, but it was a steamy Jamaican night, the beginning of the hurricane season. The moon was setting bloodred in the west, half-covered with clouds; mosquitoes flew into the room, surrounding me with their maddening whines. Bertha—two rooms away—still screamed curses at me, at her father, at God, at whomever or whatever she could imagine. *What kind of life is this?* I asked myself. *It is hell. She is as sound of body as she is unsound of mind. She will live for years and years, and I will have to endure it all.* I suddenly felt I could not. I could not go on living in that hell, and I wished I had not talked Richard out of a duel, wished I had stood before him and let him shoot me as many times as it would take for him to find the target and kill me. For I felt, at that moment, that only death would relieve me of a burden that had become too heavy to bear.

I pulled a little trunk from under my bed and unlocked it and took out the case with the loaded pistols. I had placed it there after Richard had left, for safekeeping. Now I lifted one, heavier than I would have thought, and I held it in my hand for a time, thinking how easy it would be. I put it to my temple. So easy.

But then a breeze came and brought with it a rainstorm. The skies opened and rain poured down, cleansing the air. I closed the window, pistol still in hand, and watched the rain pelt against the casement. As quickly as it had come, the storm was gone, moving off to the west. I opened the window again and the air felt purer, and with it came a new sensibility. I laid the pistol back into its box and locked it away.

I left the house then, my mind already working, and I strolled across the wet grass to the orchard, where I walked again among the trees. A sweet breath of wind from Europe was on my face. I could sense the thunder of the distant Atlantic against the shore and my heart swelled within me. *There is a way,* I thought. *There has to be a way. If I must, I will take Bertha with me. She can be cared for as well at Thornfield as she is here.* For England—*Thornfield*—pulled on me, now that I knew it could be mine, *was* mine.

In the morning, I doubted my decision. How could I do such a thing? Did I not have a good life at Valley View? How in God's name would I make a life for Bertha at Thornfield? But my heart had already fled there, and I slowly came to understand it fully: Thornfield-Hall had always been my home in ways that Valley View had never, and would never, become.

In the following weeks, as I anxiously waited for Everson's response, I shared with Osmon my situation. It was only fair that he should know, since he would have full management responsibility if I returned to England. We had often spoken of the future of Jamaica and the life we led. He was a keen reader of history. "Men wait and watch and take advantage when they can," he said one evening. "It will be no different when the negroes finally rise."

"Then why do you stay?" I asked him.

"Because I, too, seek my best interest," he answered. "I am closer to the negroes than you are. I can sense the tension. But in the meantime I am saving money. When the sugar estates are gone, opportunities will come to the men who have the experience and the funds in hand."

"How soon do you think it will be?" I asked.

He gazed absently at the cigar in his hand. "Who knows?" he said, turning away and staring out over the cane fields. "You will be lucky if it's another eight or ten years," he murmured.

"And what then?"

"God knows," he said.

God knows, I thought. "Are there rumors of an uprising?"

"There are always rumors," he responded.

"But still you stay."

"I am a single man."

I nodded. He was alone in the world, with no wife or children or possessions other than the savings he had accumulated. But I; I had Bertha. And Bertha would go nowhere without Molly and Molly would go nowhere without her Tiso.

He rose finally, bade me good night, and made his way to his cottage, but I sat for a time by myself on the veranda, wondering how it would come. In the distance I could smell the remainders of the cooking fires from the negro quarters. If they rose in rebellion, would it be on a quiet night like this? Or would it be later in the year, when the rains came every day and sometimes the wind whipped trees back and forth and the sea rose in a fury that damaged boats and buildings alike? Or would they wait until winter, when the weather was calm and dry and the fields would burn more easily? Or would they plan it at all—would they simply rise at the least expected moment and for no reason, like Bertha, lash out in a passion that could not be sated until all was destroyed? And perhaps not even then.

CHAPTER 13

Despite that I had anxiously awaited Everson's response, when I actually held it in my hand I could barely bring myself to open it. It was my future. My entire life-to-be was inclosed in that slim packet. I took it into Jonas' room—a room in which I still felt his presence—and I sat at his desk and held the missive in my hands. Finally, I forced myself to break the seal.

> Mr. Rochester—
>
> You ask about your brother, Rowland Howell Rochester: perhaps your father did not inform you that Rowland Rochester was seriously wounded by a careless shot during a grouse-hunting expedition in Scotland in the month of August last year.
>
> Your father was quite distraught, but the seeming culprit was a Scottish earl, and the barrister was of the opinion that pursuance was inadvisable, given the lack of available witnesses. If I may say so, I believe it was that blow that weakened your father's constitution and made him even more susceptible to the dropsy to which he was already inclined. I am greatly sorry to be the bearer of such unpleasant news.

You ask the extent of the Estate that had once been your father's, and then your brother's, and now has fallen to you. Thornfield Estate is as it has been for the last many years, consisting of something over thirty-five hundred acres. It includes a residence, Thornfield-Hall by name, and the village of Thornfield and its chapel, as well as the village of Hay. And of course there are the usual outbuildings suitable for such an Estate, most of which have been reasonably maintained, as well as the farm cottages, also in acceptable condition, although that is the responsibility of the tenants. The property in all provides a comfortable living of ten to twelve thousand pounds per annum.

In addition, there is Ferndean Manor, a residence including some five hundred acres, mostly wooded, a distance of thirty miles or so from Thornfield Estate, a property that the late Mr. George Howell Rochester used as a hunting retreat.

The Hall has not been occupied for the last year, since the unfortunate accident that took your brother's life, and the servants—only a few remained at any road—were dismissed.

I await your instructions as to your intentions for Thornfield Estate and the ways in which I may be of further service to you.

In addition, there are a number of other ventures that had been your father's. You will find them listed on the accompanying page.

Sincerely,
Paul W. Everson, Esq.

I sat back in Jonas' chair, the letter still in my hand. Beyond the window was the lush expanse of the cane fields. I felt I should be grieved over the loss of Rowland and my father, and I suppose I was, but what grieved me more, I realized, was the absence of any sense of deep feeling toward either of them.

And, as well, I understood that despite all my fretting those last weeks about what path I should take, I had only been waiting for what this letter affirmed. Thornfield was mine. I had not lived there in nearly twenty years, had not seen it in nearly ten, and even back then I had come to it almost as a stranger, an intruder in a place where I had no right to be. Cook had greeted me then with tears in her eyes, and I had sat down at that familiar, worn kitchen table with trepidation. My father would not have wanted me there; Rowland would also almost surely not have wanted me there, and it was only by the grace of God that he was absent when I came.

It was for Thornfield itself that my heart longed most. With Rowland dead for more than a year—Rowland, dead! I still could not fathom it—Thornfield had been standing empty. I could not imagine it: empty. If I could have flown there within the hour, I would have. But, in fact, there was a great deal for me to do in Jamaica before my journey could become a reality.

It was already nearly November. The skies would have turned gray over Thornfield, and the cold would have descended on the moors, and the Hall would be damp and cold with no one living there to keep up the fires. It was one thing to completely disrupt Bertha, to take her to an unfamiliar place with unfamiliar sounds and smells and food and people. But it would be downright cruel to do so in weather she had never known, in a chill that would creep into her bones in ways she had never experienced. And Molly: Bertha would go nowhere without Molly, and yet the moment Molly set foot on England's shore, she would be free. I could, as her master, force her to leave Jamaica, but if she were unhappy in England, I could not force her to stay.

No, I would have to be patient. I would have to wait until spring, wait so that we could arrive in June with its pleasant weather, its lark-filled skies and flower-strewn meadows. I had to bring them both, Bertha and Molly—and Tiso, too—at a time that had the best chance of enticing them.

The thought of it excited me so that I even began to imagine that a new place could perhaps enthrall Bertha and cure her mind. *It could be, could it not?* I told myself.

I wrote back to Everson, thanking him, and engaging him to make a visit to Thornfield and find a suitable housekeeper and begin looking for a butler and cooks and maids, to make ready for my arrival in early June. I urged him to see if he could entice Mrs. Knox and Cook to return, and perhaps even Holdredge, and any former housemaids and footmen. I was giddy with the thought of bringing them all back, just as it had been, but in another moment I knew that could not be. They would be gone, scattered to other houses; they would have no reason to come back to Thornfield, save for my desire to have them there. To them, I was still just a wild little boy.

And I asked Everson to send me the name of the neighborhood physician as soon as possible.

The next day, my plans forming as I went, I rode to Kingston to check the sailing schedules of my ships, though I knew them by heart. Of my five ships, only the *Calypso*'s schedule could be worked to make such a passage possible. I would need her in port in Kingston for at least an extra week to prepare for our passage.

I had decided to ask Whitledge to be the plantation's attorney on my behalf, and to that end, I invited him to visit Valley View, and to meet Osmon for the first time since our journey from England. I needed to assure myself that the two of them could put their original distaste aside and work together.

The evening Whitledge arrived we sat together on the veranda for a time, spending the night in true West Indies style: passing the sugar and limes around, each of us mixing our own drinks, lighting our tobacco and drinking our grog and catching one another up. The two had greeted each other warily, Osmon in part because he felt quite capable of taking my place himself, but, as I hoped, the Jamaican style of congeniality worked its magic, and soon we were all three chatting amiably. Whitledge proudly displayed the miniature that he carried of his wife and their baby daughter, but Bertha went nearly unmentioned, except that I told them that I would be taking her and Molly with me. I gave Osmon what I hoped was a meaningful look when I revealed that information, and he nodded. I had already confirmed with him that he was not to mention our leaving to anyone, for if anyone else were to know the plan, it would be all over the plantation before sunrise the next day.

I noticed a lessening of the strain between the two men as the evening progressed, and the next day, when we made a tour around Valley View, I purposely allowed them to ride beside each other while I brought up the rear. As well, I kept my silence so that Osmon could point out salient features and respond to Whitledge's questions. The tactic worked quite well, and soon the two were engaged in a quiet conversation in which I had no part. It was important that I could trust the two of them in my absence, and, if that day were any measure, it seemed Valley View would surely prosper in their hands.

The next morning, after breakfast, Osmon and I stood on the veranda and watched as Whitledge mounted his horse for his trip home. "You two will do well together, I think," I said to Osmon.

"What about you?" he asked. "How will you fare?"

I gazed over toward the sugar mill, where negroes were on the rooftop, patching the cane-lattice roof. "I think it will be good for me," I said.

"And for your wife?"

I had already started toward the door, but I stopped and faced him. "How could things be worse for her?"

But of course, things can always be worse. I had hoped the change would be a good thing, though God knows why I thought so.

———

Everson's response arrived in February, assuring me that he was diligently seeking appropriate persons for employment at Thornfield-Hall, although he regretted the fact that none of the old servants whom I remembered were available. Holdredge was now the landlord of the Thornfield Inn in

Hay and had no interest in becoming a butler again; Cook had passed on; and Mrs. Knox was elderly and infirm and living in York with her sister. He did, however, send me the name and address of a physician, Mr. Daniel Carter, a young man of "sterling reputation," who would be most happy to assist me in whatever ways I desired.

I composed a letter that very same day to Mr. Carter, requesting his assistance in assessing the Grimsby Retreat, of which, I told him, I had heard. Truly, it had been years before, when I made my short visit to Thornfield, that Cook mentioned to me that my childhood playmate had worked there. I found it necessary to reveal to Mr. Carter—in strictest confidence, I urged—that I was returning from several years in Jamaica and was bringing with me a relative who required the kind of care that I believed the Retreat to provide. As I wrote those very words, I felt as if I had been suddenly struck on the chest, for I had promised Bertha she would never be placed in the sort of institution her mother inhabited. I did still truly intend to hold to that promise, but I felt it necessary to know, at least, what kind of place was available if all else failed.

As I sat there at Jonas' desk, in his room, his last words came again to me: *Promise you will never abandon my daughter.* I had made promises— to Bertha and to her father, in addition to my wedding vows—and I felt myself standing at a precipice now, not knowing if I could keep those promises without destroying my own life. But I was still determined to do the best I could.

My letters completed, I sealed them, placed them in my pocket, and called for my horse. I had three final tasks. One was the selling of the last of the business interests in Jamaica that I had received from my father, including the three sailing vessels that had been his. I would keep the *Sea Nymph* and the *Dragon*. I had already made initial inquiries regarding my intentions to sell and had in hand an offer; all that was needed was to finalize the papers. Did I feel guilty, selling all that my father and Jonas had built, save for the plantation itself? No, I did not. Certainly, I could have kept it all—surely my father would have—but I was not my father. I had learned, in the years I was in Jamaica, that I indeed had a head for business, but I hadn't the heart for it, and I had no regrets in ridding myself of all of it.

The second task was to meet with Foster to arrange for the papers to be drawn up for Sukey's freedom. She would not receive them, or know anything about them, until after I was gone. And I left her the town house, to do with as she pleased. I felt a bit of regret at those arrangements, for Sukey had been a comfort, and Jamaica itself had done me no harm, had, in fact, pushed me into becoming a man. But there was nothing left for me there, except waiting for the day the slaves would revolt or Parliament would order them freed.

The third, most delicate task was to visit a chemist and purchase enough laudanum to quiet Bertha on our journey. I would have to receive instructions from the chemist as to its use, that was certain, as I needed to take care that she not become addicted. But I could imagine no other way to accomplish the journey that lay ahead of us.

When I had done all that, I could mail the letters I had written. I would be fully committed and fully prepared to quit Jamaica forever. There was, as I rode the familiar road from Valley View, a gnawing feeling in the pit of my stomach. I was about to burn my bridges behind me. I wanted to feel a release, but instead I felt only trepidation.

BOOK THREE

CHAPTER I

In all the years of my life, this return to England was my first important decision—beyond the purchase of the *Sea Nymph* and the *Dragon*—that had not been orchestrated by my father, and I took substantial joy and confidence in that fact. I kept this decision to myself, save for Everson in England and my solicitor in Jamaica, and, of course, Osmon and Whitledge, and I made sure they understood the importance of confidentiality in this matter. Even Molly would not know until absolutely necessary.

I was determined to ensure that Bertha would be as comfortable as possible on the tedious sea journey to England, both for her sake and for the sake of the other passengers aboard the *Calypso*. Keeping her calm, quiet, and content would be a significant part of that, so late in March I started visiting her regularly in the evenings, bringing a mug of grog, and sitting with her for a time. Bertha was always happy to imbibe, and I had learned to carefully measure out the laudanum, pleased to note how it quieted her just at the hour she was most agitated. Often, she grew dreamy and seemed to enjoy recounting her reveries. Sometimes she was convinced that she had ten or twelve babies of her own, and she would spend much of her time counting them in her imagination, as if she expected some of them to go missing, and I would feel a pity for her, she who so wished for a child and would never have one. Occasionally she spoke of her father, seeming unaware that he had passed away. She never mentioned her mother.

In fact, Bertha grew so docile that I have to admit that I thought a time or two how easy it would be to keep her forever in this dream state. But I had studied the dangers of that path, and I had no wish to put her into a permanent addiction, no matter how convenient it might at first appear.

When the date of departure at last came, I gave Bertha a slightly larger dose in the evening and then turned to Molly and revealed my plan. She was to pack up three valises for a journey; I told her we would be leaving Valley View early in the morning and by noontime we would be on a boat. Her eyes widened. "Leave Jamaica?" she asked.

"Yes," I responded. After all my careful plans, I hadn't realized until that instant that Molly might refuse to follow Bertha.

"Me cannot," she said.

"You may bring Tiso, if you choose."

"Me cannot."

"Why?" I demanded.

"Me only know Jamaica," she said, and I knew exactly what she meant.

And yet, I had something to offer her. "Come with us, to England," I said. "You and Tiso. You help me get my wife to my home there. If..." I paused, for I did not really want to make the offer, yet I might as well, as it was true whether I wanted to suggest it or not. "If you do not want to stay, you may come back here, to Jamaica. But"—I moved closer and held her with my eyes—"in Jamaica you are a slave and always will be. In England there are no slaves. In England you and your daughter will be free."

She caught her breath at that. "No slave?" she asked.

"No slave."

She shifted her eyes away from me, as if she were trying to see herself in the future as a free woman. "How long?" she asked.

"Six weeks, more or less, to get there," I said. I did not emphasize the *more*.

"After?"

I did not want to give her the after, but I knew I must. "After, you do as you wish. After, you are free."

"And Tiso?"

"Tiso also."

She stared at me straight on, as if deciding whether she could trust me.

"Have I not always treated you well?" I urged. "With honesty? Have I not?"

She nodded then, and relief overwhelmed me. If Bertha was to be wholly my responsibility after we arrived at Thornfield, so be it. At least the worst would be over. Or so I thought.

———

The journey, though not easy, was, thank God, uneventful. Molly and Tiso and I managed to get Bertha on board early, when the few onlookers simply saw a gentleman and an obviously unwell woman settling into the first stateroom. Although Bertha asked several times into what house I had moved her, she seemed as content there as she had been in her chambers at Valley View.

As for myself, I had a stateroom of my own, at the far end of the saloon. I would still come in the evenings to soothe Bertha with a mug of grog and a bit of laudanum, but for the rest of the time, I was able to move about as if she were unknown to me. Otherwise, I spent a great deal of my time making plans.

Of course there were whisperings among the passengers about the mysterious woman in the first cabin. There were speculations that she was an illegitimate daughter of Bonaparte, returning to cause trouble in France, or perhaps even the Infanta Isabel Maria of Portugal—poor Bertha, if she had still had her senses, would have enjoyed such an elevation in status. Others suggested she was a dangerous prisoner of some sort, off to meet her fate. Those who noted my evening visitations to the stateroom eyed me with curiosity and suspicion, but I ignored them. The one or two gentlemen who eased close to me in conversation did not get from me any satisfaction, and eventually they gave up, but the distance that I forced myself to maintain from them made the journey frightfully tiresome.

In the first week of June, we heard the cry of land being sighted, and nearly all the passengers scrambled up to the deck to see for themselves, I among them—I, perhaps, more excited and more anxious than the rest. I had not quite expected it, but when I heard that cry, when I saw for myself that dim strip of darkness at the horizon that I knew to be England, my heart fairly burst out of my chest.

Everson met us at the port of Liverpool, which was a frenzy of activity. It was, I realized, markedly different from the West Indies, where almost no one felt the pressure of time or the urgency of accomplishment. I had forgotten the pace of life at home.

Since I had visited Bertha's room before debarking the boat, with what I hoped was one last dose of laudanum, the four of us—Molly and Tiso and Everson and I—contrived to move her, leaning heavily on my shoulder and already beyond consciousness, from the boat to the waiting coach with a minimum of difficulty. The crew and lingering passengers stared after us, disappointed, I imagine, to see that the sequestered passenger was only an oddly dressed woman with wild black hair, and not some fiend destined for the gallows.

Everson waved us off as we left, the whipcrack and the rattle of the coach telling us we were on our way. We were traveling as the mail coaches did, at maximum speed, changing horses every hour or two, and with any luck we would be at our destination before nightfall. I sat back, satisfied that all had gone so well.

Though it was well past teatime when we drove through Millcote, twilight still lingered; but it was nearly dark when we came upon the road to Ferndean. By then my heart was pounding so strongly in anticipation that I could barely hear the footman's question: "Shall we enter, sir?"

"Yes, indeed," I called to him.

Nearly there, I thought. Everson had assured me that the house was ready, with heavy draperies at the windows and strong locks on all the doors. There was also to be a woman from the village, Mrs. Greenway, staying there as housekeeper and cook, who would teach Molly and Tiso the ways of the Yorkshire countryside.

I still held hopes of enticing Molly with her freedom and with the run of Ferndean Manor, to stay on at length in England. If Molly stayed at Bertha's side, I assumed, things could remain for Bertha very much as they had been at Valley View. I could have my own life a half day's ride away at Thornfield-Hall: close enough to Ferndean for me to be able to respond to emergencies, yet far enough that I might even forget from time to time that I had a mad wife ensconced there.

At last the lights of Ferndean appeared, and when we approached, Mrs. Greenway opened the door as Molly and I helped Bertha into the house. Tiso ran ahead of us, darting from room to room and up the stairs and back down, wonder in her eyes and a broad grin on her face. She poked at the fire in the grate, opened cupboards in the kitchen and chests in the bed-rooms, rubbed her bare feet on the rugs—she had never seen a rug before, for in the climate of Jamaica, no one save the governor had rugs—and she even tested a dipper of water from a bucket to make sure, I presume, that water in England tasted the same. From the expression on her face, I gath-ered that it did not, though I myself had never noted the difference.

I had assumed that I would be able to leave for Thornfield-Hall the next morning. But it became clear, from the way Bertha clung to me as I tried to pay the coach driver, that my plan would have to wait. As soon as I could, I took her up to her room and began undressing her for sleep. She was only half-conscious, but awake enough to reach for me and try to pull off my clothing as well. I pushed her unruly hair back from her face and tried to lock her eyes with mine. "It is late, Antoinetta," I said urgently. "You must sleep."

"Fuck me," she whispered, reclining on the bed.

"It is too late for that." I kept my voice steady.

"Fuck me, you ugly bastard!" she screamed.

Suddenly I was filled with hate: the crudeness of Bertha's language, the wildness of her hair, disgust even for the life I had lived for the past five and a half years—a slaveholder, married to a madwoman. I wanted it over; I wanted to be shut of Bertha forever. I could have screamed as loudly as she had—but I pressed my lips together and left her in her new bed, in her new house, screaming at me as I left for a walk around the grounds. It felt unforgivable: Ferndean and Thornfield now defiled by what I had done in bringing Bertha to England.

———

Before Bertha awoke, I returned to her room. Just outside her door I found Molly and Tiso curled up on the floor, a rug over each of them for warmth. In my rage, and to my shame, I had forgotten all about them, about the fact that they would not have understood that beds awaited them in Bertha's chambers—that they indeed were expected to sleep in beds. They did not know so many things, and it was up to me to make sure their way was made smooth; I could in good conscience do no less.

Indeed, although I wanted nothing other than to hurry off to Thornfield-Hall, I saw that I would have to stay at Ferndean much longer than planned. I remained with Bertha that morning since she seemed distraught by her new surroundings, and later I had a long conversation with Mrs. Greenway, who, I learned, was fearful that "the people from across the sea," as she called them, would make unreasonable demands of her. "It is only that I am suddenly a widow with no savings and no other source of income that I am here," she confided to me. "I have no idea what West Indian people eat. And the black ones—do they speak English?"

"Yes—they are servants to the white woman, and I imagine they are as afraid of you as you are of them," I told her. "The white woman is not well. Did you know that?"

"Yes, sir, I did, sir. But in what way unwell I was not told."

"She is, to put it bluntly, a bit mad."

"A bit mad?" She took a step back, looking around as she did so, as if searching for the nearest escape route.

"Not *dangerous*—she sleeps much of the day and keeps mostly to herself at night." I hoped that description could be made true. "The two servants"—I could not bring myself to use the word *slaves* in England, and, indeed, in England they were not slaves—"will need to learn English food and how to prepare it, and of course how and where to get it. They are used to gardens supplying most of what they eat."

"We have gardens," she said stoutly, as if I could not know that.

"Yes, but here gardens are seasonal. In Jamaica, crops grow all year round."

"Oh," she said. "Will they eat eggs?"

"Yes, and bacon as well. They are used to big breakfasts."

"Porridge?"

"Not so much porridge. But they will eat soup."

"For *breakfast*?"

It was just then that Tiso peered into the kitchen, and Mrs. Greenway, seeing her, gave a start. Tiso slipped back out of sight. "Tiso," I said, "come here. Meet Mrs. Greenway."

Accustomed to doing as she was told, Tiso stepped back into view, but not into the kitchen.

"Mrs. Greenway," I said, "this is Tiso. She is a good child, well behaved."

Mrs. Greenway smiled cautiously, but for a moment she hardly knew what to say or do. Then she recovered herself and said, "Good morning, Tiso."

"Tiso," I said, "are you hungry?"

The child was startled: she had never been asked such a question by a white person before.

"I am sure Mrs. Greenway can fry up some eggs for us both," I offered.

Tiso stood stock-still, staring at her feet. A white man had offered her food; a white woman was to cook it for her. She had no idea what she was to do.

The next day, having assured myself that Mrs. Greenway was capable and sensitive to the situation, I sent for a hired horse and set out for Thornfield. It would have to be a short visit, I knew, but I could wait no longer. This was what I had worked toward for the last six months; indeed, it had been my greatest dream from the moment I was sent away three days after my eighth birthday. I had not known it as a child, but now I did: there had never been another home for me, only way stations on a homeward journey that I had somehow always dreamed of making.

And now I was taking the final leg of that journey, riding across the meadows and fields and woods, seeing that dark shape in the distance that was again to be my home, then—coming closer—the outlines of it: the chimneys at its four corners, the stonework balustrade defining its roof, the wide, plain front, even the stables and outbuildings. Suddenly I spurred my mount, dashing headlong toward Thornfield; I could not reach it soon enough. And when I did, and tied the horse and lifted the latch and opened the door, a flood of emotion overwhelmed me, and I stood just inside the door in awe, as if I had entered a cathedral, and I wept.

CHAPTER 2

I was not inside the door more than a minute before a man appeared, whom I took to be the newly hired butler. "Munroe, is it?" I asked him.

"Yes, sir," he said. "I am sorry, sir. I did have knowledge from Mr. Everson that you could be arriving one of these days, and I apologize that I was not at the door to greet you."

"Never mind, Munroe," I said. "In fact, I was pleased to be able to open the door for myself, to step on my own inside a place that is so special to me. And if you do not mind, I will take my time, on my own, renewing my acquaintance."

"Of course, sir." He stepped back, excused himself, and left.

I stood there, taking in the familiar scene: the portraits and the pendant bronze lamp, the great clock standing sentinel—at the sight of which my fingers felt again the childish urge to trace its carvings. Then into the dining room, and the drawing room with its same ivory-colored rug bordered with flowers. I glanced above the fireplace, but the only painting that hung there was the same hunting scene that had tormented my days as a motherless child. I paused in that room, memories flooding my mind, nearly overwhelming me. And slowly I climbed the broad, curved staircase to the second floor. To the right was a guest bedroom, and another, and another, until, at the end of the hall, the nursery and the schoolroom, and then I turned the other way and strolled down the hall. To the left of the staircase was the room that had been my father's, and afterwards, I supposed, my brother's, when Rowland came of age and my father moved permanently to Liverpool. It was the room that now would be mine.

But when I opened the door, the world stilled. There it was: the portrait I had so hoped to recover, hung above the bed as if it had never been anywhere else. I walked closer, almost unbelieving. My mother, whose memory to me was only in this portrait, gazed back. Rowland must have brought it back from Jamaica and hung it here above his bed—for she was his mother too, and he was the one who could remember her.

I stood before that painting, my mind numb, then moved closer and took it from its place above the bed. I carried it out of the chamber and down the stairs and into the drawing room, where I removed the hunting scene and hung my mother's portrait there, where it belonged. In that moment I came to fully realize not only how much I had always loved Thornfield, but also how much I had lost: Carrot and Touch, dead. My father and my brother—and my mother—all dead. Even Mr. Wilson and Jonas, dead. Now Bertha—my pitiful, hateful bride—was all the family I had in the world.

——

Back in the entrance hall, I returned to Munroe, who stood silently in a corner, awaiting my orders. "If I may," I said, "a light lunch. Nothing heavy."

"Yes, sir," he said, and disappeared.

As I waited in the dining room, the new steward stopped in to greet me. His father had been my father's longtime steward, and this younger Ames had worked side by side with him for some time, taking over fully two years earlier, when his father passed away. We talked of my concerns and his, and I was pleased to find that he seemed as competent as his father had no doubt been. Afterwards, I took a walk into the fields—now that I was not in Jamaica, it did not seem an extraordinary thing to do. The haying had started, and I watched the workers, their scythes swinging in rhythm.

I almost envied their simple, backbreaking labor. The sweet, grassy scent of new-cut hay hung in the air, and I closed my eyes and listened to a lark as it rose high in the sky, and, from a distance, the call of the cuckoo. I stopped in to the little church at the gates to Thornfield Park and strolled through the graveyard there, the last resting place of my ancestors—and of my father and my mother. Even Rowland's body had somehow been brought back from Scotland. Rowland. When I saw his gravestone, when I thought of him, I felt neither sadness nor joy, just an emptiness.

That night I slept in the room that had once been my father's. I felt strange in that place, as if I were an interloper, for the only bed I had known before at Thornfield had been in the nursery. When I awoke, the sun was still low in the sky, but I could not force myself back to sleep. I knew I must return to Ferndean and take care of my responsibilities there, so I rose and threw on my clothes and pulled up my boots, and, unshaven, I hurried down the broad front stairs. I had not even reached the ground floor when Munroe appeared.

"Mr. Rochester, sir," he said, striding forward, nodding a bow.

"Is it likely that Mrs. Keen has bread and jam in the kitchen?" I asked.

"I am sure she is preparing a proper breakfast. If you will allow me—"

"Please...I will just go into the kitchen myself and see what she has there."

"Sir..." He looked at me in puzzlement.

"We will sort it all out, I am sure, Munroe, but for now I must hasten back to Ferndean." I was already walking away from him.

"Yes, sir," he said.

Hearing the note in his voice, I turned back to him. He looked quite forlorn, as if bereft of all responsibilities. "I apologize if I seem abrupt," I said. "I shall just take a bit of breakfast in the kitchen and then be off."

"In the kitchen, sir?" He had no way of knowing it was for me one of the most comfortable places at Thornfield.

"Yes." I nodded.

I found Mrs. Keen in the kitchen, where she was already frying up bacon and cooking eggs. After I had turned down her offer to send them to the dining room, she studiously avoided any more discussion, surely thinking her new employer strange. So be it. She was thinner than the only cook I had known at Thornfield, which had seemed to me a bad sign, but her tea the night before had been very tasty, and the breakfast turned out to be perfectly cooked.

When I made to leave, Munroe appeared at the door to see me off, as a good butler should. "When shall you be returning, sir?" he asked.

"I am not sure," I responded. "But I will send word."

"Very good, sir."

I wished I could stay. I wished Ferndean did not weigh so heavily on my mind. I wished I had a better plan. I wished I had a choice.

———

At Ferndean I found a silent house, except for Mrs. Greenway working quietly, with Tiso lingering uncertainly in the doorway. I took a seat at the table.

"Is your mother with Madame?" I asked her.

Tiso mumbled something.

"And Madame Antoinetta?"

"She sick," she whispered.

I sprang from my chair. I had completely forgotten about the laudanum; Bertha would be suffering grievously from the lack of it. I ran up the stairs, but the door was locked. I pounded on it until Molly opened it. Beyond her, I saw Bertha lying on the bed, bedclothes and rugs mounded on top of her as if she were trapped in an ice cave in January instead of a comfortable room in the middle of June. I could see that she was shivering and hear her anguished moans.

"Get coffee," I said to Molly. She darted from the room as if she knew where coffee was to be found.

I sat on the bed beside Bertha, reached my hand beneath all her coverings, and found her arm and her shoulder, and I stroked them gently. "It will be all right," I said to her. "I will make it right." I talked like that, as if I could make well again everything that had gone wrong in her life and mine, with words alone. Would that I could.

When Molly returned I dropped just a bit, but almost all I had left, of the laudanum into the cup and urged Bertha to sit and drink, and afterwards, she stared at me as if I were a stranger and then blessedly slipped back into her own world. I turned away and caught Molly watching me. "We will have to make her right again," I said.

I asked Mrs. Greenway to send for Mr. Carter, but she insisted on going herself. Perhaps she was just as happy as I for an excuse to leave Ferndean. Meanwhile, I sat with Bertha and pondered our situation: how long it would take to wean her from the laudanum, if indeed it could be done. What if it had permanently worsened her condition, and she remained ill—or, worse, became even more unmanageable? Back at Valley View, I had imagined the worst would be the ocean journey. It had not occurred to me that that was only the beginning.

Oh God, I thought, *what have I done?* Would Molly and Tiso accommodate themselves to life in England? And what if they simply refused? What if Molly, now that she was no longer a slave, decided to leave? Or insisted the two of them be returned to the only home they had known? Would they not miss Jamaica as much as I had pined for Thornfield? And could I expect Mrs. Greenway—or any other cottage woman—to stay in a household such as this?

Feeling overwhelmed, I rose and walked to a window and gazed out, but all one could see from Ferndean's windows were trees, and then I finally left the room. Molly and Tiso were just outside the door, sitting on the floor and playing their game of bones and pebbles. The two of them did not acknowledge me as I walked past, as slaves would not, though, I realized, servants would have done. England was so different from Jamaica in so many ways, and yet it was essential that Molly and Tiso remain with us, for I now saw that I could not manage Bertha without them.

When Mrs. Greenway returned, red-faced from her exertions, she announced, "I have sent a cottage boy. I told him to make sure Mr. Carter understood it was urgent."

"Thank you," I said. Then I added, "Have you had dealings with Mr. Carter?"

"Oh no, sir. He is for the gentry. The apothecary is good enough for me. But I have heard good things of him."

"Mrs. Greenway," I said, "the white woman—"

She waited, expectantly.

I had thought to say, *The white woman is my wife.* But what came out of my mouth was: "The white woman is the daughter of a friend of my father's. He has passed on, and I have the care of her. She is English, but she has never been here. Neither she nor the other two know much of our way of life. They are used to different foods, different weather, different customs to some extent, even somewhat different clothing. The two negroes are not used to shoes, for example."

She was nodding at all I was saying, though I had no idea if she did so as my employee or if she really understood the half of it.

"There is a great deal for them to get used to," I added. "You could be of immense help in that respect."

"Yes, sir. And they will understand me when I talk to them? The child never says anything."

"Did you not hear me speak to the child, in English?"

"But—but she seems to have so little facility in it herself."

"They speak in patois—a dialect. You will get used to it. They understand what you say. And the child is shy."

She took a breath as if to speak, but then did not.

"As for . . . the woman," I said, "she cannot help the fact that she is mad. She can be difficult. But Molly and Tiso are used to her; they will deal with her. If you will just be kind enough to help them learn their way."

She straightened: a soldier receiving orders. "Yes, sir." And then she added, "Are they...are they...?"

"In Jamaica they were slaves. They know that here they are not. To be honest, I do not know what will happen with them. For that reason"—I leaned closer to her over the table—"it is important to me that they feel at home here. That they find a decent life here."

"Are they mother and daughter?" she asked. I nodded. "And where is the father?"

"In Jamaica, things are different, as I said. There is not always a husband."

"Oh."

"You will not disdain Molly for that," I said, rather more sternly than I meant. "They are used to being slaves. It is a harsh word, but it is the truth. They do not understand exactly what their roles are. To them, disobedience has always meant the whip. Therefore, if they are unhappy, or fearful, they may run away." I gave her a meaningful look. "We would not like it if that were to happen," I added.

"Oh no, sir."

"Then I think we understand each other."

"Yes, sir, Mr. Rochester."

"It may actually be, Mrs. Greenway, that little Tiso could be of help to you in your work."

She nodded solemnly, and I left, with that seed in her mind. Tiso was old enough to need occupation and young enough to adjust to new ways. I hoped it would work.

———

Mr. Carter arrived at Ferndean that afternoon. He was impeccably dressed, with a warm and pleasant way about him that made me feel immediately at ease as we greeted each other. I led him into the library as if it were my own home, though it was almost as unfamiliar to me as it was to him.

"It is a pleasure to meet you at last," I said, motioning him to a chair.

"You have just arrived, I understand," he said.

"Three days ago. But as you know from my letter, I have immediate concerns regarding my wife."

"Your wife?" he said, and I remembered too late that I had referred only to "a relative."

"Yes, indeed. My wife." I cleared my throat. "She is, unfortunately, the victim of some familial disorder. You may recall that I asked you to look into the Grimsby Retreat."

"Yes, and I did. You are not, by any chance, a Quaker, are you? It's a Quaker institution, designed primarily for members of their own persuasion."

"For Quakers only?"

"Not exclusively, but nearly. I believe that funding is sometimes difficult; perhaps if a person were to offer a generous gift, they might consider..."

I settled back in my chair. "Tell me about the place."

"It has a fine reputation; they exercise what they call the 'moral treatment' of their patients, believing that if a mad person is treated as if he were a rational being, whatever spark of rationality remains will be nourished."

"And they have cures?"

"Yes, of course. But you must realize that not everyone is curable. May I see her?"

If the Grimsby Retreat could offer a cure, I thought, it might be worth taking her there, despite my promises. Surely both Jonas and Bertha herself would have wanted me to follow that path. But first I must deal with the immediate issue.

"Actually," I told him, "I have a more pressing need of help with her." I explained about the laudanum, and that she needed treatment for her addiction to it. And I went on to tell him of her habit of sleeping in the day and roaming at night, her need for secure surroundings, even her rages and her occasional violence. It was not necessary to tell him so much, I am sure, but once I began to unburden myself I could barely stop, and he listened, calmly, quietly, without judgment.

When I had told him everything, including my intention to keep our marital connection a secret, at least for the time being, I led him upstairs to her room and he saw her lying there, not even slightly restless. He asked me when she had had her last dose. I told him, and he nodded again and opened his valise and measured out something into a bottle and gave me instructions. He would be back every day, he said, to monitor how she was doing, and he urged me to send for him if there was a crisis and warned me never to give more of the medication than he advised. She would, he said, be quit of her addiction in a month or six weeks, if I obeyed his instructions.

But those six weeks were among the worst I could have imagined.

CHAPTER 3

Mr. Carter was true to his word: he came every day, shortly after noon. Bertha was at first usually asleep, but as the effects of the medication became less and less, she grew more and more agitated, her rages and visions and screaming continuing for hours on end. I could not imagine what Mrs. Greenway down in the kitchen thought; Tiso generally stood in Bertha's chambers with her back against the door, not quite willing to leave her mother, but staying as far as she could get from the terrifying creature Bertha had become. For her part, Molly followed Bertha around the room, murmuring, singing, caressing, trying all sorts of tricks to distract her, to soothe her to sleep. Sometimes they worked, but more often they did not. The first time Mr. Carter saw Bertha's outbursts, he suggested to me that I tie her down to keep her from hurting herself or others, but I could not bring myself to do that.

At Valley View, I had relied on Molly to tend Bertha, and I had gone to her apartment each day for only a short time, but at first at Ferndean I made it my business to be with Bertha as much as possible; it was my fault, after all, that she had become addicted and that she now suffered from withdrawal of the medicine. Only now and then did I ride back over to Thornfield for respite. When she slept, I would slip away to find some peace: I could not have kept my sanity if I had had to stay constantly locked up with her as Molly did. As for Molly, I urged her to give herself a rest, to leave Bertha for a while and go to the kitchen or out into the garden. But she would not leave Bertha's side, sending Tiso to fetch the meals or a jug of water when Bertha demanded it, or to empty the chamber pot.

And Mrs. Greenway was true to her word as well. As much as she could, she took Tiso under her care, luring her from Bertha's bedchamber with sweet treats and promises to teach her how to cook in the English style.

After those initial weeks, when it became clear that the laudanum addiction had run its course, it was also clear that Bertha had further regressed. She rarely slept now, neither in the day nor at night, and she roamed her bedchamber with a fury, grumbling and murmuring to herself, telling herself incoherent tales, laughing wildly. Once, left alone for just a moment, she pounded her bare hands against the mullioned windows until one shattered, and she cut herself quite severely. When Molly returned, Bertha was in the process of licking up her own blood as it ran down her arms.

In desperation, Carter and I rode to the Grimsby Retreat to speak with Mr. Mitchell, who was in charge there. I had regained my hopes for the place as time had passed, realizing more and more each day how futile and mistaken had been my plan to house Bertha permanently at Ferndean. As we rode through the grounds, I began to feel optimistic. Grimsby was a grand estate, with handsome spired buildings and walkways across the gardens and green lawns. It was nothing at all like the gloomy asylum in Kingston.

Inside, as we were led to Mr. Mitchell's office, I noted the tall windows, the bright rooms, the lack of unpleasant odors. Bertha could be cared for here as well as anywhere, I told myself. It was not at all what Jonas was thinking of when he exacted that promise from me, and my spirits rose at that thought.

Mr. Mitchell was a compact man whose dark curls surrounded a round face, making him look younger than his years. He sat in his office and listened patiently as Carter and I explained Bertha's situation, and when we had finished, he just nodded his head as if confirming something. I looked uneasily at Carter, but he was staring out of a window.

At last Mitchell spoke. "She seems like a difficult case. A mother in an institution always portends badly."

"She has not always been so," I said. "Six years ago, when I first met her—"

"She is how old?"

"Thirty-two years."

He nodded. "They often have twenty or twenty-five years of normalcy, these ones with a familial connection."

"But I understand your institution—"

"The Grimsby Retreat, as you may or may not have been told, has always been designed for people who have an upbringing in the Society of Friends."

"But you do make exceptions," Mr. Carter countered.

Mr. Mitchell looked down at his desktop. One hand went to a silver letter opener on his desk, and he turned it over, and then over again. "We do, yes," he said finally, nodding again, his eyes fastened on the letter opener in his hand. "But only when we perceive that the prospective patient would benefit by being here. From the way you describe your wife's circumstance, in all honesty, I do not see that as a possibility."

"Mr. Rochester is prepared to pay—" Carter began.

"Yes, I understand that," Mitchell replied, looking at Carter, not at me, as if I were not even in the room. He rose from his chair. "But I do not see that this is a possibility for his wife." He strode toward the door, to usher us out.

"Why not?" I demanded, remaining seated.

He sighed. "The Grimsby Retreat is an institution that intends a cure for each of our patients. It is not a holding pen for incurables."

Incurable. The word struck me like a blow. "What in God's name is there, then?" I cried, suddenly seeing only an abyss for my future.

"There are other institutions. I can recommend—"

"Man, for God's sake, have pity!"

His tone did not change in the slightest, despite that I was nearly on my knees. "I am very sorry, but I have the welfare of our patients to consider. You are wealthy enough: hire caretakers for her." He opened the door. The interview was over.

Carter and I rode back in silence for a time, and then he said, "Mitchell makes a point. There are other institutions."

"Not like that," I ventured, and he nodded agreement.

Promise you will never abandon my daughter, Jonas had said, and I knew what he had meant. I saw in my mind's eye Bertha's mother in her cell, raging endlessly.

———

As I was caught up in my private dilemma at Ferndean, word had spread throughout the county that the younger Mr. Rochester was newly arrived from Jamaica. Notes appeared from neighbors expressing their dismay at the untimely deaths of my brother and father, inviting me to tea or other social outings. Clearly, all were eager to meet Thornfield's mysterious and apparently eligible new heir.

At first I sent my sincerest regrets to all invitations that came my way. Instead, to fill my days and bring myself some comfort, I replaced the piano in Thornfield-Hall, which had never been played in my memory, and I took great pleasure in playing it when I could get away from Ferndean. I found in the attic a few faded music books, marked, I imagined, in my mother's hand, and I took them downstairs with tears filling my eyes at the thought of the songs she might once have played.

But life at Ferndean, and even at Thornfield, had become so barren, so taken up with my concerns for Bertha, that I knew that unless I was willing to go mad myself, I could not continue forever as I was. And so, once, and then again, I began to accept the social invitations, and I found myself enjoying the respite they provided, the forgetfulness they permitted. I astonished myself when I eventually began to flirt with some of the young women who were present. It was not honest and it was not right, but it was such a relief to be in the company of people with whom I could have an actual conversation.

Sometimes those conversations turned coyly to the Jamaican women who lived at Ferndean, and I knew that the neighborhood gossips had been at work, and I nodded and described Bertha once more as the daughter of a friend of my father's, a woman left orphaned and alone whom I had brought back from the West Indies, since she no longer had family there. It was all true, of course, except for my omitting the fact that I had married her. On several occasions a woman or two would venture the possibility of calling on my guest, as they referred to her, but I told them she was very ill, and possibly contagious from some rare tropical affliction, and they soon left off the notion of socializing with her.

Though Bertha was in truth not contagious, caring for her remained a struggle. Molly and Tiso tried to keep close watch, but even so, a few times she escaped, fumbling her way through the unfamiliar house. On one occasion she even threatened Mrs. Greenway with a poker from the hearth and was only prevented from doing real harm by little Tiso. Twice she managed to get all the way outside before she could be brought back. The fear of fire was always upon us, for if Bertha mindlessly dropped a candle or knocked out an ember from the fire and set the house ablaze, everyone could be burned alive in bed. Secretly, I worried as well about more deliberate destruction, for in her madness Bertha was insensible to the consequences of her acts.

Two or three more times she put her fists or an elbow through windows, cutting herself so badly once that we had to send for Mr. Carter in the middle of the night. On that occasion he spoke to me dolefully after bandaging her arm. "This cannot go on, Rochester. She will not improve. Ever. You do understand that? And she is a danger to herself and to others. You must find another place for her."

"I cannot." They would not take her at the Grimsby, and I could not allow myself to think of sending her anywhere else, where the practices were bound to be less humane.

"Have you thought of divorce?" Carter asked me once.

I had, I confess. But Parliament allowed divorce only if the man had two witnesses to his wife's adultery, and—while Bertha had surely been no angel at those Jamaican balls—I had no such witnesses to bring forth. So I simply said, "I promised I would not abandon her." And what kind of man would I be if I did not keep my vows?

"Rochester. Think. What kind of life have you here?"

How many times had I asked myself that same question? Mr. Wilson's words about his wife's sister had echoed back to me in my periods of despair. *Even the fiercest of beasts—wolves and bears—take care of their own.*

But Carter was right: Ferndean did not suit for Bertha. It was too large, with too many furnishings and windows too accessible, and it would be damp in the winter with so little sun. She needed a smaller space, someplace more confined, someplace with windows that allowed in light and air but that she could not reach and break, someplace where she could be safely kept, but not abandoned.

Then it came to me.

———

Yes, oh God, for better or worse I moved her there, to the largest storage room on the third floor of Thornfield-Hall itself, where the windows were too high to see out of—or reach—where the entrance could be made secure, and where I would be within immediate reach if she were to take sick or something disastrous should happen. Within a handful of weeks I had it rebuilt into an apartment with a sitting room and a bedchamber, walled off from the rest of the third floor and with a separate staircase at the opposite end of the hall from the one the servants used. It was perfect, I thought. The door to the staircase was hidden by a drapery hanging from floor to ceiling, which to the casual observer would appear to be some sort of wall tapestry.

At the time I thought the move to Thornfield was a masterful stroke, and Carter did as well. I was sorry to have to let Mrs. Greenway go, although in truth I think she felt relieved, but she did admit that she would miss Tiso.

Tiso was thirteen, old enough to want to spread her wings, to explore, but I could not give her the run of Thornfield-Hall as she had had at Ferndean, for that would raise too many questions. Occasionally she slipped out of Bertha's chambers, and more than once I found her rooting in the storage rooms, as I had done as a child. I could not be harsh with her for that, but nevertheless I had to order her back. She always went, reluctantly, and I thought, *This will not last. A child of that age will not stay cooped up forever.*

And she did not. Once, and again, and then again, she slipped out at dusk when her mother and Bertha were still sleeping. I caught her at it myself when I was returning one evening, and I marched her right back to the apartment, where Molly, just awakened, gave her a look of fire. I knew what she was thinking, but I did not stay to hear her say it.

Despite the scoldings, the child could not be contained, and a week later she slipped out again. I knew nothing about that latest excursion until I next visited Bertha's chamber, and there was Tiso, sitting on the floor, her legs stretched out in front of her while Molly applied a poultice of tea and leaves to Tiso's foot. Bertha was sitting in a corner, shaking her head and muttering to herself.

"What happened?" I asked.

"She out again," Molly said angrily. "She step on something."

I bent and touched Tiso's foot, and she gasped and jerked it from my hand, but not quickly enough that I did not feel the heat of the inflammation. I took her foot more firmly, and this time she did not try to draw it away. It was a puncture wound. A rake? A nail, perhaps?

I sent for Carter, who examined her foot and ordered hot soapy water to wash it well, and he made another poultice. He took me aside, but by then I knew as well as he, from the burning heat of her foot and the swelling creeping up her leg, that she was in trouble. Molly knew too, and she refused to leave Tiso's side. I begged Carter to do anything more that was possible, but he just shook his head, powerless to prevent the inevitable.

I stayed most of the time in Bertha's apartment, keeping watch over her, so that Molly could tend Tiso. I urged Molly to move the poor child to a proper bedchamber, but she would hear nothing of it. I did what I could for the two of them, but the sallowness of that feverish little face was an accusation I could hardly stand. I was barely man enough to confront it.

Tiso lasted weeks, unable to eat, and in time convulsions set in—it was a horrid way to die, and there was nothing Carter or Molly or I could do to ease her suffering. She grew delirious at the end, with Molly hovering over her, and even Bertha paced the floor and moaned in sympathy.

When it was all over and the little girl had breathed her last, Molly remained still, holding Tiso, the tears running down her face. I could barely bring myself to look at her: I had brought such misery upon her, and upon little Tiso, by moving us all to England, and now I could not think of a way to make things right.

That evening, Molly came to me and announced, "I go back to Jamaica."

"What will you do there?" I asked.

She stared at me then in silence, with a steady gaze unlike any I had ever seen from a negro in Jamaica.

"I will give you money," I said, "and your papers. You will not be a slave, at least."

She nodded. She did not thank me. Why should she?

CHAPTER 4

I asked of Molly only that she remain until I could find a replacement to care for Bertha. I had no idea how I would go about doing such a thing, but it was necessary, for I did not see how I, by myself, could manage daily care for that madwoman for the rest of my life. Molly seemed skeptical when I offered the deal, recognizing, I am sure, that it would be nearly impossible to find someone to replace her. But she said nothing.

Both of us knew full well that I could not find anyone in a month or two months or probably even a year. But I had not reckoned on Mrs. Greenway. She had become, in the wider neighborhood, somewhat of a recognized authority on Mr. Rochester and the women he had brought back from Jamaica. Kindly, she kept my secrets, though she did enjoy her elevated position.

One day, she came to see me at my visiting hours. Almost immediately on my arrival at Thornfield I had revived my father's practice of meeting on Wednesday afternoons with Ames and my gamekeeper and any cottagers who wished an audience. Few cottagers came, and those who did seemed to have mostly manufactured issues, created to make an appraisal of the new master of Thornfield and weigh him against the previous Mr. Rochesters. Sometimes I wondered how I stacked up against those two: my imperious brother and my demanding father.

When it was her turn, Mrs. Greenway settled herself into the chair in my study, wearing her best bonnet and newly blackened shoes, and after a few pleasantries she informed me that she had had a visitor. Did I remember a girl from my childhood named Grace?

"Yes, I do," I responded. "She was some kind of scullery maid here at Thornfield, I think, in those days. And her little brother, Jem, helped in the stables—he was my age and we sometimes played together when he was not busy."

"I have known Grace much of her life, poor thing," she said. "She has not had an easy time, though in all truth, I must say, life is not easy for many folk. But Grace worse than Jem, I imagine, because she was a girl. Her mother was dead and her father a hard man. She ran off to marry just to get shut of him, I think. But the man she took turned out worse than nothing. He beat her; even when she was with child he beat her most awful. When her son was born, Grace took the infant and left. This was a long time ago."

I had an idea where all this was going, but there was really not work enough at Thornfield for more than the staff I already employed.

"Grace is shy with people," she went on, "always has been, and she is worse now. But she is no fool. I gave her tea when she came and we talked for a time—I talked mostly, for visiting over tea is more my way than hers. But in the end she asked the question she must have been pondering. 'Is it true that Mr. Rochester has a madwoman in his care?' she asked me. Now, sir, as you know, I have been as discreet as ever you could wish for, and I must have sat for a moment with my mouth open, so astonished I was, and not knowing how to reply. 'What makes you ask such a question?' I finally said.

"'I saw him at the Grimsby Retreat,' she said. 'He did not seem to me to appear as a benefactor, but instead as someone asking for help. I have often seen them come, the families of the mad.'"

I could imagine Mrs. Greenway leaning forward in her chair at that.

"I asked her what she was doing at the Grimsby," she went on, "and she told me she worked there, had done for years, as does her brother and her son. And she said she knew you from childhood and she had recognized you, as you look so much like your father. I didn't know what to say, for I knew you required secrecy in this matter, but I did tell her that she must speak to you herself. I don't know if she has come to you. She is an odd one and you might not take her seriously, but I think you should, as she might be able to help you."

"She has not come to me," I said.

"Yes." Mrs. Greenway nodded. "I feared that would be the case."

"Have you a way to encourage her to come?"

"I don't see her as a matter of course. It's only that she came to me, and I thought...I suppose I could..."

"Never mind," I said. "I shall handle the matter. But I am grateful that you came to me. Tell me: you have seen the states that Bertha experiences. In your opinion, could Grace...manage her?"

Mrs. Greenway straightened, tucking back her chin. "Grace is sturdy; she has had to be. She has had her share of ill treatment. She is far stronger than she might appear. And she is not stupid."

"Thank you for telling me these things," I said.

She rose, understanding the dismissal, but she had one more thing on her mind. "I wonder what you have heard of our Tiso."

Our Tiso. My heart seized at the thought of that child. "I'm sorry, I should have informed you," I said, for Mrs. Greenway had thrown herself into mothering that little girl. "Tiso—you remember how she never wore shoes—she stepped on something and cut her foot, and it became infected"—Mrs. Greenway gasped at the word—"and she died."

Mrs. Greenway's eyes filled, and she pulled out a handkerchief. "Poor little thing," she whispered.

"I'm sorry I didn't tell you sooner."

She rose wearily, and as she left, she turned to me. "The last name is Poole," she said. "Grace Poole."

The very next day I rode to the Grimsby Retreat, and when I was told that Mr. Mitchell was not available, I announced that I would wait until he was, and I sat down in his office. It was more than an hour before he appeared, and when he did he had the abrupt demeanor of a man who had seen a supplicant too many times already.

"I come not to beg you to change your mind, but to ask you some questions regarding one of your staff here," I said to him.

He sat down at his desk.

"Grace Poole, by name," I added.

He frowned at first. Then he said, "Yes, she is a keeper here."

"What can you tell me of her?"

He pulled a record book from the shelf behind him and paged through it until he found what he was searching for, then nodded in confirmation. "She has no marks against her. Are you thinking of hiring her?"

"Would you recommend her?"

He paused for a moment, and then he said, "I would not *not* recommend her."

I waited.

He leaned forward over his desk. "It is not an easy task to find good persons for a place like this. The most compassionate sometimes do not fully understand the requirements of their positions, and the hardest cannot seem to...to—"

"And where would Grace Poole fall?"

He shook his head. "She is a bit of a mystery. She is pale, and one might assume she is weak, but in fact she is very strong—I have seen evidence of that. She is not a Quaker, and so we cannot give her greater duties, for she does not understand our philosophy here. For you, that should not be a problem. I honestly do not think, from what you have said, that there is hope for better for your wife than what she is now, and in fact most likely her condition will only deteriorate. If you require a keeper, someone who will make sure she is safe and secure, Grace could manage it, I am sure."

"Could you spare her?" I asked.

"Spare?" He chuckled. "People come and go here, especially those in the lower ranks. If she is looking for a position with you, she is surely already on her way out."

I rose. "I assume you will not take offense, then, if I approach her."

"She has not already approached you?"

"An intermediary only."

"Ah." He nodded. "That would be Grace. I wish you well with her."

"Thank you," I said, taking up my hat.

"It is a Christian thing you do."

I turned in surprise.

"Many is the man who would rid himself of such a woman as you have described to me, and think the better of himself for it."

"Good day, sir," I said. I could not wait to leave. I could not pretend to be such a man as he seemed to think me; I had come precariously close to abandoning Bertha, despite my promises, and I would have done so if he would have taken her in.

A few days later I interviewed Grace, who, true to her nature, said little, but what little she said comforted me that Bertha would be in capable hands. I brought her with me to visit Bertha, who on this occasion, and sadly not for the first time, appeared not to recognize me. Indeed, the sight of me seemed to enrage her—and as she moved to attack me I discovered firsthand that Grace Poole was indeed competent to deal with her. I arranged for Grace to move into the apartment immediately, so Molly could train her in Bertha's care.

There remained only to have papers drawn up for Molly's freedom, and I secured her passage on the first ship back to Jamaica.

By the time Molly was ready to leave, Grace Poole had a firm enough grip over life in the third-floor apartment that I had no longer reason to fear for Bertha's safety, nor that of Thornfield-Hall itself. The rest of the servants had known little about Molly's duties and less about the woman she tended. No doubt they were curious, but there was a kind of respect for the place—and perhaps for me—that precluded their gossiping beyond the walls of Thornfield-Hall. As for the rest of the neighborhood, I let it be known that the women from Jamaica were returning to their home there, and I hoped that that rumor would put to rest any further inquiry about my unusual guests.

It appeared to work, for the most part. It was now partridge-hunting season, and the surrounding estates were alive with hunting parties and teas. Though I tried never to appear *too* eligible, I made a point of accepting and reciprocating just enough invitations as was proper, for I knew I could not avoid society forever. And, beyond that, I craved the normalcy that came from a world away from Bertha.

At Thornfield, as the time drew near for Molly to depart, I sensed a kind of regret in her. I wondered how she would fare on her own back on her island. She had been Bertha's body servant from childhood, but she would return a free woman—yet freedom does not guarantee a living. When the time came for her to leave, I pressed two hundred pounds into Molly's hand and wished her well and thanked her for her devotion to her "missus." I could not trust myself to say more.

She stood silently before me for a long time, and I perceived she was struggling inwardly, and I waited.

"Sir, I think you do not know—of the baby," she said, gazing past my shoulder.

"What baby?" I wondered suddenly if Molly had been mistreated by someone at Thornfield, if she were fleeing England in shame. "Yours?"

She frowned, and she must at first have thought I meant Tiso. "No, no. If missus, if she cry for her baby, her little boy, tell her he is fine— sleeping."

I was dumbfounded. "Bertha had a baby? She was...she was married before?"

"Not marry. She a child. Tiso age."

"What happened to the baby?" I asked, my heart pounding in my ears.

"He gone."

"Where? Where did he go?"

"People came. They took him."

I stared at her, my mouth dry. "Who was the father?"

Still looking beyond me, she shrugged, as if there was no more to tell.

———

As the days passed after Molly's departure, I tried to establish for myself a routine of riding out in the morning, overseeing my fields and cattle, enjoying the peace of my holdings, without worry for Bertha. I was no longer concerned for her immediate safety, but I could not rid my mind of Molly's parting news: Bertha had a child, a son. And he would be grown now, nearing twenty years of age, if he were still living. Ought I to try to find him? I wondered. Did he know who his mother was—*what* she was? Would he want to know? The thought of his birth, and loss, tormented me. If only I had known sooner. She had spoken of lost babies, but I thought it was only one of her delusions. The anguish she must have felt—a child herself, weeping for her lost baby. Surely this was part of what had driven her to madness; I could not help but wonder if a reunion with the child might once have stopped her decline.

I began sitting with her again, as often as I could, hoping to speak with her about the boy and offer some sort of comfort. But she was already too far gone. Sometimes in her garbled rants, I still heard that word—*baby*— but her tirades had become so nonsensical that I could never be sure. Perhaps I only imagined it.

I wrote to Richard—to the last address I had for him in Madeira— asking about Bertha's child, but a reply never came, only the letter itself, returned to me. And I wrote to Mr. Arthur Foster, my solicitor in Spanish Town, who still kept an eye on business related to Valley View, and though he responded promptly, he, as well, knew nothing. It was what I had half suspected, for in a case like that, would they not have done it all clandestinely, given the infant to someone who was leaving the island, for—for where? Madeira? Saint Thomas? England? The Americas? Or could he have remained in Jamaica somehow, hidden safely away from the family? What if the child had died? It was a mystery I had no idea how to unravel.

As I hit wall after wall in my attempts to trace the baby, I grew increasingly frustrated and tried to put it out of my mind. To what end, after all, was I searching now for this motherless boy, to reveal to him the monster his lost mother had become? Why torment myself this way?

Yet, often I couldn't sleep, and I paced the floor, roaming around the rooms. Above me, my wife roamed as well, watched over by Grace Poole, trapped inside her head and trapping me there with her, neither of us free. Thornfield-Hall had been my dream since I had left it as a child, but in these months it had transformed into a kind of nightmare. And a prison, for the both of us. I began to realize that there was nothing for me at Thornfield, none of the joy or peace it had once promised, as long as Bertha—poor Bertha—weighed on my soul.

That thought, and the future it promised, pressed upon me those dark nights until I felt that it would pull me under. *Have I not a right to a life?* I asked myself. *Have I not as much a right as the next man?* Time and again I had tried to do the moral thing, had I not? And how had that worked out for me? *No,* I told myself, *this stops here.* I was done with it, done with Bertha, or as much as I could be. I would start over, and find love on my own terms.

The next morning, I sent for Ames and gave him instructions, and I sent letters of explanation to Everson and Carter, and then I packed a bag and took a coach toward Southampton, leaving Thornfield in my wake.

CHAPTER 5

I am not proud to say it, but those next few months proved a happier time for me. In Paris, I found a place in the Faubourg Saint-Germain—an apartment suitable to my station in life—and I hired a housekeeper and assigned her to find a cook and whatever else was needed. Since I would not be in residence there, I had reduced the number of Thornfield's servants to a minimum, just enough to provide for Bertha and Grace, and I arranged for Ames to send regular reports on the estate and my business holdings.

I had at the time some vague idea of seeking out in Paris a good and intelligent woman who would be my companion, someone who, knowing my position with Bertha, would understand and love me anyway. I imagined that if I made myself known, sooner or later a suitable match would appear. To that end, I made the acquaintance of my neighbors: on the one side, a widowed woman of great class whose recently deceased husband had been a general under Bonaparte, with whom I hoped to enjoy conversation about that great military mind. But I soon learned that she recalled little. On the other side lived a *vicomte* and his wife, the *vicomtesse*, who was much younger than her husband and a perennial flirt. Through them, I became acquainted with the younger, fashionable set with whom Madame la Vicomtesse de Verteuil socialized.

With them, or occasionally by myself, I went to nightly entertainments: the opera, the ballet, the *bouffons*, and again a theater for a play or two.

I went to fetes at the Prado and balls at the Odéon. With my new acquaintances, I learned to order the finest dishes and to drink vermouth
and cassis, to speak about the finer points of an opera or ballet, to catch
a woman's eye and smile at her over the rim of my glass, and I learned,
too, that if one has money enough there is no limit to what one may do.
Perhaps this was the kind of life Rowland had sought, and I was enjoying it thoroughly. I stayed out most nights and slept through the mornings
and half the afternoons, and on sunny days, paraded in my carriage on the
Champs-Élysées, or I walked in the Jardin des Plantes with a woman on
my arm. And again in the evenings I went to entertainments and gambled
and danced.

I could enjoy myself in ways I had never imagined: I was talking politics and business with the men, and flirting and writing my name on
women's fans at balls and having affairs with one and then another. If all
of that brought me no closer to the woman I had imagined meeting, I told
myself it was no matter. In short, unlike at Thornfield, in Paris I felt free,
and if my life there did not bear close inspection, it was certainly more enjoyable than remaining at Thornfield would have been.

One cold night in March I found myself standing in the Grand Foyer
of the Paris Opéra, disappointed at the notice board announcing that Lise
Noblet had taken ill and would not be performing the title role in *La
muette de Portici*. I would have left the theater in disgust, for Noblet was
an exquisite dancer and had already become a particular favorite of mine,
but Monsieur Roget sidled up to me and said, "You must see this new
dancer. She is a marvel."

Roget was a man who made it his business to know all the performers
at the Opéra. He held court every night at the Café d'Or after the performances, and if he said a dancer was worth watching, then she surely
must be. So I stayed, having no alternate plan in mind, and I suppose I
thought I could spend the evening critiquing her. Instead, however, from
the moment the mute Fenella first appeared onstage I was entranced. She
danced like a feather floating on air, her blond curls barely contained, her
hands and feet as graceful as the wings of a butterfly. Watching her, I

was mesmerized; I could not get enough of this petite marvel. The opera felt dull each time she left the stage.

On the one hand, I wished the evening would go on forever, and yet on the other I could barely wait until it was over, so anxious was I to find her in the Foyer de la Danse, where the dancers met with their admirers. I barely waited for the curtain calls, dashing down the stairs, running to buy camellias from a flower girl, hurrying to the foyer. I did not yet even know her name. I pushed myself as close as I could to the front of the waiting crowd, and when she finally appeared I shoved the others away until I stood right before her, and I placed the bouquet into her hands, kissing her fingers as I did so. Her face was as porcelain, lightest cream. She smiled at me and nodded at the flowers, and I placed my card into the bouquet before I was jostled away by another admirer and another, and when I turned back her arms were burdened with flowers, and all of them seemed more glorious than the ones I had given her. I left and walked back to my apartment in a spitting snow.

Despite my anticipation I heard nothing from the dancer—by then I had learned her name was Céline Varens—and the next evening Noblet returned to the stage. I attended anyway, searching the dance company for the luminous Varens, but did not see her. For days after that, I waited for a message from her, or for her name on another playbill or for any word at all of her, but there was none.

And then one day I was on my way to the Palais-Royal for a solitary stroll in its gardens. Solitary? You may wonder, and rightly, but sometimes I did so, for I am not ashamed to say that sometimes the best conversations one can have are with one's own self, and that had more and more frequently become my situation. That day, the sun was warm on my back and the sky was blue and I could not have been more content in anyone's company, when a carriage suddenly pulled up beside me, and the passenger inside opened the door.

Curious, and not a little annoyed, I imagined some acquaintance interrupting my reverie. But when I glanced inside, there was the golden nymph I had so wanted to see again: Céline Varens herself.

She smiled as I stepped inside, the aroma of her scent enveloping me—it was the fragrance of camellias. "I have been searching for you," she said.

"And I you," I responded, hardly able to breathe. "How did you find me?"

Rose-colored lips parted into a perfect smile. "Silly," she said. "I found you walking toward the Palais-Royal. God must have sent you to me."

No, I thought; *he sent* you *to* me. "But I gave you my card," I said.

"There were so many cards, so many flowers."

So many other men, I thought. But her dimpled smiles and her fluttering hands entranced me. "Where were you going just now?" I asked her.

"Silly," she said again. "I was going to find you, since you did not find me."

"But no one knew where you lived. I tried everything—"

"Ah, *mon petit chouchou,* you did not know where to look, did you?"

It came to me then: someone kept her—some man other than I, luckier than I—and I should not have been surprised. "Does he know what you do when you are not with him?" I asked.

She laughed lightly, and her hands took my face and drew it close and her lips met mine and her tongue came into my astonished mouth, and I could have ravished her there, right there, in her carriage, but she gently pushed away from me. "You are a gentleman, no?" she whispered.

"Of course I am."

"You have another card, no?"

I drew a card from my pocket and she gazed at it, as if appraising me. "I will send for you," she said, "and you will come?"

"Indeed, I will."

She smiled again, her perfect lips, her perfect teeth, her little tongue. I could have stayed with her forever, but she motioned toward the door, and I understood and left her, though it was as if I had awakened from a dream. The carriage pulled away, leaving me in the roadside, watching.

Within a week, she sent for me twice. Her apartment was not far from mine, and I wondered that I had not been able to find her, that she had instead found me nearly by chance. I never knew the man who kept her there; he was a wealthy merchant of some sort who traveled often.

Céline was a delight. She was childlike without being childish; she was quicksilver; she could listen. She was not well educated, but it was clear she had an active, lively mind. Her merchant-lover was *old*, she said, emphasizing the word, and it soon became obvious that she was looking for someone younger, with whom she could attend the theater and balls. But we did not go anywhere those first few times, perhaps because she was known to be attached and it would not have done for her to be seen with another man.

I was insanely jealous of her merchant, though I had no real cause. Although I could go to her only when he was away on business, when I was with her I was the center of her attention: I was in heaven. She sent for meals from a nearby café, and sometimes she fed me as if I were her child, and sometimes we ate together from the same plate, and sometimes the food grew cold while we made love.

Before autumn I had moved Céline out of the merchant's apartment and into another that I provided for her. She had not wanted to move in with me, as I had hoped, and I could not force her, for I knew that in the world of Paris, one was lucky to have such a woman at all, under any circumstances, and that I was even more fortunate that an angel like her could give her heart to someone like me. When she danced, I went to her every performance, most often at the Opéra, but sometimes elsewhere. I installed a piano in her apartment and played for her while she danced for me. Sometimes she urged me to sing, and, flattered, I held her in my arms and sang love songs into her ear.

We ate dinners at our favorite restaurants and we often went to the theater or to a ball, but sometimes we stayed home by ourselves, which was my preference, though her choice would have been to go out every night. That was her life: to see and be seen in the most fashionable of company. I bought her things: the finest gowns of silk and cashmere, jewels for her lovely throat and arms and for her hair, even a full equipage, complete with matching horses and a coachman and footman, and she rewarded my gifts with love and attention, calling me her *chouchou*. I entreated her to call me by my given name, as no one ever had, but she pouted that Edward was a hard name—like feet stamping, she said—and instead whispered *chouchou* into my ear, licking my earlobe, giggling softly, her breath against my cheek. I could not deny her anything. Because her very name—Céline—meant heavenly, I called her *ma petite ange*.

Amid our bliss, I did not confide in her the burden I carried. I told myself it was because of fear that she would leave me, but that surely was not the full truth; in Paris, especially with Céline, I had simply found for myself a refuge where I could forget Bertha, and her long-lost child, and all that I had left at Thornfield-Hall.

CHAPTER 6

In Paris, there had been no need for me to return to England. Ames was a fine and trustworthy agent, and Grace Poole had never given reason for concern. I had long since given up hope of any reversal in Bertha's condition, and because I had been unable to locate any further information on her son, it was enough now to know simply that she was safe and secure and receiving adequate care. She had even almost grown to appreciate Grace—as much as she could appreciate anything or anyone—and after the first few weeks she no longer tried to attack her caretaker, although she still could not be trusted to wander at will through Thornfield-Hall. But because she had always preferred dark and inclosed places, the third-floor apartment, with its hidden entrance, was a perfect sanctuary. No one came, save Grace, to disturb or anger her.

In early summer, however, I made a hurried trip back to Thornfield because Ames had written that Munroe had given notice. It came as no surprise, for without the master in residence, there was little need for a butler. There was still the cook, Mary, and her husband, John, who did whatever was required; and Leah, the parlor maid; and young Sam, the footman. All that was needed in addition was a housekeeper. I could have left the responsibility for hiring such a person to Ames, but the situation at Thornfield was delicate, and the personality of the housekeeper was crucial, so I returned, telling Céline I might be gone for a week or more.

Because Thornfield was rather remote, and a madwoman residing there made the place seem even more daunting, Ames had suggested that we not inform the new housekeeper of Bertha's presence. *How can we not?* I wondered. *The housekeeper has the run of the Hall, and the responsibility for it; how can she not know of its peculiar inhabitant?*

But when I arrived, I discovered that Ames, who had lived in the neighborhood his entire life and knew nearly everyone, already had a plan. First, he voiced a strong concern that keeping servants would always be a problem, unless Bertha's presence was a carefully guarded secret. He revealed to me that a distant relation lived nearby, a discreet and respected widow, Mrs. Fairfax by name.

The name caught me straightaway. "Fairfax?" I asked.

"Oh yes," he said. "She would have been married to your mother's second cousin. Caroline Fairfax Rochester, your mother was."

The revelation stunned me. I had not known until then the provenance of my second name. "I was named for her," I said. "Did you know my mother?"

"I never met her," he said, "though I saw her a time or two when I was a boy. A lovely woman. And this Mrs. Fairfax is a widow of great reputation but with very little to live on. It would be of benefit to you both."

"But she would be my relation! And you propose I not tell her of my wife? How could I do that?"

"You simply tell her—or I will, if you prefer—that Grace tends to private concerns of yours and is not to be interfered with. Stranger situations than that have happened in great houses such as Thornfield-Hall."

"But—" I could not think what to say, except that it felt unseemly to keep such secrets.

"She is a proper woman and would be just right for what you require. There is no need for her to know all your family secrets," he countered.

Perhaps I had become jaded in Paris, where, in the circles in which I lived, secrets more often than not were willfully flaunted. Every man, it seemed, had a mistress, and his wife, if he had one, ignored that blatant fact; and every woman, married or not, had her own dalliances, which were common knowledge to all.

Yet in England secrets are held close to the breast—the more dangerous the secret, the closer it is held. One may call such a state hypocrisy, and perhaps it is. But: "Hypocrisy is an homage vice pays to virtue," La Rochefoucauld wrote, and there are few secrets as dangerous—or as shameful—as a mad wife.

Ames arranged for Mrs. Fairfax to come for an interview the very next day, and she seemed to me indeed the very epitome of rectitude and discretion. I could immediately see that she might well have balked at the knowledge of Bertha in the hidden apartment, as well as at the idea of working for a man who would keep his wife in such a state, especially while he lived like a will-o'-the-wisp abroad, and I was certainly of no mind to explain in detail my history or my choices.

I confidently offered her the position, but before our interview ended, I could not resist asking her if she had known my mother.

"Not well," she answered, "for Mr. Fairfax and I married late, and your mother died young. But she was beautiful, an elegant lady, well regarded and the darling of the county. Yes, it was a pity she died so young that you never knew her."

"But what was she *like*?" I pressed.

"As I say," she replied, "I did not know her well; I only saw her a time or two. But I do know this: she was kind, and it was her kindness that made her beloved."

"Thank you, Mrs. Fairfax," I said, and she nodded to me and tightened her bonnet and left. But I hung on to those words and played them again in my head: *She was kind.*

———

After a disastrous and heartrending visit to Bertha, in which I perceived that her decline had become even more pronounced, I felt I was ready to fully commit myself to the new, happy life I had found in Paris. I could not wait to return to Paris, to Céline's apartment, where, I imagined, she would fly into my arms and smother me with kisses. I spent nearly all my time on the return journey imagining the scene, working out the most romantic things to say. We would continue to live in Paris, where Céline had her dancing and her admirers, and I would, if necessary, return to England now and then. Perhaps the time would come when we could, as a change, go to Thornfield as well. Yes, I am ashamed to say, I imagined that too, though Bertha was of a hearty constitution and could go on for decades. *Decades—God,* I thought, *have mercy.*

The coach horses could not travel fast enough, the ferry could not cut through the water fast enough, the horse I hired at the dockside could not gallop fast enough, to return me to my Céline. Evening was falling when I arrived at her apartment, where I was stunned by its silence, its emptiness. Even Annick, her maid, was not there. I hoped Céline would be returning soon, but of course life for Céline began in late afternoon and ended only when the last establishments closed, at three or four o'clock in the morning. There was no telling whom she was with.

After a few impatient moments, I laid my card on her toilette table and left the apartment and wandered the streets in a daze of disappointment. *Where was she?* I told myself she could be at tea or having her hair done, clinging desperately to the idea that she was mine, as I was already hers. As I walked, I found myself growing more and more anxious, angry even, that she had not been there waiting for me. Foolish man that I was, I still desired the world to revolve around me and my wishes.

But when I returned a few hours later, the apartment was still empty. Perhaps Céline was at a private party, I thought, and Annick had been given the evening off. I waited in her boudoir, breathing in her camellia scent, and after a time I opened the French doors and stepped out onto the balcony. The evening air was fresh, the moon shone full on the street, and the gaslight at the corner made a comforting glow. I sat there smoking and eating chocolate bonbons, imagining how it would be when Céline was my wife and we could spend quiet evenings by ourselves on summer nights like this, watching the carriages rolling past on their way to the opera.

One of those carriages drove up to the front of the hotel, and I recognized the equipage that had been my gift to Céline. I sat forward as the horses stopped, shaking their heads restlessly. My *ange* was dressed in a hooded cashmere cloak that I recognized as one I had gifted her, though it seemed too warm for a June night, and there was her tiny foot peeping out from under the skirt of her dress, as, with a light movement, she skipped down from the carriage. I rose, all smiles, ready to call out a greeting, when another figure emerged behind her. It was cloaked as well, but wearing a man's spurred heel that rang on the pavement and the hat of a cavalry officer. He and Céline disappeared, passing under the *porte cochère* of the hotel.

Suddenly my chest felt pressed with a great weight. I remained rooted in place, though at the last moment, before they entered the apartment, I thought to reach through the open window and draw the curtain across it, with just the barest of openings, that I might view and hear their assignation. Annick came in first—I had not even heard her return, so enamored was I of the evening—and she lit a lamp, then withdrew. A moment later the couple entered, laughing softly at some joke. There she was, in all her glory—in a rose-colored silken dress and jewels I had given her—and he in his officer's uniform. I recognized him as a young roué— someone I knew to be beneath her. Céline saw the card I had left, and she pointed at it and laughed, deriding my personal defects, she who had over and over told me she found me handsome and charming, but now I heard that I was as ugly as a stray dog, and just as graceless. All the love I had thought I felt for Céline fled in those few moments, and my new sentiment was confirmed as their mindless chatter continued: frivolous, stupid, mercenary.

I could not bear to hear more, and I stepped through the window and without preamble freed Céline from any obligation to me and gave her notice to vacate the apartment as soon as possible. I threw down a few francs for any immediate need and made to leave, disregarding her screams and protestations, as she was suddenly intent on revealing to me that she did truly love me after all and was sorry, etcetera, etcetera. At the door, I turned and told the *chevalier* that I expected him the next morning at the Bois de Boulogne, and then I closed the door on Céline's continued hysterics.

In the morning, though it was the first duel I had ever fought, I made quick work of the fellow, wounding him in the arm. His shot went far wide of the mark, a good example of the state of the French military.

One might forgive a single night's mistake, but it is quite another to hear your lover belittle you to another in the crudest of language. I was finished forever with Céline, and I vowed I would never again give a woman power over me as I had done with Céline.

CHAPTER 7

Leaving Paris as quickly as I could, I traveled: Rome, Naples, Florence, Saint Petersburg, even Baden-Baden, where I spent hours—no, days— at the gaming tables, as if winning or losing were an antidote. I cared little which city I was in, or with whom I spent my time. I was in those days a very changed man from the one who had first left England at the age of twenty-one. Then, I had been a child, seeing things in black and white, assuming there must be a satisfactory moral solution to any prob- lem, assuming that what one saw on the surface was all there was to see. I marveled at my past self: what had become of that naïve, softhearted boy who had wanted to believe the best of everyone?

Though the angry wound of Céline's betrayal never fully healed, as time went on and my bed grew cold I did occasionally find in my travels a woman who at first I thought could be a partner for me, but each time I was disappointed. There was an Italian who was charming and beautiful and alive with verve. I enjoyed her company, her passion, her very Ital- ian sense of humor, and she struck me as the sort of woman Bertha might have become, with a different family history. But the more time I spent with her, the more doubtful I became, for while Giacinta was not mad, she had a violent and unprincipled side that disturbed me. I also dallied for a time in Saint Petersburg with the daughter of a German merchant there, an innocent young girl not yet into her twentieth year, who stirred in me the same sympathies as Alma had, back in Maysbeck. But as time passed, I saw that what I had taken for quietude and calm was really ignorance and mindlessness. I left her with a gentleness I had not bestowed on Giacinta, and I gave her enough money to open a shop of her own. There were others, to be sure, but we never seemed to fit together as I imagined a man and his wife should, although God knows I had little enough experience in what that would mean.

At the same time, events were roiling in Jamaica. Six months after I quit Paris, disappointed that their demands for more freedom had been rejected, tens of thousands of Jamaican slaves rose in revolt. The rebellion was short-lived and the subsequent punishment brutal, but it was the beginning of the end. Two years later, while I was romancing Clara, slavery ended for good. I was late in hearing the news, for such information was not welcomed in Russia, where the serfs were inclined to believe in freedom themselves. But Osmon managed to get word to me, and I remained confident he was doing his best under the circumstances, so I went back to the gambling tables, for, indeed, what could I have done from so far away, and what point was there in returning to Jamaica?

———

Some years later, I drifted through Paris again. I happened to be sitting at table with Monsieur Roget at the Café d'Or when Céline arrived, holding a little girl by the hand. It was far too late for such a young child to be about, but the whole table made over her as if she were a princess, and in fact she was remarkable looking—fairylike in a shimmering pink dress with a large pink bow in her blond curls. She moved her hands as she spoke, as a dancer would, and it was clear that she delighted in being the center of attention. Céline nodded meaningfully at me, but I stared stonily back, for, I thought, if she meant to claim that this creature was mine, it must certainly be clear to all that she was not.

As I made my excuses to leave, attempting not to create a scene, Céline held her hand out to mine and I could do nothing but take it, and she slipped me her card. To my regret, I accepted her invitation.

She greeted me the next day with kisses and embraces, and the child, whose name was Adèle, was well trained in the art of coquetry. She climbed into my lap and held my face in both her little hands and planted kisses on my cheeks. I had brought a doll for her, and I suppose she was thanking me, but I was repulsed by such a forward manner in one so young. I stayed at Céline's apartment as short a time as I could, determined not to give the impression that I had forgiven her. She tried to imply that Adèle was my own, but she must have known I could easily deny it—there was nothing at all about me in that little face. I fled the apartment, insistent that both mother and daughter were gone from my life forever.

From there I continued my travels, my gambling, my liaisons with unsuitable women. I am not proud of that rootless life. But even so, changed as I was, more cynical about human nature, more hard-hearted—more, perhaps, like my father than I had ever wished to be—the boy I had once been lived on in one undeniable way: I continued to yearn for Thornfield. Not as it had become, barren and warped in secrecy, but the Thornfield of my childhood imagination.

My self-imposed exile was not without comfort, however. Once, in Baden-Baden, I picked up a companion who has, so many times since, warmed me with his presence. One day, having grown tired of casino games, I set out for a change of pace and caught a coach going toward the Badener Höhe, where I aimed to take a long walk in the Schwarzwald. And quite a walk it turned out to be, for I lost my way, and God knows what would have become of me if a scruffy-looking, half-grown dog hadn't appeared as I leaned against a fallen log to tear into my lunch. The animal gazed at me with such intelligence that I was moved to offer him the rest of my bun. He stood at my knee, chewing with gusto, and when he had finished, he looked expectantly at me again, as if I could conjure more, which made me laugh. When I rose to try to find my way back, though my food was gone, he followed. But he must have judged me an inferior guide, for after an hour of wandering in the darkening forest he suddenly set out ahead of me, glancing back now and then as if to make sure I was still there, until we had reached civilization. The next morning he was waiting for me outside my hotel, and he has been my constant comrade ever since. I named him Pilot, for he surely led me back that first day, and has often given me succor when no one else could.

I seemed to have little luck in quitting troublesome women, however, for a few years later, when I was again in Paris and passing an evening with Monsieur Roget, Céline's name came up. "Ah yes," he said, nodding. "Céline: what a pity."

"Pity?" I repeated.

"She ran off with some Italian. A person of little account, unfortunately; she did not always have the best taste in men."

I said nothing, choosing not to include myself in that slight, and he went on: "A musician, I think. He sometimes performed with the opera. He took her to Italy."

His terminology suddenly struck me. "*Did not* have the best taste? Is she..."

"Well, yes, I understand she went only a year after she left for Italy. Consumption: she ignored it for months before she left."

I was stunned. Céline, so full of life: dead? "And the child?" I asked, unthinking.

He laughed then. "If you were to run off with Varens, would you take her child along?" His face suddenly went serious. "The little girl—Adèle is her name, is it not?—she can't be yours—?"

"She is not."

"Ahh." He nodded. "Perhaps the Chevalier du Bellay."

"I would believe *that*," I responded, a certain bitterness resurfacing.

"So," he went on, "Varens left her with Madame Frédéric. Do you know her?"

Oh yes, I knew her. She had been a neighbor of Céline's, a former courtesan turned sometime procurer. *What had Céline been thinking, leaving a child with that woman?* "Does she still live on rue Favart?" I asked.

"Yes, but she is now in reduced circumstances, I am afraid. Varens left little enough money for the girl's care. The *madame*"—he said the word with an ironic tone—"is in a tiny flat now."

I turned away and left, compelled to find the child, if only to assuage my conscience.

Madame Frédéric's rooms were on the top floor of the building. Pilot waited for me on the street, and as I climbed the stairs I reminded myself that I had no responsibility for this child. I had not seen myself in her, and neither had Monsieur Roget, and certainly there was no place in my life for a child, a living reminder of the second biggest mistake I had ever made.

When I knocked on the apartment door, there was no answer for so long that I was just making to leave as the door opened and a woman peered up at me. The thick powder and rouge on her face failed to hide the tangle of lines that webbed it. "Madame Frédéric," I said.

She looked at me, nodding. "I knew you would come," she said.

"You have Varens' child," I said. "Where is she?"

"Where? Where do you think, at this hour of night? In bed."

Only then did I realize how late it was. "Ah," I said. "I should have waited until morning. I only just learned—"

She smiled a nearly toothless smile. "And you are so anxious to see your daughter."

No, I was not. I still did not believe she was mine. Perhaps the only reason I was there at all was to prove it to myself, once and for all. "Excuse the disturbance," I said, backing away. "I didn't think of the time. I will return in the morning." I made a fast retreat, with the old woman calling after me. She was, I am sure, afraid I would not return at all.

But I did, and the next morning Adèle was there to greet me, dressed in a pink frock that seemed a size or two too small, a tattered pink ribbon in her curls. She had been prompted, it was clear, and she smiled, and I saw again the dimples in her cheeks, her fair skin, her flaxen hair, her hazel eyes, and the curve of her chin. She was definitely Céline's child, but just as definitely not mine. I had seen those eyes before, large and wide-set, and that nose as well, but not in my mirror. They were those of the secret lover. But her little lips were moving already, silently forming the word by which she had been instructed to know me: *Papa*.

"She is yours," the old woman croaked, reading my thoughts on my face. "Her mother always said so, and I have no reason to doubt. And as her father—"

I shook my head. "She is not mine," I whispered. "You must know that."

"Do you not find her beautiful?" she asked, her eyes narrowing.

A chill ran through me, and I leaned closer to her. "I can see what will become of her if she remains with you."

She shook her head slowly.

"You know it will," I said. "How did you find that life, eh? How does any woman find that life? Because it is all she has, is that not the truth? And is that what will become of Adèle?" I had no interest in adding to my responsibilities. But how could I leave Adèle to the fate I could foresee? "Is this what you have been waiting for?" I continued. "For me— or anyone else—to come and claim her? Or is it"—the thought was still dawning as I spoke—"just that you have not yet found a man who will pay your price?"

"You threaten me?" she asked, defiant.

"How much?"

She smiled cautiously. "You will take her?"

"How much?"

She named a figure. It was far too much, but I was in no mood to bargain over the life of a child I did not even want. "I will return in three hours. Be ready to bring her to a solicitor's and we will make it legal."

"She is to be your child?"

"She is to be my ward. I will house her and feed and clothe her and make sure she is educated to be a proper kind of young lady." And that would be all.

———

By the end of the day, Adèle was mine, though I had no idea what to do with her, or even how to speak to her. As unused to children as I was, I did, thank God, have the wisdom not to immediately disrupt Adèle's life any more than it had been already, and so I determined we should stay on in Paris for some time. I found an apartment with two bedrooms and moved her there. The very first thing I did was go to a convent school and make arrangements for a nurse for Adèle, as it was clear that I could not bring up a child on my own. And the second thing was to inform her, as gently as possible, that I was not her *papa*, which would have been a great trauma for her if it hadn't been for the presence of Pilot, whom she petted and fondled as if he himself had been her parent. That great beast had grown to a massive adulthood with a patience with Adèle that outlasted any human's. Even so, and despite the nurse's capable, loving presence, Adèle so desperately clung to me if I tried to leave the hotel without her that I made sure to bring new clothes and toys and books when I returned. It was the only way I could think of to get her to allow me to leave.

Finally, after a few weeks, when I felt Adèle and the nurse and I were more comfortable with one another, I arranged for our departure to England.

CHAPTER 8

We stopped for a few days in London, where I thought Adèle would feel at home, having lived in a city all her life, but she found it disagreeable—filthy and common—and she was not afraid to say so. Having just come from Paris, I had to admit I felt the same, and therefore as soon as I had completed my business, I hurried her on to Thornfield, accompanied by Sophie, the nurse. I had high hopes that Adèle would find the Hall as warm and inviting as I had as a child, and indeed she did. She ran from room to room when we first arrived, enthralled and impressed by the size of the place and by its furnishings. Adèle was, in so many ways, her mother's daughter.

As soon as we arrived in England I tried teaching Adèle rudimentary English, for this was to be her language, but she said she found it *"difficile et détonné,"* and she refused even to try. Nevertheless, I went on speaking to her in English, which she sometimes pretended not to hear or understand, and she carried on her conversations almost totally with Sophie. I felt sorry for the child but also on occasion found her as aggravatingly silly as her mother had sometimes been. The sooner she made the best of her new situation, the better, and I tried to impress this on her as firmly as I could. It is possible that, on occasion, I was too gruff—as yet I had so little experience with children. Fortunately, once Adèle was at Thornfield, Mrs. Fairfax's unassuming gentleness won first Sophie and then Adèle herself. And it did not hurt that Pilot was always ready for a retrieving game or a belly rub.

Mrs. Fairfax had the good sense to say nothing until we were alone, when she asked after Adèle's provenance. "She is the daughter of a friend of mine, now recently deceased," I responded. I reassured the widow that I expected to put Adèle into a school as soon as I found one suitable.

Mrs. Fairfax raised her eyebrows. "Is it indeed wise to send her off to school when she is so recently removed from all she knew, and where she does not even speak the language?"

I was not used to being questioned, and I am afraid I was rather harsh with my response. "It will be good for her, and God knows I cannot imagine having her here all the time."

"If you will pardon my saying so—"

"I will not, as a matter of fact," I snapped, and turned on my heel. I had thought, when I took Adèle on as my ward, that it would be merely a legality, a charitable act to keep her out of the clutches of anyone who would make her into a miniature strumpet. Why should she not be sent off to school? That was what my father had done with me, when I was not much older than Adèle was now, and that experience had turned out well enough.

The very next day, I paid a call on Everson for recommendations of a suitable school for Adèle, but he frowned when he heard that she spoke only French, and when I explained that she had been brought up in Paris and had some distinctly Parisian ways, he frowned further and suggested a governess instead.

A governess! *What a terrible idea,* I thought. Adèle at Thornfield, and Bertha upstairs? I remembered Tiso's escaping Bertha's chamber, exploring the attic storerooms—I remembered myself doing the same. Bertha's chamber only yards away from where Adèle might innocently wander. Absolutely not! But when I visited several schools for young girls in the county, at each one I saw prim and neatly uniformed children, two to a desk, heads bent over their lessons. Much as I wished to see Adèle ensconced in such an ambience, it was plainly impossible to drop her into such a place now. I returned to Thornfield disappointed, and I called Mrs. Fairfax into my library that evening and allowed that it would indeed seem best for her to find a governess as soon as possible.

"I, sir?" she asked.

"Well," I said, "who else is there?"

"Is that not your responsibility, as her guardian?" she responded.

"You are twice the guardian that I am," I said, and I walked off. It was true; she had a way with Adèle that I could not fathom. Though Adèle spoke little English still, she chattered incessantly in French to Mrs. Fairfax, who would smile and nod and go about her business.

A week or two later Mrs. Fairfax came to me with a notice from the *Herald*—a young lady, an experienced teacher, it seemed, looking for a position with a family. Mrs. Fairfax appeared content with the applicant's qualifications, and thus I considered the matter closed. I would be coming and going and have little contact with any of the women now suddenly filling my Hall.

—•—

By mid-August, half the titled folk and the gentry of England are in Scotland for the grouse hunting, and when that is finished they return for the start of partridge season, then pheasants. And lastly, in November, comes the fox hunting. It is a movable party in which I had sometimes participated, the whole group residing for a time at one manor. That year, I had already missed the grouse, but I was back at Thornfield for the partridges, and decided to join.

Lord and Lady Ingram of Ingram Park were hosting; their eldest daughter, Blanche, seemed a more interesting and complex young woman than many others in the neighborhood. She could shoot with the best of the party and she sat a horse as well as any man. She was beautiful too, and her gregarious nature perfectly masked my own disinterest in the gossip that is so common in those circles. In short, though I resisted seeing it at the time, she complemented the man I had become.

The hunts were grand indeed, and a welcome distraction from the vexations back at Thornfield. I was able to give a good accounting of myself, though Miss Ingram frequently teased me that my mount was lacking in the steel and daring of her own. The horse was not, she insisted, acceptable for a man like me, for he sometimes hesitated at the hedgerows and shied away when other riders veered too close. What kind of man, exactly, did she think I was? I asked, laughing. She replied, with a wink, that she expected me to have charge of my steed.

As we exchanged banter, I noticed that the other young ladies had fallen back in deference to her supposed claim on my affections. I had no intention of taking any of it too seriously, though I did find it amusing that she was a dark-haired Amazon, a veritable Greek statue of womanhood, just as Bertha and Giacinta had been. I told myself I must be destined to form attractions to such sensual women.

The truth was, I wanted neither Miss Ingram nor any other woman in a serious way. I had lost any conviction that I would ever find a true companion, and I was certainly in no position to be courting someone so close to Thornfield. Bertha's existence made marriage in England impossible; in fact her mere presence at Thornfield made my own happiness equally elusive. Only distance had given me the freedom I needed to keep my own mind still.

Yet, I sometimes wondered, what was there for me anywhere—at Thornfield or abroad? I had long ago grown tired of the life I'd led in Europe, and my life in England had been constricted to such surface pleasures as hunts and parties and meaningless conversations.

But before the hunts had ended, a letter for me arrived, sent over from Thornfield-Hall. It was from Geoffrey Osmon, writing that he was back in England for a while and would like to meet with me in January, if that was agreeable. It was by then a few years since abolition in Jamaica, and from all reports Valley View had weathered it fairly well. Many of the former slaves had stayed on, receiving payment now for their labor, and I assumed Osmon's presence in England meant he was ready to move on. At any rate, I was pleased at the thought of seeing him again and learning how he was faring. I responded to his address in London, asking if he could meet me at Newmarket, just after the first of the year, for I had a plan in mind.

CHAPTER 9

I arrived at Newmarket three days before my meeting with Osmon. Though I would not have confessed it to her, I had been thinking in recent days of purchasing a new horse, one that met Miss Ingram's exacting standards: big and handsome and daring. I wanted to feel that way myself, as if I could take hold of my life and make it to be as I wished, instead of the purposeless procession of days I saw stretched out ahead of me.

It was impossible, of course, to walk through this town's streets without thinking of my old friend Carrot. If he had still been alive, I knew, he would have reminded me, *Jam, you can do anything you put your mind to.* In my younger days I had not seen that as possible, and perhaps it still wasn't, but I was at least ready to try. I could buy a stunning horse; I could live life on my own terms and not be constricted by the ugliness at Thornfield-Hall.

I wandered onto the downs, where close to two decades before Carrot had passed his last moments, and I confess my eyes misted as I strolled around, thinking of all he had taught me in our too-short time together. In the distance, I saw a rider on a black horse, larger than any horse I had ever seen, and I stopped to watch. The rider was putting the creature through its paces while two gentlemen stood near, watching. I ambled closer, trying to guess what was going on; was it possible they were discussing the purchase of that splendid animal? Something in my breast arose; how wondrous I would look on that horse, what a figure I would cut. *Foolish,* I told myself in the next moment. *Do I really intend to buy a horse just to impress Miss Ingram?*

"He is too big," I heard one of the men say. "He will never win a race."

"There's no such thing as too big, and he has good breeding—out of Zanzibar."

"He could never win the Derby. Never."

"Are you selling him?" The words came out of my mouth before I could stop them.

The two men turned and studied me. Then they noticed Pilot. "Get that animal out of here."

Pilot placidly returned the gaze.

"Are you selling?" I asked again. "I might be interested in buying."

One of the men stared at me. My traveling clothes, I realized, must have made me seem like a cottager. "I daresay you couldn't afford him," the man said.

"I daresay you are mistaken," I said, rising to the challenge.

"You haven't even ridden him," the gentleman said.

"Indeed," I said. "Bring him here and I shall."

He raised his eyebrows at that, but signaled the jockey, who brought the horse over. When I had mounted, I turned to the man who seemed to be the horse's owner. "What's his name?"

"Mesrour," the jockey offered, when the owner didn't speak.

"Mesrour," I repeated. "From *The Thousand and One Nights*. How appropriate." And with that I touched my heel to his flank and we were off, racing across the grassy down, and I knew I had to have him.

"What do you think, fellow?" I asked Pilot when Mesrour and I returned. "Shall I buy him?"

Pilot ambled over and sniffed at the horse's fetlocks, then nuzzled my leg.

"Yes, I agree," I said, dismounting. "Five hundred guineas," I said to the owner.

He glanced at his companion. "I could make that up in one season."

"Not likely," I said, "unless he wins the Derby."

"Who are you?" the owner asked.

"Edward Fairfax Rochester. Of Thornfield-Hall in Yorkshire," I replied.

"Yorkshire!"

"Why not?" I asked, knowing full well what the rest of England thought of the North Country.

"Would you race him?" he asked.

"Not for money. I would ride him across the moors."

"Foxhunting? He will never be a jumper."

I laughed. "Nor will I, I imagine."

The owner came forward and took Mesrour's bridle from me, and my heart fell. "Seven hundred and fifty," he said.

I walked around Mesrour, feeling his legs, sensing the power in them and in his hindquarters, looking into his mouth. "His age?" I asked.

"Two years."

"He's massive for that," I said, and then added, "A bird in the hand—"

He said nothing.

"Six hundred," I said.

The owner looked at me seriously for the first time. "I will see your money," he said at last.

"Of course," I responded.

The deal was done by noon the next day. Mesrour, the most magnificent horse I have still ever seen, was mine. Foolish purchase, perhaps, but I seldom give in to frivolity, and this was a horse I had to have. Mounted on him, with Pilot trotting along beside us, I felt a new man. Suddenly all things *were* possible once more.

———

It had been ten years since Osmon and I had seen each other, and we had both aged, I probably more than he. Yet even so, we greeted each other as brothers when we met at the inn. I insisted on taking him first thing to admire Mesrour at the stable where I was keeping him. Osmon knew horses better than I, and I was pleased that he thought I'd made a good purchase, though he asked me what I intended to do with such an animal.

"Ride him!" I replied, and he laughed.

Back at the inn, mugs of rum before us, Osmon reported in great detail about Valley View, lamenting that now that laborers must be paid some kind of wage, the estate was not nearly as profitable as it once had been, though he was making do as best he could. As I had suspected, however, he had grown restless with his position and was ready to move on, but there was the difficult issue of what to do with Valley View. Because it was entailed, it could not simply be sold.

As we talked over possible solutions and the difficulties of the Mason inheritance, Osmon suddenly paused in our conversation and gazed into his mug. I wondered, too late, if he had arranged this meeting with something else on his mind. "Osmon?" I prompted.

"A young man came," he said. "From America." His eyes flicked up to mine and then dropped again to his mug, until, with what seemed like a force of will, they rose again to meet mine. "He says he is your wife's son."

My hand froze with my upraised mug—for a moment, it seemed, nothing, and no one, moved. So there *was* a child. And the boy had lived. The shock of Molly's story, the horror of Bertha's madness, the rage and frustration of that fruitless search years earlier—all of it rushed back at me in a moment, and I felt the room spin. "From America?" I asked.

"South Carolina, I believe."

"He has a name, I presume."

"He calls himself Gerald Rochester."

A fresh wave of emotion hit me. He shared my name—or had taken it—born of my wife, and yet I was not the father. Who, then? Another suitor of Bertha's? No, she had been too young, still a child herself, Molly had said. A slave? Unthinkable. Some criminal act, kept secret from the neighborhood? But no, the child would then have had no cause to use the Rochester name. Surely, it had not been my own father. No, but perhaps Rowland: the unwelcome product of Bertha's childhood crush on my brother?

And further, how did the infant get to America? Who had raised him there and what did they know of his parentage? What did *he* know, beyond the name of his mother? Would he find me at Thornfield? I stared across the table at my old friend, my mind stuck in a jumble of thoughts. Osmon's sympathetic eyes were on me. "How old is he?" I asked him. "What does he look like?"

He toyed with his mug before responding. "In his late twenties, I suppose; tall, slim, good-looking, I imagine one would say. Dark—but not as dark as you. Curly hair. He has a kind of arrogance about him. To be frank with you, I didn't care for him."

Rowland, I thought. *Rowland and Bertha. God have mercy, this is Rowland's bastard son. Unless...* "Where is he now?"

"I sent him to your solicitor—and the late Mr. Mason's—in Spanish Town: Mr. Foster. I would not be surprised to see him turn up here in England. He seemed a determined young man."

"I don't suppose he has proof of a marriage."

Osmon gave a quick shake of his head. "Not that I saw."

If he had it, I knew, he would be Rowland's heir—and Bertha's. He would inherit Thornfield and half of Valley View. If he didn't, he would have no claim to anything. He would be legal son of no one, heir of no one.

If Molly were to be believed, it was unlikely there had been a marriage, else the infant would not have been sent away. No, it was clear that pains had been taken to hide Bertha's pregnancy—because she had given birth to a bastard? I allowed myself to be satisfied that that was the whole of it. It did not yet occur to me that there was more.

Osmon had no additional information to offer, and seeing my distress he kindly tried to steer the conversation in other directions. After a few more rounds of rum, we relaxed once more and talked late into the night. He had married a widow who had brought a little property into the marriage, as well as two children; he had an exporting firm in Kingston in mind and was hoping to accumulate enough savings to purchase it. He asked, gently, after Bertha, and, grateful for his openness in this difficult situation, I told him as much of the truth as I had told anyone, and he nodded and laid a consoling hand on my arm. I praised him for the way he had handled my affairs all those years, and I asked how much more he needed to purchase the exporting firm. With great hesitation he told me a sum that must have seemed huge to him but seemed quite reasonable to me, and in return I shared with him an idea that had been forming in my mind as we spoke. While Valley View could not be sold, it could be rented. "Rent the land to whomever you trust to be good stewards," I told him. "I will pay you to oversee the arrangements and to be my land agent. In exchange, I will lend you enough to buy your new business, and instead of paying you a salary, I will put it to your account." Neither he nor I mentioned that such a business deal could be voided by Gerald Rochester's proof of legal birth.

In addition, Osmon told me he still saw Whitledge from time to time, and that Whitledge had sent his greetings and that he now had a daughter and three handsome sons. I envied that: those two married, with wives and families, with children. I looked down at Pilot, curled at my feet, and reached down to pat him.

Although it had grown quite late, when we parted I walked for some time afterwards, Pilot at my heel. I was pleased that Osmon seemed to have done so well for himself, and was glad to have played a part in that. On the other hand, what was my life? I had just purchased a stunning horse, and I should have been in good spirits. I had all the trappings: ownership of Thornfield-Hall, the interest of the beautiful Miss Ingram, freedom to travel when I wanted or stay home when I chose. Yet still, my life seemed empty, except for the burden of Bertha. And Adèle. And now, for the question of Gerald Rochester.

CHAPTER 10

It was January and bitter cold. Most of the gentry—the Ingrams and the others—would be in Bath by now, if not farther afield in Europe somewhere, and eager as I was to show off Mesrour, I had no mind to join them. It had been months since I had been in residence at Thornfield, and despite the burdens I had there, I felt it was time to make an appearance, to assure myself that Bertha was still in good care and that Adèle was in good hands as well, that her new governess was not ruining her. And, perhaps most important, I needed to assure myself that this so-called Gerald Rochester had not somehow materialized at my home in my absence. Osmon's revelation had bothered me, I realized, much more than I cared to admit.

The journey to Yorkshire took almost two weeks, for there was snow on the roadway and, despite my hurry, I had no intention of ruining Mesrour in the first days that I owned him. Yet, as we neared Thornfield, coming down the causeway from Millcote in the late afternoon, I was deep in my own head, where my emotions were at war with themselves. Even as I dreaded what I might find at the Hall—Bertha's further disintegration or the presence of this mysterious, unwanted stranger—nonetheless I still felt that old familiar longing to see the distant outlines of Thornfield-Hall against the darkening sky, to be home again. In my distraction, I was not paying the attention I should have to Mesrour's footing, to the telltale slips of the hoof that foretell disaster. We came around a curve in the pathway, where moisture from a recent rain had frozen into a thin sheet of ice. Suddenly, Mesrour's hooves lost their purchase, and before I could react, we were both of us falling onto the frozen causeway with the kind of crash that shatters bones.

I was dazed for a moment, as was the horse, but when I came to myself I discovered I was entangled with him, and he groaned as if he were near death, a sound that frightened the deuce out of me. I struggled mightily to remove myself from my entanglement, swearing to myself as if it would help the effort, as Pilot snuffled around us both. I thought I heard a voice and peered about into the gloom, but seeing no one, I was put in mind of childhood tales of woodland sprites haunting this vicinity. Then the voice came again, more clearly: "Can I do anything?"

I looked toward the sound and saw a little thing, barely half my size: not a sprite after all, but a child. I ordered it to one side, afraid it might get hurt, and managed to scramble to my feet, a sudden pain flashing through my ankle. As I helped Mesrour stand and checked him for injuries, Pilot leaped and barked around us in either joy or concern. I had just limped my way to a convenient nearby stile when I was surprised to hear the voice again, for I had forgotten that I was not alone on the path.

"If you are hurt, and want help, sir, I can fetch someone, either from Thornfield-Hall or from Hay."

"Thank you," I said, without glancing up, feeling instead at my twisted ankle. "I shall do: I have no broken bones—only a sprain." Hoping to prove those words, I stood again and immediately felt a fiercer stab of pain in my ankle.

"I cannot think of leaving you, sir."

It was only then, at this last insistence, that I truly saw the creature and realized that it was neither a sprite nor a child proper, but a young woman with a pale, otherworldly face, all bundled in a beaver bonnet and a merino cloak and a muff. I could not fathom what she might be doing on the path all alone at twilight. "I should think you ought to be at home yourself," I said, "if you have a home in this neighborhood: where do you come from?"

I was surprised to hear her tell me she came from Thornfield itself. The warm familiarity with which she spoke the name of my home struck me as both charming and rather improper—clearly she had no idea I was its master, yet she harbored evident affection for it, as I once had. When I tried to draw out her identity without revealing my own, I was astonished to learn that she was the new governess.

"I cannot commission you to fetch help," I said to her, "but you may help me a little yourself, if you will be so kind." She had no umbrella on which I might lean to make my way to my horse, so I asked her to fetch Mesrour to me. I saw too late that she had no experience with horses—and Mesrour, proud beast, could tell that too. Yet she was a determined little thing, and fearless, and knowing Mesrour was well trained and would do her no harm, it brought me great pleasure to witness a stubbornness in her nature that seemed to match that of my spirited horse. God knows how long she would have kept at it if I had not in the end intervened, for her efforts had brought me near to laughter and it would have been cruel to keep on with it. "I see the mountain will never be brought to Mahomet," I said, and I begged her to assist me to the horse instead.

Apologizing, I leaned quite heavily on this slight creature, and with her help I managed to limp to Mesrour, whom I mounted without much difficulty. Once astride, I looked down at her, struck again by something haunting in that little face, and I thanked her for her aid. She had a letter to mail in Hay, and so we parted ways. She did not know me still, and though I supposed she would learn soon enough that I was her master, there was something unyielding in her little spirit that made me unwilling, yet, to play my hand.

Over the rest of the way to Thornfield-Hall, despite the pain in my ankle, the encounter stayed in my mind. It was an incident of no great moment, yet I felt somehow as if it marked a change, however slight, in my life. The act of accepting her help had been both discomfiting and curiously pleasant. I could not help but wonder if I had been right at the first, that she was nothing but a woodland sprite, taken shape in the garb of a fragile governess. Her face was dissimilar to all others I had known—quiet, obedient, yet undeniably marked with intelligence and strength. Her tranquil expression stayed in my mind until I reached the estate. There I lingered at the gates; I lingered on the lawn.

I found, suddenly, that I did not like reentering Thornfield if it meant merging the world of this dreamlike sprite into one governed by the madwoman there. How could two such different women exist under my own roof?

Soon, though, Pilot could not help but announce our arrival, and John swiftly appeared to help me inside. He sent a boy for Carter and stoked a fire in the dining room, while Mrs. Fairfax hovered over me, Adèle caressed my leg as if such ministrations would cure the sprain, and Leah scurried to the kitchen to bring tea. I learned from Mrs. Fairfax that, to my relief, there had been no unexpected visitors in my absence, so Gerald Rochester, wherever he was, had not yet come to disturb my home.

Amid the excitement I might have forgotten the governess, but I did not. Such a delicate thing out alone at nightfall—I could not explain how I could have left her, knowing who she was, out on that icy path in the gathering gloom. I had a sudden need to know she was safe.

I turned to Adèle, at my arm. "What of your new governess, Adèle?" I asked. "What is her name? She is a small person, thin and a little pale, is she not? Tell me what you think of her."

"*Oh, Monsieur! Oui! Elle est—*"

"In English, please."

"Miss Eyre, she is fine. She is an *artiste*!"

"An artist?" I asked. That was not a good sign; I had had enough of artist types in Paris.

"Yes, but she is! Let me show you!"

She started to run off, but I stopped her. "Tomorrow," I said. "I will see her work tomorrow."

Just then Carter appeared, tutting over my accident and opening his case and setting to work. When he had finished and given me a sedative to ease the pain, sturdy John helped me up to my room. As he turned to leave, I thought to ask, "I have not yet seen the governess; surely she is about somewhere?"

"She has recently returned from a walk to Hay," he said. "She is in her room, I believe. Did you want to meet with her this evening?"

"Oh no, John," I said carelessly. "There is plenty of time for that another day." And I settled myself in bed, closed my eyes, and drifted to sleep forthwith.

CHAPTER 11

I slept late, a drugged sleep, and when I arose, Ames and some of my tenants were already waiting to see me. I meant to have a quick cup of coffee and a boiled egg and then set to business, but suddenly Adèle flew into the room with a portfolio of Miss Eyre's drawings under her arm. I was impatient to get on with the business of the day, but it seemed her excitement could not be contained. With a sigh, I flipped through the drawings quickly, or at least I meant to, but indeed, they turned out to be much more interesting than I had expected. Still, I had tenants waiting, so I handed the portfolio back to the child and sent her off, assuring her I would look at them again in the evening when I had more time.

My meetings ended up lasting most of the day, with Mrs. Fairfax popping quickly in and out, bringing tea to the guests. Eventually I signaled to her and confided that I desired to have Miss Eyre and Adèle with me for tea, for I thought it was time for a proper introduction.

Carter returned in the afternoon, and while he felt at my ankle I winced in acute pain. He glanced up at me. "That hurts?"

"Indeed, yes," I responded.

He muttered something to himself that I insisted he repeat. "That is not a good sign," he said. "Is it possible that you have injured this before?"

"Years ago, when I was a boy, I twisted it."

"And what was done for it?"

"Nothing. Rest; it was just a twisted ankle."

His experienced fingers probed more carefully. "I think we shall bind it," he said.

"Bind it?"

"If we keep it immobile for a week or so—"

"A week!"

"I suspect the original injury was worse than had been supposed, and now, if you don't take care of yourself properly, you might be permanently affected," he said.

"Oh, for pity's sake!"

He looked at me full on. "It shall be as you wish, I'm sure," he said.

"Get on with it, then!" I growled, angry at the prospect of being an invalid for God knew how many days. "I am sorry, Carter," I apologized, "but this puts me in a foul mood." He merely nodded.

When my meetings had finished, I limped into the sitting room and positioned myself on a couch there, feeling sour. Adèle bounced in just before six, all hugs and kisses and caresses, chattering to me in French despite my insistence she speak English. Finally, I dismissed the child, who ran immediately to Pilot in the corner and prattled to him in whispered French, caressing him with an affection he readily returned. I was pondering that free and open exchange of fond attachment when Mrs. Fairfax interrupted my thoughts. "Here is Miss Eyre, sir."

"Let Miss Eyre be seated," I said brusquely, feeling out of sorts still, and exhausted, suddenly, by the abundance of women in my house who had expectations of me. I had been interested to learn more about the strange little governess, but that was before my blasted ankle promised to keep me prisoner in my own home. Now I simply wished to be left alone.

It's possible Miss Eyre found me rude—and indeed more so for having concealed my identity the evening before—for which I intended to apologize. Yet the calm self-possession with which Miss Eyre entered the room and took her seat made me think her less a prisoner of common social niceties than many women I'd met. That unsettling fact in itself began to rekindle my curiosity.

Not wanting to reveal my interest, I glanced at her once, briefly, while her attention was on Adèle—and indeed she was just as small and determined looking as I had ascertained on the path, yet the sight of her face made me uncomfortable. I reminded myself that she had done nothing to hurt me, and in fact had helped me a great deal, and yet I could not shake the feeling that this Miss Eyre would expect more of me than the foolish gossip of the Ingram crowd, and I could not at first think what to say. Perhaps I had lost all ability to engage in intelligent conversation with a woman.

Mrs. Fairfax, sensing the tension, chattered on and on about this and that until I was driven to distraction, and I asked her to ring for the tea, as much to employ her with other thoughts as from my own hunger. As Miss Eyre served me my tea, Adèle spoke up—in French—asking if I had brought a gift for Miss Eyre. Of course I had not—but the child had not yet begged for her own present, I realized, a bit of good manners for which I was wont to give Miss Eyre the credit, although at the same time I knew that it had been only Adèle's way of hinting for her own present. Did she think I was so stupid as to not recognize the ploy? She remained so much her mother's child—and it annoyed me, too, that she still spoke in French, despite clear instructions to use English.

Ignoring my gruffness, Miss Eyre, for her part, assured me that she had not had much experience with presents, nor did she expect any from me. I turned my attention fully to her as she spoke, and studied her. She did not wince from my gaze, nor, to my surprise, did she give any hint of having met me the previous evening. I had thought to apologize for my rudeness but saw immediately that there was no need—in her eyes there had been no insult. Her face was mild, but her eyes—a color between hazel and green—stayed steadily on mine: deferential, but with that same uncanny self-possession. I went on to nudge her on the issue of gifts, mostly to see how she would respond.

She replied with answers that intrigued me, for they were honest and thoughtful, and yet she almost seemed to be parrying with me, as if it were a kind of game. I looked closely at her: this interesting little woman. She was dressed as plain as a Quaker, save for a very small pearl brooch; her brown hair was braided and bound up neatly at the back of her head.

I took my tea in silence, trying to understand what kind of woman had entered my home, and when I had finished, I urged her to join me closer to the fire for I was curious to learn more of her.

I could see that she was used to carefully parsing her words, which I took to mean that she had not had a particularly pleasant upbringing, and that she had learned to guard herself. And yet, she had no artifice; she was plainspoken and earnest. It came as no surprise when she told me that she was an orphan, brought up in a charity school, where food was rationed and lives were Spartan.

The physical poverty had clearly not impoverished her mind, however, for there were depths there that intrigued me. In talking with her I was gripped by a warmth I had not known for a very long time.

Feeling my spirits returning, I bantered with her a bit, teasing her for causing my injury like the sprite she was. While she kept pace with me, much to poor Mrs. Fairfax's confusion and dismay, Miss Eyre did not tease back, and I reminded myself that a governess is closer to a servant than to a guest.

Clearly Miss Eyre's physical tastes were not extravagant, and I wondered what other gifts she might possess. I asked her to play for me, which she did, serviceably if not particularly well—her modesty in that area was fully earned. But I knew there was another realm in which she rightfully excelled: "Adèle showed me some sketches this morning," I said, then provoked her with the suggestion that a master had helped her.

"No, indeed!" came the reply, and I had to suppress a smile at such sharp pride in one so delicate. I asked her to fetch her portfolio so I could see more, insisting that she vouchsafe it all as her own hand. She did so, in her quiet and unassuming way, but she was staunch in her determination; obviously she could not easily be intimidated.

When she brought the pictures, I looked at them once more, this time not so hurriedly. I had trouble focusing on them and relating them to the artist herself, for the emotion in them did not seem to match this tidy little governess. At last I pulled out three of the most arresting. They were peculiar and striking indeed, each a tragic human figure set against a fierce landscape. In the first one, the figure was clearly dead, a corpse in the water. She insisted that she had pulled the scenes entirely from her own imagination, which surprised me both for the clarity of their evocations, and for the desolation they appeared to contain. What a strange life she must have led thus far, this orphan governess! Where had she gotten her ideas, I asked her. "Out of that head I see now on your shoulders?"

"Yes, sir," she replied stoutly.

"Has it other furniture of the same kind within?" I asked, eager suddenly to know more of her.

"I should think it may have: I should hope—better." In response to more of my questions, she explained each drawing graciously and without self-consciousness.

As she spoke, I found myself thinking of Touch, whose imagination held that same vividness and darkness—but when I challenged her she said she had indeed been happy in her painting, only frustrated not to bring more of the reality of her vision to the page.

I took far more time with her than I had anticipated, and soon it was late. The pain in my ankle, the provocative paintings, the memories of Touch, this pale, steadfast paintress—all these overwhelmed me, and I dismissed the company and made my way to bed.

It seemed strange at the time—much less so now—but in the ensuing days I was always aware of Miss Eyre. Much as my own business pulled at my attention, nonetheless it was as if that small brown presence carried a magnetic charge within her that attracted the iron within me. Sometimes, when she and Adèle were in the garden or walking through the orchard, examining the trees for signs of new life, I lingered near the window of the library or my bedchamber and watched them. Slowly my ankle healed, and more and more often I found reasons to pass near the nursery door, that I might hear the lessons in progress. Her voice was low and calm, and even Adèle, who was always fluttering about like a butterfly, sat still and quiet as Miss Eyre taught her. She did not make the lessons a game, as Mr. Lincoln had, but she did know how to engage the mind of a child of Adèle's upbringing: she spoke of fairies and goblins and quoted poetry and drew sketches of mystical beings. There was nothing at all in her voice to suggest the drama and emotion in her drawings. It beguiled me to listen to that quiet voice, so confident, so calm. I took pains to conceal her growing power over my attention when I met her in the gallery or on the staircase, which appeared successful since she seemed completely oblivious to my distraction and maintained her reserve. At other times I tried to draw her out, asking more than once to see her entire portfolio, which would not release its hold on my imagination. But she remained reserved with me. I remembered something Mr. Landes had said: One must keep one's inferiors at a distance, or else one will lose all authority, and I guessed that perhaps someone might have given a reverse admonition to Miss Eyre.

One evening, at the request of my land agent, I hosted a gathering of landowners for the purpose of discussing how best we might control the poachers who seemed to have overrun the neighborhood. At the end, over glasses of sherry, the conversation turned to lighter topics, and I shared Jane's portfolio with them, for I was still in thrall with her work. They were suitably impressed, and I confess it gave me more pleasure than perhaps it should have to hear them praise her, and me for having her in my employ. I toasted with them my good fortune in having such a talented governess for my ward, and when my guests took their leave, I sent for Miss Eyre and Adèle, for whom a box from Paris had lately arrived. As soon as they stepped into the room, Adèle ran for the carton, exclaiming: "*Ma boîte! Ma boîte!*"

"Yes—there is your *boîte* at last," I said. I did try to be kind with the child but would often be thrown off course by sudden, unwelcome reminders of Céline. I sent her off to disembowel the package, and I came to myself and glanced around. "Is Miss Eyre there?" I asked, and then I saw her, tucked in a corner, as was her way. "Well, come forward; be seated here." I pulled a chair closer to my own for her, for I had no intention of being distracted by Adèle. I sent for Mrs. Fairfax to attend to the girl's joyous chatter, while I conversed with the governess.

It seemed the sort of moment I had enjoyed far too seldom in my life: a moment of relaxation, with the opportunity for true conversation of real depth, with a worthy—or so I hoped—conversationalist. But I could not think what to say. For a time there was only the sound of Adèle's chatter, and the rain driving against the window pane, and the crackle and hiss of the fire. I grew aware of Miss Eyre's eyes upon me, as so often I had observed her when she was otherwise occupied. I wondered what she saw there, since I could not remember when I had felt myself truly seen and contemplated in such a way. "You examine me, Miss Eyre: do you think me handsome?" I asked her.

Perhaps I was craving more simple praise, as I had earlier received from my dinner guests. But in that case it was a question foolishly set forth, for her response seemed to surprise us both: "No, sir."

There is no gracious recovery from such a response, but her honesty startled me—so different from the craven flattery I'd too often heard since I joined society. So I challenged her to announce what specific faults she found in me. It was not so much that I wanted to hear my failings recited— both Bertha and Céline had done that sufficiently—as it was simple curiosity to know how I looked to those lovely eyes. In all, I could not remember the last time I had been spoken to so frankly.

Was I handsome? I knew I was not, no more than she was beautiful. But she was cast in a different mold from the majority, and I found myself eager to hear her assessment, kind or cruel. But now she equivocated, worried no doubt that she had overstepped her bounds. We talked anyway, of other things.

It quickly became evident that, though her mind was sprightly and deft, she held to a moral core that could not be swayed, and was outspoken in its defense, occasionally to the point of insolence. I did not mind—indeed, this only further lit the fires of my curiosity. I discovered that if I played the role of master too broadly, and pushed her too imperiously, she became stubborn and annoyed, so I took care to apologize where I could, to treat her not as an inferior but as a younger, inexperienced equal, for there was something in this Miss Eyre that I could not resist prying into. Then, of course, she began to challenge *me*, and I found myself engaged in a wide-ranging philosophical debate on my own sins and conscience and truth—strangely enough, one of the most satisfying, provocative, and engaging conversations I had had in many years. This little governess was a rare creature indeed, and I found it impossible to be conventional with her. We talked this way deep into the evening.

CHAPTER 12

For the first time since Bertha had taken up residence in Thornfield-Hall, I found myself no longer tormented by the idea of remaining within its walls for more than a handful of days. It is not that I forgot Bertha; indeed, I slipped upstairs every day or two to check on her and affirm to myself that Grace Poole had her care well in hand; on that point I was always satisfied, though occasionally Grace appeared somewhat distracted. Bertha continued on as she always had, alternately raving and sleeping. I thought of telling her that her son lived, that he seemed to be thriving and well, but I could not be sure she would have understood me, and the news, to be frank, now brought me little joy. So I said nothing.

No, the change in the oppression I felt at Thornfield came not from Bertha, but from Jane Eyre, the peculiar young governess herself.

The more time I spent with Jane—yes, I had already begun to think of her as Jane, although I knew better than to call her that openly— the more I valued her presence. I spent more time at Thornfield than I had previously, and I had taken to inviting Jane to come to me after tea on the evenings that I was not away with the Ingrams or the others. At those times we read to each other while Adèle played with her dolls nearby, or we chatted lightly, or more often seriously, for she was a serious person, and was well-read and could argue cogently. She seemed to delight in vexing and then pleasing me by turns—it was an unusual arrangement for a master and employee, perhaps, but I had no cause to complain.

I enjoyed Jane's company immensely, but the more comfortable I became in her presence, the more ominously I felt the weight of Bertha's presence overhead. I could not imagine what Jane, with her strict moral vision, would think of me if she knew of the inmate on the third floor; I was sure she would not stay one more day in my employ if she were to find out. Yet I believe she sensed I was withholding something, and, further, that she was moved by my burden, despite having no idea what troubled me.

One evening, however, she came dangerously close to finding out. That afternoon, during my usual visit to Bertha, my wife had been more disturbed than usual, begging me to bed her, and when I refused she became violently enraged, her eyes flashing with a dark fury. It made me wonder for a moment if she, too, could sense a change in me, a peace and happiness attributable to another. But, surely, jealousy was now too complex and rational an emotion for this creature in my house, was it not?

I left her to Grace's calming influence and fled to the lawn, where I found Adèle and Pilot playing, with Jane watchful nearby. Jane agreed to stroll with me and, driven perhaps by a need to confess—even if I could not speak the true weight on my mind—I unburdened myself to her about Adèle's history and my relationship with Céline. It offered me an unfamiliar but refreshing feeling of relief.

The whole time, Jane walked beside me in silence, her eyes on my face as I spoke, offering neither absolution nor censure. But at one point during our walk I made the mistake of looking up at the house, where, despite that the windows in Bertha's room were far above her head, I swore I could feel my mad wife staring down at Jane and me.

Guilt and worry tumbled through my head as I tried to sleep that night, tortured by a nagging regret over how despicable my life had often been, especially to imagine, now, how it appeared to Jane's steady, righteous eyes. Finally, I took a small portion of the draught that Mr. Carter had

328 • Sarah Shoemaker

left for me when I had sprained my ankle, and at last I fell into a heavy sleep.

Hours later I was roused by the sensation of drowning in a deep well. I struggled to gain the surface, only to discover that I was in my own bed, entangled by the sodden bedcovers. "Is there a flood?" I cried out.

"No, sir," came Jane's voice, sounding as ethereal as it had on the causeway; "but there has been a fire: get up."

Still half-asleep, I imagined elves, witches, even demons as I rose from the bed, and looking about, I finally grasped the truth: someone had set fire to my bedclothes, and it was Jane herself who had saved me, pouring water from my ewer and hers to stanch the flames. It did not take much more for me to understand who must have been the culprit.

Leaving Jane safe and warm in my room, and entreating her to send no further alarm in the household, I took the candle she had provided me and rushed up the staircase to Bertha's apartment. I had thought to confront her—give release to my fury and fears that she had endangered me and the rest of the household, including Jane—but as I flung open the door I found my wife struggling fiercely against Grace Poole. I managed to pry Bertha's fingers from Grace's throat and, with no other solution at hand, captured her in my own arms. I swallowed my anger and murmured soothing words until she quieted and could be put to bed. She demanded that I lie with her, that I "be a man," but it was all I could do to remain calm, not to scream at her. As soon as I could I left her there, locking the door behind me.

In the front chamber, Grace was holding a cloth to the sore flesh of her neck. "She has been disturbed all day, since you left," she said. "She insists someone has invaded her house. But I thought she had calmed—"

I interrupted her. "See that it does not happen again."

"Of course." She nodded.

"It *cannot* happen again."

She stepped back as if I had struck her. "I understand," she said. I thought I smelled alcohol on her breath.

"Were you drinking?"

She paused. "Just my mug of porter."

I felt my anger spiking once again, but I tamped it down. Surely, Grace's life here was difficult—shut into this apartment with a madwoman—but Grace had come into it with her eyes open, knowing the ways of the mad, understanding what it would be. And now this carelessness, her drinking, had moments ago nearly cost me my life. I could not allow it. And yet, I reminded myself, even as Bertha had worsened, Grace had never asked to be relieved. Her life had been a hard one, and this was most likely not the worst of it. I sighed. "Make sure it is never more than one," I said, and left that wretched place.

I paused on the stairs, wondering if I must bring Jane into my confidence—reveal Bertha to her. And if I did? She would leave my employ immediately. Her moral conscience would never allow her to work for a man who kept his wife secured upstairs like that. I would lose this ray of light that had so recently come to shine on my life at Thornfield. No, I could not risk that.

When I returned to my chamber, Jane was still there, as I had ordered her, sitting in the dark, probably terrified, but safe. She confirmed, to my relief, that she had seen nothing; for some reason she seemed to think it had been Grace Poole's doing. Well, I thought, there could be worse explanations.

"Good night, then, sir," she said, and started to leave.

"What!" I said, for I was reluctant to let her go without some assurance that nothing between us had been jeopardized by Bertha's evil act. "Are you quitting me already: and in that way?"

"You said I might go, sir," she responded.

"But not without taking leave; not without a word or two of acknowledgment and goodwill: not, in short, in that brief, dry fashion. Why, you have saved my life!—snatched me from a horrible and excruciating death!—and you walk past me as if we were mutual strangers! At least shake hands." Obediently, she put her small hand in mine and I covered it with my other hand. If we could have, I would have stood there the rest of the night, her hand in mine, her eyes on my face. I was barely able to speak to her then, though I know I said more of what I owed her, and, too soon, she fled when we heard Mrs. Fairfax stirring.

She had saved my life in more ways than she knew. I would keep Bertha a secret from her, no matter what. I would do whatever I must to not lose Jane Eyre.

CHAPTER 13

I slept only fitfully for the remainder of the night, and rose from my couch before the servants began their work. Immediately I climbed to Bertha's hidden apartment and let myself in. Grace was dozing in her chair, but I could hear Bertha pacing and mumbling in the adjoining chamber. Soon after dawn, I knew, she would fall into sleep and Grace would take her daily respite away from that terrible place. I shook Grace awake, and she startled in agitation, as if she expected to see Bertha bearing down on her at any moment.

"A word, Grace," I said.

"Sir?"

"Take this," I said, handing her the rest of the sedative that Carter had given me. "Give this to my wife in her usual cup of tea if she seems to you unusually disturbed. It will not make an addict of her if you give her the correct amount. I will get more from Mr. Carter, and perhaps I shall have a stronger lock installed on the door." I studied the two windows high on the wall—they were indeed too high to see out of...unless... "Have you ever seen her pull a chair over and look out those windows?"

"No, sir, I have not, but it is not impossible. I sometimes must leave, for food or to empty chamber pots."

I stared up at the windows. I could not paint them over: that would leave the rooms forever dark and airless, more like a cell than I could bear to think. "You must be sure to lock her in her chamber whenever you must leave, even if she is sleeping. *Always*. Today you will be needed to help repair the damage done in the night: that will be a welcome change for you, I should think. And don't speak to anyone of this. You know nothing of what happened in the night—whatever tales you hear, *you yourself* know nothing. And one more thing: I have brought you this length of rope. If there is ever a need, we will use it to bind her to keep her from doing real damage. You understand?"

She tried to stammer an answer.

"It was Mr. Carter who suggested it," I added, for, indeed, he had.

"Yes, sir," she said.

"Thank you. I am in your debt; I am well aware of that."

She nodded. "And I in yours." A curious response, I thought then and think still.

"Good day, Grace," I said.

"Good day, sir," she responded.

———

I wanted nothing more than to see Jane that morning, and I feared nothing more, as well. I wished, in those stolen moments in the night, she had given me more reassurance of our common feeling, had spoken to the companionship I had felt growing between us. But she did not, and I found myself increasingly disturbed by the horror of having both Bertha and Jane under the same roof, risking the chance of discovery, or something worse. I needed to solve the problem, and quickly, but was unable to clear my head.

I confess that in my distress I succumbed to my old habits and fled Thornfield altogether. I told myself that this was for the best, that time away would allow me to avoid any questions regarding the fire and let the whole thing be finished and forgotten before my return.

Fortunately, that very evening there was to be a gathering at the Leas, the home of Mr. Eshton, the local magistrate, and his wife. The major families in the neighborhood had been invited, including myself. I had sent my apologies a few days previous, preferring instead to spend my days in conversation with Jane, but now I sent a message ahead that I would be coming after all. I hurriedly packed my things, went down the back stairs to the kitchen, and had a quick breakfast and was off on Mesrour. My trunk would follow in the cart. It was cowardly, I knew then and admit still, but at the time it seemed the cautious thing to do. And, if I am being honest, a small part of me also wished to make Jane feel my absence, to show her how easily I could leave her, too, after her almost emotionless farewell in the night.

As it happened, it might have been better had I remained at home.

Riding across the countryside, I purposely turned my mind to Miss Ingram and reminded myself that this was where my affections should lie. She was beautiful, charming, accomplished in every way, an established and admired member of the neighborhood society. Yet, I did not feel a sympathy with her in the way that I had come to feel with Jane. She did not have the power to intrigue me, as this young girl had, did not bring me the same pleasure—or pain. Still, is it ever wise to let one's emotions rule one's life? Did I not do that for all those regrettable years in Europe?

I told myself—sternly—that Blanche Ingram was my fate. That I should value her for her social charms and beauty as I was valued for my name and land and income. With her as its mistress, Thornfield-Hall could once again be bright with candles and elegant women and music. What more could a man want? What more, indeed.

When I arrived at the Leas, the group was just finishing a lazy breakfast. They had all arrived the night before and had stayed up late gossiping, I suppose, and had slept nearly till midmorning. Miss Ingram's eyes caught on me as I entered the room, and she smiled broadly and patted the back of the empty chair beside her. "I knew you would change your mind," she called out. "You could not possibly miss the fun!"

Eshton rose and indicated the same empty chair. "Sit, Rochester! So good you could join us after all."

I gazed around the room: Lord and Lady Ingram and their son, Theodore, and their other daughter, Mary; Lord and Lady Lynn and their sons; Colonel and Mrs. Dent; Mrs. Eshton and the two Eshton daughters. They all greeted me warmly in one way or another, and immediately folded me into their conversation.

This is where I belong, I told myself. *These are the people whom I was bred to join.* I filled a plate at the buffet and sat down beside Miss Ingram. She was telling a story of the vicar of the local parish, a meek man of limited talents, and imitating his lisp with remarkable accuracy.

"Why, Blanche, do you not indeed find his sermons stimulating?" her brother asked in a mocking tone.

Miss Ingram laughed. "Stimulating to sleep, I would say!" She turned to me, her eyes sparkling with laughter. "What would you say, Rochester?"

"I have only heard the man once or twice," I responded. Indeed, he had seemed a fool, but a harmless one.

"That is enough for an opinion, surely," she pressed.

"Well, I suppose he is good for an hour or so of sleep," I admitted, reluctantly.

Ted Ingram let out a loud guffaw. "At least. *At least!* Would he not be good for a nightly sleeping draught?" I did not care for Ted; he was tall and slim and elegant, and he had a way of dismissing anyone he did not think worth his time. I could not see him without thinking of Rowland.

"And his wife," Miss Ingram pressed. "Have you ever seen anyone so mousey? Brown hair, brown clothes, and she never speaks a word without his permission first."

"That last part is not so bad, actually," Colonel Dent observed.

"Oh, really?" Miss Ingram parried, leaning forward across the table. "Do you think all women should be silent unless spoken to?"

"Present company excepted," he responded. "But a woman like that, what possible ideas could be floating around in her head?"

"No doubt she is worrying herself over what woman might steal her husband away from her, such a *marvelous* catch he would be!" Miss Ingram said with her eyes fully on me. I nodded uncomfortably and the whole company laughed.

Lady Lynn, who was seated nearby, leaned over just then to ask: did I not have a ward under my care?

"Yes, I do," I responded mildly. "A French child, but she is learning English."

"Learning?" said Lady Lynn. "So she must have a tutor or a...a governess?"

"A governess, yes."

"And is she pretty?" Miss Ingram interjected.

"She's only seven, but yes, I suppose—"

Miss Ingram laughed. "The governess, I meant. Is *she* pretty?"

"Ah." I hesitated, unsure how best to halt this line of inquiry. "In a way, I suppose."

She laughed again. "Not such high praise, I think." She leaned closer to me, in confidence. "My father had an eye for every governess we ever had. He seemed to think it his prerogative. My mother ignored it, but we all three hated every one of them."

"Adèle seems to like this one well enough," I said, and I left it at that.

My father had an eye for every governess we ever had. I could not shake the comment. As my time at the Leas lengthened, my opinion of Miss Ingram soured and my respect for Jane grew. But how true were my feelings? Did I find her appealing only for her dependence? No, decidedly not—she was hardly of a dependent spirit, whether or not she accepted a salary. But I could see how it would look if I seemed to favor Jane—to Jane first of all, but also to Miss Ingram and all the rest as well. Even to Mrs. Fairfax, no doubt. I, the master of the house, exacting pleasure from an underling—that's how it would appear, and how many times had that happened? I thought back to Jamaica, where many men *owned* girls and they so often took advantage of the fact. Had not I myself, at the age of fifteen, tried to claim the affections of a girl in the mill's employ? No. If there were to be anything between me and Jane Eyre, I would have to convince her to come to me. I must reveal to her my affections without expressing them directly; *show* her how she suited me far better than any other; then extend my hand and wait for her to take it. For this now seemed immutable: *she* must make the movement—I could not.

I could almost laugh at the irony: I had spent years in Europe, hoping for a woman who would suit me. Now here I was, faced with one woman who suited me better than any ever had, but whom society would not accept as my equal; and another woman who pleased society to no end but not me; and still a third woman with whom no one cared to spend two minutes unless paid handsomely for the duty. And it was this last to whom I was married. Oh, God in heaven. Jane was my only hope for relief, for regeneration.

But how to manage it? How to convince Jane, first of all, that I preferred her company above these others', that I was not merely dallying with her as a man in my position might? How to break through that composure and provoke a reaction that would allow her to reveal what she thought of me, she who guarded herself so closely?

———

As I contemplated all that, the days flew by; there were riding parties and excursions and picnics and every evening a dance or an entertainment of one sort or another. Though it did not give me quite as much pleasure as it once would have, I enjoyed showing off Mesrour to Miss Ingram, who did at first seem to be suitably impressed. She admired his size and his vigor but seized immediately on the fact that, as I had been warned, he was not a good jumper. "You should have taken me to see him before you made the purchase," she scolded me. "I would have told you he wasn't suitable."

"Well," I responded, "he's suitable for *me*."

"Really, Rochester," was all she said.

I did try to flirt when the occasion called for it, but my heart wasn't in it. In the rare moments that we were alone together, Miss Ingram asked me about Thornfield—she seemed already to know the extent of its acreage, but she was curious about the number of cottagers and the amount of land under cultivation and the number of servants I kept in the house, all of which she approached in such circuitous ways that I believe she thought I would not notice her interest. I was reminded again of Rowland and his calculations and was surprised this had not struck me before.

I was reminded of someone else as well, a figure even more loathsome in my life than my callous brother. I watched Miss Ingram make her grand entrances, determined to be admired in all things: the best markswoman, riding the finest horse, dressed in the most beautiful clothes, noted as the best dancer, the best singer, the best pianist. The others, I noticed, always made way for her to go first. It was that familiar determination to be the envy of everyone present that completely, irredeemably finished her for me, and after that I knew I must withdraw myself from her inner circle. That was the easy part; the other—provoking Jane to act—was much more difficult, but perhaps, I realized, I could use one to accomplish the other.

I waited until after dinner to broach the subject. Miss Ingram had been at my side all evening. Sitting in the Eshtons' drawing room, listening to Miss Ingram play the piano, I thought again of Jane, of her amusing lack of skill at that instrument, but also her lack of embarrassment about it. It was time for me to return to Thornfield: I yearned to see Jane again, and I worried over Bertha. I knew I would receive word from Thornfield if another event occurred, but I also knew I could not afford to wait for that to happen. I needed to be on hand, I told myself. I needed to make sure that all was still well. And I could not keep Gerald Rochester out of my mind. Someday he would appear, I was sure, and I could not leave those at Thornfield, who knew nothing of him, to deal with him alone.

When Miss Ingram finished her piece, I vigorously applauded, and before anyone else could say anything, I rose. "Miss Ingram, perhaps you don't know that I purchased a new pianoforte when I returned from Jamaica. While I have dabbled at playing on it, I would like nothing more than to have you christen it properly. Why don't we all"—I cast my gaze around the room to include all present—"why don't we all move on to Thornfield-Hall, where it has been many years since a party of this significance has entered our gates." How could they decline such an invitation? As I expected, Miss Ingram was the first to gush her enthusiasm, and the next morning I sent a message to Mrs. Fairfax to prepare for our arrival.

———

I may have fled like a coward from Thornfield, but a fortnight later I returned like a king, and what a procession we must have seemed as we rode up the drive to Thornfield-Hall: the carriages polished and shined, the coach horses trotting briskly with braided manes and ribboned tails, and the rest of us on horseback leading the way, with Miss Ingram and I in front, she resplendent in purple with a matching purple veil surrounding her black curls, and I sitting proudly on Mesrour. I only hoped Adèle might have dragged Jane to the window to watch our approach.

I did not see Jane the day we arrived, nor did I expect to. She would have, as a matter of course, kept Adèle and herself invisible to the company unless they were summoned. But I did catch Mrs. Fairfax to ask if all had gone well in my absence, eager for assurance that Bertha had remained safe in her chambers.

"All was tranquil, Mr. Rochester," she responded.

"Nothing unexpected occurred?"

"No, sir, except for a man who came looking for you, shortly after you left."

I drew a quick breath. "Did he leave a name?"

"I asked his name, but all he said was that he was a relative, on the Rochester side. And he did not say what he wanted—only to speak with you."

"It was only you who spoke to him?"

"Yes. A handsome man, I must say."

"Did he say . . . that he would return?"

"Oh yes, indeed. And as he claimed a relation, I told him he would be welcome anytime."

I paused, unsure how to instruct her without showing my alarm, and finally I turned away.

———

The first dinner at a hosting house is always a magnificent affair, and Thornfield's was no different. The polished lustres gleamed, the plates sparkled in the candlelight, village men hired for the duration as footmen stood proud and straight in their finery, and the food was excellent. Mrs. Fairfax had, in all ways, done a superb job. The party lasted well into the night, and I wondered if we were keeping Jane from her slumber. I would be sure to have her in attendance tomorrow.

The next day an excursion was planned to an ancient stone circle, famous in the neighborhood. Before we left, when Mrs. Fairfax was making sure everything was in readiness, I stopped her for a moment, asking after Adèle and Miss Eyre.

"Oh, sir," she said, "you should have seen Adèle last evening! She was dressed to the nines, hoping to be invited downstairs."

"Well then," I said, "have Miss Eyre bring her to the drawing room this evening after dinner."

"Mr. Rochester, sir, I don't know about that. Miss Eyre is not so used to...to...such company. I can't imagine she would like appearing before so gay a party—all those strangers."

"Nonsense!" I replied. Though Mrs. Fairfax spoke the truth, I would hear nothing of it. "If she objects," I added, "tell her I will come and fetch her myself in return for her rebellion!" Jane *must* attend the gatherings; there could be no discussion. She held the most essential role in my play.

And come she did, but hidden in a corner, nearly behind some window draperies, while Adèle allowed herself to be petted by the ladies. Jane was working on some handwork, and I could tell that she chose not to look at me unless she felt sure I was occupied elsewhere. So, for my part, I stood beside the mantelpiece, watching the scene before me: Lord Ingram flirting with Amy Eshton; the other men gathered in a corner talking politics or rent-rolls no doubt; Adèle vying for attention from whoever would give it; Louisa Eshton sitting with one of the Lynn brothers, who was trying to speak French to Adèle; Mrs. Dent acting the grandmother she someday would be; and Lady Ingram, haughty and proud, sitting on the settee and nodding in conversation with her daughter Blanche, who seemed to be just waiting for me to approach. Of all of them, it was only Jane Eyre, sitting patiently in a corner, whom I did not watch; yet it was she on whom every fiber of my attention was focused.

And yet, to my shame, I knew the evening was painful for her, especially when Miss Ingram and her mother began an overloud and odious dissertation on children and, more to the point, their governesses, indirectly pointing their blunt conversational daggers at Jane herself. Ted Ingram, of course, could not refrain from adding his bit, making the conversation even more distasteful. While my first instinct was to protect Jane, I suppressed it: Jane had a sturdy sense of self and did not need my protection. Instead, I chose to let my distinguished guests parade in front of her their grotesque opinions and smallness of mind, showing at each turn how unworthy they were compared to the steadfast little governess in their midst.

It was Miss Ingram herself who changed the subject, for she, so unlike Jane, reveled in attention. Shooing Louisa Eshton away and seating herself at the piano, she called for me to sing with her, and I fell into her game—a game she believed she was winning, even as I mocked her with overwrought obedience and excessive praise. She, so used to being spoiled, thought it genuine emotion, I am sure. How I wanted to sit with Jane one day and laugh at Miss Ingram, the same way Miss Ingram had mocked the vicar and his wife so mercilessly, though on second thought, I could not imagine Jane laughing at anyone's frailties. But Jane could see, I was sure, the artifice beneath nearly everything Miss Ingram said or did: the way that woman treated Adèle, the absence of any originality of mind and the shallowness of conversation, no matter how showy she was in presenting herself. It would be immediately clear to Jane that she was far better suited as a companion to me than Miss Ingram would ever be.

I moved away from the piano when I had finished in a sign that I had had enough, and as the talk turned to something entirely different, I noticed Jane attempting to make a quiet exit. I followed and caught her just as she was about to mount the staircase.

"Miss Eyre," I said gently, "how do you do?"

"I am very well, sir," she responded.

"Why did you not come and speak to me in the room?"

She replied, as I could have known she would, that she did not wish to disturb me when I seemed otherwise engaged. I longed to hear her say she had missed me, but she did not; I pointed out that she looked pale, yet she would not confess to jealousy, too polite to give any reaction at all to the odious scenes played out before her that evening. As ever, she kept her own counsel. I tried to urge her to return with me to the drawing room, but I saw that the thought of it nearly drew tears to her eyes. Aha—there was feeling in there for me after all. I did not wish her to suffer, only to allow that I belonged with her, not with Blanche Ingram. But this evening I had pushed her too far already, I saw, and regretted it.

"Well, tonight, I excuse you," I told her, "but understand that so long as my visitors stay, I expect you to appear in the drawing room every evening; it is my wish; don't neglect it. Now go, and send Sophie for Adèle...Good night, my—" I swallowed that final word and fled, having nearly played my whole hand at once.

CHAPTER 14

The next few days continued in a similar vein: the assembled guests entertained themselves in one way and then another, the younger group flirting ridiculously—Miss Ingram and I among them. I hesitate to confess that some cruel part of me enjoyed tormenting Miss Ingram in this way, drawing her on with my pretended affections, whose hollowness she was too self-absorbed to perceive. I could never have treated a true heart in this way, but the Janus-faced Miss Ingram—who had served up her own fair share of duplicitous praise and gossip even within my own hearing—deserved little better. I looked forward to the day she would learn I had chosen the unassuming Jane over her haughty excesses.

But regardless of what I did or said, Jane sat quietly, stoically, in the corner. It soon became clear that she would not be provoked this way. If I wanted a reaction, I must force an engagement. As my guests prattled on around me, I scoured my mind for every battle plan I had learned at Mr. Lincoln's table, seeking perfect deception and surprise. At last, I landed on the great genius himself: William Shakespeare. Like Hamlet, I would prepare a play to catch my mark.

One evening, as if it had suddenly occurred to me, I suggested a game of charades. I did offhandedly suggest Jane join my party, but she, as I knew she would, chose to remain an observer, sitting quietly, reacting to nothing, yet watching us all with her uncompromising eye.

The first portrayal was my suggestion, and it was the easiest and the most daring: a marriage scene, with myself as the bridegroom and Blanche as the bride. I confess to a measure of mischief, knowing that the scene would excite Miss Ingram every bit as much as I intended to provoke Jane. The second scene was more obscure, but still I hoped that "Eliezer and Rebecca at the well" might open Jane's mind to the possibility of love from an unexpected source. The opposing party did not correctly guess the scene, but I felt sure Jane had.

The third scene was guessed immediately and correctly as "Bridewell," and that completed the theme. As I was being complimented on my acting, I loudly reminded Miss Ingram that she was now my wife, for we had been married an hour since. Secretly I watched Jane's face in these moments, hoping that her reaction would reveal her thoughts. I had no doubt that she had seen and heard enough of Miss Ingram by then to know how inferior a specimen she was, that Thornfield-Hall would be a miserable place with Blanche as its mistress. And yet, Jane did not react.

What was I to do? Had I been wrong to think that in her heart Jane returned my interest, that I had charmed and intrigued her the same way she had me?

I will admit that it required a sleepless night before I understood how unfeeling I had been. How could I fairly have expected her to speak her mind in front of the whole company, this plain, polite little creature who held her emotions so thoroughly in check? Of course she would not have spoken. Clearly I needed both to increase the urgency for her, to drive her to confess, but also to do so in private. I set to thinking.

One morning, I managed to absent myself on the excuse of business in Millcote. The ladies were talking of going to Hay Common to visit the Gypsy camp, while I slipped upstairs to pay my usual visit to Bertha and Grace Poole, keen to assure myself there would be no more surprises while my guests were at Thornfield. Before I left, I begged of Grace some old ragged gowns and shawls of Bertha's, which would suit me nicely, as Bertha was as tall and large as most grown men. I made a few more stops on the road to Millcote and then took a room at the inn. Though I entered that room as a landed gentleman, after a careful toilette I emerged and slipped down the back stairs, unnoticed, as an elderly Gypsy woman.

That evening I appeared at Thornfield's kitchen door, got up in my disguise. The performance was not difficult for me, after my theater days at Trinity College, where I was inevitably cast as the ugly character, the witch, or the depraved person. One of the village women hired as cook's assistant for the duration stared at me unblinking. It was no trick to fool her, for she was not so very used to seeing the master of the house, but when Leah came to the door as well and tried to shoo me away, I knew I would succeed. "I only want to visit the guests who are here," I croaked at her. "I only want to tell a fortune or two."

"They are busy in their own pursuits; they have no need for the likes of you," she responded, moving to close the door against me. (There was a strange freedom, I found, in being treated thus—it had been many years since I had felt what it was like to be an inferior, not a master.)

But I pushed myself into the kitchen, hobbled to the chimney corner, and sat down before anyone could stop me. "I need to rest myself," I wheezed. "I have come a long way on this dark night."

The kitchen workers crowded around me, full of conjecture. "Can she really tell fortunes?" one said. "I'd 'ave mine told," said another. "Get on with 'er," said another. "She only wants to scope the place for the plate there might be."

"This foretelling must be spoken and heard. Your guests will be pleased with what I have to say," I said.

In a moment Mrs. Fairfax entered to see what the disturbance was. She bent to me, and briefly I worried she would see through the disguise, but she did not. Poor Mrs. Fairfax, she knew only how to be kind, and she could not think of a way to dislodge me from my position; but just then Sam returned with the news that the guests would indeed see the Gypsy in the drawing room.

"Oh no," I said. "Not in a cluster like a vulgar herd. Each one should have her own chance in a private room, for I may say things they won't want shared." I told him to bring only the young and single ladies.

peR. ROCHESTER • 345

Sam left again and soon returned with word that the ladies would see me, one by one, in the library, as I had demanded. I made a great show of indignation at the treatment I had received and also a show of confusion over the location of the library.

I knew Miss Ingram would be the first to appear, for she would not want anyone else to have the first look at the old Gypsy. As she entered the room, I motioned to a chair in front of me and begged "milady" to sit down. I set my face in shadow, for although even Mrs. Fairfax had not known me, I could not risk being found out.

"Let me see your palm," I said in my rasping voice. She opened her hand for me but flinched as I reached for it. She would not let me touch it.

"Do you fear me, miss?"

Her face remained rigid. "Of course not!"

"You have great hopes for marriage. To be mistress of this great house," I said.

"That may already be well-known," she snapped.

I peered closely into her hand, as if examining her palm. "You are an equestrian, are you not? And you are proud—"

"And that is known as well. If that is all you have to say, you are certainly nothing but a charlatan."

I leaned closer to her, and she moved back in her chair. "You are interested in this place—this Thornfield. You have already made inquiries, I suspect; do you approve of the rent-rolls?" That stopped her, and before she could think what to say, I added, "You think they should be raised." That latter was a guess on my part, but she seemed so disturbed that I knew I had hit my mark.

"You are satisfied with those numbers?" I prodded.

"You tell me," she demanded. "Yours is not to question; it is to answer."

I shrugged. "You think they should be larger. You have been mulling ideas of your own, changes you plan to make as soon as you are mistress."

She was about to reply, but I cut her off.

"But you do not know the debts to the place, I think. You do not know that he is a gambler and has already gambled away half his fortune."

Her face was suddenly still.

"Did you not know he went to Millcote this morning to arrange for the sale of more land to pay his debts? And his property in Jamaica is gone."

"I did not know—"

"Oh yes. There is much you do not know."

She started to rise, but I held her back by saying, "Do you not want to know who he will marry? It is not you. No, it is someone with far greater riches and truer beauty than you will ever know."

At that she rose with a start. "You are an ugly old hag! How could you know what will proceed? The future is unknown to all."

"It is not unknown to me," I replied, and she fled from the room.

Next came the three young ladies: Mary Ingram and Louisa and Amy Eshton, giggling and shrieking from embarrassment and fear. They had refused to see me except in a group. "Welcome, and sit down," I said, and waited for additional chairs to be pulled into place.

"You thought it would be fun to tease the old Gypsy, did you not?" I said when they were all seated.

Miss Mary Ingram spoke up. "What did you tell my sister?"

"Do you think I should tell her secrets? Would you like me to tell her yours?"

"Then tell my fortune."

I leaned back into my chair, the shadows better covering my face. "First, I will tell something of your past. Yes, indeed, you and your sister and brother tortured your governesses until they left in despair: calling them names, throwing books into the air, scattering crumbs of biscuit around the nursery."

The Eshton girls sat openmouthed, and Mary Ingram winced, as if I had physically attacked her.

"Tell me: are those the actions of proper children?" I asked. Then, recalling every family story I had heard around the dinner table, I told a tale or two on each girl: how Louisa had tried to climb a tree and was too afraid to climb back down, how Mary had been thrown from a horse at the age of twelve and had refused to ride ever since, how Amy had secretly learned to cook eggs and had surprised her mother by making breakfast for her mother's birthday just last year. And I described their homes and their favorite lockets and the books they preferred to read. Through it all, they sat amazed that an old Gypsy could have seen so closely into their lives.

"What about the future?" Mary asked softly when I had finished.

"Ah," I croaked, "the future is far more difficult, for it has not yet been written in stone, as the past has. You cannot erase the past, but you can change the future."

"Will my sister marry Mr. Rochester?" Mary asked suddenly.

"Your sister does not love Mr. Rochester. She will not marry him."

The three sat silent in astonishment.

"I told that lady many things," I added, "and some of it she did not want to hear." But I didn't want to send them back with sour faces, so I gave them beautiful, obedient children; stately homes; lovely gowns and exquisite jewelry—all the things I imagined young girls dream of, and I even whispered into each delicate ear the name of a young man in their group whom I was sure held her interest. I sent them away giggling.

After they left, Sam returned to usher me out, as all the young ladies had seen me.

"All?" I said. "*All?*" Sam nodded, not understanding whom I was after. "There is one more, is there not?"

"Ah, well. But she is not a lady," he insisted.

"No? What is she, then?"

"She is just the governess—a kind person indeed, but—"

"She is a *lady*, young man, and I will see her."

"She is a private person. She may not come."

"You may tell her I will not leave until she comes."

He hurried away, and as he went, I adjusted my disguise, and gripped tightly the arms of my chair. Now came the true test.

Miss Ingram had come in imperious and defiant; the three girls had come shy and a little afraid; but my Jane came in curious and, as ever, composed. I pretended to read as she entered and ignored her at first, to see how she would act in private with a person by all accounts her social inferior. I was pleased, but not surprised, to see her wait as calmly and respectfully as she did for me in my normal guise. "Well, and you want your fortune told?" I asked her.

"I don't care about it, Mother," she said; "you may please yourself: but I ought to warn you, I have no faith."

I suppressed a smile. This was my Jane, all right.

"Why don't you tremble?" I asked.

"I'm not cold," she responded.

"Why don't you turn pale?"

"I am not sick."

"Why don't you consult my art?"

"I'm not silly."

I chuckled, for I had guessed well her responses. I pulled out a pipe and lit it slowly, and gazed for a time into the fire, letting her observe me all the while. Then I said, "You *are* cold; you are sick; and you are silly."

"Prove it."

"You are cold, because you are alone: no contact strikes the fire from you that is in you. You are sick; because the best of feelings, the highest and the sweetest given to man, keeps far away from you. You are silly, because, suffer as you may, you will not beckon it to approach; nor will you stir one step to meet it where it waits you." There, I had laid it out.

She did not take the bait. "You might say all that to almost anyone," she replied.

"But would it be true of almost anyone? Find me another precisely placed as you are."

"It would be easy to find you thousands," she responded.

"You could scarcely find me *one*. If you knew it, you are peculiarly situated: very near happiness; yes; within reach of it." What did I have to do to make her rise to my provocations? I promised her bliss in exchange for one movement. But she still would not act.

"I don't understand enigmas," she responded. "I never could guess a riddle in my life." My sturdy Jane was not going to bend, was not going to give an inch, even to a poor old Gypsy.

"If you wish me to speak more plainly," I challenged, "show me your palm."

She handed me a shilling, which I stowed away as carefully as if it were worth a guinea, and I bent over the fine lines in her flesh, wishing that I were a real fortune-teller, who would know her heart line, and what it said of her. Cautiously I raised my eyes to her. "Destiny is not written there. It is in the face: on the forehead, about the eyes, in the eyes themselves." Those eyes: how often had I wished to plumb their depths. "And in the lines of the mouth. Kneel, and lift up your head." I came within half a yard of her, and stirred the fire, whose glare lit Jane's face more fully, and more deeply cloaked my own.

I saw her watching me, and I waited for a while before saying, "I wonder with what feelings you came to me tonight. I wonder what thoughts are busy in your heart during all the hours you sit in yonder room with the fine people flitting before you like shapes in a magic lantern."

She gave a little shrug, confessing nothing.

What was she made of, this Jane? "Then you have some secret hope," I asked, "to buoy you up and please you with whispers of the future?"

"Not I. The utmost I hope is, to save money enough out of my earnings to set up a school someday in a little house rented by myself."

Alone. But independent. Was that truly all she hoped for? Solitary independence, devoid of love and family? Did she really not crave my love as I craved hers? "A mean nutriment for the spirit to exist on," I countered, "and sitting in that window seat (you see I know your habits)—"

"You have learned them from the servants," she interrupted.

"Ah, you think yourself sharp," I said. Could nothing stir a reaction? Then I had an idea: "Well—perhaps I have: to speak truth, I have an acquaintance with one of them—Mrs. Poole." I watched her face closely, and she seemed indeed startled—more so, it proved to me that all her suspicions *still* lay on Grace's shoulders, that she had learned nothing further of Bertha in my absence. I offered a few good words in poor

Grace's favor, she who had been serving me so well, but Jane was again unmoved.

We continued on like that, I trying to draw her out on the subject of courtship and marriage, she frustrating me at every turn, for she would not admit—even in relative secrecy—that she held any personal interest in her master's attention to Miss Ingram. The harder I pushed, the more clever and evasive she became.

In the end, I broke before she did. Able to bear it no more, I made as close to a profession of love as I dared, lavishing praise on those qualities in her face and form I was growing to love so well—it was all I could do not to grasp her and pull her close. As her eyes studied mine, I felt myself falling into a kind of dream. If I could have kept that moment forever, I would have.

But I could not, and I gave up. She had won. "Rise, Miss Eyre: leave me; 'the play is played out,'" I said, and, slowly, I began to uncover my face.

She stared as I did so, comprehending and uncomprehending. "Well, Jane," I said to her, "do you know me?"

"Only take off the red cloak, sir, and then—"

Back suddenly to some semblance of our former stations, the confessions of the past half hour (such as they were) forgotten, she scolded me for talking nonsense and for trying to draw her into "nonsense" as well. But I knew there had been truth there. I asked her to forgive me, but she would not until she felt clear of her own conscience.

Yet when I asked her for news from the drawing room, hoping to hear my effects on the silly ladies earlier, she confessed instead that a stranger had come, a man from the West Indies named Mason, and—*my God!*—my heart froze. Not Gerald, true, but Richard Mason—just as bad! That fool, in my own home, talking with all those gossips—what might he have said by now? And what unspeakable events would come trailing after his revelations? It was a blow. Desperation clung to me, and I hardly had strength to stand, but Jane helped me to a chair and I urged her to sit beside me. I held her hand in both of mine and could do nothing more than wish for some quiet place where she and I could dwell forever away from all cares and all disasters.

"Can I help you, sir?" she asked after a time. "I'd give my life to serve you." Ah—*now* she offers a glimmer of feeling! But my agitation over Richard was too great for me to seize on it. She continued: "Tell me what to do,—I'll try, at least, to do it."

For a moment I could think of nothing but Jane—and of Bertha, and of the need, above all else, to keep the knowledge of my shameful secret from destroying the happiness I could just glimpse on the horizon. Then, gathering my wits, I sent Jane into the dining room for a glass of wine and to spy on the group there assembled.

Jane returned shortly with word that the guests were all standing around the buffet cheerful and gay. *God give me strength to face whatever comes next...* "If all these people came in a body and spat at me, what would you do, Jane?"

"Turn them out of the room, sir, if I could," she responded. She knew nothing of my sins, knew not why I asked. And yet, she stood by me un-questioning, her loyalty fierce in the face of ruin. I nearly smiled at the thought of little Jane, standing up to them all.

"But if I were to go to them, and they only looked at me coldly, and whispered sneeringly amongst each other, and then dropt off and left me one by one, would you go with them?"

She looked straight at me: "I rather think not, sir; I should have more pleasure in staying with you."

"You could dare censure for my sake?"

"I could dare it for the sake of any friend who deserved my adherence; as you, I am sure, do."

Friend. That was more than I had heard from her before, though less than I had allowed myself to dream. But I could not dwell: there was no time to waste. Richard could even now be speaking the words that might bring my world crumbling to my feet. Much as I would have loved to hide away forever with Jane, I urged her to return to the dining room and se-cretly summon Richard to me.

CHAPTER 15

Richard Mason at Thornfield-Hall—what is he doing here? Had he, too, been approached by the so-called Gerald Rochester? What, indeed, did he know of Bertha's child and its fate?

"I've come to see my sister," Richard announced as he entered, surveying the room as if expecting to see Bertha there. "Where is she?" he demanded.

I shook my head. "You can't see her now. Not at this hour."

"You keep her in a prison, no doubt! Where is she? I shall go on my own—"

"You will tell me about her son, is what you will do."

That stopped him.

"Richard, what do you know of his provenance?" I spoke gently, for I did not want to provoke him into silence.

Indeed, he took a step or two toward me, his face darkening. "Your brother...*your brother*...seduced her."

I caught my breath on that. So it was true. "And she was...thirteen?"

"A child. A beautiful child."

"And the infant? What was done with the infant?"

"I don't know. I don't know anything about him. I only came to see my sister. I'll wager you have put her into an asylum—against her wishes and my father's. Against your *promises*." He spat this last word at me.

"She is not in an asylum. She is safe and well cared for."

"*Where?*"

"What was done with the infant? Who took him? Tell me that and I will tell you of your sister."

He sighed, still looking aimlessly about the room. "My parents had friends who moved to America," he said finally. "After the end of the slave trade in the islands, some people moved to the American South, thinking slavery would last longer there. I was only a child, and I don't know any more than that. But that is nothing to do with me: *Tell me of my sister!*"

I searched his face, wondering if I could trust him. Still, he had a right, I thought. He had many other flaws, but he truly loved his sister. "She is in care, here, in this house, not in an asylum."

"Here? Well then, Fairfax, you must take me to her now!"

"No." Despite that he frowned at me like a petulant boy, I went on: "Not now. She has always been worse at night; you know that. I will take you in the morning, I promise. She is safe in an upstairs apartment. Now, tell me: Were they married? Bertha and Rowland?"

"She was a *child*!"

"With your father's permission she could have married. Rowland would have been a good catch for her. Better than I."

He shrugged. "Rowland didn't want her, I suppose. I'm sure I don't know."

"But somehow you learned of it?"

He looked away. "Oh, you know," he said vaguely, "a child hears things."

"What kinds of things?" I pressed. He was not telling me all of it, I was sure.

"Your brother seduced my sister—is that not bad enough?" he said with renewed vigor. "Does there need to be more? When do I see my sister? Is she truly here in this house?"

"You will see her in the morning," I said, reassuring him as best I could. I was not convinced that he had come to terms with the severity of her case, nor with how difficult and unpredictable she had become. "Come, now," I added, trying to change his mood. "Have a drink with me, and tell me what brings you all the way to England."

He watched as I poured us each a glass of rum. "Yes," I said ruefully. "It's not quite grog, sad to say. But it will have to do."

We both drank in silence for a few moments. "Do you still live in Madeira?" I asked him.

"I do," he said. "Wine is a better crop than sugar. Grapes are far easier to grow."

"Ah," I responded, "that does not surprise me. And"—I looked at his glass and mine—"is it wine now that you drink?"

"Mostly. Are you familiar with Madeiran wines?"

We switched to wine after the rum, and to nostalgic conversation, reminiscing about the balls we had attended, about his father and Valley View, about the sad state of affairs in Jamaica now. It was almost as it had once been between us, the easy friendship when I had first arrived in Spanish Town, except that he occasionally raised again the issue of his sister. But each time I calmly assured him I would take him to her in the morning.

It had become late, and I ushered him up the staircase to bed. The others had already retired, and, filled with wine and spirits, we bade each other a pleasant good-night.

———

But as I retreated to my room, my mind seized again on the appalling news: it was true, then, about Bertha and Rowland. Of course, at thirteen, she could have been infatuated with my dashing brother, but would Rowland actually have taken advantage of her in that way? All elements of my soul resisted the image of the two of them entwined. I still simply could not believe that there wasn't a terrible misunderstanding. But then I thought back to that conversation on our first night in Spanish Town, and Bertha's assertions about Rowland. She had mentioned the portrait of my mother, the one that I had found hanging over my brother's bed at Thornfield—that, I realized, must once have hung over the bed, *my* bed, in Spanish Town, where Bertha had seen it with her own eyes.

Oh God. Poor, pitiful Bertha, festering in her upstairs chamber: how much of the precipitation of her madness could be laid to Rowland's abandonment, to the loss of the baby?

And now her brother was here, eager for a reunion with his sister, and I was aware of the shock he would have in the morning. Although Bertha had been in a poor state the last time he saw her, years ago, she was infinitely worse now. And I didn't believe Richard had ever visited his own mother, whom, though my heart recoiled in confessing it, Bertha resembled more and more by the year.

Unable to sleep, I tried distracting myself with happier thoughts: my Gypsy ruse, while not wholly successful, had gone well enough that Jane had declared herself a loyal friend to me, at least, and—as a friend—even offered to lay down her life in my aid. I had also felt the undeniable satisfaction of puncturing Miss Ingram's haughty confidence. I wondered how long it would take for her interest to wane.

Eventually, I faded off into sleep.

———

In the middle of the night, a startling shriek arose: Bertha, screaming into the night. *No,* I thought, *of all nights, not now, not Bertha now.* I held my breath and listened but heard nothing more. As I was drifting back to sleep, thinking it must have been some part of a dream, suddenly there came muffled sounds, and shortly afterwards desperate cries: "Help! Help!" And then, "Will no one come?"

At that I leaped from my bed and began to dress, for I knew it was Richard: despite my warnings he must have gone to his sister in the night. And then came: "Rochester! For God's sake, come!"

When I reached the upper chamber, I found Richard clutching his shoulder, his arm dripping blood, and Bertha wielding a blade and struggling against the valiant Grace Poole. I moved to subdue her, wrestling the weapon from her grasp, but at just that moment she broke free and buried her teeth in her brother's shoulder, growling and shaking her head like a tigress. It was all Grace and I could do to separate them and return Bertha to her chamber. Once there, she still would not calm, so I reached for the bonds we kept for an emergency, and Grace and I bound her as she muttered angrily. Satisfied that my wife was under control, I left that inner room.

In the outer room, Richard had collapsed, blood soaked and moaning, into a chair. I thought his wounds, though many and bleeding profusely, were not life threatening, and at that moment I began to hear voices below—it was just as I had feared: my guests had been aroused by the blood-curdling cries. With a glare, I forbade Richard from making a noise until I could return, for I had more important things to attend to.

As I ran back down the stairs I could hear Colonel Dent shouting, "Where the devil is Rochester?"

"Here!" I called, doing my best to sound unruffled. "Be composed, all of you: I'm coming." I reached the gallery to see them all there, candles in hand, clustered together in their nightclothes.

Miss Ingram ran to me and clutched at my arm. "What awful event has taken place?" she asked. "Speak! Let us know the worst at once!" At the same time, the Eshton girls rushed over and clung to me as if their lives depended on it.

I forced a laugh. "But don't pull me down or strangle me." My head spinning, I settled on poor Grace again as my scapegoat, since the company had seen me arrive from the third floor.

"All's right!—all's right!" I shouted so that everyone could hear. "A servant has had a nightmare; that is all." I explained her away as an excitable, nervous person, troubled by a nightmare and an overactive imagination. I did my best to coax the group back to their beds, bargaining that Miss Ingram's pride would override her affection for drama, and prevent further excitement. She cast me a knowing look, plainly suspicious of my feeble explanation; I suppose I could not fault her for that, since only hours earlier the old Gypsy had given her plenty of reason to doubt the word of her dashing Mr. Rochester. But I had neither time nor inclination to play her games just then, and I was grateful that she said nothing as the others, even Jane, returned once more to their rooms.

As soon as they had all dispersed, I returned to Richard, who was sprawled in the chair where I had left him. He seemed in a stupor of some sort, but whether it was a faint from loss of blood or an overabundance of fear I did not know. I tore his shirt away to take stock of his wounds, shuddering at the horror of the bites, but I cannot say I was surprised, for I had seen Bertha in acts of savagery and destruction before, and I could no longer put anything past her.

I tried using shreds of Richard's own shirt to stanch the bleeding, but it would not be stopped, and then I dipped the cloth into a basin of water and tried washing the blood away, but he had begun to bleed so rapidly that I could not keep up with it. Thanks to my time at Black Hill, I was quickly able to fashion a tourniquet and stop most of the bleeding, but I also knew it was dangerous to keep the device in place too long. It was becoming clearer that he needed more help than I could give.

I took off my shoes and, before leaving, bent close to the half-conscious Richard. "I will return with help," I said.

I intended to send Sam for Mr. Carter, but as I began to cross the second-floor hall toward the stairs up to the servants' quarters on the opposite end, I saw in the darkened far end Blanche Ingram at the door of her room, candlestick in hand, as if waiting for me to return. No—I could not risk getting caught by her, of all people. *But where to turn now?* Richard's condition would become serious if he lost much more blood.

Hidden in the shadows, I looked desperately about: the schoolroom was across from me, and the room where Adèle slept beside her nurse—Sophie might help, but I could not risk waking the child; beyond that was the room the Eshton girls shared. And next to me: Jane's room.

Jane: the last person I could risk learning my secret. Besides, as I knew from her first meeting with Mesrour, she had no facility with horses—I could not send her on a dark ride alone to Carter's house. No, Jane was out of the question.

But as I hovered in the hall, wracking my brain for an answer, another low, desperate moan erupted from the wounded man upstairs. I had to act swiftly, or I might have a dead man on my hands. Even in my panic, I understood that Jane was exactly the sort of steadfast, coolheaded person I needed beside me in this emergency; I knew she, more than anyone, could be trusted to do what I asked of her.

Well, she had said, had she not, that she would risk danger for me, as a friend? I would have to test that now. I would have to leave her with Richard and make the ride to fetch Carter myself. Without giving my doubts time to surface, I stepped closer to her door and tapped softly.

"Am I wanted?" I heard from inside. She was awake. My heart warmed at her voice, though a part of me had hoped I could still have spared her, and myself, the dreadful task ahead.

"Are you up?" I asked softly.

"Yes, sir."

"And dressed?"

"Yes."

"Come out, then, quietly, without a light, please." The door opened slowly. "I want you," I whispered. "Come this way: take your time, and make no noise." I took her hand and led her to the hidden door, but as we reached the third floor, I had a thought. "Have you a sponge in your room?"

"Yes, sir."

"Have you any salts—volatile salts?"

"Yes."

"Go back and fetch both," I whispered, and I handed her a candle and she hurried back the way we had come. Even if Blanche were still holding vigil, I figured, she would think nothing of seeing the governess alone at the far end of the hall.

Meanwhile, I stepped into the room and confronted a whimpering Richard. "Someone is coming to sit with you," I said. "It is no one of import—just the governess. But on pain of death, you will say nothing to her, nothing about your wounds, nothing about your sister, nothing at all. If you want to live, you will obey me on that, no matter what."

Frightened by my words, he nodded silently. I hoped he would obey. I hoped I could keep Jane from learning about Bertha, keep her suspicions on Grace Poole. I hoped I wasn't making a terrible mistake.

I hurried down the steps to wait for Jane. It was only moments until she returned, and she followed me wordlessly to the door of Bertha's apartment, where I tried to prepare her for what she would see inside. "You don't turn sick at the sight of blood?"

"I think I shall not," she responded. "I have never been tried yet."

"Just give me your hand," I said. "It will not do to risk a fainting fit."

She placed her small hand in mine. It was warm and steady, like Jane herself. Though I dreaded the consequences of what I was about to do, at the same time I felt some peace, for, standing there beside her, I could not at that moment have wanted a better companion.

As we entered the outer chamber, I saw Jane's eyes wandering over it. The door to Bertha's chamber was open slightly, and from behind it came an animalistic snarling. Leaving Jane, I walked quickly into the room, where Grace was attempting to soothe Bertha as she lay bound on the bed. Bertha gave a loud, wild laugh at my entrance. With as fierce a gaze as I could muster I made it clear to Grace that she must keep Bertha contained—and quiet—at all costs, and administered a dose of sedative to ensure it. Under no circumstances was Bertha to be allowed anywhere near Jane. I locked the door behind me when I left.

"Here, Jane!" I said, moving to the chair where Richard had collapsed. I held the candle over him so that she could see who he was and that he had been wounded. What remained of his shirt was soaked in blood. True to her word, she remained calm and clearheaded.

I handed her the candle, and together we bathed his wounds and revived him with the salts, until he opened his eyes and groaned. "Is there immediate danger?" he asked in a weak voice. *What a coward,* I thought. I assured him he was fine and that I was about to fetch the doctor.

"Jane," I said to her, "I shall have to leave you in this room with this gentleman, for an hour, or perhaps two hours." I tried to sound confident; I was removing the tourniquet as I spoke. And I was determined to leave no detail to chance, give the two of them no reason to speak a question or command between them. "You will sponge the blood as I do when it returns; if he feels faint, you will put the glass of water on that stand to his lips, and your salts to his nose. You will not speak to him on any pretext—and—*Richard*—it will be at the peril of your life if you speak to her: open your lips—agitate yourself—and I'll not answer for the consequences."

With that I gave the bloody sponge to Jane and watched her take up the task I'd given her. "Remember!—No conversation," I said, and I left them there.

What else could I have done? Should I have let him die for his own foolishness, to protect my secrets? And yet: to think of Jane sitting there, mere yards from Bertha—was I myself a madman?

Thank God, Miss Ingram appeared to have given up on me. I dressed swiftly for the journey and raced to the stables for Mesrour. Pilot barked once to be allowed to come, but I quieted him with a word and made off in a state of both panic and exhilaration.

Though it was hours before dawn, I found Carter attending a dying patient, and despite that I sent in a message that my own errand was a matter of life and death, I still had to wait until he felt he could leave the suffering woman. In the meantime, I rounded up a post chaise for the surgeon and finally we were off, I still on Mesrour and urging the driver to whip his horses to a faster pace. It was one of the longest rides of my life; and I confess it was the uncertainty about Jane in that dark chamber alone for hours with Richard—so close to Bertha herself—that made my blood run cold.

Dawn was just announcing itself when we arrived. The driver waited below while I hurried Carter through the silent Hall.

"Now, Carter," I said as we entered the chamber, "be on the alert: I give you but half an hour for dressing the wound, fastening the bandages, getting the patient downstairs and all." As I spoke, I could not bear to look at Jane, dreading to think what she might have learned in my absence.

"But is he fit to move, sir?" Carter asked, bending over for a closer look.

"No doubt of it; it is nothing serious: he is nervous, his spirits must be kept up. Come, set to work." I pulled back the curtain and drew up the Holland blind, letting in more light. Then I turned to Richard. "Now, my good fellow, how are you?" I asked him, feigning cheer.

"She's done for me, I fear."

"Not a whit!—courage! You've lost a little blood; that's all. Carter, assure him there's no danger."

"I can do that conscientiously," said Carter, who had already undone the bandages; but in the next moment he discovered the torn flesh where Bertha's teeth had been, and he frowned at me.

"She bit me," Richard murmured. "She worried me like a tigress—"

I hurried to stop him from saying too much. "You should not have yielded," I said impatiently. "You should have grappled with her at once." She had seemed so quiet, he replied; and he had wanted to see her, had believed he could do her good. His weakness made me furious; not only had he not trusted my word about her condition, but he had explicitly disobeyed my orders, and now was insisting on discussing it in front of Jane. I tried to soften my tone, to cover my own panic and fury, to keep Richard calm and Jane disinterested. But I needed him out of my house as swiftly as possible, before my guests awoke—and before Jane heard another word.

As Carter finished the shoulder dressing and turned his attention to the other bite marks on Richard's arm, the latter whimpered: "She sucked the blood: she said she'd drain my heart." *Yes,* I thought, *now you see how she has been draining mine.*

I turned away in disgust. "Come, be silent, Richard." I spoke as soothingly as I could. "Never mind her gibberish: don't repeat it."

"I wish I could forget it," was the answer.

As did I. As did all of us, I was sure, including staunch Jane, to whom I now turned, having thought to send her down to my room for a clean shirt for Richard, so that I could have a word with him in private. I thanked Carter for his willingness to leave a deathbed for this tragic scene, and to Richard I issued the threat that, should the governess or any others in the house learn of Bertha's presence, his sister would be sent away to a harsh asylum, far from my protection. I knew Richard would not want Bertha to end her days in such a place, and I hoped the threat would be enough to silence him.

Jane returned in only a few moments.

"Was anybody stirring below when you went down, Jane?" I asked her.

"No, sir," she responded. "All was very still."

Carter and I helped Richard into the clean shirt and his own waistcoat, while sweet Jane ran several more silent errands up and down the stairs in her velvet slippers. I administered to Richard a small draught of a medication I had gotten once in Italy, which would soothe pain and give strength. It was potent, though short-lived, and just the thing to get him down the stairs and into the coach.

Jane led the way, keeping a lookout as we escaped down the back stairs. "Take care of him," I said to Carter as we helped Richard into the coach, "and keep him at your house till he is quite well: I shall ride over in a day or two to see how he gets on. Richard, how is it with you?"

"The fresh air revives me," he said, his voice weak. Then he said, "Fairfax..."

"Well, what is it?" I said, impatient for the coach to be gone. Jane was still standing nearby, listening, and I was afraid for what Richard might say.

"Let her be taken care of; let her be treated as tenderly as may be; let her—" And he burst into tears. *Enough,* I thought. *See how he suffers after only one night, while I—I have had her on my soul for nigh on fifteen years!*

I signaled the driver to be gone and he cracked the whip and the coach started off. I barred the yard gates behind them, wishing to God that Bertha could be gone from my life.

Once they had left, I could not bear to reenter that cursed Hall, and started toward the orchard, needing solace from the burdens of the night. I had hoped that Jane might walk with me, but when I turned I saw her retreating instead to the house. I softly called her back, and together we strolled down the walk, inclosed by the boxwood hedge, a private island for the two of us, full of flowers coming into bloom. I was feeling more acutely than ever the pain of Thornfield's accursedness, yet there is something about trees—about an orchard—that is calming to the soul. I bent and plucked the first rose of the season and offered it to Jane. It was slim enough thanks for all she had done in the night, and our eyes rose together toward the sky and the sun, appearing in the east.

"You have passed a strange night, Jane," I said to her. Much as I feared what truths she might have learned in my absence, it was better that I know them now. "Were you afraid when I left you alone with Mason?"

"I was afraid of someone coming out of the inner room."

"But I had fastened the door—I had the key in my pocket: I should have been a careless shepherd if I had left a lamb—my pet lamb—so near a wolf's den, unguarded: you were safe." *My pet lamb*: it was the first endearment I had allowed myself to speak to her, and, I confess, I wanted her to notice it. It seemed an innocent and mild enough evocation of my feelings—though the term did little justice to the strength of character I had witnessed in the night.

Her words interrupted my thoughts. "Will Grace Poole live here still, sir?"

Ah, so she did still believe Grace to be the monster. I was glad of it, may Grace forgive me; and I would let her continue to believe that. It moved me to hear Jane so concerned for my well-being, and after the traumas of the night, I wanted, for just a moment, to bare my soul to her sympathies. But all I could do was allude to the precariousness of my daily life, the crater crust on which I stood, capable of spewing fire at any moment.

Jane did not—as she could not—understand the danger Richard Mason posed to me, especially given the weakness in his own character that we had both that night witnessed. At that time I still believed that Richard could hurt me only accidentally (it was from Gerald Rochester that I feared a deliberate attack), and Jane did not see why I could not simply request—or command—Richard not to harm me. In her goodness, Jane did not yet understand that good intentions and moral truth might inflict as dangerous, as painful—indeed as *fatal*—a wound as malicious intent.

Indeed, I wished suddenly to hear her opinion of my own case, to see myself through her clear and honest eyes, and to know how harshly she might judge me if I confessed the truth about Bertha, and about my desire for Jane herself. I sat down on a little bench in the garden and bade her sit next to me, but she remained standing. "Sit, sit," I urged. "You don't hesitate to take a place at my side, do you? Is that wrong, Jane?" I wanted to again hear her call me her friend—or more—but now I worried that this endless night could have changed all that.

Yet, she assured me that she was content to stay with me, and sat by my side. I tried to cast a portrait for her of my situation: "Imagine yourself in a remote foreign land; conceive that you there commit a capital error, no matter of what nature or from what motives, but one whose consequences must follow you through life and taint all your existence." I saw her start at the words *capital error* and hurried to correct them. "Mind, I don't say a *crime*; I am not speaking of shedding of blood or any other guilty act, which might make the perpetrator amenable to the law: my word is *error*." I described in vaguest generalities my mistakes, my sins, my miseries, wandering foreign lands seeking solace from my "error," until at last, heart weary and soul withered, returning home and making an acquaintance who had all the good and bright qualities that had been lost, and of feeling regenerated, alive again, and my desire to spend the remaining days in the company of this "stranger." And then I asked the question: To attain that end, did she not believe one is "justified in overleaping an obstacle of custom—a mere conventional impediment"? Could I not, I begged obliquely, pursue my happiness with Jane, despite that she was a governess in my employ, and despite that Bertha lived?

I waited for her absolution, but she did not respond. I tried again, but she spoke only of relying on divine, not mortal, solace. Oh, my difficult Jane, did she not see that to me her own little self was more than mortal, was, indeed, a window into heaven itself?

"But the instrument—the instrument!" I insisted. "God, who does the work, ordains the instrument, and I believe I have found the instrument for my cure in—" *Jane Eyre!* I nearly choked out the words but stopped myself just in time. She had listened to my story and remained unmoved—how could I believe, then, that she felt the same for me as I for her? I would not bare my soul to her if she would not deign to have it. No—I saved myself humiliation in the final moment; she would speak first of love, or neither of us would.

She said nothing, and I felt the gates of my heart close up once more, that I had so recently made vulnerable to attack. I would not make that mistake again. "Little *friend*"—I spat the word back at her—"you have noticed my tender penchant for Miss Ingram; don't you think if I married her *she* would regenerate me with a vengeance?" And I rose and left her with that thought.

Walking the path for a few moments, I felt my head clear again, my pulse calm, and I realized how close I had come to the brink. I returned to her once again the master of my emotions. "Jane," I said lightly, "you are quite pale with your vigils: don't you curse me for disturbing your rest?"

"Curse you?" she asked. "No, sir." She was as calm as ever, as if she had witnessed none of the passion that had coursed through my veins.

I took her hand as if to shake it in confirmation of her words. "Jane," I said, "when will you watch with me again?"

"Whenever I can be useful, sir."

"For instance, the night before I am married! I am sure I shall not be able to sleep. Will you promise to sit up with me to bear me company?" I was determined, this time, to *make* her angry, to shake her out of her complacency, to provoke her to speak. "To you I can talk of my lovely one," I said, "for now you have seen her and know her. She's a rare one, is she not, Jane?"

"Yes, sir," was all she said.

"A strapper—a real strapper, Jane: big, brown, and buxom; with hair just such as the ladies of Carthage must have had." The sarcasm was thick in my voice, but still Jane did not rise to my words.

At that moment then I saw Dent and Lynn at the stables, and I dismissed her—there seemed nothing else I could say that would move her, at least not then.

CHAPTER 16

I did not see Jane again until the afternoon. Everyone had slept later than usual after having been roused in the night, and they drifted down to breakfast still disturbed. I suggested a picnic to distract them, but Lady Ingram begged off, saying she had a headache, and Mrs. Dent said she did not think her nerves could take such an outing. Only Miss Ingram—despite her late-night vigil—seemed little bothered by the night's events, and dared me to a gallop over the moors. I took her up on that, curious to know what she might say to me in private. As I could have expected, she asked about my business in Millcote that had taken me away, and about Richard Mason's visit and swift disappearance. Though she had not made the connection to the disturbance of the previous night, she seemed to believe he was in some way tied to my supposed debts, and I was just evasive enough in my responses to confirm her suspicions. I imagined her interest in me would now cool quickly; she might even spread rumors about me in the neighborhood, but I cared little enough for that. It would be interesting, indeed, to know how I was viewed by society without the veil of wealth surrounding me. At that point, my whole attention was on winning Jane.

Miss Ingram and I returned in time for lunch, and then someone proposed billiards. We were in the midst of the game when Miss Ingram suddenly snapped, "Does *that person* want you?"

I turned and saw Jane. Alarmed—for it was not her way to interrupt like that—I threw down my cue and followed her into the schoolroom, where we could talk in private. "Well?" I asked, as I closed the door.

"If you please, sir, I want leave of absence for a week or two," she said. *She was leaving me.* "What?" I blurted. "You would just leave, without any warning?" Immediately I could see that she was taken aback by the vehemence of my reaction, but I did not care. I would not let her leave me so easily. "What to do?" I demanded. "Where to go?"

"To see a sick lady who has sent for me."

"What sick lady?—Where does she live?" This was an invention, I was sure. I had overplayed my hand. She was fleeing Thornfield after what she had seen in the night and after my confession, for she refused to live under the same roof as a monster and a sinner. I was losing her!

"At Gateshead in ——shire." The lady was the widow of Reed, the former Gateshead magistrate, Jane told me, who was Jane's own uncle.

Then I knew I'd caught her. "The deuce he was! You never told me that before: you always said you had no relations."

But she had an answer for that, too: when she was orphaned, Reed had taken her in, but Mrs. Reed had cast her off after Mr. Reed's death because Jane was poor and burdensome—*Jane, burdensome!*—and because she had disliked Jane. But now John, the son, was dead by his own hand, and his mother had had an apoplectic attack and was asking for Jane.

Perhaps, if the story were true, I should have been more sympathetic to the widow Reed, but in my panic I could think only of Jane. "And what good can you do her?" I asked. "Nonsense, Jane! I would never think of running a hundred miles to see an old lady who will perhaps be dead before you reach her: besides, you say she cast you off."

"Yes, sir, but that is long ago," she said, "and when her circumstances were very different: I could not be easy to neglect her wishes now." Her compassion: it was so Jane, and I began to believe her, for it was exactly how she would think, with a degree of loyalty that, as proven just that morning during my ride with Miss Ingram, was lacking in so many of her "superiors" in society.

If this summons were real—and I wanted to believe it was, not least because I could not believe Jane would lie—then her absence would be painful, but not unbearable. "How long will you stay?" I asked her.

"As short a time as possible, sir."

"Promise me only to stay a week," I demanded. More than that I could not stand.

But she would not make that promise for fear she might have to break it. However, she did promise that she would indeed return as soon as she could.

I had schemed to rid myself of my guests so that I could be alone with Jane, but instead, it was she who was leaving, and they who were hanging on. I could not think what to say—after all my manipulations, to be defeated by a sick woman a hundred miles away. My dear Jane, opening her generous heart to someone who had treated her badly. Would that I could match her. "Well," I said, "you must have some money; you can't travel without money."

I tried to give her fifty pounds for her expenses, but upright Jane refused to take more than she was owed; she refused to be in my debt, while I would have given her the world merely to ensure her return. Honest Jane—how could I have imagined she would try to deceive me? *But—was I not deceiving her?*

I hardly had time to think of that before she surprised me with a further statement: "Mr. Rochester, I may as well mention another matter of business to you while I have the opportunity. You have as good as informed me, sir, that you are going shortly to be married?"

My God. "Yes, what then?"

"In that case, sir, Adèle ought to go to school: I am sure you will perceive the necessity of it."

"To get her out of my bride's way; who might otherwise walk over her rather too emphatically. There's sense to the suggestion," I said, nodding, wanting to force her out with it, wanting her to know I could see my so-called bride as clearly as she. "Not a doubt of it: Adèle, as you say, must go to school; and you, of course, must march straight to—the devil?"

"I hope not, sir: but I must seek another situation somewhere."

"In course! And old Madam Reed, or the Misses, her daughters, will be solicited by you to seek a place, I suppose?"

"No, sir; I am not on such terms with my relatives as would justify me in asking favors of them—but I shall advertise."

"Not on such terms," I thought, *but they make you travel a hundred miles to see the old hag.* "You shall walk up the pyramids of Egypt!" I snapped at her. "At your peril you advertise! I wish I had only offered you a sovereign! Give me back nine pounds, Jane; I've a use for it."

She was leaving me after all: perhaps not immediately, but she was already making plans. It wasn't Bertha who was driving her away, but *Blanche*, and at my own stupid hand! I was desperate, and furious at myself. I swore I'd solve this, but for now, I most urgently needed assurance of her return. For that, I managed to get her to promise not to seek a new position on her own, saying that I would find one that would suit her, for I had no intention of ever letting her go. In return, she made me promise to allow Adèle and herself both to be safe out of the house before my bride entered it, and I pledged my word on that.

As the conversation drew to a close, I could not bear to say good-bye, and told her so, hoping to draw her into a confession of fondness that I might cling to during her absence. "How do people perform that ceremony of parting, Jane? Teach me; I'm not quite up to it." *Not up to it*: I had spent my life losing those I cared about.

"They say, Farewell; or any other form they prefer."

"Then say it."

"Farewell, Mr. Rochester, for the present." There it was again, that calm coldness. How easy farewells seemed for her!

"What must I say?" My back was against the door; I could have taken her in my arms and prevented her from escaping.

"The same, if you like, sir."

"Farewell, Miss Eyre, for the present: is that all?"

"Yes."

"It seems stingy, to my notions, and dry, and unfriendly. I should like something else: a little addition to the rite. If one shook hands, for in-stance; but no,—that would not content me either." Could I goad her into embracing me? But she stood in front of me determined and steady. "So you'll do no more than say farewell, Jane?"

"It is enough, sir."

Did she truly not understand what I was asking? Well, whether she did or not, I had to face the fact that, once more, she had bested me at my own game. Another battle lost, and I could think of nothing more to say, and so I opened the door and left.

I rose early the next morning and watched from my bedroom window as the coach rolled down the drive, and I stayed there until long after it was out of sight.

Before the others awoke, I rode to Carter's home, where he was tending to Richard Mason, who lay, still weak, in bed. "It was a fearful night," Richard moaned when he saw me. "I could never have anticipated my own sister would come at me with such vengeance."

"In her mind, she is not your sister," Carter reminded him, as he helped him to a draught, which Richard drank deeply. A few moments later, he was snoring lightly, and Carter turned to me. "How did she get a blade?"

"She is locked up all day, day after day," I said. "She has more than enough time to fashion a weapon from some stray object—a spoon, for example."

"Perhaps you need a better caretaker, or more of them," Carter said. "Grace Poole is fine, but perhaps she is not enough—"

It was not the first time I had wondered about that. "One Grace Poole can be explained," I said. "More climbing those stairs every day would arouse suspicions that must not be aroused."

Carter looked at me seriously. "Perhaps it is time to make it known who resides in that apartment," he said. "People are apt to be kinder than one imagines."

To Carter it seemed simple, but he had no idea about Jane, or my hopes for a future with her. And yet—perhaps he was right on one count: the situation with Bertha must change, and change now.

As I rode home, a plan began to take shape: I would see Everson about finding a new place to house Bertha, discreetly. The location must be far enough away to allay suspicion, yet close enough for me to visit occasionally; but that was the easy part. Finding a place with light and fresh air, yet without windows that could be broken, would be much harder. It was not something one did in a week or two, or even a month, perhaps, but I vowed to begin immediately, during Jane's absence, so that I could begin to press my case to Jane without the specter of Bertha lingering over us both.

CHAPTER 17

$\mathcal{T}$he following days were a most anxious time: Jane had promised she would return, and, as well, that she would let me find her a new position. I wanted to trust her, and she was not one to renege on a promise. But what if something fell into her lap? Surely governess positions were not so common that she could afford to refuse. She had no idea that the whole thing was a charade, that I would never marry Miss Ingram, that Thornfield would be Jane's home for as long as she wanted it.

As soon as Jane left, it seemed to me that the life had gone out of Thornfield-Hall, and perhaps it had gone out for my guests as well, for with only a few words on my part, they decamped that very same day, leaving Thornfield-Hall quiet and me at a loose end.

In those first days without Jane, both Adèle and I were wholly out of sorts. I bought her trinkets when I could and tasked Sophie with taking the child on walks and little adventures on the estate grounds to keep her mind and heart occupied, while I tried amusing myself with rides across the moors on Mesrour, as Pilot bounded along beside.

Once I crossed paths with Miss Ingram, who archly told me she had more pressing things to do than to join me in a ride. It was clear that the Gypsy's hints had taken root and I was evidently not deemed an eligible suitor. Oddly, I was discomfited in this result, though I had planned it myself. I had once assumed the choice between Miss Ingram and Jane was mine alone to make; now I had closed a door and there would be no going back. Though I felt some satisfaction in giving up what I had once possessed, it was worth nothing—*I* was worth nothing—if I did not have Jane. But upon her return, I vowed, that would change.

In the meantime, Thornfield without Jane was barren. She wrote to Mrs. Fairfax with news of her aunt, which the housekeeper kindly shared with me, and it became clear that the visit was going to last much longer than Jane had originally implied. It was irrational, perhaps, but I began to worry again that she was gone for good. I could not simply remain in place, waiting anxiously for her return, so after consulting with Ames about issues on the estate, I packed a bag and left.

I headed immediately for London. I'd told Mrs. Fairfax I was going to buy a new carriage—which indeed I did, imagining Jane riding home on our wedding day—but I had also heard that a daughter of the Gateshead Reeds, a Miss Georgiana, had been much admired in London society a few seasons back, and, with veiled questions, I sought out what news I could of her family. Did she have a cousin Jane Eyre, in truth? And what was the standing of the family? I wondered. Would they cause trouble for me if I tried to marry Jane without first ridding myself of Bertha, if the secret got out? Unfortunately, I did not learn much—Georgiana was beautiful and selfish, it seemed, and the whole family had suffered much at the recent death of her brother, John. No one had heard of a cousin.

This last niggled at me: it fit with what Jane had told me—that the Reeds had never considered her a true relation—and yet it made me wonder again why she had been sent for. Since I was ready to return to Thornfield anyway, I made the detour to Gateshead unannounced. Of course, I did not intend to make my presence known to Jane, but I thought I could get a better picture of the Reed family and perhaps even hear some gossip about their visiting cousin.

I found accommodations in a nearby inn, telling the landlord I was distantly related to the Reed family and asking for news of them. He was a loquacious man and warmed up easily to conversation, telling me that the Reeds had experienced no end of trouble since the death of Mr. Reed. The son had been a bully as a youngster and had grown into gaming and alcohol and other dissolute substances, had played too much with women he shouldn't have, and had recently died, though, he assured me, he hated to speak poorly of the dead.

And his mother? I asked. Ah, yes, that woman was as blind as a bat as far as her son was concerned, wasting her money on him until, rumor went, it was mostly gone, though the one daughter still dressed and acted as if she were a princess. And now the mother had apoplexy and was not well, maybe even dying for all he knew, and there was another daughter, as thin as a stick and with a sour face to go with it. Was there a cousin who used to stay with them? I asked cautiously. Name of Jane Eyre? It was she, I added, who was my relative.

"You may be in luck," he told me: "I heard a young woman, a distant relative perhaps, is doing the work of a servant in old Mrs. Reed's last days. If you have any sense"—he leaned closer—"you'll get her out of there before they make a maid of her."

I left him, determined to see for myself, but they must have been keeping Jane busy, for it was three days before I saw any sign of her. The "princess"—whom I assumed to be Georgiana—was walking along the street finely attired, carrying a parasol, with Jane in her usual sober gray a half step behind, loaded with bundles. It was a pitiful sight, and immediately I decided that when I had Jane home, I would dress her in the most beautiful silks and satins and shower her with jewels. I left, then, for if I had stayed, I would not have been able to resist interrupting this charade, no doubt fully humiliating Jane.

At Thornfield, returning with my new carriage and bearing gifts for Adèle, I was surrounded by the idyllic sight of the hay harvest: laborers swinging their scythes and others with rakes drawing the hay, and haystacks in meadows all around under the warm, early summer sun.

When I set foot in the Hall, however, I was greeted with unwelcome news. "That same gentleman has been here to see you, sir," Mrs. Fairfax said as she took my hat and cloak. "Mr. Rochester, he calls himself; he says he is your nephew."

I was just removing my gloves, and I looked up sharply. Mrs. Fairfax, as any good servant would, had no expression at all on her face. "He is here now?" I asked.

"He has been here, sir. He is staying in Millcote, I believe. He said to send for him when you return."

"Thank you," I replied, retaking my things from her arms. I made directly for the stable, where Mesrour had just been unburdened of his saddle, and I ordered the hand to saddle him up again. I should have left the poor horse to rest from our journey, should have taken another mount, but Mesrour was in my heart and I needed him beneath me, and Pilot beside me. If Jane had been present, I might have wanted to take her with me as well.

———

Everson was just tidying his office when I arrived. "I've been expecting you," he said.

"Have you?"

"Mr. Gerald Rochester, he calls himself," he said.

"You have met him?"

"He came here. He says he is your nephew."

"How did he know you were my solicitor?"

Everson shrugged. "It is known in Millcote. It would not be hard for him to discover who represents you. But once he told me his business, I refused to speak further with him."

"And...what is his business?"

"He *says* he is wanting to see his mother, that he understands you are responsible for her care. That's what he says, although I have no idea how he has learned of her whereabouts. Rochester, I expect he intends to lay claim to what he would call his inheritance."

"Thornfield."

Everson nodded, and sat back down at his desk, indicating a chair for me as well. But I could not sit; I could not even stand still.

"He intends to take it from me."

"He did not say so specifically; that is only my inference."

"What's to be done?" I asked, collapsing then into the chair.

"Have you known all this time that there was another possible heir? Can he be discredited?"

"I don't know. Bertha often cried out for a lost baby, but I always assumed it was merely the ranting of a madwoman. But when Molly, her Jamaican servant, left, she told me there had indeed been a baby that was taken away. Bertha was only thirteen, poor child. And, recently, I asked her brother, Richard, and he confirmed it."

"And her brother said...," he prompted.

"That, yes, there was a male child, who was sent with friends to be raised in America. And the father was my brother. Richard does not believe there had been a marriage."

Everson nodded. "Would he testify to that?"

"I have no idea what he would testify to."

"A child born out of wedlock, or even born of a marriage that is not considered a proper one—that is, outside of a church or without the proper banns—is considered *filius nullius*: the child of no one. If he cannot provide proof of a proper marriage, that is what he is in the eyes of Chancery: the child of no one."

I sat for some time in silence. "And we do not know if he has proof," I mused.

"In the meantime," he said sternly, "I advise you not to speak with him except in my presence."

I nodded. "Have you had an opportunity to look for a suitable house for my wife?"

"I have begun, but as you know, a house as you've described is not easily come by. But my inquiries continue."

"Very well," I said. "And as for Gerald Rochester, or whatever his name is, let it be understood that he is not to come to Thornfield again as long as I am master there."

"Indeed," he said.

As I waited for news from Everson, and waited as well for news from Jane, I confess a sour mood overtook me. It felt as if she had been gone for years. *She will not return,* I thought. *She is gone.* And worse: *I do not deserve her.* I wanted to banish those thoughts from my mind, but they would not leave. I loved her—I knew that—and I wanted her; I could not see how I could live without her at my side. But for me to insist that she, unknowing, ally herself with me, a man married already to a madwoman, was beyond all bounds. She was young, innocent, pure. I myself had been that once, but I had crumbled to an ugliness that could lay no claim on one such as Jane; and, now, if I lost Thornfield, I would have nothing left to offer her.

But Adèle would not let me wallow in such dreary thoughts; once I returned from London and Gateshead, the lonely child had insistently become my daily companion. One morning I ordered Sophie to dress Adèle in her oldest clothes, for I had something in mind. I had been watching the haymakers, the rhythm of their work, as steady and insistent as a heartbeat, and although my help was not needed, an unexpected urge came upon me to become a part of that tableau.

Searching for old clothes for Adèle was like hoping to locate an oak tree growing in the drawing room, for the child carelessly discarded clothing long before it was outgrown. But finally something suitable was found, and, with Adèle's hand in mine, I led her down the lane and into the fields. There I took a spare rake and set myself to work with the laborers. I could see the stifled smiles at my ineptness, but never mind, it was good for me to be out in the sun and the open air. The work cleared my mind, and the sun on my back, the unfamiliar aches, blotted out nearly every other care.

Adèle, meanwhile, scampered here and there, gathering hay in her arms and ferrying it to stacks we laborers were forming. She delighted in the activity for a time but soon grew bored and begged me for a ride in the pony cart, not relenting until I gave up and walked with her back to the Hall, where we harnessed up the pony cart and took ourselves to the village and back.

But that was only one day out of so many. I missed Jane more than I could have imagined—that staunch little friend, as pert as a wren, as steady as a rock: how had I let her go so easily? Why had I not accompanied her? I would have made sure she was not treated badly, not insulted as she once had been at that house. And I would have ensured she did not find another position elsewhere. I would have brought her home to Thornfield-Hall, where she belonged.

On some afternoons, while the sunlight lingered, I took a book and sat on the narrow steps of a stile on a small knoll. It afforded me a view at once vast and pleasant, and, more important, an opportunity to see the road, to see if a coach came, to watch Jane alight with her small box, home at last. I tried to write but could not focus my thoughts, imagining my dear one patiently suffering through her time with her cousin Reeds, insulted and demeaned beyond all reason.

But in the end, Jane fooled me. She did not come by coach as I had expected, but walked the way from Millcote on her own, across the fields and meadows. I saw her at a distance, and she seemed to me again like the woodland sprite she had appeared at our first meeting. I did not at first quite believe the vision, watching her coming toward me as evening fell. Here she was, my familiar Jane, sound in body and, I hoped, in spirit—not gone forever, but returning home to me, and I would never let her leave again.

I thought she did not see me until she was nearly upon me, and then she seemed a bit confused when I called out to her: "There you are! Come on, if you please."

And she did come on, nearly as if in a trance, so astonished, I supposed, to find me there. "And this is Jane Eyre?" I said to her, nearly giddy simply to be in her presence. "Coming from Millcote, and on foot? Yes—just one of your tricks: not to send for a carriage, and come clattering over street and road like a common mortal, but to steal into the vicinage of your home"—*yes, Jane, yes,* I thought, *this shall be your home forever*—"along with twilight, just as if you were a dream or a shade. What the deuce have you done with yourself this last month?" She looked pale in the evening light, and I feared for her well-being.

"I have been with my aunt, sir, who is dead."

"A true Janian reply! Good angels be my guard! She comes from the other world—from the abode of people who are dead; and tells me so when she meets me alone here in the gloaming! If I dared, I'd touch you, to see if you are substance or shadow, you elf!" As I longed to do, to gather her to me and never let her go. Instead, I continued my playful banter. "Truant! Absent from me a whole month: and forgetting me quite, I'll be sworn!"

She did not contest this last, as I had wished, but instead she gazed about her, as if quite overcome, and I supposed she was. I had greeted her more effusively than I had ever done, but I could not help it: I, too, was overcome in the moment. She seemed so pure, so perfect and separate from all mortal flaws as to be inhuman—*better* than human—not susceptible to sin or worry. As I had those thoughts, she turned the conversation to my London trip; I was relieved that she knew—from Mrs. Fairfax—only of the carriage purchase, nothing more.

"You must see the carriage, Jane, and tell me if you don't think it will suit Mrs. Rochester exactly; and whether she won't look like Queen Boadicea, leaning back against those purple cushions. I wish, Jane, I were a trifle better adapted to match with her externally. Tell me now, fairy as you are,—can't you give me a charm, or a philter, or something of that sort, to make me a handsome man?" I could not help but grin at her, for of course the Mrs. Rochester I was hoping for was Jane herself. She did not believe herself beautiful, I knew, and she did not seem to understand that a loving eye is all the charm needed for beauty.

"It would be past the power of magic, sir," was all she said, and despite the insult I found my heart soaring at my little friend's familiar serious honesty, her refusal to flatter. Now that Jane was back to me, I had only to try to convince her that she was my destiny, and I hers.

I sent her on her way and she began to obey, but she turned back, suddenly, and I saw emotion storm across her face as she uttered the words that would change my life: "Wherever you are is my home," she said, "my only home." Before I could speak, she was gone.

There it was. She *knew* she belonged to me as completely as I to her. I could not contain my heart: now I felt sure she would choose to be with me, as soon as I was free to make her the offer.

———

As soon as I could after Jane's return, I sent a message to Everson, asking him to meet me at Carter's home one evening a few days hence, and I sent another to Carter, requesting him to host a gathering of the three of us. Now that I believed Jane loved me, that I was her "home," I was determined to free myself of Bertha, not just physically, but legally. I could not dream of dragging Jane into the disgusting situation in which I found myself. I had been tricked into a marriage without knowing my betrothed's full story, and to bring Jane into an alliance with me would commit the same offense to her.

Since I could not bring myself to tell Jane of Bertha, I would simply rid myself of Bertha before the need arose. There was only one recourse that I could imagine, one that I had once discarded as extremely difficult and unlikely. But I had been young then, and hopeful that life would work out well for me. Now I was more experienced, and more cynical.

Both men were seated before Carter's fire when I arrived, and they stood to greet me. Carter called for more brandy, and I sat with them.

"You know my wife's condition," I began with hesitation, and both men nodded solemnly and leaned forward as I spoke. Carter had more than once urged me to find a more acceptable accommodation for Bertha; he might even know already of Everson's as-yet-fruitless search for such a place.

"And I am wondering..." I looked expressly at Everson, for he would know the law. "What are the possibilities for divorce?"

Carter sucked in his breath, likely remembering the vehemence with which I had rejected his earlier mention of the same idea.

Everson contemplated my suggestion for a few moments. "It might be done," he said cautiously. I could feel the weight of years of worry and care begin to shift on my shoulders.

"*Might*," he repeated, turning to Carter. "What is her condition?" he asked.

"She is like an animal," Carter said. "She is healthy and as strong as an ox, but it is not possible to think of her as anything but an insentient creature."

Everson shook his head at that. "It has been done," he admitted. "But with difficulty, and I cannot imagine your doing it successfully in this case. One must go before Parliament and swear that she has been caught in flagrante delicto. There must be witnesses, of course. And you cannot have had congress with her since."

Certainly the last was not a problem, but the former would be, for I did not know if she had ever had congress with any other man after our marriage. I refused to let my hopes fall yet, though I could see how this would end.

"It's not possible," Carter said. "No man would have congress with her, for any amount of money. Nor would she allow it; she would tear him apart."

Everson nodded agreement. "Parliament has gotten quite sticky on the matter. You would not be the first man to try to rid himself of an inconvenient wife."

"Inconvenient?" Was that the way the law saw it? A mad wife, with whom one could not reason, upon whom a man could not safely turn his back. A woman who must be locked up to keep her from harming herself or others? *Inconvenient?* I rose, anger flushing my face.

"Sit down, please, Mr. Rochester," Carter said.

I turned to him.

"Sir, I beg you to be seated. Let us speak rationally."

But I could not.

"It is complicated—divorce," Everson said, staring meaningfully at me. "On the other hand, if there existed—"

But I had caught his meaning. "If there are actually documents—*proof*—that there was a previous marriage..." From the corner of my eye, I saw Carter start at my words: he had no idea what I meant, but for certain Everson did. "Then my marriage to Bertha is null and void."

"*If*," Everson said.

"If," I repeated. I still did not believe a prior marriage had happened—but what if it had? And if so, Gerald would be the rightful heir. Was this truly something I could even be wishing for?

"You understand what that means?" Everson asked me.

"I do," I said. "I would lose Thornfield." But I would gain Jane.

Carter's face showed genuine surprise, but Everson's did not; he was too good a solicitor for that.

"I will see what I can discover," Everson said. "If that is not a possibility, I have little hope for you, for there are only two grounds for a divorce: one is a prior, undissolved marriage, and the other is if a man cannot be assured that his wife's progeny are his own. As I said, Parliament is well aware of men—and women—manufacturing assignations for the sole purpose of getting a divorce. They would send out their spies, and it is known in the neighborhood that you have been courting Miss Ingram. Your names would be dragged through the mud, and after all that the divorce would not be granted."

They were thinking of Miss Ingram, but that was not who would suffer. I could not allow Jane's name to be sullied that way. "There is no hope, then," I said. None, unless I gave up Thornfield. The idea was still forming in my mind: could I trade one love, one security, for another?

———

I could barely sleep that night, my thoughts roiling, and when I did fall into a fitful slumber, my dreams offered no respite: *I was a child, wandering through Thornfield-Hall, crying out for my mother, rushing from room to room but finding her nowhere—neither her nor anyone else—Thornfield itself cold, empty, barren.*

And when at last I woke, shaken and stunned from my dreams, I rose and washed and dressed numbly. I made my way to the drawing room, where I sat down on the sofa, facing my mother's portrait. There she stood, staring down at me. What would she have me do? I tried to order my thoughts, but I could not. Caroline Fairfax Rochester. She had been known for her kindness, Mrs. Fairfax had said—how I wished for her kind hand on my shoulder now, to guide me down the right path.

But I was on my own. I was on my own—except for Jane. It was Jane who grounded me, Jane who knew me to my very soul. It was Jane whom I could never give up—not my life as a landed gentleman, not the Ingrams, not Bertha, not even my ancestral home. If I had to choose, I would let nothing, not even... not even Thornfield itself stand in the way.

CHAPTER 18

I left for Millcote without even breakfasting, At Gerald's inn, I pounded on his door until, half-dressed, he opened it. I imagine we both were surprised at this first meeting: I at the way he, even dark haired, resembled my brother, and he, perhaps not even knowing who I was, surely startled at my slightly mad appearance.

"You call yourself '*Rochester*,'" I said, the accusation clear.

"It is my name: Gerald Rochester. And you, I assume, are my uncle."

I would not acknowledge that. "Why have you come?"

"To see my mother, why else?" It dawned on me that I did not know if he was aware that his mother was my wife.

"Why else?" I repeated. "One does not go to a solicitor if one is merely trying to establish a familial connection."

He looked me straight in the eye. "But we are connected, are we not?" In a sudden motion, he stepped back from the doorway, saying, "Why don't you come in?"

I advise you not to speak with him except in my presence. I hesitated just a moment, and then, Everson's advice be damned, I stepped into the room, and he motioned me to the only chair, while he sat on the unmade bed. "Do you know where your mother is?" I asked.

"I know that she is in your protection. Does she live at Thornfield-Hall, perhaps?"

I steeled myself. "Do you know what state she is in?"

"What do you mean by that? I presume she is treated well."

"Your mother is mad. Insane. She does not take visitors. She would not recognize you; she would not know you; you might very well not want to see her in her condition."

"I would want to see my mother in any condition."

I had already opened my mouth in riposte, but this stopped me. *See my mother in any condition.* Could I fault him for that? "Have you met her brother?" I asked.

"I was at Valley View," he said, "but my uncle Mason was not there. He lives in Madeira, I was told. In Madeira they said he had come here."

"Indeed, he was here, and visited your mother and she attacked him for his trouble and nearly killed him."

He did not react to that revelation. Instead, there was steel in his eyes as he said, "And my father: your brother?"

Could he possibly know how much he resembled Rowland? But of course he could, for those who had taken him to America must surely have known Rowland in Jamaica. Still: "I have no reason to think my brother was your father," I said.

"You have only to look at me," he responded, leaning close, his face nearly in mine.

"My brother is dead, these many years ago."

"And I have come to claim my inheritance as his son."

And now he comes to it. "Son or no son, the inheritance is not yours, unless you have proof of a marriage," I countered.

"I do have proof."

That stopped me for a moment. *What kind of proof could he have?* "Show me."

"First, let me see my mother. I have a right to see her."

I could not deny that. I did not want to allow it, but it hardly seemed decent to deny a man his mother. But I did not need to tell him that yet. "You have no right to see anyone you claim as a mother but cannot prove; you do not resemble her. You do not carry her surname."

"I carry her husband's name: her husband, Rowland, your brother."

"And yet you show no proof. If you expect to see her, much less to claim an inheritance, you will show proof of legal marriage first."

"If you are looking for legal proof, the parish records were destroyed in the hurricane of October 1818; but I have a letter—two, in fact—from your father, Mr. George Howell Rochester, to my grandfather, Mr. Jonas Mason, referring to the marriage of his son to my mother."

I stifled a gasp. So the proof did exist—Rowland and Bertha had wed after all. Unless— "His son? Which son?" I demanded, before realizing I should not play my hand, if Gerald did not know about my own marriage. Then I tried covering my mistake: "You have the letters with you?"

"My solicitor has them—for safekeeping."

"In that case, tell your solicitor to arrange a meeting at my solicitor's. We will settle this thing there."

———

As soon as I could, I went to Everson, telling him what had happened, and sitting through his disgust that I had gone against his orders. But when he had finished scolding me, he admitted an interest in Gerald's supposed proof. "It is not a copy of the record," I pointed out, "only letters, because the record was destroyed." His eyebrows rose at that, but he said, "It's not usual, but letters might do. It is possible. Let us see them and do our best to determine if they are genuine. When I hear from his solicitor, I will inform you."

I turned to leave, but he stopped me at the door. "Surely you have thought this through. If he had proof of marriage between his father and your wife, he inherits all that had been your brother's."

"I know that full well," I said. Everson said nothing in response to that. It occurred to me that he might be surprised that I would be willing to trade Thornfield to secure the hand of Blanche Ingram; he seemed on the verge of advising me against such a colossal mistake. I could not help but smile to myself, a little, as I took my leave.

Three days later the four of us met in Everson's office, Gerald looking nervous and I feeling nervous. This meeting would seal my fate one way or the other; it was only with determination that I could hold my thoughts together.

Gerald's solicitor was a large man with rumpled clothing and a full shock of black hair, appearing more like a cottager than a solicitor, but Everson had warned me that he had a sharp mind. The two of them—Gerald and Mr. Ramsdell—arrived exactly on the dot of ten, and Everson got right to the point: "I understand you have letters proving Rowland Rochester's marriage to Bertha Antoinetta Mason," he said.

"We do," Mr. Ramsdell replied.

"Let us see them."

Ramsdell withdrew from a portfolio two letters, carefully unfolded them, and placed them on Everson's desk. I could not restrain myself from moving closer that I might see them as well.

The first, dated 18 June 1809, read:

> *My dear Jonas,*
>
> *I am pleased to write to you that of course I maintain my intention to conclude the arrangements I made with you for the benefit of both our families, especially your daughter, Bertha Antoinetta. My son is already on his way to Jamaica and will soon arrive, and by God's will this business will be finished shortly.*
>
> *I trust that all is well with you and your family.*
>
> > *Yours faithfully,*
> > *George Howell Rochester, Esq.*

And the second, dated 12 February 1810:

My dear Jonas,

I have now received a letter from my son, reporting that the wedding has taken place, and the two of them have made a home for themselves at Valley View. I cannot tell you of the pleasure I feel that this marriage has been achieved as we hoped and planned, and I feel now that I have upheld my end of the arrangement.

Yours faithfully,
George Howell Rochester

They were short letters—shorter than I would have expected—but clearly the two of them indicated a marriage between my father's son (and by the dates, it could only have been Rowland) and Jonas Mason's only daughter.

I turned to Everson, and he was already staring at me. "What do you think?" he asked. "Might they be genuine?"

I pulled out three letters that I possessed in my father's own hand and laid them down beside the others. There was no doubt of it: the same kind of vellum my father always used, and the handwriting an exact match.

"It seems so," I said, hardly able to believe it. Why had no one objected to my marriage at the time, if Bertha and Rowland were already wed? Why would Jonas and my father have both blessed it—indeed, encouraged it?

"So you consider this proof?" Gerald asked.

"That's for the court to decide," Everson responded, "but..."

"But?" I asked.

"One never knows," he said.

I felt suddenly cold, unable to fully comprehend what had just passed. Everson nodded and began refolding the letters, and Ramsdell reached for them, but suddenly I stopped them both. "Wait," I said. "Let me see them once more."

390 • Sarah Shoemaker

The letters were laid out again on Everson's desk and I examined them more carefully. Suddenly, I, who had been a copier of letters in my childhood, realized two things simultaneously: one, that these letters of Gerald's were falsified. My father's letters never included the full date, and the dates here were in a subtly different pen, a different hand. Gerald, or someone looking out for his interests, must have added the dates to make these letters a clearer proof.

But my attention was drawn even more strikingly to the second realization: the promises referred to between my father and Jonas. If the dates had been falsified—and I now was convinced that they had been—then there *could* be only one meaning to the words: there had been an agreement between Jonas and my father, a long-term arrangement that played out only when I arrived in Jamaica, one that culminated in my blind marriage to the young woman with whom my brother had, earlier, fathered a bastard child.

My arrival in Jamaica had apparently been planned as an *arrangement* to clean up my brother's indiscretion, my own life a payment into the account of my brother's irresponsibility. God, my whole *life*...?

I could not comprehend it, but there was no other explanation I could see. All I had believed, all I had understood, about my father and his care of my future: it was all lies; he was protecting Rowland, and I was the coin he chose to spend. And Jonas Mason as well, who had in his last years been like a father to me—he had taken me as payment for my brother's sins. At least...at least Jonas had had a reason: love for his own child. And my father? My father's reason? I could barely even think it: to uphold his business dealings, whatever they might have been with Jonas, while at the same time saving Rowland from marrying a girl with Bertha's inheritance. To save his holdings and Rowland at my expense. My whole life, for that.

I gazed around at the others, and they were all staring at me, wondering what I was seeing. It was clear that I was the only one to have noticed the fraud, and the fate of my life—and of Thornfield—lay in my hands. I could speak and save my claim to Thornfield, hold on to the Rochester heritage that had once been Rowland's but had now become mine—or I could stay silent, let my father's lands go to this Jamaican bastard, and be free to claim Jane as my own.

I could have wept. I could have bellowed. Instead I swallowed and spoke. "Yes, all right. This is finished."

"You're certain?" Everson asked, frowning somewhat, for he could see that there was more going on in my head.

"Yes."

"Then we are done here," Ramsdell said, gathering up the letters. "Good day, gentlemen."

"I will see my mother now," Gerald said.

But I was in no hurry to give his mother to him. "I will contact you when it will be convenient," I said.

"Today."

"No, not today."

He insisted, but I stood my ground, he becoming angry, far angrier in fact than the circumstances would bear, but Mr. Ramsdell reached out and touched his arm and quieted him. "Within three days," Ramsdell said to me.

"Within three days," I agreed.

Gerald nodded at Everson and led the way out the door.

"Rochester," Everson asked me when they had left, "are you really satisfied? Have you no quibbles at all with this?"

"I have not. It seems clear to me; there was a marriage. There is no point in dragging this out."

"But you will lose everything—Thornfield-Hall, your other properties, your income, everything."

"I will lose them indeed." *But I will keep Jane.* "How long will it take to receive an annulment?"

He sighed. "Four weeks, I would assume."

"Four weeks," I repeated.

CHAPTER 19

Gerald came to see Bertha two days later. I had ensured Jane's absence from Thornfield by suggesting she take Adèle on a trip for the day in the pony cart. It was a mistake on my part, in retrospect, to let him come, but at the time I was trying to do the right thing. I reminded myself that it was not Gerald who was to blame for what my father and brother had done to me, and I warned him again of her condition, but he seemed incapable of understanding.

He left his mount in the stable yard and followed me through the side entrance door and all the way up to the curtained door to Bertha's chambers. "She's like to be sleeping," I warned him. "She is more somnolent in the daytime, more violent and unpredictable at night. She will not know who you are, even if you tell her, but she dislikes strangers. Take care, she may, even in daytime, try to attack you."

He nodded carelessly, as if to say *he* was no stranger. I imagine he thought he could beguile Bertha into recognizing him.

I unlocked the door and led him into the outer chamber. Grace Poole was startled, for I rarely came at this time of day, and she made a quick move to hide the mug at her side. "Grace"—I nodded to her—"my companion has come to visit Bertha."

At the door to the inner chamber I stood for a moment on the threshold, Gerald looking over my shoulder. Bertha lay asleep, her hair matted and awry, but her face as calm as it ever was. I could still see how I had once thought her beautiful.

I stepped to the edge of the bed, but Gerald immediately knelt at the bedside and put a hand on her arm. I marveled at his lack of hesitation; it occurred to me he might be playing out a scene he had imagined countless times in his head over the years. At his touch, Bertha stirred, then fell back into sleep. "Mother," Gerald said softly.

Her eyelids fluttered. "Mother, I'm your son," Gerald said, trying to coax her awake.

"'Ware," Grace warned, her voice swelling from the doorway behind us.

Suddenly Bertha opened her eyes, seeing me first, frowning as if unable to decide if she knew me. Then her eyes swept to Gerald, and she flinched sharply at the unfamiliar face, batting his hand away from her arm.

"Mother, it's me," he said more forcefully.

"Took my baby, where's my baby, where's my baby, where's my baby," she muttered almost incoherently. Should I have warned him that she would not understand? Yes, undoubtedly. But I did not. I was curious as to how this would play out.

"I am he," Gerald insisted, his eyes searching his mother's face, which was growing more feral by the minute. "I am your son and I have—"

His words were swallowed by her scream. Again he persisted, his voice rising to match hers, as if her understanding were only a matter of hearing him. "I am here, Mother. I have finally found you!"

"*Gaaaa, gaaaa!*" She let out a wail that could be heard throughout the house, and she clawed at him as he stood, frozen in horror. It was only Grace's quick reflexes that saved him. She leaped across the room and pulled a snarling and growling Bertha away.

"Gerald," I said, "come."

"No," he said. He now stood halfway across the room, unwilling to approach his mother but unwilling, too, to leave her. But her cries were growing louder now, and I knew Grace would not be able to contain her forever. I took him by the shoulders and pushed him from the room and down the stairs, slamming the door behind me.

By the time we reached the gallery, he was furious and in tears. "What have you done to her?" he demanded.

"I told you. She is mad, and she cannot be cured. Her own mother was the same."

But he would hear none of it. *"You have done this to her! She was the most beautiful girl in Jamaica..."* His eyes blazed dark fury, and he swung at me, his fist barely missing my jaw and landing on my shoulder instead.

I tried to guide him toward the stairs, but he swung again and this time hit his mark, and then came another blow, and by the third I was swinging back, and we tumbled to the floor, two grown men fighting and tussling like common ruffians.

I was less skilled, perhaps, but stronger, and I rose from him, straightening my clothes, but he stayed at my feet, staring furiously at me. *"What have you done to her?"* he demanded again, his voice steely.

I shook my head and walked away, for there was nothing I could say in response to that. I waited at the top of the staircase for him to regain his mind. But when he did, all he could do was stomp past me and down the stairs and glower back in at me from the door in that dark fury, before he dusted off his hat and left.

What had we been thinking, two gentlemen brawling like villians? Or was that how things were done in America? It seemed an eternity to wait for the proof to go through the courts; but, I reminded myself, in four short weeks, I would be free of Bertha and her whole accursed clan forever.

That very evening I was reading in the library, waiting for Jane to join me after putting Adèle to bed, when I happened to catch a movement from out of the window. I raised my head, and there Jane was, walking toward the orchard. It had become a favorite place for her, as it had always been for me, and I stood at the casement and watched her small figure disappearing into the beech avenue on the other side of the gate.

I followed. She was not in sight, and her soft step was impossible to detect among the evening birdsong and the wind rustling in the beeches. But she was there in the garden still, I knew, for though I could not see or hear her, I felt her presence. As I wandered, I popped a cherry from an espaliered tree into my mouth, tasting its refreshing sweetness; I bent closely to a rose to smell its fragrance. Oh, how I would miss this garden! It was strange to think of it as Rowland's before me, and Gerald's after. But such is the life of an object; it is the human connections that are irreplaceable, and I had come, tonight, to claim mine.

I could feel Jane beyond me; I touched the velvet petals of a yellow rose and saw a drop of evening dew slide down. Evening had always been my favorite time of day at Thornfield; I could have lived my life in it. A brightly colored moth caught my eye, and I bent to watch as it lighted as delicately as a breath on a patch of pinks.

"Jane, come and look at this fellow," I murmured.

When the moth flew, I looked up and caught her retreating. "Turn back," I said to her. "On so lovely a night it is a shame to sit in the house; and surely no one can wish to go to bed while sunset is thus at meeting with moonrise."

She came and walked with me but remained a step behind, as if her mind were on other things. We strolled like that in comfortable silence for some time. Troubled as I was by the bittersweet knowledge that I would soon have to take my leave of Thornfield, I nonetheless felt the delicious anticipation of tonight's task. But how does one begin?

We continued down the laurel walk toward the old horse chestnut, and, cautiously, I broached the subject that had been much on my mind. "Thornfield is a pleasant place in summer, is it not?"

"Yes, sir." The abominable *yes, sir*, when I yearned for something more intimate.

"You must have become in some degree attached to the house,—you, who have an eye for natural beauties, and a good deal of the organ of Adhesiveness?"

"I am attached to it, indeed." *As am I,* I thought, *but I have chosen you.*

Instead of falling into sentiment, though, I teased her, putting the fortitude of both our hearts to the test. She had made it seem easy for her to say farewell to me—I would call her bluff. She had said, had she not, that I was her home? She freely admitted how sorry she would be to part with Thornfield, and Adèle and Mrs. Fairfax, but neither of us spoke of her parting with me.

"Pity!" I said with an evident sigh. "It is always the way of events in this life: no sooner have you got settled in a pleasant resting place, than a voice calls out to you to rise and move on, for the hour of repose is expired."

"Must I move on, sir? *Must* I leave Thornfield?"

"I believe you must, Jane. I am sorry, Janet, but I believe indeed you must."

"Then you are going to be married, sir?"

I nearly laughed. Yes, I hoped I was! "Exactly—precisely: with your usual actueness, you have hit the nail straight on the head."

Remembering that of course, poor Jane had no reason to know how things had fallen out between myself and the Ingram ladies, I launched into a comical rendition of Blanche Ingram's supposed blessings, expecting Jane to interrupt me at any moment, but somehow it appeared she believed me still. Sweet, honest Jane! I was touched to see how it affected her, how she turned away to hide a tear. I should have stopped, it's true, but knowing that I had the power to make us both exquisitely happy, I could not help but prolong the pain a moment or two, to make sweeter the relief.

"In about a month I hope to be a bridegroom, and in the interim I shall myself look out for employment and an asylum for you. Indeed I have already, through my future mother-in-law, heard of a place that I think will suit: it is to undertake the education of the five daughters of Mrs. Dionysius O'Gall of Bitternutt Lodge, Connaught, Ireland."

"It is a long way off, sir," she said, struggling with her emotions.

"From what, Jane?" I pressed her.

"From England and from Thornfield: and—"

"Well?"

"From *you*, sir."

The sweetest phrase I knew.

My blood surged at the words, but like an addict I needed more. "It is a long way, to be sure; and when you get to Bitternutt Lodge"—the name so idiotic it was a wonder she believed it—"Connaught, Ireland, I shall never see you again." I could see she was near tears, but I craved a declaration from her that was stronger still, a commitment that would carry us through the years together, in our exile from Thornfield. I threw her own word back at her again: "We have been good friends, Jane; have we not?"

"Yes, sir."

"And when friends are on the eve of separation, they like to spend the little time that remains to them close to each other." I walked her over to the chestnut tree, an old thing I had known since childhood and that soon would be gone from my life forever, and sat her down beneath it. "Come, we will sit there in peace tonight, though we should nevermore be destined to sit there together." Not at Thornfield, at least. I confess I rattled on for a time, extending the sweet agony of the moment, heaven forgive me. Finally, I asked, "Are you anything akin to me, do you think, Jane? Because I sometimes have a queer feeling with regard to you—especially when you are near me, as now: it is as if I had a string somewhere under my left ribs, tightly and inextricably knotted to a similar string situated in the corresponding quarter of your little frame. And if that boisterous channel, and two hundred miles or so of land come broad between us, I am afraid that cord of communion will be snapped; and then I've a nervous notion I should take to bleeding inwardly. As for you,—you'd forget me."

"That I *never* should, sir: you know—" Between her tears, she told how she would grieve mightily to leave Thornfield. My heart skipped for a moment, worrying that she would not stay if Thornfield were no longer mine, until I realized she loved it for the same reason I did, for the happiness it offered, not for the walls themselves. She went on, "It strikes me with terror and anguish to feel I absolutely must be torn from you for ever. I see the necessity of departure; and it is like looking on the necessity of death."

"Where do you see the necessity?" I asked. I sensed we were close to finished—here was my final provocation and, at last, at long last, she spoke her heart to me.

"In the shape of Miss Ingram, a noble and beautiful woman, your bride."

"My bride! What bride? I have no bride!" I looked directly into her eyes. I had thought by now she understood.

"Do you think I can stay to become nothing to you?" she nearly shouted. "Do you think I am an automaton?—a machine without feelings? Do you think, because I am poor, obscure, plain, and little, I am soulless and heartless?—You think wrong!—I have as much soul as you,—and full as much heart! And if God had gifted me with some beauty, and much wealth, I should have made it as hard for you to leave me, as it is now for me to leave you. It is *my spirit* that addresses *your spirit*; just as if both had passed through the grave, and we stood at God's feet, equal,—*as we are!*"

"As we are!" I echoed her, and I wrapped her in my arms and I kissed her. "As we are, indeed," I whispered, "and have always been." I kissed her again and looked into those lovely eyes of hers. "So, Jane!" I said.

"Yes, so, sir," she responded, "and yet not so; for you are a married man."

I gasped: had she known all this time?

"Or as good as a married man," she continued, "and wed to one inferior to you—to one with whom you have no sympathy—whom I do not believe you truly love; for I have seen and heard you sneer at her." *Miss Ingram, it was Miss Ingram she meant.* "I would scorn such a union: therefore I am better than you—let me go!"

Oh, you are better than I, Jane. You are.

"I have spoken my mind, and can go anywhere now," she said.

She continued to fight against my arms, but I held her tight. "Jane, be still; don't struggle so, like a wild, frantic bird that is rending its own plumage in its desperation."

"I am no bird; and no net ensnares me," she insisted. "I am a free human being with an independent will; which I now exert to leave you." And with a final, great effort, she pulled herself away from me.

"And your will shall decide your destiny." This is what I had waited for all those months: a declaration of feeling that held us not as master and employee, but as equals. "So," I said, "I offer you my hand, my heart, and a share of all my possessions." *Such as they may be.*

She stared at me in silence, unbelieving, and suddenly I realized I had played the game too far. My serious Jane refused now to listen as I promised, again and again, that it was *she* I intended to marry. I explained that I had driven Miss Ingram away with tales of a lost fortune, that I had never loved her, that we were finished.

"Are you in earnest?" she asked. "Do you truly love me?—Do you sincerely wish me to be your wife?"

"I do; and if an oath is necessary to satisfy you, I swear it."

"Then, sir, I will marry you."

"*Edward*," I whispered. "Say Edward—give me my name—*Edward*, please, my little wife."

"Dear Edward!" she whispered.

Edward. "Come to me—come to me entirely now," I said, holding her close, her cheek against mine. "God pardon me," I whispered to myself, "and man meddle not with me: I have her, and will hold her, and I will give my life to make her happy."

But even as I said those words, the wind came up, and the trees began to creak with the force of it, and a streak of lightning darted across the sky, and a crash of thunder jolted us to run, for the rain was already beginning to fall. We dashed through the grounds and into the house, and I helped her remove her sodden shawl and loosened her hair, and then I could not resist kissing her again and again. I had eyes only for her: her cheeks rosy from the sudden chill and the exertion, the hair falling down her back into whose tresses I buried my hands. She thought herself small and plain, but to me she was warmth and light—life itself—and in my joy I could not have enough of her.

When she made to draw away from me, I understood, for it was late and Adèle would be there in the morning, vying for Jane's attention, and there was much that I must do as well. I led Jane upstairs to her chamber and kissed her again good night and went on to my own room.

The storm went on for two more hours, rain pelting against the casements, lightning flashing across the sky, thunder roaring and cracking and rattling. In the night I rose two or three times and went to Jane's door and knocked softly, making sure she felt safe.

In the morning, the sun shone out clear and bright. The storm had gone, with nothing to show for it but the felling of the old horse chestnut at the bottom of the orchard.

CHAPTER 20

I was late in rising that morning, having lain awake in bed the full duration of the storm, my mind as tossed as tree branches in the wind. I
would marry Jane in a month, as soon as the courts cleared me of the
weight of Bertha's bond, and I would take her away soonest possible on
a honeymoon, then to a new home. I hadn't told her of that part yet—I
hadn't even thought where we might live: let Jane decide that, I thought,
for I was hardly used to the idea myself. I would arrange for Adèle to be
taken into a school—no, Jane must see to that too, as she surely would
have a better idea of Adèle's needs and capabilities than I did.

I would send for the family jewels immediately—they had been locked
in a safe at a London bank since my mother's death—and never mind that
they were part of Gerald's inheritance: they had been my mother's. *My*
mother's. I would take Jane to Millcote and buy her the finest of fabrics
for dresses. As long as I possessed the inheritance, I would spend it as I
pleased, and I had promised myself in Gateshead that Jane would have
only the best of everything. That would not go on forever, but for the next
month, it would.

Jane was at breakfast with Mrs. Fairfax when I came down in the
morning, and I dared not face the two of them together, for I realized
how it must look to the proper old lady to see the master of the estate
marrying the governess. Instead, I returned upstairs to the schoolroom

and waited there. Adèle bounced in shortly. She was surprised to see me, but, taking advantage of every opportunity for affection, she leaped into my arms.

"You have become too big a girl to jump into men's arms—into anyone's arms," I scolded her. But I did not put her down immediately.

She placed her hands on my cheeks and held my face close to hers. "Did you hear the storm?" she asked. "Were you afraid?"

"No, of course not. It was only wind and rain."

"And did you see? The big tree has come down!"

"Indeed, it has," I said putting her down. "Now, run along, and find Miss Eyre and tell her I am waiting for her here."

"Will I not have lessons this morning?" she asked, with the joy every child feels at the prospect of freedom.

"We shall see," I said, though I could not summon my usual gruffness on a morning so happy.

Jane came in shortly afterwards. "Come and bid me good morning," I said to her, and she came, and we embraced and kissed, the sweetest of kisses.

"You look blooming, and smiling, and pretty, truly pretty this morning." My heart was full, overcome with the sunshine of her presence. "Who is this sunny-faced girl with the dimpled cheek and rosy lips?"

"It is Jane Eyre, sir," she said.

"Yes, indeed, but soon to be Jane Rochester: in four weeks, Janet; not a day more. Do you hear that?"

Her face turned a sudden white, and I saw something like panic—or fear—pass across her face. "You gave me a new name," she said, "Jane Rochester; and it seems so strange."

"Yes; Mrs. Rochester; young Mrs. Rochester—Fairfax Rochester's girl-bride. Surely you can become used to it."

"It can never be, sir; it does not sound likely. Human beings never enjoy complete happiness in this world. I was not born for a different destiny to the rest of my species: to imagine such a lot befalling me is a fairy tale—a daydream."

But it was, indeed, that very fairy tale, that dream of complete happiness, that I intended to build for her, while it was still in my power to do so. But to my surprise she responded to my offerings with horror. I explained that I wanted to treat her as a peer, to make her my equal in society's eyes, to shower her in jewels as nature had endowed her with spirit. But she would hear none of it.

"And then you won't know me, sir, and I shall not be your Jane Eyre any longer," she said.

I wanted the world to see her beauty as clearly as I did, and I tried to make her understand. "This very day I shall take you in the carriage to Millcote," I said, "and you must choose some dresses, and we shall be married in the little church at the gates of Thornfield, and then I will waft you away at once to London. And after we have been there, we will go on to all the finest places in Europe—everywhere I took my lonely and jaded self, I will revisit with you, and you will turn them into magical places and heal them in my eyes."

She laughed. "I am not an angel and I will not be one till I die: I will be myself. Mr. Rochester, you must neither expect nor exact anything celestial of me—for you will not get it."

That blasted *Mr. Rochester* again! Could she not understand how much I wanted to be called by my first name, the name my mother gave me?

We bantered back and forth, she laying out a rather woeful portrait of a capricious and cold marriage as a matter of course; I assured her my ardor would not cool in six months, as she claimed—indeed, I was sure it never would. "I think I shall like you again and yet again," I said, "and I will make you confess that you do indeed know that I do not only *like* but *love* you," I said, "with truth, fervor, and constancy."

However, she was not finished with teasing me, and she went on, calling me *sir* at every opportunity until she nearly drove me mad, finishing with, "Well, then, *sir*; have the goodness to gratify my curiosity, which is much piqued on one point."

Grace Poole, I thought. *Good God, woman, just give me a few more weeks and we will be clear of Bertha forever.* "What? What?" I asked.

At least I had not yet sworn to answer every request, though I was surely eager to prove my love in any way I might. Still, the more I panicked and attempted to overrule her, the more delighted and sprightly she became.

But finally she came out with it, asking why I had taken such pains to make her think I wished to marry Miss Ingram. I was surprised that one so intelligent as Jane might need this explained. "I feigned courtship of Miss Ingram," I told her, "because I wished to render you as madly in love with me as I was with you; and I knew jealousy would be the best ally I could call in for the furtherance of that end." For I had thought that she surely would realize that she could never bear the thought of seeing me with another woman. But, she asked, was it fair to play with someone's emotions like that? I responded that I had done it for the best of reasons: to bring her to me.

She chastised me for acting disgracefully, but I was surprised that it was not *her* emotions she defended but those of her rival, Miss Ingram, whom she imagined pining for the prize Jane was now enjoying.

I laughed at that. "Her feelings are concentrated in one—pride; and that needs humbling. Were you jealous, Jane?"

She would not concede the point, and went on to impugn my principles. I smiled to think of all the years of joyful battle ahead of us. Not even at Cambridge had I experienced so worthy and quick-witted an opponent.

When I asked her to make ready for a trip to Millcote, she made one last request, sending me off to put Mrs. Fairfax's mind at rest as to my intentions, for it seemed she had seen Jane and me kissing in the hall the previous night.

I found that good woman in her sitting room, mending an apron. I could have summoned her to my office, but I wanted to approach her at her most comfortable. I hoped she would be happy for us, as perhaps my own mother might have been; I hoped *Jane's* happiness, in particular, would win her over.

"Good morning," I said, as if surprised to see her there.

She put her mending aside and rose. "Sir," she said, her face betraying nothing.

"May I have a word?"

"Of course."

I sat in the chair facing hers, and she seated herself again. "You knew my mother far better than anyone else I know," I began.

She stiffened. "I did not know her well at all, sir."

"Still, she was a lady in every meaning of the word, was she not?"

"Yes, sir, she was."

"When she married my father—George Howell Rochester—were there whisperings that she had married beneath herself?" This was treacherous ground, I knew, but it seemed the best. "He had the Rochester name, but he had put himself in trade, which made him a kind of pariah, no? I cannot imagine what must have been said of him in those days."

Mrs. Fairfax's eyes lowered.

"Did you ever hear gossip of that sort?" I asked.

"It could have happened," she allowed.

"She was your late husband's second cousin, I understand."

"Yes, sir."

"And he never said anything? That she had married beneath herself?"

"Of course not. Your father was a gentleman, despite..."

I nodded. "Despite that he was in trade."

She cleared her throat, and her eyes wandered away from mine. "I really don't recall, sir."

"I never knew my mother, as you are well aware. So I have only a child's dream of what his mother might have been, but I assume that she was a fine woman. However"—I cleared my throat—"in all my life, and in the many, many places I have traveled, I have never met a woman as admirable as our Miss Eyre."

If I had imagined that I would catch her unprepared, I was mistaken. "If I may say so, sir," she said, "she is a child—only eighteen."

"Many women of good family marry at eighteen."

"As I say, sir."

I had to smile that she did not dare to point out I was twice Jane's age. "Yes, she is young," I agreed. "But she is wise beyond her years; surely you have seen that."

She said nothing in response, for she could not deny my words.

I continued: "Would that I were younger, or she older. But that is not the case. Is that the only reservation you might have? You should know I shall marry her regardless, but I—and Jane, I am sure—would welcome your blessing. So again I ask, is her youth your only reservation?"

She looked at me straight on. "It will indeed be said, sir, that you are marrying beneath your station. Eyebrows do rise when a man allies himself with his child's governess."

"You do not admire her?"

"I think she is a fine young woman, sir. But a *governess*, married to the master of the house, it does…it does not…"

"It does not bode well for the governess, you are saying. You have concern that I would take advantage—"

"Oh no, sir! No. It's just…she is very inexperienced, sir."

I would have laughed if I had not felt so put out by the rest of the conversation. "On that count, you will not have to concern yourself," I said to her, rising. "Miss Eyre is perfectly capable of taking care of herself." I started toward the door, but I stopped and turned. "At any rate," I added, "I am determined to marry her. Whether you accept her or not is your affair, I suppose, but in one month, she shall be my wife."

After that, Jane and I—and Adèle, who despite my original wishes charmed her way into our carriage—took off for Millcote. I urged Jane to agree to the loveliest of fabrics, but she was a stubborn little thing, and instead chose only a black satin and a pearl-gray silk. The harder I tried to lavish her with gifts, the harder she resisted, saying, "I only want an easy mind, sir; not crushed by crowded obligations. Do you remember what you said of Céline Varens?—of the diamonds, the cashmeres you gave her? I will not be your English Céline Varens. I shall continue to act as Adèle's governess: by that I shall earn my board and lodging, and thirty pounds a year besides. I'll furnish my own wardrobe out of that money, and you shall give me nothing but—"

My God, I thought. *Such independence in her! Cannot she simply let me spoil her while I still have the means?* "Well," I asked, "but what?"

"Your regard: and if I give you mine in return, that debt will be quit."

"Well," I responded, "for cool native impudence, and pure innate pride, you haven't your equal." I shall say this for her: certainly, unlike some women, her view of marriage was not dictated by the fanciful romantic vision of a Jane Austen novel.

As we were approaching Thornfield, I asked her to dine with me that evening, for she had not yet done so in all the past months. But she declined, for, as she insisted, she had come to Thornfield a governess and she was determined to remain so until the day of our wedding.

I gazed at her, sitting primly beside me, her hands folded in her lap. *She is a puzzle,* I thought; *she is a puzzle to be unwrapped one piece at a time until she is completely revealed. Well, then, so be it,* I said to myself. *I will have the rest of my life to discover my Jane.* Difficult, contradictory, maddening as she might be, she was my whole world, almost my hope of heaven.

But if she could be difficult, so could I; and as soon as I had a chance, I ordered the finest wedding veil to be had to grace Jane's head.

CHAPTER 21

I had not seen Gerald for some time after our fight, and I can't say it disappointed me, for I didn't care if I never saw him again. In less than four weeks' time I would have my annulment, and Gerald would press his case to have the courts declare him Thornfield's legal heir. And Jane and I? Jane and I would find ourselves in an entirely different life. We would be without Thornfield, but we would have each other, and I believed it would be bliss. Perhaps I would buy her a school while I had the means, for I knew she had always wanted her own school. It would not be one like Mr. Lincoln's, but it would be a place where young ladies would be educated to be independent. In the meantime, my time at Thornfield was bittersweet. At least, I realized, it was not necessary now to move Bertha, for with Gerald taking over at Thornfield, she could remain in the only place she had known for years.

Shortly before the wedding, I went to Millcote for a meeting with Everson on some other business, but while I was there Everson brought up the question of the inheritance, urging me to protect myself. He did not understand that I could upend Gerald's case if I chose but had chosen to keep silent and let it go forward, and by the time I left his chambers, he could barely find the words to say farewell to me.

I left Everson's office in a sour mood, and as I walked through the town I heard insistent footsteps behind me. Turning, I saw it was Gerald. It was an effort to give him a civil greeting.

"I want to see my mother," he announced.

"Oh no. You have done that once. You can see her all you want when Thornfield is yours."

"I insist!" he demanded. "*I insist! She is my mother!*" He was shouting now, and passersby were turning to watch.

Bertha had been relatively quiet since her previous attack on him. And she was his mother. Still, I refused, not feeling inclined to humor him for the absurd, ungentlemanly scene he was making.

Gerald's face grew dark and, angry beyond words, he spewed out a torrent of invective at me, and I again saw that familiar dark fury in his eyes. In a moment, I understood too clearly: *He is going to become like her,* I thought. *He will become her.* I feared he might try fisticuffs, right there on the street, but he did not. Instead, he continued to yell at me: "She is not my mother! What have you done with my mother?"

"She is your mother if your mother was Bertha Antoinetta Mason," I said as calmly as I could manage. "I have had her in my care for fifteen years."

"Then you are a madman yourself! No one in his right mind keeps an animal like that in his home."

"It was her wish. And her father's. I made promises."

"Then you are a fool. When you leave, you may take her with you, you who are so ready to make promises. *You* take care of her, or I will put her where she belongs."

I stared at him in horror. I, whose life had been ruined for the sake of my family reputation, for the sake of my brother—I had given years to this woman, whose own son, at first so anxious to see her, was now just as anxious to throw her away. A son who, as I was seeing before my very eyes, would no doubt grow to be as mad as she was. I turned and walked swiftly away from him, and he chased me and struck me from behind. I was tempted to respond in kind, but I ignored his provocations and left the scene. He did not follow.

I stewed over that for a night and a day, barely able to contain myself, even in Jane's presence. She noticed my mood but I told her it was nothing, just a troublesome cottager on my land. But it was not nothing; it was a madman set to take control of Thornfield, and I could not bear it. I knew that when Jane discovered the truth—for at some point she would—she would hate that I had done such a thing. It was six and two threes: whatever I did would be wrong. But I knew what Jane would want me to do.

The next day I told her I would be gone for some time, perhaps overnight, but not to worry, and I rode back to Millcote and told Everson of my business. He sat at his desk in silence until I almost thought he had not understood; finally he said to me, "They are examining the letters tomorrow morning, I believe."

With that, I rose, but Everson stayed me. "I will accompany you, but we must let Ramsdell and Gerald Rochester know, for they have a legal right to be there." After that, I could not wait, and I was off, trailing Everson, and I am sure Ramsdell and Gerald as well, behind me.

I slept poorly at an inn that night, and in the morning the magistrates were angry when I barged into their session, demanding a hearing, pulling out my proof while the chief magistrate pounded his gavel. I emptied onto their tables the letters I had found in the desk in the library: a total of nineteen of them. I straightened each one so they could see it well, the judges sitting in dour and mystified silence all this time. "Look at the letters you hold in your hands, and look at these that come from my father's desk. A guinea for the man who sees the difference first." Two of the three almost smiled, and they set to their task.

Everson stepped in just at that moment and stood in amazement, not knowing whether to upbraid me or praise me. The judges took longer than my patience lasted, and so I gave them a hint: "Notice the dates." As these letters made clear, my father, for whatever reason, was in the habit of including only the day and the month—in all of the letters I had provided, but not the two that Gerald had presented as evidence. "What say you?" I asked, pulling out a guinea coin.

"Forgery," said one judge.

"He took the genuine letters and added a year," admitted another.

"Indeed," I said.

"Indeed, he did," Everson said. "But when—"

"Never mind," I silenced him. "The annulment cannot stand."

"It cannot indeed," said Everson. "We withdraw our petition."

I walked out of there in a flurry of emotion, encountering Gerald and Ramsdell on the street.

"It's over," I said. "It was clever, Gerald, but it didn't work. Perhaps you didn't know, but the letters were regarding me, not my brother. Whoever falsified the letters perhaps did not know that I was the Rochester son who married your mother."

Ramsdell, confused, began to stammer a response, but I saw that fury rise again in Gerald—his eyes darken, his hands clench—and I mounted Mesrour and rode away before Gerald could strike out. I knew the law would hold Gerald for at least a short time for presenting forgeries to the court. Jane and I would be married and gone by the time he was free to bother anyone again.

———

It was late when I left, and I did not need to put my heels to Mesrour, for he knew we were bound for home, and he galloped those many miles as if I were a highwayman escaping arrest. I knew full well what I was doing, but I didn't care. Man's laws can be manipulated to dishonest ends. God's laws can be used in ways I was sure God had not intended. I would marry Jane; Everson would find a place where I could move Bertha, where she would be safe, and no one would know. I could have it done while Jane and I were on our honeymoon.

It warmed my heart more than I can admit when I spied the first lights of Thornfield-Hall in the distance—home at last, and marriage tomorrow and Bertha to be removed. It was as if every care in the world had suddenly vanished as we sped homeward in rain and driving wind.

Then the moon, which had been passing in and out of rain clouds all evening, revealed to me a figure standing in the lane outside the gates of Thornfield, and I knew immediately it was Jane. *Jane?* Out so late at night? What could have happened? *God, not Bertha,* I thought. *Please, not Bertha!*

As I came closer, she ran to meet me, and I stretched out my hand to her and pulled her up to join me in the saddle. Holding her close, I asked if anything was wrong that she should come to meet me at such an hour, but she insisted it was nothing.

I did not believe her, for I felt a strong foreboding beyond the emotion that had that day occurred, but Jane would say nothing more until after I dined. As nighttime drew on, I tried to cheer her with a reminder that she had promised to sit up with me the night before my wedding, but she smiled only a wan smile.

I managed to coax her into telling me what had disturbed her. She'd had nightmarish visions of a destroyed Thornfield-Hall, and of a child, clinging to her for dear life. I tried to reassure her that all was well, certain that she could not know anything of my fevered idea, abandoned less than a day earlier, to move us out of Thornfield.

But she could not be deterred. "On waking," she said, "a gleam dazzled my eyes: I thought—oh, it is daylight! But I was mistaken: it was only candlelight, Sophie, I supposed, had come in. There was a light on the dressing table, and the door of the closet, where, before going to bed, I had hung my wedding dress and veil, stood open: I heard a rustling there. I asked, 'Sophie, what are you doing?'

"No one answered," she went on, "but a form emerged from the closet: it took the light, held it aloft and surveyed the garments pendent from the portmanteau. 'Sophie! Sophie!' I again cried: and still it was silent. I had risen up in bed, I bent forward: first, surprise, then bewilderment, came over me; and then my blood crept cold through my veins. Mr. Rochester, this was not Sophie."

My own blood chilled at her words.

"It was not Leah," Jane said, "and it was not Mrs. Fairfax—no, I was sure of it, and am still—it was not even that strange woman, Grace Poole." It was not, she said, anyone she had ever seen; even in the half darkness she had been certain of that.

"It *must* have been one of them," I said, for I could say nothing else. Perhaps the force of my words could convince her.

But in the next moment she described, in slow and fearful words, the savage image of Bertha herself. I dared not breathe as she described how her midnight visitor took up Jane's bridal veil and placed it on her own head to gaze in the mirror, and in a spasm of violence tore the veil from her head, ripped the lace in two, and threw it to the floor and tramped on it. I imagined Bertha somehow understanding in her own confused way my intentions toward Jane. And, oh God, there was more! When Bertha had finished with the veil, she approached Jane herself with the candle and looked into her eye, and still staring closely at Jane, extinguished the candle and remained there until Jane fainted from terror.

I swallowed deeply and forced calm onto my face. "Who was with you when you revived?" I asked.

No one was there, she said, and as it had become broad daylight, she rose and did her usual ablutions, and while she felt weak, she was not ill, and then she asked who or what that could have been. It was a nightmare, I told her, surely just a creature of an overstimulated brain, and I was relieved that such a vision could be explained away. But she insisted that her nerves were not in fault, that the thing had been real.

I reminded her gently that none of her other dreams had come true, and half succeeded in convincing her, I thought, that it was a matter of nerves. But then she rejoined: in the light of broad day, she had seen her fine new wedding veil, lying on the carpet, torn in half.

I clung to her, wishing I could erase the event from her mind, erase it from time altogether. Now it was clear: it was not just I who was in danger from the madwoman—Jane herself was at risk. How could I protect her now? *Would this terror never end?*

Struggling to control my voice, I offered an explanation: It was—it must have been—Grace Poole, I said. She'd seen how oddly the servant had acted in the past. In her half sleep, Jane had imagined Grace as a monster. I comforted her in as cheery a voice as I could muster, making it up as I went, desperate to hide the truth for one more day. After the wedding, when we were on our honeymoon, Bertha could be moved away somewhere—anywhere. Grace Poole's good name deserved better than this, but there was little to be done for it now, knowing my clear-sighted, rational Jane would wonder why Grace was allowed to remain at Thornfield-Hall. I hinted that Grace's tenure at Thornfield represented a burden and debt I had taken on and must repay, but that when we were married a year and a day I would tell her the whole of it. I would have liked to tell her immediately, to hear her lift my burden with the blessing of her trust and love, to have her tell me that I was not wrong in the clear eyes of God and morality to think I deserved a better life than the one I had been dealt. But I dared not tell her now, while I could still lose her.

Jane, bless her, seemed content with what I had to say. I urged her to sleep with Adèle in the nursery and to lock the door. If I could just get her safely to morning, to our exchange of vows, we would be off to London for our honeymoon and a happy life together.

She did as I suggested, and as soon as she was settled, I climbed to the third floor and let myself into the chamber. All was quiet there, Bertha pacing in silence in her room, and Grace sitting up in the outer room, relishing the one mug of porter I allowed her each night. "She was out again last night," I said quietly.

I could tell by Grace's expression that she had not known. "Does the porter make you sleepy?" I asked.

She rose in umbrage at that. "I keep my promises. I do my duties."

"She nearly attacked Miss Eyre," I hissed at her.

She shrugged. "In another day you will be shut of us, off on your honeymoon."

Indeed. I held her eyes, torn between rage at her impertinence and the knowledge that I could not risk losing her service the way I had lost Molly's.

"Thousands of people better off than her are kept in asylums," she added, and I think I saw pity in her eyes.

"You have served me well all these years, Grace, and I appreciate that." She nodded.

"And have you saved enough by now?"

She smiled her gap-toothed smile. "It is never enough."

I left her with that. Nothing is ever enough. One thinks one has done enough, and it turns out not to be so; one thinks nothing else could go wrong but is mistaken in the end. And yet, as I left the chamber, the big clock downstairs chimed and I told myself that in a few hours, my new life would begin.

CHAPTER 22

All night, half-awake, half-asleep, I dreamed of our future. Our travels in Europe, a happier place now that we were together; our return to Thornfield, which would remain my own. I imagined, even, children exploring the woods as I had once done and dawdling their way through the orchard, picking cherries or plums; running recklessly through the rooms and up and down the stairs; dragging mud through the kitchens; laughing and squealing in delight; Mrs. Fairfax, perhaps frowning in disapproval but silent, because Jane and I were delighted simply in the life we were afforded. Bertha would remain my secret, and I would guard Jane well and secure our happiness, no matter what man's law might think of me. Had I not earned this? Had I not acquitted myself as well as or better than any man in my position would have done? Jane and I loved each other as equals: I had been willing to give up Thornfield for Jane and had convinced myself her love for me was surely stronger than her moral stubbornness. If she knew, she would forgive me. But she need never know.

I rose that morning with the sun, watching the deep shades of the orchard lighten, the shadows shorten. I made my ablutions and dressed, slowly and carefully, letting the import of the morning enter fully into my mind. In less than three hours, and then less than two, Jane would be at my side in the little church. She would be mine—all else be damned. She would want this; she loved me. I could not believe my fortune.

I fairly skipped down the broad oak staircase and peered into the dining room. The buffet was laid, but Jane had not yet made an appearance. I felt too agitated to sit and eat. I strode into the library and immediately back out, then to the drawing room. I nodded at my mother's portrait above the mantelpiece, suddenly flooded with emotion. Then, patient no more, I went to the bottom of the stairs and called out for Jane.

She was there in a few moments, and was a vision: even in her modest silks and the simple lace square on her head, she was the most beautiful creature I had ever seen. I could not even mourn the loss of the other veil. I took her elbow and hurried her to breakfast, but it seemed, as I, she was too overwhelmed to eat and sat only with a cup of tea before her.

Finally the footman informed me that all was in readiness, and at those words I nearly dragged Jane from the table and across the entrance hall, where Mrs. Fairfax stood, as still as a stone carving. She nodded a curtsy as we passed, and I returned the nod, and Jane would have paused, but I was all in a rush. It seemed that time could not fly fast enough. I wanted only for the wedding to be behind us, and Jane safely mine and I hers.

Her small hand in mine in the morning sunlight, we raced down the long drive to the wicket gate of the church, where I discovered she was out of breath. Poor wren! "Am I cruel in my love?" I asked her. "Delay an instant: lean on me, Jane."

After a moment, I gave her a little caress on her shoulder and we walked forward. As we took our place at the communion rail, the clergyman, Mr. Wood, opened his book and began to read. In this place, where generations of Rochesters had worshipped, my heart filled with gratitude to God and to Jane for giving me this chance at happiness. I felt secure that Providence had seen my good intentions for Bertha, and my pure, true love for Jane, and was smiling on our union.

I watched my little Jane, her face on Mr. Wood's as his voice echoed within those stone walls: "...any impediment why ye may not lawfully be joined together in matrimony, ye do now confess it; for be ye well assured that so many as are coupled together otherwise than God's Word doth allow, are not joined together by God, neither is their matrimony lawful."

He paused, as I suppose was required of him. The words did not arrest me, so sure was I that God himself had brought Jane to me.

But just when Mr. Wood moved to continue, a voice from behind me said: "The marriage cannot go on: I declare the existence of an impediment."

No, I thought. *No.* Not with my prize seconds from my grasp. I almost turned to confront the unknown voice, but I stopped. I would will it gone.

Mr. Wood must have been as shocked as we: for how often could there have been a response to those old, familiar words? Yet he stood by his duty. "I cannot proceed without some investigation," he said.

"The ceremony is quite broken off," came the voice again. "I am in a condition to prove my allegation: an insuperable impediment to this marriage exists."

I would not, I could not, turn and allow for this to be happening. I glanced down at Jane beside me, and she was staring wordlessly in return. I took her hand in mine; if the speaker revealed my secret, Jane would be lost to me forever. *We shall not be overcome by this,* I told myself. *I forbid it.*

"What is the nature of the impediment?" Mr. Wood asked, his voice hopeful. "Perhaps it may be got over—explained away?"

"Hardly," came the voice. "I have called it insuperable, and I speak advisedly." The speaker came forward then, and I saw he was a stranger. From whom could he have heard my secret? Not Gerald. "It simply consists in the existence of a previous marriage," he said, slowly and clearly, so there could be no mistaking his words. "Mr. Rochester has a wife now living."

I gripped Jane tighter still, twined my arm around her waist as if fearing the man might make her vanish with his words. "Who are you?" I thundered.

"My name is Briggs," he said, "a solicitor of —— Street, London."

"And you would thrust on me a wife?" I was in a fever dream—I would stave this off by force of will if I must. After all those years with Bertha, surely God had given me what I deserve!

"I would remind you of your lady's existence, sir; which the law recognizes, if you do not."

No, by God. No. I would not retreat. Perhaps this was a bluff. "Favor me with an account of her—with her name, her parentage, her place of abode."

"I affirm and can prove that on the twentieth of October, A.D. 18——, Edward Fairfax Rochester, of Thornfield-Hall..." His words swirled through my head, the full account of it: my marriage to Bertha, and the place, etcetera, etcetera. "Signed, Richard Mason."

All was lost now if I could not remove this last impediment. I scrambled for any last footing. "That—if a genuine document—may prove I have been married," I said, "but it does not prove that the woman mentioned therein as my wife is still living."

"She was living three months ago," the lawyer rejoined.

"How do you know?"

"I have a witness to the fact; whose testimony even you, sir, will scarcely controvert."

Richard. It could be none other, and damn him to eternity, after all that I had done for him. "Produce him—or go to hell."

I heard Mr. Wood suck in his breath—such language in the house of God.

"Mr. Mason, have the goodness to step forward."

At the name, I felt a shudder as if an earthquake had erupted beneath my feet. I clung to Jane still—I would not release her!—and I turned to face Richard. In a fit of passion I raised my arm as if to strike him, and he, seeing the movement, scuttled back away from me like a frightened spider. Pathetic, witless coward, how dare he stand in my way now? "What have *you* to say?" I demanded.

He, who had abandoned his sister more completely than I ever had, who had depended on my efforts for his living, could only mumble inaudibly.

"The devil is in it if you cannot answer distinctly. I again demand, what have *you* to say?" *Goddamn it, man! Make this right—after all these years, you would not do this to me now.*

"Sir—sir—" interrupted the clergyman, "do not forget you are in a sacred place." Then he turned toward Richard and asked if he was certain that Bertha was still living.

Richard still shrank back, for he knew he owed me much, but the lawyer urged him on. "She is now living at Thornfield-Hall," he said in a stronger voice than I could have imagined possible. "I saw her there last April."

And she would have killed you, I thought, *if I hadn't saved your life.*

Mr. Wood, too late, seemed to take my side. "Impossible! I have never heard of a Mrs. Rochester at Thornfield-Hall."

At that, I could not help a grim smile—to have succeeded all these years, to be mere *seconds* from happiness, only to be brought down by one who owed me his life. Indeed, this was not an act of man but one of God—Providence had checked me. I had never been anything but a sinner, and I was wrong to believe in forgiveness. *Out with it, then!*

"Enough," I said. "Wood," I said to the clergyman, "close your book and take off your surplice." I turned to his clerk: "John Green, leave the church; there will be no wedding today." *Or any day.*

Once started, the truth came bursting out of me, as if from a dam; if it had not been so painful I might have been relieved to be done with the secrecy after all these years. But in the moment my misery, my self-loathing, was too deep. As I spoke to those around me, my words were meant for Jane. I could not bear to look her in the face, she who had trusted me, and whom I had brought into shame. I confessed it all: I had a wife, and she lived, and knowing this I had still intended to marry another—yes, I was a devil. I felt like one, through and through. I tried, too, to have them know that she had been thrust upon me by my father and hers, without my knowledge of her family history of madness. I bitterly wanted to have them understand the nature of this "wife"—and in the end, with nothing left to lose, I dared to bring them back to the house to see her for themselves, in the flesh, for she was the greatest evidence of my desperation. And even as I clung to her with an iron grip, I absolved Jane of all knowledge or responsibility for my plan. "Come, all of you, follow!" I demanded, and I led the way back to Thornfield-Hall.

The servants, knowing nothing of the drama in the church, crowded forward to congratulate us, but I shooed them away and stormed upstairs, with a trail of bewildered men behind me, until we burst into Bertha's private chamber. Grace, surely as shocked as anyone, handled the intrusion with perfect aplomb.

As soon as Bertha was aware of our presence, she rose from her crouch in a corner and uttered a ghastly scream that shattered the small group behind me. None of them had ever beheld such I sight, I'd wager.

"Ah, sir, she sees you," Grace warned. "You'd better not stay."

Bertha bellowed and advanced, and the men shrank back. Grace moved forward to distract her, but I wanted to face her myself. I was determined to give them what they'd asked for: proof of my marriage. "She has no knife now, I suppose?" I said.

"One never knows what she has, sir," Grace responded. "She is so cunning: it is not in mortal discretion to fathom her craft."

"We had better leave," a frightened Richard whispered behind me.

"'*Ware!*" Grace cried suddenly, and Bertha lunged forward, scattering the men behind me.

I shoved Jane behind me just as Bertha seized my throat and sank her teeth into my cheek. She was a goblin; a devil as large as I and almost evenly matched—she had lost none of her strength. We grappled—she trying to throttle me while I did my best to avoid hurting her: she growled wildly the whole time, until I was able to wrestle her to the floor, when Grace slipped me the cord, and I bound her hands together with it, and with another I tied her to a chair.

Then I faced the small assemblage of onlookers. "That is *my wife*. Such is the sole conjugal embrace I am ever to know—such are the endearments which are to solace my leisure hours! And *this*"—I gently touched Jane's shoulder, and to my lasting gratitude she did not shrink away—"this is what I wished to have: this young girl, who stands so grave and quiet at the mouth of hell, looking collectedly at the gambols of a demon. Wood and Briggs, look at the difference! Compare these clear eyes with the red balls yonder—this face with that mask—this form with that bulk; then judge me, priest of the Gospel and man of the law, and remember, with what judgment ye judge ye shall be judged! Off with you now. I must shut up my prize."

CHAPTER 23

$\mathcal{T}$he others hurried away, while I remained in that chamber of horrors, alone but for Grace Poole and her demonic charge. This, I supposed, would be my life from here on, trapped with this "wife," unless Jane would forgive me. "Grace," I said, "you and Bertha will not be moving to other quarters. The whole world is now aware that my mad wife lives here; there is no point in hiding the truth anymore."

"She will move out of this chamber now, sir?" Grace asked.

"I suppose not," I said. "This is as safe for her as anywhere, and safer than most."

Still, I tarried, afraid to step outside and face the destruction of all my hopes. We untied Bertha as soon as she calmed, and with Grace beside her caressing her arm, Bertha dozed off in bed a few minutes later.

Numbly, I left that ghastly place and walked down the stairs, glad not to encounter Jane or Adèle. Mrs. Fairfax was in her sitting room, and I stopped there, for I owed her an explanation. "I am sorry to have deceived you," I said.

Her eyes rose to meet mine. "I was aware of some of it," she said simply, and turned back to her sewing.

We both remained silent for a time, and then I asked, "Is Miss Eyre in her room?"

"I imagine she is, sir," she said, still not looking at me.

I rose and left her there. *That is how things shall be now,* I thought: the averted eyes, the stares behind my back. *People will conjecture all kinds of scenes of mayhem—and worse—hidden behind these walls.* Thornfield-Hall would now be a place haunted by my shame and sins, its great reputation forever tarnished. And how could I continue to live at Thornfield myself? Would that I had let Rowland's accursed son take the place off my hands!

I mounted the stairs slowly and turned toward Jane's room. At the door, I paused: *I cannot disturb her,* I thought; *it is not my right. I can do nothing but wait for her to enter the world again, and forgive me.* Silently, I pressed my hand—and then my forehead—against the wood of the door panel. I don't know how long I stood there, feeling a flood of remorse and exhaustion wash over me as the waters came into my soul. Eventually, I went to the nearest room and brought out a chair and quietly set it down in front of Jane's door.

I had betrayed her, just as my father had betrayed me, and I knew, better than anyone, that a trust once broken is never again the same. I sat there for hours—replaying times we had spent together, happier times; surely they had meant as much to her as they had to me. After a time I began to worry that something could have happened to her—that the recent events had made her ill—but just then I heard soft sounds of movement, and then the bolt was withdrawn, and a pale, rumpled Jane collapsed into my arms.

I gathered her close and held her. "You come out at last!" I said. "I have been waiting for you long, and listening; yet not one movement have I heard, nor one sob: five minutes more of that deathlike hush, and I should have forced the lock like a burglar." She moved slightly in my arms, as if trying to escape, but I held her to me, waiting for her to scream at me and pound my chest, to release the anger that meant she still cared. But she was silent while I blundered on: "Jane, I never meant to wound you thus. Will you ever forgive me?"

Still, she said nothing. Would she never speak to me again? "You know I am a scoundrel, Jane?" I said. Even rage would have been better than this stubborn, gruesome silence.

"Yes, sir," she said, her first words to me.

"Then tell me so roundly and sharply—don't spare me."

But she could not: she was too weak to do more than lie in my arms, and I realized she had had nothing to eat since the night before. I carried her down to the library and plied her with water and wine and sent for nourishment for the both of us, for I had not eaten, either. Slowly she revived, regaining color in her face and limbs, and regaining as well her willpower. I was sure she felt comfort in my arms, as I did in hers, yet she would not allow a kiss or even an endearing touch.

"Why, Jane?—because I have a wife already? You think me a low rake?" I asked her, but I knew the answer before she could give it. And I could have repeated her other arguments before she gave them as well. Nothing I could say would move her. I challenged her to consider my dilemma: the husband of a mad wife, the necessity of keeping my secret in order to hire and keep servants, and even a governess!—but she chastised me, saying it was not Bertha's fault she was mad.

I tried reason; I challenged that she didn't truly love me; I told her my entire story, from childhood to my ill-considered, disastrous marriage and my realization of what Bertha really was, and my decadent, wastrel life in Europe, all of it up until I met her that dark January evening, hoping that she would see me anew, sure that she would admit I had done the best that could be asked of any man in the same place. I brought her and myself near to tears more than once.

But as she grew stronger, the power of her will increased all the more. I went through every weapon in my armory—patience, love, forgiveness, anger, reason—but nothing could pierce the steel of her will, nothing could break down the walls of what I had most admired in her: her resolute independence, her moral compass. I was powerless against her.

This was not like the previous times in which we had enjoyed parrying with each other, challenging each other, the wordplay that had once so amused me. But this was not a game: this was my life, for without Jane, I had nothing; I *was* nothing. And yet I saw her slipping away from me, and, try as I might, nothing I could say would move her.

Still, I was convinced there must be some way to bring her back to me. It tore my heart when she announced at last—so sternly it made me weep—"I am going, sir," and made to return to her room.

Devastated, I could not bear to watch her go.

In the morning, I told myself, *in the morning I will find a way to persuade her.*

CHAPTER 24

$\mathcal{D}$awn came in a bleak July sky. I had paced all night. As I watched the light strengthen, I told myself Jane would be mine again before the sun set. I clung to that thought, for surely moral laws were not so immutable that Providence would have brought her to me and then denied me her love. I rose and dressed and hurried to the door of her chamber, not to wake her but to assure myself of her presence. I touched it softly with my fingertips, and then I slipped away and down the stairs.

I went into my library and looked out, watching an early-morning haze rise from the meadow. What else could I tell her to show her that we belonged together? How to make her understand that our love broke no law of God? I wandered down into the kitchen, where I had often felt most comfortable. Mary was already shaping the day's bread, and she bobbed a curtsy at me and kept on with her work. She, at least, did not appear changed by yesterday's calamity. I picked up a piece of ham—a remnant of what was meant to be yesterday's supper—and popped it into my mouth, and as its cool, salt taste lingered on my tongue, I realized what I'd left missing. Fool that I was! I needed to tell her the rest—tell her about Gerald, about Bertha's suffering at the hands of my selfish brother, tell her that I had been willing to give up Thornfield for her, and still would, if I could be sure Bertha would be cared for and the estates were in safe, stable hands. Surely Jane, sweet Jane of all people, would understand this! My spirits soaring, I turned to go and wait by her door for her to awake, when Mary spoke: "Something odd, sir," she said.

"What's that?"

"The side-passage door was already unlocked when I went out to get the eggs this morning." She shook her head in confusion. "I was sure I had locked it last night."

My mind refused to consider the worst. "John had not already gone out, perhaps?" I asked.

"No, sir."

Oh God, I thought, turning, but her next words stopped me. "And there was bread missing, I'm sure of it." Then she shrugged. "Probably an unfortunate wanderer passing by. I'll make sure the house is better secured—"

Those last words came to me from behind; I was already running. Up the steps from the kitchen, across the hall, up the grand stairs, turning to Jane's room, and stopping abruptly. Dare I risk waking her? I hardly gave it a second thought. I did knock, but immediately opened the door, envisioning her in bed, turning sleepily in surprise at the intrusion.

The bed was neatly made, the room in order, and Jane was not in sight. I opened the cupboard: Jane had so few clothes, and they all seemed to be there. No—her black silk dress was missing. I searched the meager rest of her things: she had taken nothing I had given her, and her trunks remained packed and locked, just where John and a stableboy had brought them back upstairs the day before. Perhaps she had just gone out for a morning stroll to clear her head? But even as I thought it, I knew it couldn't be true, for why else the unlocked kitchen door, the missing bread? No, Jane had removed herself from temptation. From me.

I ran from the room, my mind at once full and blank, if such a thing is possible, and down the stairs and to the back entry, where I exchanged my ordinary boots for riding boots and threw on a jacket and made for the stable. A few moments later Mesrour and I were clattering out of the stable yard, with Pilot bounding beside us. But where to go? *Where?* I hesitated a moment, asking myself where Jane would go but finding no answer. Jane was, in some ways, still a mystery to me.

Not to a city, I thought. Not even to Millcote. Where? *Where?*

"Find Jane!" I ordered Pilot, knowing it was useless. He looked back at me, tongue flapping, joyous at the chance for a romp across the moors, but insensible to my pain. No, I would have to find her myself. Would she take the road or would she set off across the moors? Surely she was too smart to cross the moors, where she could so easily twist an ankle and fall, where the bogs could devour her. And so I spurred Mesrour into a gallop down the estate road; at the gate I turned instinctively not toward Millcote, but the opposite way. How far would she get? She had little enough money, I knew, since her salary would not yet come due for two more months. She must have had in hand only a pittance—not enough to survive on, not even for my resourceful Jane. God, we allow our people little enough; what do we expect them to live on? *Damn it all!*

I galloped ten miles at least on the road but saw no sign of her, and I knew it was impossible for her to have gone farther on foot, even if she had started out well before light. Did she go toward Millcote? *Could* she, in her desperation, have set out across the moor? Was she lying now in a gulley, having turned her ankle, unable to walk? Had she been accosted by someone living rough and been taken away against her will? I reined in Mesrour and looked about me. All was silent, save the cries of a pair of larks and the wind in the heath and the pant of Pilot at my foot.

"Jane!" I shouted, rising in the stirrups. "*Jane!*" But there was only silence to carry her name across the moor.

Witlessly, I spurred Mesrour onward, aimlessly, down into one dale and up onto another fell, until slowly it occurred to me that she might not be on foot at all. She might have taken a ride on a passing coach, or a farmer's wagon bound for market. She might, by now, be past Millcote or on her way to Harrogate; she could be halfway to Doncaster or nearly to Leeds. She could be anywhere.

She could be lost to me.

She could be lost. How could I give up the search?

I could not. I rode this way and that. I stopped a coach-and-four with an irascible passenger but a more kindly coachman to ask if they had seen her; I queried a passing tinker; I spoke to a couple of ruffians who were more drunk than alive; I asked at the George Inn in Millcote and at the Royal Oak at the crossroads. No one had seen her. It was as if she had vanished from the face of the earth.

I returned home well after dark, tired and hungry. I told myself I would find her there: perhaps she had had second thoughts. Perhaps it was all a misunderstanding, and she had only gone for a long walk after all.

But, of course, she had not returned, and no word had come from her. She had forsaken me; my love for her had not been enough. She did not love me as I loved her. She had been within my grasp and now was torn from me—forever. And it was *Bertha* who had caused this, my manic *wife*, the woman I was stuck with for eternity. In a frenzy I stormed up the stairs and burst into her chamber. I ignored Grace and charged straight into Bertha's bedroom. She had been sleeping, but my angry shouts wakened her, and she cowered in her bed as I screamed at her that all this was *her* fault, that her dalliance with my brother had ruined my life, her madness had cost me my one chance at happiness, that I was sorry that I had ever laid eyes on her, that I wished I had never come to her blasted Jamaica, that she and her greedy, selfish son had destroyed me.

Grace, horrified, tried speaking sense to me, but I was beyond reason—and when I wouldn't listen she seized me by the shoulders and forced me out of that place and I stumbled down to where Mrs. Fairfax stood, wringing her hands in the second-floor hall, having heard my angry shouts. She gathered me to her bosom, and, after a few moments, led me to the kitchen and gave me tea and spoke calmly to me until—desperate, miserable, and now ashamed—I grew quiet. She told me that Sam and the others were all out looking for Jane. Surely, she murmured, Miss Eyre will be found by morning, safe and sound, and brought home where she belonged. She tried to give me a sleeping draught but I would not take it; however, I did finally allow her to take me, now exhausted, up to my bedroom.

As soon as she was gone, and before I succumbed to sleep, I left my chamber and made my way to Jane's room, where I searched her belongings, looking for any indication of where she might have gone. I opened her trunks and rummaged through her neatly packed clothes, and I searched her dressing table. There I found the little pearl necklace I had bought her in Millcote, and holding it clasped in my hand, I returned to my bed and fell asleep.

In the morning I woke and was immediately hit with the memory of Jane's disappearance, and my own sorry state. I wasted no time in riding to Millcote to find Gerald. I was ashamed at what I had said and done the previous night in Bertha's chamber, for I knew none of it was her fault. But I did have a grievance against Gerald, for I was convinced he had something to do with breaking up our wedding—no doubt out of vengeance for my showing up his manipulations of my father's letters.

He was not at the inn, but as I was walking away from there I heard his voice behind me. "*Oi! Rochester!*" he yelled. I turned around to see him advancing on me in a fury, his eyes wild. "You scoundrel!" he went on, accusing me of taking his rightful inheritance away from him with lies and insinuations.

"I am no scoundrel," I replied with a calmness I did not feel, "and it is you who doctored those letters with false dates. And you who broke up my wedding—"

"*You scum! You dog shit!*" Gerald yelled. "*How could you marry another while my mother still lived?*"

I turned away to leave, and he would have followed me, no doubt, but by then the owner of the inn had come out to see what the trouble was, and held him back while I left.

It is not over, I thought, for I was sure Gerald would not let it go at that. Infuriated, Gerald's words still ringing in my ears, my mind reeled. I needed calm. I needed peace, and there was only one place I could hope to find it.

All was quiet in Jane's room; no one had been there since I had left it the night before, her trunks still standing as they had been. I searched her belongings again, hunting for any indication of how I might find her. I opened her trunks once more and scoured her dressing table. I even went to the schoolroom and looked there. I found her painting supplies and leafed slowly through her images, seeing there a portrait of almost preternatural perfection: a dark-ringletted goddess that it took me several moments to recognize as Blanche Ingram. Jane's artistry had rendered her far more beautiful than in life, with a sweet, delicate expression that had never graced that actual face. Did Jane imagine *this* was how I saw her rival? What had I done to her with my cruel, useless games?

A few sheets later came an even greater shock: a portrait of myself that was both honest and loving—she had placed a gleam in my eye that was surely meant for her, and, as always, my hair falling over my forehead. I touched my finger to it; she had seen into my soul and drawn this. She knew me. I was hers. She *did* love me, and had spoken the truth; there could be no doubt of it now. And yet the man on the page was far better, more beautiful, inside and out, than the man holding it. How could I have treated her so? I held that drawing in a shaking hand and wept.

Before I left the room, I paged through the rest and was arrested by another image. It was a representation of Jane herself. Yet she was almost as unrecognizable as Miss Ingram had been, but for an opposite reason—instead of the sprightly, intelligent passion that illuminated Jane's face and cried out daily to my heart, here was a visage of dullness and despair. This was not my Jane. I wondered if this was how she felt: deceived, taken in, her loyalty mistreated. *Oh God,* I thought, *what have I done to her? It is I, not Bertha or Gerald, who have driven her away. I am a monster.*

My limbs felt heavy, for I had not slept. All was quiet in the corridor, and I crept back to Jane's room and lay down on her bed, where the pillow still held the faint scent of her, and I fell, at last, into sleep.

I rode out the next day and the day after and the day after that. I rode east and west and north and south. I asked discreetly where I could, and searched carefully wherever I went. I toured the moors and the fields and the meadows and the lanes. I tracked down the horrid Reed children once more—the vain absurd one was being courted in London by a man of fashion, the other one in a remote convent—but received no fruitful reply. I wrote to Lowood School, where she had spent her childhood, but they had no news of her, either.

My last hope was that she would write, that she would at least settle my mind that she was alive and well. But a letter never came. Only once did Mrs. Fairfax give me a moment of hope, but the letter was *about* Jane, rather than a response to my inquiries—a message from that accursed solicitor Briggs, who had been responsible for driving us apart. Even if she were found, I would not allow *him* to have anything to do with her. I told Mrs. Fairfax I would hear nothing more about it.

"Where is Miss Eyre?" Adèle asked day after day. I had no response for her, and I could bear it no longer. I arranged, at the beginning of the school year, for her to be sent away to school, and Sophie back to France. Adèle did not want to leave, but I was unwilling to hire another governess and I could not care for her myself.

"You will destroy yourself," Mrs. Fairfax said more than once through that time.

I wished I could. I wished I could drive myself down to the bone and then float away like ash in the wind. I had driven Jane away, made her miserable, and I did not deserve space on this earth.

How could God do this to me?

CHAPTER 25

$\mathcal{B}$ut I went on living, and the only thing I could think to do was to keep on searching. When the folly of that had become obvious even to me, I buried myself in work. I made the rounds of all my cottagers, I helped in the harvest—to the amusement and dismay of the harvesters—and I invented reasons to see Everson. Around that time, odd things began to happen: noises on the grounds late at night, locks broken, the gardens trampled, even once a dead stoat hanging from a tree in the orchard. Ames believed someone was trying to break in, but John and Sam could catch no one. The servants became nervous, afraid to go out at night, and Mrs. Fairfax especially was deeply anxious. I was sure it was Gerald, his madness perhaps growing worse, trying to force his way back to his mother, into the house he considered his own, but there was nothing to prove since we were all unable to catch him. Eventually, Mrs. Fairfax could bear it no more and asked to be released from her duties. I was almost relieved when she did, for I had become uncomfortable in her presence: she had turned almost too kind, more mothering than I could bear at a time when I hated myself and who I had become—a liar and a bigamist. I settled a goodly sum on her and wished her well. She was all graciousness at the gift, and no little embarrassed, I imagine, but she deserved it, if for no other reason than she was my only living relative.

The same day she left, I removed the portrait of my mother from the drawing room and placed it and Jane's drawings in a closet on the second floor, for I could not bear to see these reminders of all I had done, the misery I had caused and fallen into myself.

I went out with the harvesters as often as I could, hoping to work myself to the marrow, to drop into bed at night too weary to think, to rise in the morning and take to the fields again, to allow the pain of my blistered hands and my weary back to at least in part replace my other, worse, pain, and the sun on my face to burn off a small portion of my regret.

———

It was one of those nights late in that harvest season, two months or so after Jane had disappeared, and I had fallen into bed and into a weary and miserable sleep, with dreams that assaulted my mind with unease. I dreamed that Jane had died in some lonely, forsaken place; I dreamed that I was perishing on some faraway island, bereft of all I had ever known; I dreamed that the sea had overtaken me and I was drowning; that I had died but instead of peace I was greeted by the fires of hell, which were consuming me, and I could barely breathe.

I woke, but it seemed as if I were still in the dream, for I could smell the fires and feel their heat. I rose from my bed and lit a candle to reassure myself that I was still in my own chamber, and indeed I was, but I felt surrounded by a kind of fury that I could not shake. I walked to the door and opened it and was nearly thrown back by the smoke and the flames. *Fire.* There *was* fire. This was no dream.

The far end of the gallery—*Jane's room*—was engulfed in flames. I looked up, and the fire seemed worse above me—for fire burns upward first—and I thought of John and Mary, and of Leah and Sam, and, the realization dawning, of Grace Poole and Bertha. *Bertha. Fire.* I ran to the servants' stairs and took them two at a time. I roused John and Mary, who were already nearly overcome with smoke, and pulled them from their burning room, and then hastened to Leah's and Sam's rooms and brought them out as well, and sent them all downstairs toward safety. Then I dashed up the hidden staircase for Grace and Bertha. Grace, perhaps already dulled with drink, had almost succumbed, but Bertha was not in her room, and I had no time to think. I nearly dragged Grace downstairs with me, both of us leaning on each other, gasping for air, catching her when she stumbled. Half carrying Grace, I somehow shepherded her out of the inferno. Just as we reached safety, Leah cried out and pointed, and I saw Bertha on the roof, at the battlements, like a ghost in her white shift, her hair flying wildly about her head.

Once more, I ran. I cannot say what made me turn back to the house, to risk my life to save the woman who had spent fifteen years destroying it. Perhaps it was how little I valued my life without Jane. Perhaps it was that I had spent so many years protecting Bertha that I did not know how to stop. Either way, I am no hero, for I could not save her.

Standing on that shuddering rooftop, I called her name. She half turned and saw me. Calmly, despite the crackling flames that surrounded us both, she gave me a smile. I suppose I may have imagined it, but something in her eyes seemed clear, for once, as if for the first time in years, she knew what she was doing. She gave a cry and turned from me to the edge. I lunged for her, but was too late, and I could only watch as she disappeared from the roof like a great white bird taking flight. For a moment, in my delirium, and standing in the place where she had been, that freedom beckoned me as well.

I did not see her hit the pavement, but I heard the cries of horror from the people below. Mary screamed out, "*Sir!*" and I knew that if I did not move I would follow Bertha to my death.

I ran. Down the narrow, smoke-clouded steps to the third floor, through the flames that were already licking at the stairs to the second floor, down the gallery, where every room was now fully engulfed in fire, to the grand staircase, where suddenly I stopped. I knew I had no time for indecision, but there was one last thing I had to do. I ran back to the closet where I had hidden Jane's drawings and my mother's portrait. They kept slipping from my sweaty, trembling hands as I raced back to the staircase and dove, by force of will, through the flames that were swallowing my only route of escape.

But I was a moment too late. Partway down, without warning, the staircase simply collapsed. I tumbled through the flames, losing my grip on the portraits as the edifice crumbled around me, searing my flesh. I lost all consciousness.

———

I might never have expected to awake, but awake I did, with a fierce pain all across my body. I was bandaged, even my face, and in a strange bed not my own. I must have stirred, for immediately a hand was placed gently on my shoulder. "Mr. Rochester," a woman's voice said.

I tried to speak but made no sound. There were only soft murmurs in the room and the sound of a door opening and closing quietly, and a snuffling sound that I recognized immediately. Beneath my bandages I must have smiled. And then I fell again into a fog.

When I awoke again, I recognized Carter's voice. "Well, Rochester, you seem to have come through it."

"Fire," I said, surprised at the weakness of my voice.

"Fires of hell, I should say." His voice was more jolly than usual; I suppose he thought he must cheer me up.

"How long—?"

"Two days. Two and a half. You have some nasty wounds."

"I was burned in the face?"

"Not so much, actually. Mostly on your forehead. Will give you a kind of distinction, I imagine, when it has healed."

"But my eyes are covered."

"Ahh...yes," he said.

I said nothing at first, but clearly he was waiting for me to speak. "My eyes?"

"You have lost one. The banister fell on top of you, damaging it beyond repair. The other...we shall see about that."

Blind, I thought. *Blind!* I took a breath. "And what else?"

"Burns elsewhere. But not too serious."

"Is that all?"

"You have had a very close brush with death, my friend. And you are only just now conscious. Why not take a bit of rest for a while?"

"I have great pain in one hand, but no other feeling."

"That is to be expected. Why not rest now?" But I heard the hesitation in his voice.

"Carter."

He spoke, but his voice sounded far off, as if I were hearing him in a dream. "You have lost a hand as well; I am sorry, but there was nothing I could do, it was so badly mangled in your fall. I don't know if you clung to something and wrenched it all out of line, or if something fell on it and smashed it, or what may have happened. By the time I arrived they had pulled you from the fire to the paving stones outside."

" 'They'?"

"Onlookers. I have no idea who. Perhaps John, or maybe not. The fire was seen for miles, and people came, for they knew it was Thornfield-Hall burning."

"Was anyone else hurt?"

"None, thank God. You managed to save everyone. Except of course for—"

"Bertha," I said, remembering.

"You were very lucky to survive," he added.

"Lucky," I repeated. Now I had lost Thornfield as well as Jane. I turned my head away and said nothing more, and neither did he, and after a time I fell into sleep.

———

Blinded, I found the days a monotony. I learned I was in Carter's own home, in the same room where he had cared for Richard Mason, that ungrateful wretch. That was a lifetime ago; back then Jane was within my reach and I treated her so callously, yet she loved me anyway. Now she was gone, and I did not deserve her back.

Ames came after a few days, for, like it or not, I was still master of the estate and must guide its business. There was much to discuss in the light of events, and we had the first of many conversations regarding the state of Thornfield-Hall, as well as the inevitable disruption to the harvest that the fire had wrought, and the future of John and Mary and Leah and Sam, now that there was no house for them in which to live or work.

When we had finished discussing business, he rose to leave, made a few steps to the door, and turned back. He didn't sit down again, but stood beside the bed. "It appears there may have been another body in the rubble," he said, his voice low.

I was startled. "Carter told me no one else—"

"I only just saw something this morning, sir, where a stray dog was nosing around the ruins. No one else has been informed, I don't believe."

I felt a heaviness in my chest. "A man?" I asked him.

"That was my impression, sir, from what I saw."

Gerald. "Have you asked Grace?" I asked.

"Grace has disappeared," he replied.

I was silent for a time, thinking of Grace, thinking of the years she had spent with Bertha. *It is never enough.* "Ames," I said then, "this is a delicate matter, on which I will require your utmost discretion."

"Yes, sir."

"Please pay a visit to Everson and convey to him—and *no one else*—the news you have just given me. He will know what to do. Tell him to send news to America if he can locate the proper recipient. And tell him to withdraw funds from my account to arrange for a respectful, anonymous burial near Bertha's grave."

"Yes, sir," Ames repeated.

When he had gone, I was left alone with my thoughts. Poor, mad Gerald. He must have succeeded, that night, in breaking into the house and sneaking to Bertha's chamber, where...I did not dare think of what had happened then.

The time came when I was able to rise; although the bandages were still on my eyes, I learned to move about somewhat, always with a guide at hand, and Pilot padding softly near my feet. Because I was so little able to do anything, my thoughts often went to Jane. I missed her, and would never stop loving her, but I also understood that I would never have her. I had destroyed that chance.

Though I often lost hope, I desperately wanted to believe that she was not dead. She had little worldly experience, but she was strong of heart and mind, and I felt certain she would find her way to the kind of life she deserved. I placed all my hopes on that certainty, for Jane deserved happiness and contentment. I could not provide it for her, so I prayed to God that she would find it on her own.

Autumn fell into winter, and one day the bandages were removed from my eyes. I imagine that it could have happened sooner, but I think Carter was attempting to be kind, to delay the reality that my sight was gone for the rest of my life. I discovered that I could see faint light with my one good eye, and the occasional shape, but that was the extent of my vision. Carter had been wise, I suppose, for even though I should have been used to the idea, when the bandages came off I was so overwhelmed with misery that I begged Carter's housekeeper, Priscilla, to hasten me back to my room and shut me in, alone.

Carter came in sometime later. "There is many a blind beggar who would give both his legs to be in your position," he chided me.

I lashed out. "Would he give his hand as well?"

"You have money. You have a house at Ferndean, if you choose to live there until you find something more suitable. You have a friend in me. Everson, too, stands by you, as you know."

"You will not allow me to wallow in self-pity? Even for a day?"

"Not even," he said, almost laughing, and I heard the echo of Jane's voice, for she would not have allowed it either. "You have much to be grateful for," he added.

"And much to regret."

Carter didn't respond, and I lay there, knowing what he was doing, but refusing to be jarred from my self-pity. And then a thought of Jane came to me, and what she would say, and I sighed, and rose from the bed and sat on its edge, and he and I began to discuss what was in store for me. I asked him to send for Ames, and for Everson, and then I began, in earnest, to prepare for what was to be the rest of my life.

I moved to Ferndean Manor, hidden away in its wood of oak and pine. I imagined bluebells and wild garlic in abundance in the spring, though I had been there with Bertha and Molly and poor little Tiso in that long-off June, and I did not recall anything blooming. It was too shaded for sun to stream into the windows, except for winter, when the oaks were leafless. I would never see the sun anyway, but I would be able to feel it, once the trees had lost their leaves. Carter disapproved of the place, for he said it would be too damp and cold, even in the summer, but I rather liked it, for it gave me good reason to avoid company, and I felt it brought me closer to God.

Ames was able to find places for Sam and Leah and the scullery maid and the stableboys. John and Mary came with me, the only people I needed, for she cooked and cleaned house and John did the heavier chores. And, of course, Pilot stayed with me, that faithful friend.

I kept Mesrour, too, for a time. Though I could not ride, I loved to stroke his neck and feel the power and warmth of his presence. But he deserved a rider who let him race, and I was no longer that man. With a heavy heart, I sold him. I had the rest of my life to live with my regrets. Mesrour, and Jane, deserved better lives.

That winter I sat as close to the fire as my chair would allow, and I began to doze away my days. At night my thoughts ran wild, not unlike poor Bertha's used to do. Often I wondered what, exactly, had been the agreement between my father and Jonas Mason. Given time to think, I imagine that Jonas may have noticed, even back when she was only twelve or fourteen, the early signs of Bertha's illness. He would have wanted her kept safe, and that would take either a husband or money, and Richard Mason could not have been depended upon. A husband—a dependable husband—would have seemed a good solution, and perhaps that was what he had seen in Rowland. But Rowland, despite having brought Bertha into maternity, wanted nothing to do with her, or Jamaica, for that matter. And perhaps my father, recognizing an opportunity to bring a much larger plantation into the family, offered his younger son as a replacement. It was not the first time he had maneuvered to do such a thing. Of course, there was that long wait for me to come of age and to have an education, but my father would have considered the investment worthwhile, never guessing that he would die young and Rowland even younger. From time to time, I wondered what would have become of me if I had refused to go to Jamaica, but I shall never know that, and, as Carrot was fond of saying: *You have to play the cards you were dealt.*

Carter came often and tried to cheer me in his own way. Sometimes he read to me, though I was like as not to fall asleep as he did so. It was not that I had suddenly become an old man—I was still in my thirties—but the loss of my eyesight brought a lack of stimulation that I had not yet adjusted to. I could not escape the irony of my confinement there, in the same place where I had once tried to house my lunatic wife. I, too, was strong in body yet unable to care for myself, destined to live out a dreary life, trapped inside my own head.

But my friends would not leave me to my sadness. With warmer weather, John began rousing me for walks around the grounds. There was no orchard, which I had loved so much at Thornfield, but John would guide me to bend down and touch snowdrops, and anemones, and finally reach up and feel the hazel catkins. The earth was coming to life and, as much as possible, I was too. Memories came with spring as well: last year's hopeful days, my fireside banter with Jane, our walks in the orchard, the sound of her laugh. That life was gone: Thornfield-Hall a ruin, Bertha and Gerald dead, I a broken man. And Jane: pray God she was safe.

The day was cloudy, as despondent as my mood. For how many years, I wondered, would I be moldering away in these woods? That was my feeling all that day, a grief that knew no bounds. Even in the evening it did not lift, and I took myself to my room early, but could not sleep. That was just as well, for my nightmares had been worsening: I was vividly haunted by a lifetime of sin and regret. There were so many people, irretrievable now, who had been lost and wronged. Not just Bertha and Gerald, and Jane herself, but Touch and Carrot and Alma and little Tiso and Mr. Wilson and so many others who had suffered, whom I wish I might have saved. Sitting beside my opened window, feeling the air on my face, I imagined the moonlight, and Jane somewhere, laying herself down from a busy day. "*Jane!*" I called out suddenly. "*Jane! Jane!*" And then, more quietly, "Oh God, Jane."

I expected no answer—of course I did not. But, in my mind I thought I heard a voice: "*I am coming,*" it seemed to say, "*wait for me.*" And a moment later, as if the wind in the pines itself was speaking: "*Where are you?*" The sound of it echoed as if across the fells, though there were none near.

"Here," I said aloud. "Just here."

But there was no response, though I sat at the window for nearly an hour more. It was as if it had happened in a dream: Jane's spirit and mine calling across some wild and lonely distance. I wanted to believe that it was a sign that God was setting me free.

The next morning I arose as usual to the birdsongs, and again the next day and the next, but nothing in my life had changed. It seemed that God had not, after all, heard my prayer, or perhaps he had more misery in store for me.

But on the fourth day, as darkness was starting to fall, I felt an urge to step outside on my own. Down the one step to the grass, cautiously. A step out. And then another, my arms outstretched for balance and because I knew there were trees even that close. As the first drops of rain descended

I thought I heard a footstep, or a voice. "Who's there?" I whispered, but no one responded. A woodland sprite, perhaps, waiting for me. If only it were real. The only sound I could hear was the wind in the trees, but I stood there anyway, for I felt a kind of comforting presence that I had not felt since coming to Ferndean.

Just then I heard John's voice coming from my side. "Will you take my arm, sir?" he said. "There's a heavy shower coming on: had you not better go in?"

"Let me alone," I said impatiently, for I felt as if there were something just out of reach, and for a few moments I tried to walk toward it, as if I could find it and hold it in my hand, but it was useless, and finally I turned and made my way back into the house, feeling worse than I had before.

I had only just returned to my chair when Mary came in. I thought at first she was bringing my tea, but instead she said, "Sir, there is someone asking to speak with you. What shall I tell them?"

I was annoyed. It had been a difficult few days, and was growing worse. Besides, Mary knew I did not see strangers. "Who is it at this time of night?"

"I—I did not ask a name, sir."

"Well, if he cannot give his name and his business, I certainly have no desire to see him. And bring me a glass of water. Please."

She hurried away, her shoes scuffing against the floor.

When she returned, she had no more than entered the room before I heard Pilot scramble up from beside me with a soft yelp and leap upon her, splashing the water. She whispered a quiet order. The commotion was so unlike Pilot—or Mary—that I turned toward the noise, straining. This *damnable body!*

"Give me the water, Mary." I sighed. But as I waited for the glass, I heard again Pilot's excited paws on the floor. "What is the matter?" I asked, having begun to fear an intruder.

Then came a voice that was not Mary's: "Down, Pilot!"

I *knew* that voice. But it could not be: I was hallucinating. "This is you, Mary, is it not?"

"Mary is in the kitchen," the voice said, and hope and fear clashed within me. Inadvertently I put out my hand, as if to touch the apparition, as if to assure myself she was real. Oh, that I still had my sight!

"Who is this?" I demanded. "Who *is* this?" I half rose as if I could force an answer. "Answer me—speak again!"

"Will you have a little more water, sir? I spilled half of what was in the glass," came the calm reply.

"*Who* is it? *What* is it? Who speaks?"

"Pilot knows me, and John and Mary know I am here. I came only this evening."

Jane. *Jane.* I would know that voice anywhere—had heard it in my fever dreams for a year. But it could not be. "Great God!—what delusion has come over me? What sweet madness has seized me?"

"No delusion—no madness: your mind, sir, is too strong for delusion, your health too sound for frenzy." It was she, for certain. The water she had brought me, the water I held in my hand: that was real. How then could she be a dream?

I cried out and reached to touch her, and I felt her small fingers encircling mine. "Her very fingers!" I cried out. "Her small, slight fingers! If so, there must be more of her." I reached for the rest of her, seeking the form I knew so well in my heart. I wrapped my arm around her waist and drew her close. My heart pounded in my chest, and as I brought her ever closer I could feel hers as well.

"Is it Jane?" I asked stupidly. "*What* is it? This is her shape—this is her size—"

She laughed at my disbelief, and I knew it was my Jane. "And this her voice," she said. "She is all here: her heart, too. God bless you, sir! I am glad to be so near you again."

"Jane Eyre!—Jane Eyre!" was all I could say.

At first we just held each other close in silence, and then the words poured out of us. She insisted, over and over, that she was not a vision, not a dream, not an echo of the moors. But without my sight, how could I be sure of her? She laughed and kissed my eyes, which had been so sore for human touch. "Is it you—is it Jane?" I asked, still unbelieving. "You are come back to me, then?"

"I am."

"And you do not lie dead in some ditch, under some stream?"

She laughed. "No, sir; I am an independent woman now. My uncle in Madeira is dead, and he left me five thousand pounds."

I must have smiled at her, for this was Jane. This was my practical Jane. I could not have dreamed that. "But as you are rich, Jane, you have now, no doubt, friends who will look after you, and not suffer you to devote yourself to a blind lameter like me?" I teased her, yet the worry was real. She had money, and I had nothing else to give her.

"I am my own mistress," she responded. My heart rose at her words: she was promising to stay with me, to love me, to be my companion. But then she talked of neighbor, nurse, and housekeeper—what was this? This was not love, but pity. Not passion but, at best, devotion to a father past his prime. I sighed—I should have understood that perfect happiness would never be within my grasp. If she would not be my own wife, I should release her.

But, sensing my gloom, her voice changed, and she began to tease me again as of old. I thought she would be revolted by my scars, but instead she claimed she was now in danger of loving me too much. I could not believe her words, but over and over again she laid herself out to me: she was mine, if I wanted her. *If I wanted her—my God!*

We dined together that evening, still talking—the first time we had ever shared a meal—and it was as it always should have been.

I could barely believe it: my Jane—despite what I had done to her, she was still—*always* mine.

And I hers.

———

Reader, she married me. I cannot still believe it. The evening she returned, I held her in my arms, and I showed her the necklace I had worn since the day she left, and with her help I took it from my neck and returned it to hers. And I asked the one thing I had to ask her again. "Jane," I whispered into her ear, "please. Call me Edward."

I am sure she smiled at me, and she laughed until she recognized the seriousness in my face. "Edward," she whispered. And then again, "Edward." And finally, a kiss on my lips and: "Edward."

I held her. It was all I could do. I could not speak. I could not silence my pounding heart. I could only hold her tight against me and think the words that had become truth: *You are my family, and I am yours.*

Two days later we were married, and at last—*at last!*—she was my wife, and I promised her that our honeymoon would shine our whole life long; its beams would only fade over her grave or mine.

EPILOGUE

Ferndean Manor was suitable for a miserable wretch living out his lonely life, but it was not a fit place for a married couple, nor a family. I told Jane we should find a better place, but she insisted not, because I had become used to Ferndean, where I could find my own way independent of her, or Mary and John.

"But it is not *I* for whom we need a house," I said to her. "We need a home for our family. And a family home should never be for the oldest and least able, but for the young, for the generations to come—the home they will pine for when they are far off, and cherish when they have returned, a home to hold all the memories of a lifetime. We must build a house, Jane, that has sunshine streaming in the windows, and nooks and crannies where children can hide, and lawns where they can play. We must be sure to have rooms that are not always square or rectangular, but unusual in shape and aspect, and that lead to each other in surprising ways, and there must be attics that children can explore on rainy days, and..."

She laughed. "And banisters they can slide down?"

"Yes! Absolutely!"

"Did you do that? At Thornfield-Hall? Did you slide down the banister?"

"I never dared."

"Ah! You were not such a ruffian as you like to pretend!"

"Did you? At the Lowood School? Surely not at the Reed house."

"I never dared, either."

"We will build the world's best banister," I responded, "and we will slide down it every day."

———————

It took five years, deciding exactly where such a house should be situated, and how large it should be and what it should look like: the entire planning and building of it. After two years of our marriage, I had regained a bit of sight in my one eye, and although I could not see the house plans well enough to decipher much, I could see it all in my mind, and Jane drew what we agreed upon. By the time the house was built, I knew it so well that I did not need to be guided through it, and it has become the house where our sons were born and the house where Jane wrote her life story and where she insisted I tell mine.

And now there is sunshine coming in our windows, and ponies in the pasture, and the orchard blooms in the spring with fruit trees, and I wander in the garden, and there are still some woods left, and beyond them there are meadows where sheep graze and our sons can play at being soldiers or pirates or warrior chiefs, and there is Adèle, more English now than French, who comes home on her school holidays, and has become, truly, a daughter to us, and a blessed relief, sometimes, from our boisterous sons.

And there is Jane, my dearest heart, who walks with me and reads to me and talks and laughs with me and teases, and sometimes slides down the banister when no one is about, and who calls me "Edward" every day of my life.

ACKNOWLEDGMENTS

There are so many people who have, in one way or another, contributed to the writing and the publication of this book that I will no doubt mistakenly omit some names. Still, I would like to thank Jennifer Weltz, of the Jean V. Naggar Literary Agency, for her steadfast support and encouragement. And, as well, Millicent Bennett of GCP, who shared my vision of what this book could be and was so instrumental in helping it bloom into what it is, and Millicent's assistant Jessie Pierce, publicist Andy Dodds, and many others at Grand Central, including Jamie Raab, Deb Futter, Brian McLendon, Carolyn Kurek, cover designer Liz Connor, copy editor Eileen Chetti, and Tracy Dowd, Karen Torres, and the rest of the sales team.

My deepest gratitude to Kent, my first reader always, whose early enthusiasm kept me going; to Pamela Grath, bookseller extraordinaire, whose initial reaction buoyed my hopes; my two early readers, Sue and Betsy, and my writing group: Alison, Karen C., Mary, and Karen M., who gave valuable advice and encouragement; my many other writer friends, who, before even reading the book, cheered me on: Elizabeth, Dorene, Marilyn, Barbara, Trudy, and Susan. And finally, thanks to my favorite librarian, Deb Stannard, and her assistant, Mary, who have indulged my often unusual requests, and the terrific Michigan eLibrary, without which I, who live in a very small village, could not possibly have done the research required for this book; and thanks to all teachers and librarians and booksellers who make it possible for those of us who love reading to get our hands on books and read.

And, of course, to Charlotte Brontë, who masterfully invented this terrific character who has kept readers wondering for so many years.

ABOUT THE AUTHOR

Sarah Shoemaker is a former university librarian and lives with her husband in northern Michigan.

READING GROUP GUIDE

DISCUSSION QUESTIONS

1. Edward Rochester is an iconic literary hero. Did your impression of him change in reading his side of the story as told in *Mr. Rochester*, especially in contrast to *Jane Eyre* or *Wide Sargasso Sea*?

2. What was the most surprising or memorable thing you felt you learned about Rochester, his character, or his motivations in this retelling of the story?

3. "I could not get Jamaica out of my head." Even as a young boy, Rochester is fascinated by Jamaica. Discuss its depiction in the novel and what it represents.

4. Who—or what—would you say is the greatest influence on Rochester's life as he grows up? How do his friendships with Carrot and Touch shape him? How different do you think he might have been if he had never met Carrot or Touch, or if either of them had remained in his life longer?

5. "But then I remind myself that if I had turned my back on my father's plans, my journey would have been entirely different, and while I might have found a satisfactory sort of life much sooner, I would

never have found Jane." What does the novel say about past experiences shaping your future?

6. Think about Rochester's relationship to his father. How does that change over the course of the novel, and how does it shape the boy Rochester is and the man he becomes?

7. "I felt as if she saw into my soul, saw all that I was, and when she smiled, I felt the kind of approbation I had always hoped for." This is how Rochester describes his first meeting with Bertha. Compare and contrast this with his first meeting with Jane and his impressions of the women who play such a pivotal role in his life.

8. "It was for Thornfield itself that my heart longed most." How important is Thornfield as a character in the novel? What does it signify to Rochester?

9. "There were depths there that intrigued me. In talking with her I was gripped by a warmth I had not known for a very long time." What do you think most attracts Rochester to Jane?

10. "Jane was my only hope for relief, for regeneration." Rochester falls very quickly for Jane. What do you think of his unorthodox method of pursuing her? Do you agree or disagree with his tactics?

11. "And there is Jane, my dearest heart...who calls me 'Edward' every day of my life." Discuss the importance of names in the novel.

12. How do you think Rochester's perception of love changes throughout the novel?

Q & A WITH SARAH SHOEMAKER

Edward Fairfax Rochester is one of the most beloved and controversial characters in literature, but somehow his story has never been told before now. Where did the idea for this novel come from?

We were discussing *Jane Eyre* in my book discussion group, and the conversation circled around Mr. Rochester. What are we to make of him, we wondered. This man who is sometimes angry and sometimes tender, who keeps his mad wife secretly in an upstairs apartment—who is he, really? What did Charlotte Brontë think of him? Is he a hero or an antihero? Do we not admire Jane for her independence, her moral integrity, her perceptive instincts? So what does she see in him? In the midst of all that, I began to think that someone ought to write Rochester's story, someone ought to read *Jane Eyre* closely and figure out who and what this man really is. Before I reached my home that day, I had already decided: I was going to write that book.

Did you do special research to capture the voice, setting, and atmosphere of Brontë's era?

I read and reread *Jane Eyre*, of course, looking to understand Rochester, but also trying to get a sense of the period, the rhythm of the language, the expressions that we no longer use, the personalities involved. Then I read more widely from fiction that is of the same time period as *Jane Eyre*—Brontë's *Shirley*, Charles Dickens, Mary Gaskell, Harriet Martineau, Mary Russell Mitford—looking for the same things until I had those sounds and rhythms and atmosphere clearly in my mind.

The novel maps perfectly against the original Brontë, in terms of not only action and spoken word but mood and style. What was it like to try to inhabit, and bring to life, such a well-known character by such a classic author? Did it give you *more* freedom to let your imagination loose within those constraints, do you feel, or less?

One of the things that surprised me most was how little freedom I felt I had. There is much more in *Jane Eyre* than the casual reader realizes, and one has to read *so* carefully, so as not to miss anything. It is like playing a role in a play or movie: one has to *be* that person. Of course that is true in any novel, but perhaps more so when the story and the character and the mood and all is already known to the reader, and the writer has to respect that and work with it.

Jane and Mr. Rochester have one of the most famous, opaque, and complex love stories in English literature. Having spent so much time inside their heads to write this book, what do you think drew them to each other with such intense chemistry? What does he love in her? What does she love in him?

This question is a complicated one! I'm not sure I can do it justice here. In the first place, we have to keep in our twenty-first-century minds the very important issue of class. Even Jane Austen doesn't deal with people having romantic relationships beyond their class, at least not in her major characters, and that would have always been at the back, if not the front, of their minds. For example, Blanche Ingram talking about how her father always was going after the governesses—and that was not uncommon in those times.

And yet on their first meeting (not including their evening encounter on the pathway) he asks her a very personal and surely inappropriate question: "Do you think I'm handsome?" Why? Perhaps he has already "read" her honesty and forthrightness. And she answers honestly: "No." What an incredible moment—each of them stepping beyond propriety to be open with the other. Brontë makes little of this moment; I call a little more attention to it, but in my mind, this is the beginning of an unusual relationship, one in which they can engage as equals and experience the pleasure of mind play which neither has ever done before with a member of the opposite sex, to say nothing of someone of such a different standing in society. For both of them, this is a world-changing experience: to be "seen" and respected for who they really are by someone of the opposite sex. How could they not fall in love?

The whole first half of the novel is your own invention, before Edward crosses paths, literally, with Jane halfway through the book. Where did you find inspiration for these characters and events?

I started out with an understanding of where I needed the character of Rochester to go. Since in *Jane Eyre* Rochester mentions his father and brother but not his mother, I assumed his mother had died early; and since what he tells Jane of his father and brother seems to make them distant and unpleasant in his mind, I began with that—a lonely childhood. There's only so much one can do with that all by itself, so I imagined him going to school relatively early. I read *Nicholas Nickleby* to understand what a school at that time might be like, and it was so horrible, so *Dickensian*, that I decided that the school in my book would be wonderful. So I imagined what young boys might like a school to be and wrote that. From then it was a matter of bringing young Edward up toward what I wanted him to become: a man who longed desperately for a place to belong, for home, for true companionship in the old meaning of the word—someone with whom one can share intimacies. Again, it's like staging a play: one has to create the characters and the events that will help move the protagonist in the way the writer needs him to go.

As many novels are, this was a multiyear project, from the original idea to the final book. What surprised you during that time? How did your feelings about Rochester, or Jane, or even Brontë change or evolve during that period?

First and foremost, what surprised me was how hard it was. I thought it would be simple: just follow along what Charlotte Brontë wrote and show it from Rochester's viewpoint. But I soon realized that would not work. The reader already knows that story; I had to create another story that would keep the reader's interest. Readers of *Jane Eyre* already know part of Rochester's story, for he tells her far more than one might at first reading guess. So with that structure in mind, I had to create a new story, with new characters, with things going on, even toward the end when we think we already know everything, that Jane—and therefore the reader— never knew. That was crucial and really important to create tension at that point. I would say that while I began with very positive feelings regarding Rochester, as I "watched" him grow and struggle, I developed an ever closer relationship with him. There are two very tender moments from the Brontë book that particularly struck: the time Jane announces that she is leaving to go to see Mrs. Reed, and you can just feel how bereft Rochester is and how desperate he is to insure that she will return. And the other is the scene where he is trying to get her to commit herself to him, and he is so desperate for her to do so, and she won't, she just won't.

What will be the biggest surprise for readers of your book who are big *Jane Eyre* fans?

I think, because of what is so generally thought of Mr. Rochester, that his treatment of Bertha—what the reader knows from *Jane Eyre*—developed over time, that he did not suddenly throw her into an attic and lock the door, that what we see in *Jane Eyre* is the result of a long and difficult process for the both of them.